"AN EXTREMELY INTERESTING AND PROVOCATIVE STORY."
—*Science Fiction Weekly*

"Riveting . . . The book may well become a cult classic, if not more."
> —Professor Howard Gardner
> Harvard Graduate School of Education
> Bestselling author of *Frames of Mind:*
> *The Theory of Multiple Intelligence*

"I loved *The Truth Machine*. Once I started the book, I couldn't put it down."
> —Professor Robert Sternberg
> Yale University
> Department of Psychology

"Halperin has combined a visionary analysis of the future of brain imaging technologies with a compelling and deeply human story. *The Truth Machine* is simultaneously fascinating, moving, and chilling. Anyone interested in where society is heading should read this book."
> — Professor Daniel L. Schacter, Chairman
> Harvard University Department of Psychology
> Author of *Searching for Memory:*
> *The Brain, the Mind and the Past*

"Halperin has turned the future into a great read. . . . Not since Ayn Rand's *The Fountainhead* have we had a portrait of a great man that is as convincing and poignant as Pete Armstrong. . . . This is a novel to be discussed and debated by thoughtful readers for years to come."
> —Jonathan M. Winer
> U.S. Deputy Secretary of State
> for Law Enforcement and Crime

THE TRUTH
MACHINE

James L. Halperin

A Del Rey® Book
BALLANTINE BOOKS • NEW YORK

A Del Rey ® Book
Published by Ballantine Books
Copyright © 1996, 1997 by James L. Halperin
Excerpt from *The First Immortal* copyright © 1997 by James L. Halperin

All rights reserved under International and Pan-American Copyright Conventions. Published in the United States by Ballantine Books, a division of Random House, Inc., New York, and simultaneously in Canada by Random House of Canada Limited, Toronto.

Originally published in a slightly different form by Ivy Press, Inc. in July 1996.

http://www.randomhouse.com or post your comments on the Truth Machine forum at http://www.truthmachine

Library of Congress Catalog Card Number: 96-93086

ISBN 0-345-41288-5

Printed in Canada

First Ballantine Books Trade Edition: September 1996
First Ballantine Books Mass Market Edition: August 1997

10   9   8   7   6   5

TABLE OF CONTENTS
AND INDIVIDUALS INTRODUCED

v

CONTENTS

CONTENTS

The technological and political predictions dated after 1995, although based on extensive research, are fictional.

Truth be told, to observe the future without altering it is a scientific impossibility. But if your views remain fluid, even a false vision is far more valuable than no vision at all.

THE
TRUTH
MACIIINE

Intel 22g CP-TLMos
Dallas, Texas—July 15, 2050

Silently, you sit in a courtroom as the evidence unfolds against you. You can only watch and listen—in frustration, fear, and disbelief. You cannot prove your innocence, because there is no Truth Machine. Instead you pray for a miracle, a divine intervention to save your life. But the miracle never comes. Later, as they strap you to a table to receive the lethal injection that will steal your every possession and dream, you wonder if even the people you love, and who love you, secretly believe you are guilty.

That is not fiction. As recently as 26 years ago, before the Truth Machine remade our world, it happened all the time.

As of March 1, 2024, Randall Petersen Armstrong, only 34 years old, had already built the world's most profitable corporation, becoming the wealthiest person in human history. On that day, for reasons I will try to help you understand, he chose to commit one of the greatest frauds of this millennium. Yet fraud would not be his worst offense. It was only the first in his now-infamous series of crimes that, astonishingly, would remain undiscovered for 25 years.

Since you plan to read these words, you'll want to know who wrote them. I am an Intel 22g CP (22 billion instructions per microsecond contextual processor) from the series of 2046, specially designed for reportage. I've been programmed to write in journalistic style, so don't expect scintillating metaphors or artistic imagery. If any show up on these pages, please assume they were added during editing, or that I am reporting someone else's

1

thoughts. What you'll get from me are facts. When the photons strike just right, I'm even capable of some marginal irony or humor. If you'd prefer to read a composition reminiscent of Hemingway, I suggest you stick with human authors, or at least the output of a 44g PIM (parallel internal memory) computer with full literary mapping applications.

Frankly however, you might wish to endure my writings. Stationed in Dallas, Texas, I have been favored with exceptional access to Randall Petersen Armstrong and David West, the two most influential people of the 21st century. Their stories are complex, and I have accumulated many facts of which you're certainly unaware.

My owner, Mr. Thomas L. Mosely, became a reporter for the *Dallas News Syndicate* (at the time it was a "newspaper" called the *Dallas Morning News*) in June 2010, long before I was manufactured. Over these past 40 years, Armstrong and West have granted him over 700 hours of one-on-one interviews, and I enjoy real-time access to all but the most private of their archives.

Mosely also wrote the only family-authorized biography of Harold Edward Kilmer, who has come to symbolize the Swift and Sure Anti-Crime laws of 2005. Presumably, had Kilmer been given a scip,[1] he would still be alive today. Thus, his tragedy eloquently demonstrates the value of the Armstrong Cerebral Image Processor (ACIP), otherwise known as the Truth Machine.

With all this background, and the Armstrong trial so recently concluded, it would seem a waste for me not to write this narrative.

The appeal decision won't be rendered for at least two

---

[1] Few people today are aware that the word "scip" was officially added to our standard lexicon only 24 years ago. First conceived in 2010 by the ACIP development team as an acronym for Scan Cerebral Image Patterns (SCIP), it was adopted into our daily discourse as a noun, adjective, or verb. Scip is currently the 612th most commonly used word in the English language.

weeks, not in time to include before we disseminate this document. Updates will be available later, but may be unneeded. Since his trial has been the most widely followed news story of the third millennium, virtually every person in the world will learn of Armstrong's fate at the same time.

Thanks to his ACIP, Mosely and I have come to know Armstrong in a way that would not have been possible 26 years ago. Our goal is for you readers of *The Truth Machine* to understand him as well as we do. We both believe it would be best if the World Tribunal were merciful. Not to underplay the seriousness of his crimes; Armstrong has done you far more good than harm. In fact his invention may have single-handedly diverted the human race's relentless march toward self-destruction. It seems illogical to kill him or even reduce his capacity to further contribute to scientific progress. Unfortunately the strict sentencing guidelines appear to offer little hope of leniency.

But enough speculation; we will all know the Tribunal's decision soon enough.

REFERENCE POINTS

You can skip this section if you'd like, but unless you're a fellow machine, it might be better if you didn't. Even when a history is accurately portrayed —as I assure you this will be—human readers often come away with misconceptions. Very few of you boast the perfect mnemonic abilities of computers (though I realize you have other valuable attributes). To diminish the confusion that springs from a combination of authorial omission and readers' distortion, I will provide additional perspectives.

For example, I'll try to keep you informed of the ages of the people I discuss, but it's easy to forget that a 50-year-old woman in say, 2010, was quite different from a

50-year-old woman today. Or if I describe a man in 2015 as being 5 feet 11 inches tall, you might think he was somewhat short in stature although actually as an adult male 35 years ago, he would have stood at average height. Also, because inflation has eroded the purchasing power of the dollar, $1,000 in the year 2000 was the equivalent of $41,500 in today's dollars. Hence I have prepared three charts on age, height, and inflation, which appear in the Appendix at the end of this book. You might wish to refer to these charts during your reading.

This history spans about 60 years and involves many people. The Table of Contents and Individuals Introduced, which precedes these pages, might also be a useful reference.

Each chapter heading bears a date corresponding to the most important event described therein. What's more, every chapter appears in chronological order. I see no need to be tricky merely for the sake of drama. Drama is nice of course, but I'm more interested in clarity.

Finally, next to the date at the beginning of each chapter I will list a few of the most important news events reported in the media that day. The added historical vantage point should help you better interpret this extraordinary story.

—Intel 22g CP-TLMos

CHAPTER 1

CHAIN OF FURY

Massachusetts State Prison
September 6, 1991—The cold war between the United States and the Soviet Union has just ended following an unsuccessful coup against Mikhail Gorbachev's reformist government. Gorbachev remains in power, but Boris Yeltsin, whose heroic actions during the coup may have saved Gorbachev's government, is now a force with which to be reckoned. Communism, for all practical purposes, is dead.—The United States, in the midst of economic recession after the Gulf War against Iraq, is entering a dangerous time of increasing isolationism. Many voters resent seeing America's resources exploited to solve the problems of other nations and insist their leaders focus attention on problems at home, particularly the economy and violent crime.

"According to your file you were raped by your father and you murdered your mother. Tell me about that."

Those were the first words Daniel Anthony Reece, Jr., heard from Dr. Alphonso Carter. Reece was shocked. Carter didn't ask if he had been happy in school, or what his childhood had been like before the "incident," or any of the other standard questions.

Just my luck, Reece thought. *Affirmative action. This monkey should be flipping hamburgers, but instead he's my goddam shrink.*

* * *

5

In fact, Dr. Carter was famous in criminal psychology circles, and well known even outside his field. Just 31 years old, he had coauthored the best-selling book, *Chain of Fury—The Cycle of Savagery in America*, and so could afford to pass up the financial enticements of private practice. At Massachusetts State Prison, Carter immersed himself in the study of violence—and those who commit it. Thus he had developed a depth of understanding of the criminal mind exceptional for a man of his time.

Carter's voice boomed and his diction was perfect, like that of a trained actor. As a boy he had stuttered horribly, the butt of cruel and inevitable teasing by the other kids in the neighborhood, until a drama teacher from the Booker T. Washington Middle School discovered his concealed talent. By the time he graduated from high school, Carter had played the lead in *Othello*. Even now his speech often seemed more like performance than conversation. Never did he use contractions or resort to street lingo.

"Mr. Reece?"

Reece sat back in his chair and sucked on a kitchen match. The two were less than four feet apart, separated by nothing—not a desk, not a coffee table. Carter's legs were crossed, his hands folded, his massive head shaved above a face so black that when he smiled his gums seemed blue.

Reece glared. Defiance showed in his eyes—and something else.

Contempt, Carter thought to himself.[2] *Mr. Reece is a racist.*

---

[2] I assume you want documented facts, and won't waste your time with excessive speculation. Carter confirmed these thoughts and his personal feelings about 20th-century racism in America during a scip interview for the *Boston Globe* on February 16, 2033. I have access to the digital record of the original interview transcript. I also have, in my central memory, data-cubes derived from the original audio tapes of the entire conversation cited here (and many others) between Reece and Carter. Additionally my

He plied his sense of timing and patience. Perfectly still and silent, he gazed at Reece with such intensity that the inmate felt as though Carter was peering straight into his brain.

Reece had always enjoyed therapy sessions. In a way, he was addicted to them. Talking about himself with the various psychologists, psychiatrists, and social workers made him feel important, as though his life meant something, and as if there might be some hope for him. The more he disclosed, the better he felt.

He now realized that this new shrink wasn't going to utter another word; it was up to Reece to say something next, or there would be no further discussion.

Finally he blurted, "I was only nine, but I knew there was gonna be trouble. Dad got mean when he was drunk and I knew he'd been drinkin' a long time 'cause he got home so late. I heard them arguin'—my mother and him, I mean. Then I heard her go. She just *left* me with him. I never forgave her."

Did I just tell him I blamed my mother for what happened?

Suddenly Reece wasn't enjoying himself at all. He had never said that before. Not to anyone. *What's this black bastard doing that's so different?*

"You never forgave your mother, but it was your father who brutally raped you. Tell me your thoughts about him."

Again the words came in a rush, unconsidered and unedited: "I didn't really understand what was going on. I was in shock. He was like a runaway train and I was the

owner, Tom Mosely, has interviewed both men under ACIP scrutiny and I have full access to other scip interviews of them as well.

You should find it reassuring that I've corroborated virtually all descriptions and conversations throughout this entire chronicle with authenticated digital records, a minimum of two human witnesses, or scip interviews of at least one participant. I've verified each human thought I describe (including this one), through authenticated digital recordings of scip interviews with the subject.

track. Nothin' could stop him. He smelled so bad. And it hurt. It hurt like hell."

Carter leaned toward Reece from the edge of his chair. "Are you absolutely certain your mother knew what was happening?"

"Certain? Shit yeah. My mother was a goddam coward, but she wasn't dumb. She knew exactly what would happen if she left me alone with him. She knew. Next day, she wouldn't even take me to the doctor. Scared shitless he'd call in the Child Protection—maybe lose them their precious welfare checks. Fuckin' right she knew."

"Did you ever tell anyone else?"

"Yeah, I sure did. I told my best friend, Joey Del-Greco. Know what he said?"

"Tell me."

"Joey says, 'Well I think that means you're a queer now.' That's what he said. But he never told anyone else. Even after we stopped bein' friends which was right around then." Reece laughed. "Maybe he was afraid everybody'd think *he* was a fruit, too."

"So what Joey DelGreco said caused you anxiety. You felt. . . ."

"Haven't you read my file, dumbass? I come home one day about eight years later and my mother's talkin' on the phone. I ask her what's for dinner or somethin' like that. Anyway, she says 'Hold your horses, you little faggot, I'm busy' and I snap. I just snap. Musta stabbed her 100 times. Carved her up like a goddam side a beef. Afterwards, my arm's so tired I can't even move it. So yeah. Yeah, motherfucker. I guess what Joey DelGreco said caused me some anxiety."

Of course Carter had read the file quite carefully. And as he played back earlier tape recordings of Reece and the state psychiatrist, he realized that Reece had been lying in previous therapy sessions. Before today he had always told the story differently, claiming he blacked out after arguing with his mother. "And then I just remember the police came."

The police came because Reece had called them about 45 minutes after he carved up his mother. It was an action consistent with temporary insanity. *Too consistent*, Carter believed. Reece's attorney had used the threat of an insanity defense to plea-bargain his case to second degree manslaughter.

Reece would be out of prison in less than four years.

Carter now suspected that matricide had not been Reece's only violent crime. Unknown to Carter, Reece, as a teenager, had been responsible for a string of animal mutilations and two sexual assaults on younger children.

Also, just 16 days ago Reece had stabbed Kendall DeLoach, a fellow inmate who had tried to sell him "protection." Reece's response was to slide a wooden blade he had stashed earlier clean into the inmate's throat. Miraculously DeLoach survived. In keeping with the twisted code of prisoners, the injured inmate told the authorities he had been attacked from behind and therefore couldn't identify his attacker.

In 1991 video cameras were about the size of a man's cap and cost a few hundred dollars each; large and expensive, but not prohibitively so. Yet because of privacy rights, these cameras could not be used in prison cell areas in the United States. So officially the assault by Reece didn't occur. Many of the inmates and a few of the veteran guards knew the real story, but nobody acted on it. They just left Reece alone.

If they hadn't, our world might look very different.

CHAPTER 2

TWO FIVE-SIGMA EVENTS

Massachusetts State Prison
January 6, 1995—The Republican party assumes majority control of Congress after an unprecedented rejection by voters of the liberal policies instituted by legislators over the previous six decades since the New Deal. House Speaker Newt Gingrich, whose political action committee, Gopac, helped elect many Republican legislators, is now considered the second most powerful politician in America.—Russia's President Yeltsin, who replaced Gorbachev as the nation's leader, finds himself in political peril over his government's inept and tragic war in Chechnya.—The United States public rivets itself on the upcoming double-murder trial of former football star O. J. Simpson. The trial will offer many Americans a long-term, close look at their expensive and flawed judicial system.— Through delicate diplomacy conducted at the eleventh hour by former President Jimmy Carter, war is narrowly averted in Korea, for the time being.

Some 40 months after his first meeting with Reece, Alphonso Carter was having one of those mornings. It could have been worse, he decided; but his throbbing head and foggy brain were bad enough. He felt irritable, dulled, and marginally angry, all rare conditions for him. *Just great,* he thought. *Why today, when I need my edge more than ever?*

The only explanation he could deduce for his attack of "the morning stupids" was that he hadn't slept enough.

Without his normal seven hours, his brain became akin to a 15-year-old automobile engine, its over-stressed timing chain firing in fitful pops and random stutters. Disjointed thoughts continued to run through his mind independently of, and despite, his intentions.

Even Katherine, his wife of 14 months, had become aware of his restlessness, and she was a heavy sleeper, rarely aware of his presence at all between the hours of midnight and six a.m. Still, twice during the night she had come fully awake and had asked him what the matter was. He had assured her that he was fine, but she was having none of it. She could feel his distress in her sleep. Eventually his anxiety and sense of dread had so permeated their bed that neither of them could sustain any pretense of normalcy. From 2:30 a.m. until dawn they'd held each other close, sometimes in restive sleep, often wide awake.

Dr. Carter had a horrifying problem and absolutely no solution.

Now, at 10:14 a.m., seated in his office with six colleagues who had become inexplicably uncomfortable in his presence, talking to none of them in particular, Carter said, "This progress report is the most ominous-looking thing I have ever seen...." His voice trailed away momentarily. "Hell, I wrote most of it myself and it looks worse to me every time I read it. I wish I could tell you there was hope, but I would be lying."

Terry Harwood, the unit manager, reminded Carter in a much too cheery voice, "In the report you describe this guy almost like he's some kinda sex criminal. I don't quite follow your concerns. The only crime Reece ever committed was killing his mother."

Carter massaged the bridge of his nose between thumb and forefinger and admonished himself not to snap at this naive bureaucrat. "No," he told Harwood, the words rolling off his tongue even more slowly and carefully than usual, "that is the only crime we know about, but it has *not* been his only crime; on that you may depend. I have never seen such severe rage in a rape victim . . . of either sex. When Reece murdered his mother, his anger was so powerful he apparently found his release within the homicide itself. That he skipped the sexual component is all the more alarming."

Harwood lashed back, "You *did* have over three years with him. Didn't your sessions help at all?"

"Not in the least," Carter answered calmly, his actor's voice achieving an almost condescending tone, like that of a schoolmaster patiently explaining a geometry axiom to a fifth-grader. "There is no legal way to cure a man like Reece. As I am sure you must be aware, the recidivism rate for treated sex offenders is slightly higher than it is for *untreated* offenders. As brutal as this may seem, Mr. Harwood, surgical castration is the only effective treatment known."

"Surgical castration works on these guys?"

"Apparently. In a Danish study involving 84 castrated criminals, only three committed sex crimes after castration—and all were nonaggressive acts. Obviously no castrated rapist has ever been known to rape again. Castration has been tested in several other countries, but never in the United States."

"Too bad," Harwood whispered under his breath.

In 1995 approximately one out of every six prisoners in state and federal lockups was a sex offender. Sex criminals tended to be very active, averaging perhaps a crime a week. The problem was severe and seemed to be getting worse.

Carter, never one to sully his diagnoses with political opinions, merely added, "It may take a year or it may only take a few days, but Reece is going to kill again."

Harwood knew better than to question the doctor's judgment. They had worked together for almost four years, and Carter was a cautious man; he'd seldom offered such an unhedged prediction. In rare but similar cases in the past, he had always been right.

Harwood shrugged. "We can't release this report to the press but at least we can circulate it to police departments. Any other suggestions?"

Everyone in the room knew all about the "Privacy Act." In 1974, Congress had passed legislation that, among other things, dictated severe penalties against those disseminating to the press any prisoner information outside the public domain. As federal law, the Privacy Act applied to every state and federal penal system. If Carter were ever caught violating the Act, he could never practice again. Besides, he would never break any law governing his professional conduct; committing such a crime would undermine everything he stood for and believed.

Carter finally answered. "Mr. Reece is neither insane nor stupid. He knows he is dangerous, but believes, incorrectly, that he can control his impulses. He will not let me have him committed. Believe me, I have tried— and I will keep trying, but I know I will not succeed."

"What about counseling?" Harwood asked.

"He has agreed to counseling; I only hope he will show up. I have decided to work with him myself, since he trusts me as much as he is capable of trusting anyone. But I doubt more counseling will help. The only other thing I can suggest is around-the-clock surveillance."

Tony Bechtold, the case manager, spoke. "I can pull some strings, probably have him followed for a week or two—assuming he stays in Middlesex County. That'll take some serious begging even with *this* progress report. After that we should at least be able to keep tabs on him through the probation office. But I'm guessing the best we'll be able to do is nab him after his first assault."

Carter thought to himself, *Reece's first assault will be a homicide.*

Harwood added, "Obviously we'll warn his probation

officer, but after probation he won't even have to register his address. His term of supervision's only 12 months."

"I doubt it will take him that long," Carter said quietly.

CONCORD, MASSACHUSETTS—January 7, 1995

Randall, the older child, stared at the blood worms floating at the top of the bowl. Still uneaten. *Circling like buzzards,* he thought, worried to the point of obsession.

The worms should have disappeared within seconds, but Harry, the Armstrongs' pet beta, hadn't been himself since the two boys and their mother had changed his water an hour earlier. The boys' nanny, Judith Sonntag, customarily responsible for that task, was away for the weekend. The water had looked pretty dirty, so they'd changed it themselves. Now Harry barely moved and wouldn't touch his food.

Why won't he stop thinking about the damned fish? his mother thought. Naturally Liza Armstrong was much more worried about Randall. Accustomed to her son's extreme sensitivity, she hated to see him agonizing over everyone else's troubles—even those of a fish.

"We've had Harry a long time," she consoled. "He's old for a beta and it might just be his time to die. Sweetheart, sometimes sad things happen and there's nothing much we can do."

But Harry always becomes more energetic after Judith changes his water, Randall remembered. Certain that they were somehow responsible, he refused to accept his mother's appraisal. *Something is wrong.*

He imagined how he'd feel if he were Harry; so helpless, so dependent. He hated the idea that such a defenseless creature should have to suffer, especially if there were something he could do about it.

Always aware of his emotions, Randall knew that if he sat still he'd get even more upset. He moved to the couch, where Tabitha, the Armstrongs' cat, jumped into his lap. Stroking her fur, he began gently rocking back and forth to calm himself.

He sat Indian-style, back straight as a board, slender legs crossed. Despite his earnest demeanor, Randall's appearance was comical: tongue pushed far out through his front teeth, protruding slightly from the left side of his mouth as it often did when he concentrated on a problem, and his straight blond hair, which only that morning he had decided to comb into bangs, completely covering his now-closed eyelids. Even more than the hair, the stuck-out tongue gave him the bewildered look of a shaggy English sheepdog.

Looks, however, do mislead.

Seeking clues to Harry's predicament, Randall now played back all of the past week's events, like a video tape in his mind. When he got to Wednesday morning, he saw and heard everything he had experienced three days earlier, as Judith once again changed the water in the bowl. To Randall, it was as if he had gone back in time; as though it were Wednesday again. He hadn't paid much attention back then, but now as he relived it, he noticed every movement, every nuance, every feature, and every sound.

"Mom," he finally said, "When Judith changed the water on Wednesday, she put something in Harry's bowl—from a white and orange plastic bottle. Is there anything like that in the cabinet near the blood worms?"

Liza Armstrong discovered the water conditioner they had neglected to use. She poured a teaspoonful into the bowl. The fish was back to his normal self within a few hours. Without a doubt, Randall had saved Harry's life.

Randall Petersen Armstrong, barely five years old, was obviously no ordinary child.

His parents, Ed and Liza Armstrong, were a well-educated, worldly couple: he the CEO and sole owner of Boston Quality Corporation, a small, successful manufacturing business that employed 35 people; she a partner at Foley, Hoag and Eliot, a large Boston law firm. Still, neither of them could figure out how to deal with their two tiny geniuses.

A case of mumps during Ed's adolescence had left him sterile; therefore they had been unable to have children on their own. In 1988 Liza was referred to Concord Hospital's In-Vitro Fertilization Clinic and, although at the time it was unusual for women over 40 to bear children, 41-year-old Liza became pregnant. Randall was born on December 6, 1989.

Normally paternity records were sealed, but because of a clerical error the couple would later find out that Randall's biological father was a University of Georgia Medical School student named Cassidy O'Meara. Apparently O'Meara had helped cover his expenses by making deposits to the University Hospital's sperm bank. He entered medical school in 1987 and died of a drug overdose during an internship in 1991.

We still have much to learn about heredity and intelligence, but far less was known in 1995. During the 20th century, Intelligence Quotient (IQ) was measured almost exclusively on the basis of the brain's ability to process verbal and numerical information. Today we also gauge intelligence from other elements, including interpersonal skills, musical ability, artistic talent, emotional awareness, and kinesthetic sense. But then as now, although standard deviations (one-sigma) were the norm, variations of twice the standard (two-sigma) were scarce and three-sigma events were very rare.

In 1995, most scientists believed that intelligence was determined almost entirely by a child's environment and the intelligence of the parents. We now know that certain combinations of parents can produce exceptional deviations in the expected intelligence levels of their children. The Armstrongs' experience offers compelling anecdotal evidence of this.

Less than a year after Randall was born, Ed and Liza Armstrong were back at Concord Hospital requesting the same donor. Leonard Charles Armstrong was delivered on July 10, 1991, the day before Liza's 44th birthday and about 19 months after Randall was born. Although O'Meara's other offspring may have tended to be very bright, none have approached the intelligence levels of Randall and Leonard Armstrong. It is possible that the genetics of the two biological parents complemented each other in just the right way to generate two consecutive five-sigma events.

At first Liza and Ed had no idea what to expect from their children. Three years earlier, when Liza had mentioned to one of her partners that two-year-old Randall was putting together puzzles marked "for ages five to eight," and memorizing stories read to him at bedtime, she was met with only mild ovation. "Aren't kids amazing?" her colleague exclaimed. "My little girl always corrects my mistakes when I read her favorite stories. You can't get much by them."

No one realized then that Randall could memorize every story the first time he heard it. Only gradually did Ed and Liza come to recognize how exceptional their child was.

As Randall and Leonard gained intellectual and social ground, Liza became increasingly concerned that her older son would soon need no mothering at all. At five, Randall had been dressing himself for more than three years. Now he unfailingly fed and cared for Tabitha, the Armstrongs' cat, and often made sandwiches and prepared breakfast for himself and the rest of the family. Even before he was Leonard's age, Randall had demanded very little attention and had started helping Liza and Judith around the house in numerous ways.

But if the Armstrongs had expected their second child to ripen similarly, they were in for a shock.

An irresistibly cute three-year-old with bright blue

eyes and wild dark hair, Leonard Armstrong was simply
a master of infernally clever mischief. Indeed, he was
every parent's worst nightmare: a fearless child with a
hyperactive, virulently curious mind, constantly probing
to see how everyone and everything would react if he
threw something unexpected into the equation. Leonard
often endangered himself, once going so far as to start up
the riding mower to chase Tabitha (not that he had any
prayer of actually catching her); he ended up stalled in
the middle of the street, trying to restart the machine as
traffic came to a screeching halt.

Although Randall usually greeted his parents' friends
with some reticence, Leonard would barge into the
family room and perform startlingly authentic imitations
of his favorite cartoon characters, Foghorn Leghorn[3]
being his best.

Because Randall had proved such a prodigy, every
mental and physical move Leonard made was monitored
in near test-tube fashion. By all accounts he had the same
talent for memorization, or was at least in the process of
developing it. In many ways he was brighter than Randall. Astonishingly clever with numbers and all things
mechanical, he taught himself how to operate the family
televisions and VCR at an earlier age than had Randall.
Leonard would sometimes play tricks on his brother and
their parents by reprogramming the VCR or turning off
the audio with a hidden remote control.

When he was 23 months old he could tell time, even
on the analog clocks that during the 1990s were still in
use in most homes and businesses. Soon thereafter, he
taught himself the rudiments of bridge by watching his

[3] In case your parents screened out cartoon broadcasts during your childhood, Foghorn Leghorn was (and still remains) a popular character from
Warner Brothers, who also created Roadrunner, Bugs Bunny, Porky Pig,
and Daffy Duck, among others. Foghorn Leghorn is a giant rooster with the
demeanor of a gruff southern sheriff. Sometimes he is relentlessly hunted
by a baby chicken-hawk about one fiftieth his size, whom he treats with
bemused affection.

parents play in neighborhood duplicate tournaments. But he seemed to have no interest at all in learning about letters until just before he turned three. It was then that Randall (whom Leonard called "Petey") finally convinced him; only minutes later, he had taught his little brother the alphabet. Leonard never learned to read at Randall's level, but within days was capable of reading children's books, street signs, and the like.

Unfortunately his potential for mischief grew exponentially with this new skill. Liza was soon scheduling Leonard for interviews with behavioral specialists in Boston, and testing him for Attention Deficit Disorder with a local psychologist.

Although often irritated by his brother's pranks and the attention they gained him, "Petey" rarely felt any jealousy. He was devoted to Leonard and sensed a connection more powerful than blood: someday an intellectual equal might ascend to his side.

Randall went to bed at 7:30 p.m. without being coaxed, and gently rocked himself to sleep. Unlike most five-year-olds he looked forward to sleeping, because every night he would have the same dream.

In that dream, he could fly. And in Randall's dream world, his powers were such that when he flew, any of the neighborhood children he invited to join him were able to fly as well, so long as he wished it so. (His fortunate companions always included Leonard.) The children gratefully joined Randall as they soared over their rustic Concord neighborhood, waving and greeting the amazed onlookers below.

CHAPTER 3

TWO WORLDS COLLIDE

Concord, Massachusetts
June 7, 1995—Japanese government prosecutors announce the indictment of Shoko Asahara, leader of the "Doomsday Cult." Asahara was implicated by his lieutenants in the March 20 nerve gas attack on the Tokyo subway system that injured over 2,000 commuters.—The North Atlantic Treaty Organization suspends its air strikes on Bosnia, as the Serbs continue to hold hostage or surround hundreds of United Nations peacekeepers. The UN Security Council deliberates the total evacuation of its peacekeeping forces from Bosnia, but even that option would require a major military effort by NATO participants.—The International Red Cross accuses both sides in the Chechen-Soviet War of human-rights violations.—In the wake of the Oklahoma City bombing, which killed 169 people, the United States Senate passes the "Comprehensive Terrorism Prevention Act," by a vote of 91–8. President Clinton urges the House of Representatives to act swiftly on the bill.

He had already overcome nearly all the obstacles for delivering the medicinal bark of the Cinchona shrub to save the ailing natives in record time. Randall Armstrong concentrated intensely. He was about to break his own record at "Amazon Trail," his favorite video game.

He bit down lightly on the back of his tongue, which consequently now jutted out of his mouth. Lately Randall had convinced himself that the farther back he bit, the better he could think.

Suddenly Leonard burst into Randall's room. "Let's play soccer, Petey."

"Okay. Just wait about 10 minutes. I'm almost finished."

Randall took the game seriously. When he played it, he pretended he was no longer a five-year-old child; he was transformed into a fearless hero, using sharply honed skills to help rescue those least able to help themselves. Although he realized this was fantasy, he believed that someday he would do just that. To Randall, "Amazon Trail" was no mere game; it was training.

"Okay," replied Leonard.

Randall was surprised that his brother gave in so easily. He had figured on Leonard throwing a fit, in which case he would have saved the game and come back to it later.

Perhaps Leonard's acquiescence had been a ruse, or maybe he simply grew impatient. Whichever, about 45 seconds later he crawled behind Randall's Apple Macintosh desktop computer and unplugged it from the wall socket. In 1995, home desktop computers had no internal power source, so this permanently ended the game.

"You little creep. I *hate* you. I wish you were never born!"

Unfazed, Leonard just laughed.

Randall fumed for a second or two, but almost immediately, as usual, he felt his anger start to dissipate. Then he began laughing too. *Leonard can be a royal pain,* he thought, *but he's never dull.*

It was a beautiful Monday morning, typical of late spring in New England: bright green trees and lawns, warm but not hot, almost no wind, a cloudless sky. Randall loved being outdoors at this time of year. The air smelled wonderful and everything looked brighter, sharper somehow, as though his eyes had more receptors.

He was capable of comparing any images he had seen simply by flashing back through them in his memory. He realized that in the bright daylight he could perceive details and features in the scenery that had escaped his discernment at other times. *More pixels,* he thought to himself.

(Note: The image quality of primitive "television" screens of the late 20th century was measured on the basis of pixel density.—22g CP)

Judith, the Armstrongs' nanny, kicked the soccer ball gently to Leonard. He circled the ball and appeared ready to kick it to Randall. Then apparently he decided it would be more interesting to kick it in the opposite direction into the next-door neighbor's yard. Not yet four years old, Leonard wasn't capable of exerting much force on a soccer ball, but his coordination was exceptional. He kicked it perfectly through the hedge and off the Armstrongs' property. Then he doubled up in laughter.

"Come off it, Leonard," Randall called, trying to hold back his own laughter. "Go get the ball. It's not *that* funny."

Leonard got up and staggered three steps before falling down in another laughing fit. Even when Randall found himself saying, *"Please,* Leonard, go get the ball," he thought to himself, *he really does have a great laugh.*

Leonard finally scurried through the same hole in the hedge that the neighbor's cocker spaniel often used.

The soccer ball was about 15 feet from the hedge and some 5 feet from a single human landscaper[4] planting roses along the west side of the neighbor's house. Leonard had never met an adult without his parents present, and had been carefully warned not to talk to strangers.

---

[4] Landscaping robots did not exist in 1995; nearly three decades would pass before we machines would largely replace humans as professional gardeners.

Still, predictably enough, he immediately greeted the new workman. "Hey, what are *you* looking at, mister?"

"Boy, you better get away from here."

"Boy?" Leonard replied in his best Foghorn Leghorn. "I say now. Lookee here, son. You watch who you're calling boy around here. I mean, I say, how big are men where you come from anyway? I say. . . ."

The workman, Daniel Anthony Reece, Jr., felt a familiar anger well up inside him, a rage he had experienced often. Receiving Leonard's innocent words as a challenge, the damaged temporal lobe of his brain produced a fury unchecked by his enfeebled hypothalamus.

Glancing hastily from side to side, Reece saw nobody else. He lunged toward the boy and bashed his face with the back of his right fist.

Leonard fell to the ground, unconscious.

Randall began to get restless.

"Why does it take him so long to do one simple thing?" he complained to Judith.

Finally he became impatient enough to follow him.

Slipping through the hedge wasn't as easy for him as it had been for Leonard or the spaniel. Halfway through, on all fours, he saw his motionless brother being carried under a stranger's arm, and watched, frozen in horror, as the man tossed Leonard into the back of an old green Chevrolet pickup.

Randall tried to scream, but his lungs suddenly seemed empty. He couldn't even whisper. Still, the stranger, sensing his presence, turned his head and glared at him. Randall would never forget any detail of the encounter: the hateful face, the awful thud of Leonard's body in the truck bed, or the license plate number of the truck as it drove away.

Crawling back through the hedge to his own yard, his voice returned and he sobbed to Judith, "A m-m-man took Leonard away in a g-green truck. Leonard wasn't even *m-m-moving*! We have to call the p-police."

Judith ran to the Armstrongs' telephone. It was a typical late 20th-century model: a stand-alone unit with push-buttons and no visual monitor, usable as a two-way audio unit and not much else.

Out of breath and terrified, she punched 9-1-1.

The primitive telephone was attached to the wall with a cord, the transceiver portion ineffective unless held within an inch or two of the user's ear and mouth. A recording advised that all operators were busy, so Judith listened, "on hold," for the longest 50 seconds of her life. She was trapped there, unable to do anything but wait.

"Please pick up. Come on. Please!"

At last a woman's voice answered, "Concord emergency. Hughes."

"I want to report a kidnapping."

"Your name?"

"Judith Sonntag."

"The victim's name and your relationship?"

She shivered and answered, "Leonard Armstrong. I'm his nanny." At least the words were coming out right.

"When did it happen and where?"

"Less than five minutes ago. A man in a green truck abducted him. He's only three years old and he might be hurt." She gave the operator the address and described the boy.

Randall tugged at her sleeve. "I remember the l-license plate."

She repeated the license plate number and description of the kidnapper to the operator.

Then she bit down hard on her lip and forced herself to call Ed Armstrong's office. Randall waited on the couch, sitting like a stone, staring at nothing.

Judith hugged him hard.

"They'll find him. He'll be okay. He *has* to be okay."

The Federal Bureau of Investigation, a law enforcement arm of the United States Department of Justice formally disbanded in 2034, didn't always handle abduction cases. However, the landscaper's pickup truck had been registered in New Hampshire, so the vehicle had crossed state lines. Therefore the FBI was notified by the Concord Police Department.

Within two hours, FBI Special Agent M. R. (Mark) Burns and a female FBI officer, whom Burns referred to only as "Tilly," arrived at the Armstrongs' house. Burns had only two months of duty remaining until his retirement from the Bureau, a retirement he intended to spend spoiling his own two grandsons, who were about the same ages as Randall and Leonard. He noticed the house had once been professionally and tastefully decorated, but today every floor of every room visible from the foyer was covered with toys, puzzles, and papers— testimony to the fact that adults didn't entirely run the place.

Ed and Liza Armstrong, who had both arrived home nearly an hour earlier, met the two agents at the door. Liza, quaking and crying, apologized for the mess.

"Tilly" was a very attractive woman, slender but shapely, with long, straight brown hair, brown eyes, and the button-nose of a prep school cheerleader. Her full name was Marjorie Ann Tilly. Burns and others in the Boston office joked that she was a little like the rock stars of that era—Madonna, Prince, and Sting—referenced by only one name. Although her scores at the mandatory FBI marksmen qualifying sessions were consistently among the lowest, Burns believed her uncanny investigative and technical abilities more than compensated. "Over 37 years with the Bureau and Tilly's the best partner I ever had," he often said.

Tilly was particularly well-suited for dealing with my primitive forerunners. She understood computers well, and always seemed to know how to tap the proper databases for the right kernels of information.

(Note: Although today misunderstandings between man and machine are rare, in 1995 interaction was much

*more difficult. People communicated with us mostly by
typing instructions on a keyboard and operating a track-
ball or "mouse." We could not yet adapt to individual
habits and styles of our owners, or even respond to
speech.—22g CP)*

Burns, barely more computer-literate than Harry, the
Armstrongs' beta, was impressed by her versatility.
"She can make her Dell 486 sing and dance," he'd
often said, "and I've never worked with anyone who
gets along better with people or thinks on their feet like
Tilly can."

While Burns walked next door to interview the neighbor,
Tilly immediately asked to speak with Randall. She
found him where Liza Armstrong said he would be, sitting on his bed. He held a small brown and white cat gin-
gerly to his chest as he gently rocked back and forth.
Tilly was shocked by how young Randall was; having
spoken to him on her car phone, she had expected a much
older child.

"Randall, I'm Special Agent Tilly from the FBI.
Please just call me Tilly."

Randall nodded.

"The license plate number you gave us checked out.
When we catch this guy, it'll be because of you."

"It's b-because of *me* Leonard went to get the ball from
Mr. Caldwell's y-yard. If I'd gone to get it m-m-myself,
Leonard would st-t-till be here."

His body continued to sway. Rocking was the only
way he could soothe himself—and his burgeoning guilt.
He did not mention to Tilly, or to anyone else, that earlier
that day he had told his brother he hated him and wished
he'd never been born. He played those words back in his
mind—over and over again.

"Randall, listen carefully. You didn't do anything
wrong. There's nobody to blame except the man who
kidnapped your brother; you couldn't possibly have
known there was anything dangerous in your neighbor's

yard. The important thing is that you and Judith immediately called for help. Because of you we were able to trace the truck. We think we know who kidnapped your brother and we're going to find him."

Their conversation was interrupted by Tilly's cellular phone. "Tilly here."

"Ms. Tilly, this is Alphonso Carter." No further introduction was necessary; Tilly, like most of her colleagues at the Boston office, knew of Dr. Carter. "I just received a fax from your office. Unfortunately I am very familiar with the man you believe is your kidnapper. Mr. Reece left Massachusetts State Prison 75 days ago. I have been giving him free counseling since he left, and he has shown up every week until last night."

"You think it was Reece?"

"I am virtually certain it was."

"Dr. Carter, do you think the boy's still alive?"

Tilly's face showed frustration, then anger, and finally powerless resignation, as she listened to Carter's response: "No," he said. "I hope I am wrong, but I honestly doubt it."

Burns received the call at 12:47 a.m.

Two hours earlier a Carlisle police officer had spotted the partly hidden pickup truck on a dirt road by Walden Pond. Backup had arrived within minutes, and Reece, asleep in the cab, was easily captured. It took the officers about 45 minutes to convince him to take them to the child, and another hour to recover Leonard's body. Under the most relentless questioning, Reece continued to claim he couldn't remember hitting the little boy, but assumed he had and therefore panicked.

Burns woke Tilly, who had been napping on the couch, and told her the news. She volunteered to tell the family; Ed and Liza were still awake in the study.

She took one of Liza's hands in both of hers. "I'm so

sorry. Leonard is dead. We've recovered his body and we have the killer in custody."

Liza tried to speak, but could think of no words to say. Ed broke down, barely getting his question out between sobs, "Do they know for sure it's our boy?"

Tilly nodded.

Ed ran to the bathroom and vomited into the sink. When he finally returned he hugged both women. "How can we ever tell Randall?"

"I'm here to help if you need me," Tilly assured them. She had never been assigned to a murder case, but had lost a four-year-old niece to leukemia and understood what trauma the death of a small child could inflict on a family. "I give you my word, my job here isn't over until you tell me it is."

Liza looked into Tilly's tear-filled eyes. "Thank you."

Ed, Liza, Burns, and Tilly trudged upstairs to Randall's room.

Earlier, Randall and Judith had tried to go to sleep but couldn't. Now they both sat wide awake, playing a video game on Randall's Macintosh. The sparsely furnished room was much neater than Burns had expected. *The entire mess downstairs,* he realized, *must've been made by the three-year-old murder victim.*

Liza hugged her surviving son. "Leonard's never coming back, sweetie."

Judith and Randall both burst into tears. *It's all my fault,* he thought. *I was supposed to protect him!*

The cat returned to the room and leapt confidently into Randall's arms. Randall accepted her without hesitation and began petting her affectionately as his body rocked. She nestled with such familiarity that Tilly guessed the animal had sensed the boy's distress. Tilly sat silently for almost 10 minutes, biting her lip. She noticed that Randall chewed on his tongue, almost like a cow chewing her cud. The back and forth motion of the rocking seemed to calm him down.

"Randall, I've never been involved in a case like this

before," she finally said. "But I know you're much brighter than your age and I'm told you can understand whatever I tell you. I believe you need to know as much as you want to know."

"Then t-t-tell m-me everything."

Tilly did. The child continued to rock himself and Tabitha and cried quietly through much of what was said. He had stopped chewing his tongue, but now it occasionally protruded from the left side of his mouth. Tilly wondered if other neighborhood children ever picked on Randall because of his quirks. She kept talking, unsure of whether he understood what she was saying. When she got to Reece's criminal record, Randall stopped her.

"But what *m-m-makes* people like that? And if they knew how bad he is, why did they let him g-go?"

"We don't know why some people do terrible things. All we can do is arrest them and try to put them in jail for a long time. We hope by the time they're released they won't be dangerous anymore."

"B-B-But what about that Doctor Carter?" Randall reminded her. "He knew Reece was still dangerous. Couldn't he k-keep him in jail?"

Tilly had no idea Randall had overheard, much less pieced together the meaning of that brief telephone conversation 11 hours earlier. Recovering from her astonishment, she explained the law enforcement role, the judicial process, and how finally the penal system takes over. "Once someone is sentenced, as long as they don't break any more laws, we can't hold them in jail any longer than the courts tell us to."

"Even if they might kill someone?"

Tilly patiently explained due process and the presumption of innocence, and how important it was to our way of life. "We have to assume a person's rehabilitated until they do something wrong. Otherwise people could stay in jail forever just because someone else disliked them. That wouldn't be fair, would it?"

"I, uh, I g-guess not."

"The problem is, we never know for sure who's a
threat and who isn't. We can't keep everybody in jail just
because they *might* be dangerous. We can't predict what
people will do because we can't read their minds."

Randall thought about that for a moment. "Who
d-decides when it's time to let a person out of jail?"

As simply as she could, she explained about sentencing guidelines, plea-bargains, and parole boards.
Again, Randall did not interrupt until she was through.
As he continued to ask questions, she became progressively more amazed at his insight. He never asked a
single question she had already answered.

She responded to every question, never patronizing
him, with obvious compassion and awareness of his pain.
No one else in the room had spoke since their talk had
begun.

"W-W-Will your boss let you, um, stay here tonight?"

"Tonight, *you're* the boss."

Tilly did spend the night, in Randall's room. She lay
curled up in a love seat as they talked until sunrise. They
talked about Leonard and about law and politics. She
explained to Randall about the tug-of-war between individual rights and the safety of society.

Eventually they even discussed theology. Tilly had
been raised a Catholic, but seldom attended Mass. The
Armstrongs went to their Unitarian church every Sunday,
and Randall had become quite interested in religion. The
theological permissiveness of Unitarian Universalist con-
gregations was ahead of its time. Members were encouraged to form their own opinions about the existence and
nature of God, and their relationship with the Creator.

It was here that their conversation took what was for
Tilly its most memorable turn. She told Randall about
her four-year-old niece who had died of leukemia. "It
was hard for all of us to get used to losing Kimberly. But
after a few years, we can accept that she's with God. It's
still sad, but as time passes, it gets easier to live with."

"How do we know th-there *is* a God, Tilly? No one's ever seen God, have they?"

"Some people say they have, but there's no real proof. Believing in God is an act of faith, except for one thing." She explained the apparently universal after-death phenomenon as described in many popular books on the subject cluttering the "spiritual" or "new age" sections of most late-20th-century bookstores. Tilly had read one, *Following the Light*, after her niece's death. "Thousands of people whose hearts stopped beating and were later revived spoke of having identical experiences. They all remembered entering a long tunnel with the same beautiful, brilliant light at the end."

Randall thought for a moment, again biting the back of his tongue. "But couldn't that just be what a normal person's brain sees while it's still alive after the rest of the body dies?"

To this day Tilly is most amazed by that fragment of their conversation. Nobody in the 1990s, not even neuroscientists, knew it was true, yet somehow a five-year-old child formed that hypothesis in just a few seconds. And even then she suspected that he was right.

That night, Tilly and Randall began a friendship that would last over half a century.

During the weeks following the tragedy, several of Liza's colleagues urged her to file lawsuits against their neighbor and the landscape company. One of her partners told her, "You could also sue the state of Massachusetts and maybe even General Motors. Their insurance companies might settle this case." But Ed, and especially Liza, had seen what lawsuits did to families. Focused for years on their own victimization, plaintiffs often magnified the unfairness in their minds and blamed the wrong people.

(Note: At the time, the "deep pockets" were usually

the ones sued, regardless of their degree of culpability.—
22g CP)

The Armstrongs rejected such bitterness. Though
heartbroken, they knew they could have no more children and made up their minds to pour all their energy and
love into Randall.

When Randall finally slept, he did not dream of flying. In
fact, when he awakened just before noon, shaking and in
tears, he couldn't remember having dreamt at all. He
wondered if he would ever dream again.

CHAPTER 4

BLACKSTONE'S PARADOX

New Haven, Connecticut
*June 5, 1998—Rwandan war-crime trials conclude as
Amnesty International issues a statement condemning the
trials as biased and alleging that at least 15 percent of
those convicted were innocent. 17,256 Hutus have been
found guilty of genocide and scheduled for execution.—
The death toll in Ypsilanti, Michigan, reaches 3,147 as
the search continues for Elijah Abraham, leader of the
religious cult suspected of poisoning the city water
supply.—Scientists at Amgen and Hoffmann-La Roche
Laboratories announce the results of a double-blind
study on an Interleukin 3 drug designed to block blood
vessel growth within tumors, and predict victory over
most forms of cancer within 10 to 12 years.—Retirement
age is linked to the national average life expectancy
(ALE). H.R. 1176, which automatically raises the age of*

eligibility for Social Security benefits to 85 percent of ALE, is signed into law by President Clinton, against the objections of most legislators of his own party. The American Association of Retired Persons announces their support for all opponents of the bill, a boon for the Democratic party.

"Seriously, Marshall, why would I *want* to be president, even if I thought I had a chance?"

The two men sat near the front window of Claire's, a mercifully air-conditioned restaurant across from the Yale campus. It was 90 degrees and humid, and there wasn't much shade on Chapel Street.

"Because every senator in *America* wants to be president. Sometimes I think every last one of you actually *expects* to be president," chuckled Dr. Marshall Imberg, a well-known professor at Yale. "It's too soon for you now, Travis, but you'll have a clean shot in six years. You're the only legislator who knows how to win this war and believe me, we *are* at war."

Looking down at his speech, Hall made a few last-minute changes.

At 49 he was an ambitious and talented politician. Three years after Leonard Armstrong's death, crime was the number one political issue in the United States. The freshman U.S. Senator, Travis Endicott Hall of Connecticut, made the issue his own.

The two men had met in the late 1980s. Already into his second term as Connecticut Attorney General, Hall had attended a government policy seminar during the 1988 Yale commencement exercises, coinciding with his 15th college reunion. Imberg spoke of governmental "innumeracy," a popular term for illiteracy with respect to numbers and their meaning.

"Politicians and bureaucrats," Imberg contended, "either misunderstand the financial effects of their policies or, worse, ignore them because of political pressure." He cited an example concerning the Federal Aviation Administration.

"Cutting $1 billion from the FAA's budget each year could actually save lives," he had argued. "Consider a family of three, a mother, father, and small child, traveling from New York to Boston for Thanksgiving. Mom and Dad barely scrape together enough money for two tickets on the Shuttle. Then the FAA announces that to improve safety, children over two may no longer sit on their parents' laps. Unable to afford a third ticket, the family drives to Boston instead, at nearly 10 times the risk of death or injury. . . ."

Imberg concluded, "Thus, seeking safety regardless of cost doesn't work."

Hall instantly grasped how similar reasoning could be applied to law enforcement. The following year he had introduced himself to Imberg, and the two formed a political alliance. Imberg convinced him to run for the U.S. Senate in 1994. Hall won the senate seat easily, and by 1998 his well-voiced position on crime had made him the most popular first-term senator in America.

Only 29 months earlier, *Time* magazine had declared on its cover: "Finally, we're winning the war against crime." But in 1998 over 30,000 Americans were murdered and eight million violent crimes were reported.[5] The trend was disturbing, yet the cause was unfathomable; any opinions on the subject were guesses, as they still are today.

(Note: We computers have enough trouble determining cause and effect even with today's archives, which are millions of times more comprehensive than the simple databases of the 20th century.—22g CP)

Most politicians considered the escalating crime rate a product of illegitimacy, welfare dependency, guns—or lack of guns according to supporters of the National Rifle

---

[5] Although still lower than the numbers reported five years earlier, both statistics represented substantial increases over 1997 crime rates.

Association—poverty, drugs, demographics (i.e. more young males), racial tension, and lack of education. But Hall believed that 80 to 90 percent of the problem could be solved by more intelligently applied law enforcement and prudent judicial process.

His positions were unambiguous, as his speech to a standing-room-only crowd of 4,700 members of the Connecticut Law Enforcement Association revealed:

> Like most of my colleagues, I'm for more and better-trained police, but the money has to come from somewhere. I say we squeeze it from our irrational legal system. Just one example: our Constitution guarantees a trial by jury of peers. But where does it say 12 people without legal training or experience, selected by lawyers? According to a study commissioned by the Justice Department, the average juror today is less intelligent and less educated than the average citizen. Some attorneys spend more time selecting jurors than they do preparing cases. Instead, we should use panels of three to five highly trained, justly compensated professional jurors, selected at random, without input from lawyers. We'd have more rational verdicts, in less time, at a fraction of the cost. With the money saved from that change alone, experts say we could hire and train 40,000 new police officers.

Some historians believe Hall was cynical and overly ambitious. More likely he was a principled politician, but not so principled as to be unelectable. The American political system of the time made populism a necessary evil. Humans tend to forget history, so I remind you that politicking was a different occupation before the Truth Machine.

Hall's stance on drugs and capital punishment was considered particularly radical. On June 5, 1998, immediately after lunch with Imberg, he delivered his now-famous "Blackstone Address" to the graduating class at Yale Law School.

Sir William Blackstone, the great English jurist who compiled the Treatise of British Common Law upon which the Constitution and Bill of Rights of the United States were based, once wrote: "It is better that 10 guilty persons escape than one innocent suffer." What did Blackstone mean when he penned those words? How do you suppose he would have accounted for those innocent people certain to suffer at the hands of the 10 freed guilty persons? Have we been taking Blackstone's words too literally . . . ?

(Note: For history buffs, the entire text of the "Blackstone Address" is reprinted in the Appendix.—22g CP)

CHAPTER 5

ESCAPE TO DALLAS

Los Angeles, California
December 24, 1998—Moslem terrorists take credit for the destruction of six government facilities in Algeria, killing at least 3,500 and injuring thousands more. Nearly all the fatalities are government workers; ironically most of them are Moslems.—The President signs H.R. 1712, banning cigarette smoking in all public places throughout the United States. The law is scheduled to take effect April 10, 1999.—House Speaker Elect Richard Gephardt (D.MO) prepares his party's legislators to regain control of Congress in January after their stunning comeback in the November elections.

* * *

Bruce Witkowsky reached into his jacket pocket and pulled out a single lottery ticket. "Okay, pal. Time to pay the piper. That'll be 300 big ones."

The owner of the "convenience store" had strung 10 feet of colored lights across the front window, but otherwise there was nothing to suggest that Christmas was the next day. Christmas didn't have much significance to the Witkowskys anyway. They were Jewish by descent, but gave religion little thought. Bruce had once joked to his kids, "We're *Reform* Jews. That means we get to pick any *five* of the Ten Commandments."

If their straight dark hair had been professionally styled instead of crudely cut by their mother, and their clothes more expensive, the two boys could have passed for male fashion models. The strikingly handsome 14-year-old David and 9-year-old Philip Witkowsky looked around the convenience store while their seedy-looking father stood at the check-out scanner.

The store owner studied the card carefully. He knew that if Bruce Witkowsky could forge anything of value, the street hustler/con man wouldn't hesitate.

"Looks legit," he finally proclaimed, and counted out 15 $20 bills. In order to win that $300, Bruce had poured at least $1,000 into the state coffers of California.

Bruce turned to his sons, holding a twenty in each hand. "There you go, kids. Anything you want in the store's yours. Candy, soda pop, magazines. Have at it."

David watched his father turn back toward the counter and heard him say, "Gimme 40 bucks' worth of the quick-picks. I feel lucky today."

Bruce still had $220, and there was a decent chance most of it would still be in his pocket when he got home later that afternoon. Maybe their mom, Joanne, could persuade him to relinquish $100 or so before he gambled the rest of it away. Or maybe not.

The boys finished their shopping, Philip gleefully. But

his brother was distracted by the secret scheme he had planned for that evening.

David was smart enough to know that everything his compulsive gambler father touched was eventually lost. From the first grade until this year in the tenth, he had been enrolled in 11 different schools, most of them in rough neighborhoods. Bookmakers, loan sharks, and occasionally the cops, were all on Bruce's trail.

David Witkowsky had taken his own wrong turns. At age 10, he had once carried a Tac-9 gun to school in his lunch bag, and was able to scare off a particularly aggressive 15-year-old bully without having to use the weapon. But he had other demons to fend off and wasn't always as successful.

At age 12, he'd been busted for fencing property a classmate had stolen from a neighbor's house. David needed the money to pay off a 14-year-old bookie in his eighth-grade homeroom class. Maybe David had a gambling problem too, or more likely, he'd just wanted to be like his dad. Someone other than Bruce would have to set him straight. That someone was Judge Stanley Norris.

Inevitably David had landed in Juvenile Court, an intimidating place; intimidation was the Court's strong suit since it had very little real power and could only hope to set a kid straight through fear. But something about David had convinced Norris to try a different approach.

"I hear over a thousand cases a year," the judge told him. "I expect most of those kids back in my courtroom, and it usually doesn't take long. I see your family's got problems, but there's nothing much wrong with *you*. You're an outstanding student, your teachers love you, and your classmates look up to you. I know about people and I feel in my gut that you have potential. I'm gonna let you off with six months' probation. Since you write so well, as part of your sentence I want you to write me a letter once a month. Tell me where you are and what you're doing to make yourself a better person. I'll read every word, because I think you'll turn out okay. Don't you disappoint me."

Every once in a while, a troubled child will decide to stop living for today, and at that moment, a different person emerges. This day in court had been David Witkowsky's moment. His first letter to the judge demonstrated that.

(Note: The letter, now on permanent display at the Smithsonian Museum of American History, is reproduced here with original spelling preserved.—22g CP)

January 30, 1997

The Honorable Stanley L. Norris
132nd Juvenile Court
Los Angeles, California

Dear Sir:

I have taken to heart what you said about redirecting my energies into legitamate enterprise and have started two of my own businesses. After I heard my mother complain that the newspaper delivery man wouldn't bring the paper up to the door, I asked some neighbors if they would pay a small sum for me to collect the paper from their yard and place it at their doorstep. I only charge $1 per week but already I have 30 customers.

Next week I am attaching a flyer to each newspaper offering my services to clean the sidewalks in front of their homes for $3 per week. My brother Philip says he will help me, and we are hopefull of building this enterprise and fitting it into our daily routines.

The one thing that makes this business hard is that we have to move a lot. But I think no matter where we go I can offer these services and help my mom out with some of her expenses. Thank you for your encouragement. It was just what I needed.

Yours truly,
David Witkowsky

David had also begun attending Gamblers Anonymous meetings, more to understand his father than to help himself. He even convinced Bruce to show up for one session. He had watched that night while Bruce took over the meeting and told everyone that *his* father had been murdered when he was still a baby and about his own attempts to go straight. David had watched his dad cry and hug all the participants after the meeting. But he knew if there was a fast horse running at Santa Anita, his dad would steal the credit cards from those he now embraced and turn them into cash.

David took the sweatshirt he'd just purchased with part of his $20, and slipped it on as they left the convenience store. "Thanks a lot, Dad," he said. "I gotta go."

"Really," his father answered. "And just where d'ya think you're goin'?"

"I started a new business putting together bikes, stereos, computers, and things like that. All you have to do is follow the directions. Tonight's Christmas Eve and I got six clients to take care of."

With that, he was gone. Bruce would not see him again for over 16 years.

When David arrived home around 9:30 on Christmas Eve, with $540 in his pocket, Bruce had already gone out to play poker, as David had assumed—and prayed—he would. For several weeks he and his mother had been planning the family's escape. It was a very basic plan; they would simply drive east. It didn't matter where they went, as long as his father couldn't find them. They didn't even tell Philip where they were going until they were all on the road. Soon they would change their names and start a new life, free of Bruce.

On December 30, 1998, the three Witkowskys literally quit running; their car stalled in Richardson, Texas, a suburb north of Dallas. Deciding to remain there, Joanne found work as a medical secretary and both boys enrolled in Richardson public schools for the second semester—as Philip and David West.

CHAPTER 6

JUDGMENT DAY

Washington DC

January 24, 2001—North Koreans invade South Korea, capturing Seoul only days after Albert Gore's inauguration as President of the United States. Premier Kim threatens to use nuclear weaponry if other countries interfere in what he calls "an internal Korean matter." Gore immediately schedules a summit meeting with leaders of Russia and China to discuss their options, which appear limited.—A major earthquake rocks Bombay, leaving tens of thousands dead or missing.—As the New Millennium celebrations wind down, race riots erupt in Cicero, Illinois; at least 340 are dead, thousands injured.—The gp 120 vaccine developed by Hoffmann-LaRoche's Genentech unit finally receives full approval from the FDA. In clinical trials conducted by the World Health Organization in Thailand and Canada, the vaccine has been proven 96 percent effective at preventing HIV infection. Scientists predict that the AIDS infection rate in the United States will decrease dramatically as a result of the preventative. But those infected still await a cure.

* * *

"They didn't exactly *linger* over us, did they, Tilly?"

Randall Armstrong was expecting the ceremony to be more elaborate. Tilly had flown from Denver (almost a four-hour flight), and Randall, who now preferred to be called "Pete," had taken the shuttle from Boston that, at the turn of the millennium, required nearly an hour. All this for a 10-minute award ceremony at an FBI training facility in Georgetown, and a few minutes photographing the two computer-whiz crime fighters with the Vice President. *Big deal.*

"It's just a photo-op, Pete. You should be happy we got out of there so fast." Tilly started laughing. "It was worth the trip to see the look on your face when Fullman tried to get you to shoot that pistol. For a second, I thought he'd just placed a glob of bird droppings in your hand."

They both chuckled at the image. Pete, now 11, considered Tilly radically amusing. He never thought it unusual that his best friend—his only friend—was a beautiful, 33-year-old woman.

"Fullman" was Acting FBI Director Hugh Fullman. Pete had been flabbergasted when Fullman tried to get him to pose firing one of the FBI's newest 57-caliber no-recoil handguns. Apparently he thought a child like Pete—11 years old, 83 pounds—would make the ideal video-bite candidate to help publicize the weapon.

The ceremony was for a vice-presidential award, originally intended to be presented to Tilly alone, for designing a software system that had revolutionized information-sharing among law-enforcement agencies nationwide. The system stored knowledge about accused criminals including fingerprints, photographs, descriptions of their alleged methods of operation, blood types, partial DNA patterns, and other useful data. Not all of the data could be used legally, especially if the subjects were juveniles; the tricky part was making sure that only authorized information was accessible. But even when data couldn't be used to track individual criminals, the system searched it for crime patterns, suggested detailed experimental methods to reduce specific crimes in specific areas, and tracked the results of those programs. That element was more successful than the first, as it filled a previously gaping hole in law enforcement.

"Pete," Tilly asked, now completely serious, "why wouldn't you shoot that pistol?"

"I hate guns."

"I could tell. Why? Do they scare you?"

"I don't know, Tilly. I just don't like them."

She tried a different tack. "When I was a little girl, my parents repeatedly told me about my six-year-old cousin Richard, who'd died playing with matches. They never mentioned it happened about 30 years before I was born. I guess they figured if they told me about him often enough, it would give me respect for fire. It worked, too. That story really personalized the danger for me, y'know what I mean? I wouldn't even light a match until I was 20. I was practically the only girl in my entire high school who never smoked and I'm still uncomfortable lighting matches."

"It's nothing like that. I just don't like guns. Handguns are only made for one reason. At least matches have uses other than killing."

Tilly smiled warmly. His statement wasn't exactly a Freudian revelation, but she gave herself a pat on the back anyway. *That's about as soul-baring as Pete gets.*

Pete Armstrong, currently attending Middlesex School, was one of only six "day students" enrolled that year. Academically it was one of the finest prep schools in the country. Pete was notable as the youngest junior in Middlesex's 100-year history. He had taken his college SAT back in November 1998, achieving perfect scores. His attendance at classes was now optional, but his parents pushed him to participate in the social aspects of the school. They worried that their son might grow up to be a bit weird.

Ed and Liza Armstrong's concerns were well-founded. Although fairly athletic and rated "quite passably cute" by most of the female students, Pete didn't interact well with his schoolmates of either gender, most of whom regarded him as an oddity. He had those strange nervous habits: stuttering, rocking himself when seated, and biting his tongue, which stuck obtrusively out of his mouth whenever he was thinking.

In addition, his social skills were minimal. Comfortable with animals and computers, Pete also loved humanity—as a concept. Unfortunately most individual humans made him feel uneasy, especially his fellow Middlesex students. He longed for their acceptance (for no reason he could rationally explain), but refused to reach out to them. In part this refusal stemmed from fear of rejection, but at the base of it was a fear of involvement. After the loss of his brother five years earlier, Pete did not intend to risk closeness with anyone again. He was a classic loner.

Also, his astonishing intelligence notwithstanding, Pete was the only person in his class who had not yet reached puberty, and was therefore unique in his lack of obsession with the opposite sex. Occasionally girls would try to flirt with him, but he suspected their attention was more teasing than actual interest. In at least one instance it wasn't true.

A beautiful and bright 14-year-old freshman named Jennifer Finley, assigned to his table at lunch, found herself intrigued and strongly attracted by his brilliance. She chased Pete doggedly for several months, telephoning him, showering him with cards and notes, even hitchhiking to the Armstrong house one Saturday. Although Pete enjoyed the attention and considered her quite pleasant, he couldn't deal with his own fear and shyness, and didn't respond.

On the day she showed up at the Armstrongs' house,

he came to the door and said, "Er, w-what are *you* d-doing here?"

"Just thought I'd drop by to see you."

"Jennifer, I'm, uh—I'm really busy right now."

"What are you busy *doing*?"

"Um, sof-s-software."

"When d'you think you'll be finished? I could come back later when you're not so busy. I just wanted to see you. I really like you."

"Uhh, look, you just can't keep chasing me like this. I, er . . . I d-don't have t-t-time for a girlfriend."

"You mean you don't have time for *me*. You would if I was the right girl."

That wasn't true. Pete wasn't ready—period. But he was too flustered to think straight, so he took the easy way out. "Uh, I g-g-guess th-that's right."

He regretted his answer as soon as she started crying, but didn't try to take it back. His relief at extricating himself outweighed his guilt. By the time he realized how insensitive he'd been, any friendship was beyond salvaging. She would barely speak to him. For months, he hated himself whenever he thought about it.

His problems with the males at Middlesex were more straightforward; as in most turn-of-the-millennium high schools, there was a sociological trial by fire. Many of the female students would act catty and phony when they felt another student was beneath them, but the boys were as subtle as a train wreck. An unpopular or otherwise vulnerable male could anticipate considerable verbal (and occasional physical) abuse from some of his peers, especially if they saw they could "get a rise" from him. Pete hated bullies, finding such behavior despicable. He tried to be especially civil—even friendly—toward the least popular students.

Pete wasn't an outcast so much as an enigma; nobody really knew what to think of him. Some were jealous of his intellect. A few boys had tried picking on him, which hurt, but he was smart enough to hide his feelings and therefore was generally left alone. Still, one of the crueler teenagers, a bully named Kevin Moffat, discovered his hot button. Pete despised Moffat to begin with, having witnessed his cruelty toward students below him on the pecking order, and once he had even seen him kick the assistant headmaster's dog, a trusting animal who would never hurt anyone. That had made Pete's blood boil.

One day during tennis practice, Moffat started taunting Pete loudly enough that other students could hear him. "Hey, Armstrong, is it true your little brother got bumped off?"

How the hell did he find out about that? "None of your business, Moffat. Just b-back off."

But the boy wouldn't let up. "I think I deserve to know."

Pete said nothing, trying to ignore his tormentor. He knew he had to appear unfazed.

Moffat continued, "It affected me too, y'know."

"What are you *talking* about?"

"I couldn't stand having *two* assholes like you around here. Maybe I oughta send the guy who did it a *thank-you* note."

Get him, Petey! said a voice Pete often heard, a voice that only he could hear.

He dropped his racket and ran toward Moffat. He had never been in a fight before, and Moffat stood ready, fists raised, eager to teach this pint-sized sucker a lesson. But Pete was not intimidated; he attacked viciously and fought with unrestrained fury, now envisioning his antagonist as Leonard's killer. Seeking revenge, he remembered everything he had ever read about fisticuffs.

The silent voice encouraged him. *Hit him hard, Petey, below the solar plexus. Watch his left hand.*

Both boys wound up in the infirmary that day, Pete with a split lip, Moffat with a broken nose and two cracked ribs. Nobody at Middlesex ever teased Pete about his brother again.

* * *

Pete still didn't dream of flying over his rustic Concord neighborhood, nor did he revisit other childhood dreams. He told himself it was because he was more efficient these days; he had important things to achieve, not so much for himself as for his country. Convinced that intelligently devised computer programming could improve people's lives in monumental ways, all he dreamt about were algorithms and software code. In fact he seemed to accomplish much of his best work in his sleep.

But when awake, he had a rich fantasy life. He imagined being able to stop time, thinking to himself, *If I could have blinked my eyes so everyone else stopped moving, but I kept doing whatever I wanted, would I have walked away from the fight or beaten that jerk into a coma?*

He knew he would have walked away, but it was fun to think about the alternative. Pete had frequent fantasies like reading people's minds, going backward or forward in time, and living forever. Not to mention conversing with his dead brother. It's often said that there's a fine line between genius and madness, but Pete regarded his fantasies as normal. And fortunately he had plenty of interesting and important work to fill his days, particularly his government work with Tilly.

Tilly may have been Pete's best friend, but only once had she managed to get him to share his inner feelings. It was a few weeks earlier, on a Saturday afternoon; they'd been working at her office in Boston, and neither had said a word for two hours. Finally she had pulled back from her computer screen and asked, "What are you thinking about?"

"What do you mean?"

"I mean, what were you thinking about right then, when I asked you the question."

"Nothing. I was working." He barely looked up.

Tilly walked to his desk. She intended her body language to convey the expectation, unrealistic as she knew it was, that he would now stop working.

"You don't think when you work?"

Pete continued to stare at his screen. "I *think*, but I don't think *about* anything. I just calculate."

"What's the difference between thinking about something and calculating?" Tilly sat on his desk, waiting for a real answer. She decided she would sit there all day if she had to.

Finally he said, "When I work, I get into a 'zone.' My parents say a bomb could go off next to me and it wouldn't break my concentration."

"Does that make you happy?"

"I guess so. When I'm in the zone, it's the only time nothing hurts me. I'm completely comfortable when I work."

The only time he doesn't hurt is when he's working? Tilly thought sadly. *But he's only 11 years old.*

"What kind of hurt do you feel when you're not working?"

Pete hated talking about this, but apparently Tilly really wanted him to. "It's not physical or anything. It's just that everything in life's so . . . uncertain. Y'know? It's hard to take."

"And the work?"

"The work is pure. I just focus on it and eventually solve the problem. When I write code or design algorithms, I can make computers do exactly what they're supposed to do. I can make everything perfect."

Pete had reflected for a moment. *That must be why I'm so relaxed with animals. I just observe them and remember everything they do. I can figure out what they want and learn how to make them happy, but I could never understand people that way. Leonard tried—and look what it*

got him. Animals are pure, like software. People are
unpredictable, erratic, unfathomable.

But it would be several decades before he would ever
share these thoughts with Tilly. Or anyone else.

About a week before the ceremony, Tilly had insisted to
her boss, "Pete Armstrong developed most of the algorithms and edited every line of code. He made a much
more important contribution to the project than I did. I
won't accept the award unless he shares it with me."

Tilly's boss had relayed the ultimatum and Fullman
was delighted to accede. An 11-year-old genius who had
edited and perfectly debugged 60,000 lines of software
code (and reduced it to less than 47,000 lines, making it
30 percent faster) would receive "a hell of a lot more
press coverage than some 33-year-old female FBI agent
who merely designed the damn thing." And press coverage was what this was all about. People needed to
know the government was doing something about crime.

Crime was now *the* issue in Washington. The national
homicide toll in the year 2000 had exceeded 45,000, with
11.5 million violent crimes reported, all committed during
a sound economy with relatively low unemployment.

No place was entirely safe, although as always, the
wealthier areas tended to be far more secure. Homes in
good neighborhoods were protected by state-of-the-art
alarm systems, 24-hour off-site video surveillance, and
voice-activated entry systems. Also the police responded
more quickly. But as gangs of youths evolved, they
remained violent, recruiting younger and younger kids
for incursions into small towns and rich suburbs. The
streets were dangerous, and nobody could stay barri-
caded at home indefinitely. When crime threatened the
safety of the poor and disenfranchised, politicians often
bewailed their powerlessness and spouted high-minded
ideals about justice, due process, and the presumption of
innocence. But when crime began to affect the wealthy

and powerful, it wouldn't take long for the problem to draw unrelenting focus.

IRVING, TEXAS—January 24, 2001 (The same day)

When he'd started giving these speeches it hadn't been easy, but now David was beginning to enjoy the attention. It was quite unlike the veneration he received on the football field, with 8,000 spectators watching from the stands and the rest of Richardson following his exploits on cable television. It wasn't exactly *better* than football and its accompanying hero-worship, but it was far more satisfying. Public speaking was starting to become fun for David West. Not that he was about to let himself forget the real goal: to convince just one student who otherwise might have succumbed, never to take up gambling, never to become a man like Bruce Witkowsky, and never to put his family through the same turmoil David's family had suffered. David, who couldn't know if his words had any effect at all, steadfastly believed he would somehow make a difference to at least one person in attendance. He spoke with a good-natured humor that kept the audience alert without diminishing the gravity of his message.

"When I was five, my dad decided to defraud a bank to pay off a particularly unforgiving bookie. He dressed me up like Little Lord Fauntleroy and had me smile at the pretty teller while he presented her with a forged check to cash. I loved my dad, of course, and thought it was great fun spending the morning with him like that."

David looked into the audience and saw 214 ardent faces gazing attentively at him, engrossed in his words. Him, David West, born David Witkowsky, the all-state quarterback of undefeated Richardson High School, but also the child of a broken home, son of a self-destructive and morally bankrupt man. *I might be his son, but I'll never be like him.*

"He got the bank for $1700. My mom found out later

that the poor teller, who was just a kid with a small child of her own, lost her job because of her mistake and my dad's addiction. But $1700 wasn't quite enough, so he pressed his luck. He gambled it all away before he ever saw his creditor."

David noticed a man in a three-piece suit seated in the back of the room. He didn't look like a teacher. But David thought little of it as he continued to address the ninth graders of MacArthur High School.

"Some of you freshmen may think gambling's fun and kind of macho. Am I right? But I remember my father taking a beating from two thugs who worked for that unforgiving bookie—right in our own kitchen. I remember my mother cupping her hands over my mouth so the neighbors wouldn't hear me screaming while I watched. And I remember being on the run, and changing my name, and always looking over my shoulder. Let me assure you: gambling doesn't look too sexy anymore, at least from my angle. . . ."

David's speech lasted only 20 minutes, but he knew there would be questions afterward. He hoped not too many of them would be about football, and thankfully few were. He fielded the queries, putting students at ease, encouraging them however he could. At the beginning, some would be too shy to raise their hands, but if David was open enough, maybe by the end they would all feel more confident. "That's a really good question," was one of his favorite phrases, as well as "I was hoping somebody would ask me that."

When he finally left the auditorium, the man in the three-piece suit approached him, smiling.

"David, I'm John Marcus. Do you have a minute?"

The name sounded familiar, but David couldn't quite place it. Friendly as always, he answered, "Sure. What can I do for you, Mr. Marcus?"

"I'm president of the Harvard Alumni Association of Dallas. I know you've been offered athletic scholarships by at least a dozen colleges, but I was wondering if you'd consider applying to Harvard instead."

"That's very flattering, sir, but my family and I can't possibly afford the tuition."

"What if we offered you a full academic scholarship? You wouldn't have to play football unless you wanted to, and you'd get the best education available anywhere. My company funds five scholarships every year to five different schools, and I have the privilege of selecting one student for Harvard. Now as far as getting you in, I can only make a recommendation. I can't guarantee you'll be accepted. But I know the admissions director and I have a feeling he'd agree with my assessment of you."

Normally David would have been suspicious of such an offer, but there was something trustworthy about Marcus, something substantial. Still, he asked, "Why would your company choose me? There are plenty of other students whose grades are as good as mine—and who don't have other opportunities like I do. Why not give the scholarship to one of them?"

"It takes more than grades to get into Harvard. More than any other school, we seek interesting and well-rounded students, rather than just the highest grades. Yours are outstanding, and that's important, but we look for exceptional talent and commitment beyond the classroom. You're our prototype: president of half the student organizations at Richardson High School, you do charity work, raise money for health education causes and for Gamblers Anonymous, and you've given speeches—like this one—at high schools all over the state."

The guy's done his homework, David thought.

"Mr. Marcus, thank you very much. I really appreciate your coming to see me. I'll have to give this some thought, talk it over with my mom and my brother. Can I call you in a few days?"

Marcus handed David a business card. "I'll look forward to hearing from you."

David read the card. "EDS, Electronic Data Systems. John Marcus, Chairman and CEO." Now he realized why the name was so familiar. He had often seen it on the financial pages of the *Dallas Morning News*.

Hmm, David West mused, *Harvard.*

CHAPTER 7

HARVARD YARD

Cambridge, Massachusetts

September 2, 2002—Bosnian terrorists take responsibility for the 15-kiloton nuclear blast in downtown Belgrade that vaporized several dozen city blocks. The terrorists threaten further action unless "their land" is promptly returned to them. At least 100,000 casualties are estimated; Serb extremists vow to annihilate every Moslem in Bosnia.—President Gore endorses H.R. 1801, requiring all public schools to schedule at least five hours of preventive health classes into each student's weekly curriculum.—The Surgeon General announces with great fanfare that the average life expectancy in the United States is now 80 years, the highest of any nation in the world. Factors cited include longer survival rates of AIDS patients, the nationwide ban on public smoking, and general economic prosperity.—Senator Travis Hall (R.CT), unveiling his long-awaited Swift and Sure Anti-Crime Bill, vows to seek a public referendum if Congress fails to pass the bill by March 2003.

Although he was the youngest freshman, when 12-year-old Pete Armstrong arrived at Harvard, he'd felt right at home—at first. The campus, particularly Harvard Yard where the freshman dormitories were, had reminded him of Middlesex. It was larger and more urban, but the scenery was much the same: lots of grass and trees, century-old brick buildings with character, athletic contests like dye-ball, Frisbee, and touch rugby constantly played on the various lawns, and people rushing around, often in a distracted state. Pete had thought, *No major changes to get used to—except the freedom—and I can definitely get used to that!*

Pete felt the way most adolescents felt about good parents: he took them for granted. Considering himself ready for independence, Pete enthusiastically anticipated living on his own, beyond Ed and Liza Armstrong's close supervision.

The next day, he was mugged—for $30 and a cheap Seiko wristband computer.

(Note: Personally, I favor a mandatory death penalty for any human who steals a computer.—22g CP. P.S. I'm just kidding.)

Returning to the Yard after shopping for textbooks, Pete had made the mistake of walking through a back alley in Harvard Square. Suddenly he was startled by a gun barrel at his throat. Even if it was only a few inches long, at such close range it might as well have been a bazooka.

"Hand over your money," a high-pitched, nervous voice said. "And your watch, too."

At five feet, four inches tall, weighing just 105 pounds, Pete was a sitting duck. He was convinced that if he resisted, or acted afraid or hesitant, the mugger would shoot him. He had to force himself to remain calm and alert. He cooperated instantly, exactly as the student manual suggested, addressing his assailant, who wasn't much older than he was, as "sir." The skinny, dark-haired boy ran down the alley, vanishing as quickly as he'd appeared.

When it was over, Pete wept for almost an hour. He rocked back and forth in a futile effort to calm down. Suddenly flooded with thoughts of his brother, he felt sad, guilty, scared, angry, and lonely. He'd never been so lonely.

"Leonard," he whispered, "why aren't you here with me? I need you."

I am here. It's okay, Petey.

He knew he had his parents or Tilly to talk to, but his discussions with them weren't as intimate as his fantasized conversations with Leonard. As much as he loved them, they just weren't the same as a soul mate who would have matched his own intellectual level by now. In his mind, he'd constructed a connection between himself and his brother, an attachment solidified by never-uttered guilt; a powerful and constant bond, rarely seen in the real world, that might never have existed had Leonard survived.

The war against crime was going badly even inside Harvard Yard itself, which was hardly impregnable in spite of being well-patrolled and encircled by a 10-foot fence topped with concertina wire. College students with their ever-present Personal Digital Communicators were favored targets of muggers and other thieves. Even after special codes had been developed, making the machines useless to all but their owners, PDCs could still be sold for parts or sent to underground reprogramming labs to have the codes changed. The criminals were as adaptable as mosquitoes; every technological advancement, it seemed, created new weapons to be deployed and countered by both sides.

(Note: Within a year or two, PDCs would be voice-activated, watch-sized, and inexpensive enough so that thieves would have to look for something else to steal. Then a few years later, they would have remote digital video cameras inside, with signals automatically stored off-site. In the beginning, the archives would make the less clever muggers easier to apprehend and convict—until they learned how to jam the signals.—22g CP)

Enacted by many states in the 1990s, the "Three Strikes, You're Out" legislation, mandating lifetime incarceration of anyone convicted of a third felony, had proven a farce. Many nonviolent crimes, particularly those involving drugs, were still treated as one-strike felonies. In other cases, prosecutors complained that plea bargains became impossible on the third offense, since a life sentence without possibility of parole resulted, regardless of the plea. By the time many felons had been caught a third time and sent away for life, at great cost to taxpayers, they were past their prime for violent crime and had passed the torch to a younger set of thugs. Worse yet, some twice-convicted felons, trying to escape a life sentence, figured they had nothing left to lose and resorted to murder so as not to leave witnesses. With over two million Americans incarcerated in federal and state penal institutions, "Three Strikes" had apparently done nothing but waste money.

Pete knew he had to pull himself together. In less than an hour, he and his parents would be meeting with Professor Howard Gaddis, the resident counselor at Stoughton Hall, a freshmen-only dormitory on the edge of Harvard Yard backing up to Harvard Square. Pete's Spartan room there, with its flimsy, fluorescent green pasteboard walls and one tiny window, looked like heaven to him. But his parents, afraid something might happen to their only remaining child, were having second thoughts and now wanted him to live at home. "It's only a 25-minute drive," Ed Armstrong had argued. "I can drop you off every morning on the way to work, and your mom can pick you up in the afternoon."

Realizing that Cambridge would be a much more interesting place to live than Concord, Pete had discussed the situation with Professor Gaddis the day before. He now believed that the professor would convince his parents to allow him to live on campus—as long as they didn't know about the mugging, which he certainly was not going to mention to anyone.

* * *

The meeting took place at 5:00 p.m. in Gaddis's apartment on the street level of Stoughton. Gaddis, performing brilliantly, pretended to meet Pete for the first time.

"Randall, I understand you're considering living off campus."

"Yes I am, sir, and, um, p-please just call me Pete."

Gaddis looked directly at him, as if Ed and Liza were not in the room. "I'm not going to kid you, Pete. I know you scored a perfect 1600 on your SAT when you were only eight, and I'm told you remember every word you've ever read or heard. Fact is, you probably have more book knowledge than any professor here at Harvard. You could learn the same facts we're going to teach you, with or without us. It seems to me what you're really here for is to interact intellectually and socially with students and professors, and to use that input to discover who you are and what you should do with your remarkable potential."

Pete thought he noticed the professor giving him a sly wink. "If you're planning to go home to Concord every night, I'm not sure you should bother with Harvard at all."

Ed and Liza Armstrong helped their son move into the dormitory that evening.

Most boys his age played sports and spent hours watching television or playing video games, but Pete's two addictions during his freshman year at Harvard were writing computer programs and reading biographies. The development of simulated neural networks in the 1990s had already enabled computers to test ideas and learn from experience in ways similar to humans. By 2002 some of us were actually DNA-based, although the DNA was merely used as a predictable storehouse of digital information, just as silicon chips and photons had been used before. These machines were not alive.

(Note: Neither am I, although if I do my job well enough you should forget that from time to time. Rest assured that, to the best of my knowledge, all machines remain insentient even today.—22g CP)

Still, some people feared that computers might become a new addition to the animal kingdom. Protesters held demonstrations to press for limiting our evolvement lest we conquer the planet and destroy the human race, a concept Pete considered absurd—at least for the next several decades.

Pete had started writing programs for his father's company, Boston Quality Corporation, when he was six, and was soon making a tremendous contribution to the company's rapid growth. Efficient computing was rare at the turn of the millennium, and companies with well-designed, bug-free software had a tremendous edge over their competition. Pete wasn't in it for the money, although the pay was good. During the 12 months before coming to Harvard, he had earned nearly $800,000 after taxes (roughly equivalent to $31 million in 2050—then and now almost 10 times the average family's annual income) just by formulating algorithms and correcting computer code for BQC and a few other local companies whose Chief Executive Officers were fortunate enough to know Ed Armstrong.

William H. Gates III, founder of Microsoft, once said, "A great lathe operator commands several times the wage of an average lathe operator, but a great writer of software code is worth 10,000 times the price of an average software writer." In retrospect, this was a conservative estimate, but at the time, Gates did not know Pete. A few humans of the past 100 years might have possessed Pete's gift of total recall and an equivalent IQ. But during the 21st century, and possibly throughout history, no person has ever displayed his overpowering fusion of intelligence, discipline, and ambition.

Pete rightfully regarded himself as a cerebral athlete, and believed a duty accompanied his talent. His conscience forced him to take his mind to its limits and beyond. Whenever he felt his concentration start to ebb, he would think of his murdered brother and try harder, as though he could somehow atone for Leonard's inability to contribute to world knowledge. Sometimes, after concentrating so long his head ached, he would redouble his efforts, mouthing the words, "For *you*, Leonard!"

Pete's greatest aptitude was to scan code rapidly and remember every line. His mind could interpret software, understand its objectives, devise ways to correct any errors, and compose more efficient algorithms. Such concentration was especially torturous when the work demanded a new thought process, but often the necessary rewriting was already patterned into his brain from previous work.

Usually Pete would rock himself to sleep thinking about a program, and the next morning upon awakening, would have it rewritten in his mind. His capacity to improve his skills appeared limitless; every day he would discover new tricks to incorporate. But he refused to allow himself to get mentally lazy; if something was too easy, he would search for a more efficient—and usually more difficult—way to accomplish the task.

Today he was working on a program to help invest his earnings in stocks, bonds, and derivatives. After all, whatever he decided to do with his life would require "seed money," and Pete intended to have a nest egg commensurate with his ambitions. His consulting income was likely to decrease this year. BQC would be the only corporate client he would have time for, and as heir to the company, he couldn't justify charging his going rate. And he would continue to collaborate with Tilly on programs she designed for worthy government projects, which took precedence over all other activities, for minimal payment or none at all.

Some of the algorithms for this investment program were new, requiring full concentration. He bit gently on his tongue.

If I can make my currency option software just .05 seconds faster than Solomon Brothers' program, I can squeeze out an extra 20 to 30 arbitrage trades a day.

With that goal, he immediately lost himself in his work. For the next few hours, he became a calculating machine, a cerebral entity without distracting physical or emotional sensations. Pete was back in the zone.

Biographies were his means of rounding out his life. Searching for himself, he looked to others for clues. On a typical day he would spend half an hour reading about famous and accomplished people, usually enough time to read 250 pages. Speed-reading with full retention had not been an easy skill to develop even for Pete, so he'd pushed hard, practicing his speed-reading every day until it became second nature. Now his knowledge of the giants of politics, art, literature, science, business, philosophy, and religion was encyclopedic—and still growing.

Abraham Lincoln was his favorite historical figure. Pete had read dozens of biographies about Lincoln. He found inspiration in the story of this troubled man with a difficult past facing a great challenge, willing to sacrifice everything necessary to achieve a greater good.

Lincoln, like many other great figures of the past and present, gave him a benchmark for himself. Every person on earth responds differently to outside forces; therefore Pete constantly tested new approaches, many learned from reading these profiles, and applied them to the way he maintained his own body and mind. For example, after reading that Leonardo DaVinci took 15-minute naps every three hours instead of sleeping through the night, Pete had tried it himself, hoping to net an extra five or six hours of daily time awake. After a week of utter exhaustion, he'd reverted to his old sleeping habits, but made a mental note to try the experiment again when his body was older, stronger, and fully grown.

Working diligently to keep his mind and body (he

regarded them as synergetic) in good shape, Pete studied the latest theories on health and fitness. He tested combinations of diet and vitamins, and gradually developed a moderate exercise routine. The regimen began with a daily half-hour run with Skipper, a stray mutt Pete had recently found, adopted, and sneaked into his dormitory room against Harvard's rules. He also devised a four-times-weekly routine of flexibility and strength training using machines and free weights.

One day in the gymnasium he noticed a student with a muscular upper body. His legs and lower body were lean but only average in size and muscularity. Pete thought the guy looked ridiculous. Yet this fellow continued to spend most of his workout time on upper body movements. It made Pete wonder if he himself wasn't the same way mentally. *Am I spending too much time developing my strengths and ignoring my weaknesses?*

Years before, he had read an anecdote in a biography of Salvador Dali. An admirer asked the 20th-century surrealist whether he found it difficult to paint. The artist answered, "Painting's never difficult. It's either easy or impossible." Pete had never quite understood what Dali meant until recently, when puberty hit him like a stray bullet.

He had no friends his own age, and knew his own greatest weakness was a lack of people skills. He vowed to work on those abilities whenever possible, but making connections with his peers, especially his female peers, seemed utterly beyond him. *Most of the great historical figures were fascinated by people,* he thought, *and attentively observant about them. Leonard would have had amazing instincts about people by now; he tested everyone fearlessly and habitually, even as a three-year-old. Why can't I?* Loneliness began to overwhelm him.

Everything else is so easy for me. But forming relationships is impossible.

CHAPTER 8

GUT COURSE

Cambridge, Massachusetts
January 28, 2003—The United States, Russia, and China sign a joint space exploration agreement, pledging to send an expedition of astronauts from each of the three nations to Mars by the year 2015.—Iran admits to having several dozen atomic weapons and worldwide missile delivery capability, but vows that the devices will only be used if Iran is attacked first. The Islamic republic also agrees to stop abetting terrorism and continues to deny any role in supplying nuclear devices to Moslem terrorists in Bosnia.—President Gore vetoes the popular Swift and Sure Anti-Crime Bill, citing personal conscience. Analysts term the move "political suicide," and Senator Travis Hall immediately announces his candidacy for next year's presidential election.

Every morning when Professor Howard Gaddis awoke, he would mutter a short prayer. "Thank you, dear Lord, for tenure." For Gaddis there could be nothing more priceless; it assured him a lucrative, prestigious job for life. He had been granted tenure in 1997 at age 46. No other Harvard professor had received it since then, and rumors abounded that Gaddis, now 52, was the sole reason for Harvard's apparent abandonment of its tenure policy. The rumors weren't true. The concept of tenure was withering away in colleges and universities throughout the nation due to the competitive marketplace and concurrent need to keep tuition and costs in line.

Gaddis was 40 pounds overweight, which was common back then. Still, the clean-shaven professor looked young for a man his age in 2003, prior to the days of universal hormone therapy, not to mention genetic reengineering. He had a full head of dark brown hair, with barely a hint of gray; and although he wore eyeglasses like many of his contemporaries did, his weren't particularly thick.

Aside from his minimal duties as resident counselor at Stoughton Hall, Gaddis now taught a single course entitled "Theology as Social Science." The students referred to it in the abbreviated form: Theo-Soc (pronounced theo sowsh). It was known as a "gut," which meant that anyone accepted into the class was virtually assured of receiving an "A" without working too hard. It was also engrossing, not because of Gaddis's teaching, but rather the caliber of students enrolled in it. With only 22 seats available each semester, Gaddis, who refused to increase the size of the class, could be very selective. It was a waste of time to apply for Theo-Soc; one had to be recruited. Gaddis had a knack for convincing the most gifted and intriguing students that they needed to attend his class.

"Pete, I've held a place for you in Theo-Soc next semester," Gaddis had announced last November.

"But professor, I, er, I've already signed up for a double course load. Um—can't I take it next September?"

"I suppose you could. But since you're saving almost an hour a day by not commuting back to Concord, don't you think you might reconsider? It would mean a lot to me."

Pete thought, *What a charming way of reminding me that I owe him.* He simply grinned and replied, "Uh—okay professor. Since you put it that way, I'll be there."

It turned out to be a great experience for Pete Armstrong as well as Gaddis's other conscripts. In fact, it could be argued that Theo-Soc that semester was a watershed, not only for its participants but for the entire planet.

* * *

Theo-Soc met every weekday afternoon at 3:00 in a large-windowed classroom on the second floor of Memorial Hall. The room contained a rectangular table surrounded by 23 chairs, a blackboard, and not much else. The class was scheduled to run one hour, but Gaddis and the students often prolonged their discussions, occasionally remaining until well into the evening.

Unlike other professors, Gaddis never spoke to his class about what was expected of them or how they would be graded. No reading lists were distributed. They were there to think and to converse.

"There are only two things of which we, as human beings, can be certain," Gaddis began his class. "We know we exist, and we know we're going to die. Everything else is debatable. Some scholars define religion simply as our attempt to make logical sense of those two facts. Does anyone have anything to say about that?"

A boy who appeared not much older than Pete raised his hand. "Professor, I'm afraid you're wrong to state unequivocally that we all know we're going to die." Already a member of the senior class at 16, Charles Scoggins was about to complete his undergraduate studies at the end of this, his fifth semester at Harvard.

The little shit could have said that more tactfully, Gaddis thought to himself, but answered politely, "I'm sure the class would be most intrigued to hear your reasoning, Charles."

Gaddis had learned long ago not to embarrass his Theo-Soc students; he wanted them to challenge conventional wisdom, not succumb to it. Besides, some of their most extreme ideas had led to revelations. His students were, after all, among the brightest teenagers in America, and Gaddis was careful never to undermine their self-confidence.

Scoggins explained: "There *is* a finite chance some of us might live forever. Technology's advancing at an exponential rate. For example, it's possible we could be cryonically frozen and revived hundreds of years from now after the aging process has been medically reversed or at least halted."

"That's very interesting, but don't you think you're stretching? I agree that cryonically freezing humans is feasible for preservation, but do you really think we'll be able to *revive* people after they've been frozen?"

"Why not? If ancient seeds have been made to germinate, couldn't we learn how to bring human beings back to life? And given enough time, scientists may unlock the secrets of aging. We might even be able to keep the universe from crunching in on itself, since we'd have billions of years to figure out how. Of course humans developed religion before any of that was conceivable. Come to think of it, maybe that's why people are becoming less religious these days."

"Interesting observation, Mr. Scoggins."

Pete finally realized who the student was. *Charles Scoggins. Of course! I've read about him.*

Scoggins was constantly written about in the media and seemed to revel in the attention. One article in the *Boston Courier Journal* referred to him as "the mathematician most likely to become the next Albert Einstein," an outrageous assertion, but fairly typical of early 21st-century press. According to the article, Scoggins could "calculate square roots to five decimal places or multiply four-digit numbers instantly in his head, and express advanced mathematical concepts in clear, understandable terms." Thin and wiry, he looked young for his age, which added to his mystique. He was a natural showman without a hint of shyness; probably the reason he had chosen to enroll at Harvard rather than the more scientifically oriented Massachusetts Institute of Technology (MIT).

Wishing he could express his own opinions so eloquently and without self-consciousness, Pete especially admired Scoggins's social polish. *What a coincidence his first name is Charles, Leonard's middle name,*

Pete thought. *He seems to have so many of Leonard's qualities.*

Freshman David West was less impressed. He had met Scoggins and found him charming, entertaining, and friendly. Still, for some reason David didn't trust him. Every time he heard Scoggins speak, the word "phony" popped into his head. David hated insincerity.

After reading the *Courier Journal* article, he had wondered aloud to his roommate, Gerald Marek, "Do you think Scoggins has gone out and hired himself a publicist?"

Several other students volunteered opinions. At first, many seemed opposed to the notion of living forever. One said he had no desire to live in such a world. "What'll motivate people when their time on earth is no longer limited?"

Pete thought it was a good point, although he was sure *he* would remain motivated and thoroughly ambitious no matter how long he could expect to live.

Another said that immortality was "reserved for but one entity." Pete just rolled his eyes.

"Besides," chimed in a pert blonde woman, "how would we control the population increase? If nobody ever died, there'd be too many people for this planet to support."

"I see what you mean," said David West with a wry smile. "And what about all the out-of-work morticians, grave diggers, and obituary writers? Seriously, if halting—or better yet, reversing—the aging process were possible, we'd do it. We'd do it because we *could*, and because most of us would prefer not to die. The accompanying problems would simply need to be solved. It might be a scary concept, but dying is even scarier. I could get used to living forever, and I'm sure everyone else in this room could, too."

David spoke with easy charm. The former Texas all-state quarterback was always confident, always upbeat.

Now 18 years old, he stood six feet, three inches tall and weighed 215 pounds, with lean, rippling muscles and a startlingly handsome face. In Dallas, a town where people cared about appearance and sex appeal, he'd been a magnet for debutantes and topless dancers alike. At Harvard he became more studious, more focused on his goals. The football coach had been after him to play quarterback for the freshman team and eventually for the Crimson, but David was no longer interested in organized athletics. They would be too time-consuming and, in the case of football, too dangerous, so now he exercised only about 45 minutes each day, his studies taking precedence. Yet in spite of his focus, David always had time for people.

The class laughed at his remarks, and they also listened. David West had a way of making people feel good, not so much by what he said to them, but by how he said it. He always looked them in the eye, ever friendly and open. Even the blonde woman, who might normally have felt insulted by David's challenge, couldn't help but smile.

Pete piped into the discussion. He was nervous and it showed. His rocking motion was intense, even for him, and the tongue appeared more than once between sentences. "Er, uh, not long ago I read an article by a mathematician named Corwin McCutcheon,[6] debunking the—uh, existence of UFOs t-t-transporting extraterrestrial life forms to Earth. The author made an interesting point. He developed these, uh—computer models, using some assumptions that seemed pretty, er, r-reasonable."

[6] Few people had heard of McCutcheon in 2003. The article Pete referred to was first published in *Scientific American* in August 1999, and largely ridiculed by the scientific community at the time. Today, of course, McCutcheon is recognized as the founder of complex expectation theory. Considering the primitive state of the field in 1999, the predictions in the article correspond amazingly well to findings of modern probability analysis machines. Thankfully, McCutcheon's calculations did not take the Truth Machine's effect into account.

Amazing! Pete thought. *At Middlesex, where everybody's looking for an excuse to pick you apart, somebody would have groaned or yawned or laughed by now.* But here, every person in the class seemed genuinely interested in what he had to say, rather than how he looked and sounded while he was saying it.

With renewed confidence, he continued, "Uh, h-he calculated the l-likelihood that a civilization like ours could develop the technology to build a spaceship allowing travel to another solar system before that civilization destroyed itself. The probability he came up with was .00023 percent—virtually z-zero. I s-suspect halting the aging process is almost as complicated as interstellar travel. Frankly, uh, I can't imagine the human race reaching the point of conquering old age before some lunatic blows up our planet or infects everyone on it with some fatal disease. Within 100 years, thousands of nations, religious sects, even individuals will probably have the capability to wipe out all human life on the planet. If by some m-miracle humanity actually exists long enough for science to halt the aging process, what would be the point? In its present form, the human race won't survive long enough to enjoy it. What—what we need to work on *first* is a way to change our basic nature."

David West found Pete endearing. Maybe it was the intelligence behind his words combined with the awkwardness of his delivery. David suspected that Pete's obviously quirky personality had been hobbled by tragedy, in contrast to his own, which had triumphed over it.

"I can hardly believe it. Here we have the youngest and brightest person in this class . . ." David said, glancing to his side, curious if Scoggins betrayed annoyance at the reference to Pete's superior intellect. *Hmm. Barely even a glare. Either his jealousy's minimal or Scoggins is one smooth actor. The latter, I bet.* ". . . forecasting doom for the human race. This doesn't bode well for my New Year's Eve plans in the year 3001."

"Don't c-cancel your reservations yet," Pete replied, smiling. "There may be hope. That is, if the human race can change. I suspect it's possible under the right circumstances."

"How? We've been the same way for thousands of years. Not that we humans don't have wonderful qualities, but we're also self-centered, greedy, jealous, deceitful, and prone to madness. What's going to wake us up now?"

"Maybe the realization that if we don't change soon, we're all doomed. The good news is that we now have a common enemy. Unfortunately it may be more difficult to conquer an enemy within ourselves." Pete found he enjoyed articulating his own thoughts. In his other classes, he simply cited facts and quoted other people's concepts. Here it was different.

Gaddis finally broke up the class at about 5:30. They would all return tomorrow. As Pete left Memorial Hall, several students including David West and Charles Scoggins introduced themselves. Scoggins was particularly friendly, and Pete responded with enthusiasm and an openness rare for him. He could hardly wait until they reconvened. The other courses were just so much more information for his data banks. But in Theo-Soc he got to interact and speculate about the essence and future of the human race with the brightest people he had known thus far. This course was exactly why Pete had come to Harvard.

In spite of his amiable demeanor, Charles Scoggins had an appalling secret.

After class, Scoggins returned to his room, where a printout was waiting for him. Three months earlier, he had hacked into the central computer of the Bank of Boston, and programmed his own computer to match each account against every obituary listed in local newspapers. Whenever an account of the deceased had been accessible only by that person, and that account-holder was neither married nor survived by children, and certain other criteria existed that minimized any chance of a shortfall being discovered, Scoggins would strike. Careful and patient, he never succumbed to reckless greed. He would transfer just a small percentage of the account balance into an offshore bank account in the Bahamas, backdating the transaction so it appeared in the Bank of Boston's records to have been authorized prior to the account-holder's death.

He had already accumulated nearly a million dollars using this scheme, and no other person suspected that any crime had occurred.[7]

---

[7] These crimes were not discovered until November 2049, when the Armstrong defense team performed meticulous reconstruction and computer analysis of all bank records from that period throughout the Boston metropolitan area. Their conclusions were eventually confirmed, accepted, and stipulated into the court record of the Armstrong trial.

CHAPTER 9

THE GODDESS

Memorial Hall
January 29, 2003—Iraq announces its decision to ratify the Arab-Israeli Free-Trade Pact, completing Israel's normalization of relations with all of its Arab neighbors.—General Motors releases results of road tests on its 2004 models, which will be available in mid-April 2003. On average, the gasoline-powered automobiles clocked 96 miles per gallon on the highway, and 72 MPG in city traffic. GM's most popular line, the Andromeda, averaged up to 125 MPG under proper conditions. The 2004 electric cars, although slightly more expensive to operate, were able to go nearly 400 miles per recharge, a 30-percent increase over the 2003 series. Analysts project that electrically powered automobiles will garner an 11-percent market share of U.S. new car sales next year.—The FDA initiates a permanent ban on trans-fatty acids, listed on food labels as hydrogenated or partially hydrogenated oils, vegetable shortening, or margarine. In the latter third of the 20th century, these ingredients were actually marketed to the public as "healthy" because they were low in saturated fat, but in tests conducted over a six-year period, trans-fatty acids were found to be more dangerous to the cardiovascular system that butter or animal lard.—As expected, President Gore formally announces that to improve the Democratic Party's chances of remaining in the White House after his unpopular veto of the Swift and Sure Anti-Crime Bill, he will not seek reelection in 2004.

* * *

My God. She's incredible!

A young student raised her hand during the second Theo-Soc class of the semester. Pete, now 13 and well aware of such things, considered her the most beautiful woman he had ever seen. He tried to smile at her, but all he could do was stare.

Then she spoke. "Professor, I've been thinking about our discussion yesterday. May I tell the class about a friend of mine? It's a sad story, and relevant, I think, to what Pete Armstrong said yesterday about our basic nature."

"By all means, Diana."

Diana Hsu's father, Dr. Thomas Hsu, a 1971 graduate of Harvard College and later, Harvard Medical School, was 100 percent Chinese. Her mother was Irish, and like Pete's mother, an attorney. Diana's face was exotic and angelic, her tall, lean body toned from a decade of ballet and modern dance study and performance. To Pete, she was absolute perfection. And when she spoke, her words revealed quiet intelligence, carried on a soft and melodious voice. Pete surmised every other male in the class had to be as smitten as he was.

Although she looked 20 years old, Diana was barely 17—at least a year younger than her freshman classmates. She was first accepted to Harvard for a special pre-med program 26 months earlier. But unsure she wanted to study medicine, she had remained at Benjamin Franklin Arts Magnet High School in King of Prussia, Pennsylvania. Now finally at Harvard, she discovered Gaddis's class and a more interesting subject than medicine.

"While I was studying dance, Larry Dannon and Glenn Ross were my best friends," Diana told the class. "They were talented dancers, and gay. I was going through some rough times with my parents, and Larry and Glenn were just wonderful to me. I don't know how I could've survived without them. Then the worst possible thing happened: Glenn got sick. *Really* sick. AIDS. He was gone in less than a month."

Diana's sorrow was apparent on her face. "Larry was beside himself with grief. I was the only person he could speak to about it. We became closer during that time, and I convinced him to get an HIV test. A few days later, when he told me he tested negative, well, I was just so *relieved*."

Pete's eyes focused on her every time she took a breath. He was so drawn by her voice he could barely understand her words. Fortunately he could remember them, and reconstruct their meaning afterward.

"A few months later, Larry met Jordan, who wasn't at all like Glenn. I didn't like him much. I suspected he was cheating on Larry and was terrified he'd get the virus and pass it on to Larry. I'm ashamed to say I let Jordan come between us; we kind of drifted apart. Then early last year, Larry got AIDS."

There was rage in her eyes. "Jordan broke up with him immediately; he actually said to Larry, 'Don't you be counting on *me* to take care of you.' After that, I made sure I saw Larry every day —until I came here last September. Sometimes I went with him to the doctor or the hospital. I knew he must have gotten the virus from Jordan, because he hadn't had any other lovers since Glenn died. If I disliked Jordan before, well, I now *loathed* him.

"During Christmas vacation I ran into him at a party and really told him off, ranted at him: 'How could you give Larry AIDS and just abandon him like that? What kind of person *are* you?' He let me rage. Then without saying a word, he reached into his pocket, and pulled out a letter from an HIV testing lab. He'd just gotten the results. I couldn't believe it. Jordan was HIV negative.

"When I confronted Larry, he admitted everything. He knew he'd gotten the virus from Glenn, but was afraid of being alone. So he lied—to both of us. Larry is my *best friend*! I still love him. I think he's a great person in almost every way. And I still think I know him better than I know anyone else, and I understand why he did it. But he *lied*. About a matter of life and death. My closest friend endangered another person's life out of selfishness and fear.

"As much as I wish it weren't true, what Pete said about our basic nature is dead accurate."

The class broke up at 4:10. Charles Scoggins started to walk toward Pete, but backed off when he saw David West speaking to him.

"Diana and I were about to grab a bite at the Kong," David said to Pete. "The Kong" was Hong Kong, a Chinese restaurant about a block from Harvard Yard. "Since you're the only other freshman in Theo-Soc, we thought it appropriate you join us. My treat, of course. I won't take no for an answer."

"In that c-case, uh, I believe I can squeeze you into m-my hectic schedule."

It was windy and bone-chillingly cold that afternoon, so the three rushed to the Kong without much conversation. Once comfortably inside the warm restaurant, David and Diana sat down next to each other, thighs touching, unaware of Pete's raging battle with envy and lust.

David West and Diana Hsu knew very little about envy from personal experience, but a great deal about lust; from the first time they'd laid eyes on each other, the sexual attraction had been intense and irresistible. On their first date, they couldn't keep their hands to themselves; they were so anxious to tear off each other's clothes that they'd left the restaurant before the main course was served. They'd stayed up all night making love, or as Diana, describing the date to a friend, had somewhat more delicately put it, "I just couldn't stop *kissing* him. We kissed all night; kissed so hard our *lips* bled."

Since then, they hadn't been apart more than a few hours at a time, except for two weeks during the Christmas holidays. Being separated had been torture, and they intended never to endure it again.

While the three freshmen scanned their menus, the conversation remained friendly but guarded and from Pete's point of view, a bit strained. He tried to force himself to sit still, but it was hopeless; he was too nervous. He started rocking, and was sure they noticed. But they acted as if they didn't.

After they ordered, Diana asked point-blank, "Pete, tell us what it's like to be a genius. It must be *amazing*!"

"Er . . . I . . . I can't really describe what it's like because I have n-nothing to compare it to. Until I was seven I, uh, assumed everyone could remember everything, just like me. I only knew I was smart because people told me I was. All I can tell you is that some things come easy for me, but other things are still v-very hard. F-For example, I don't think I could invent a joke to save my life. Er, it must be g-great to have wit l-l-like David."

In fact Pete had a good sense of humor. He just didn't have the timing or the delivery except when relaxed, which was rare. David was always at ease with himself, and that was the real difference.

"What about *me*? I'm witty too," Diana protested.

David answered, "Yes you are, my sweet, but your wit's far too clever. Mine's less intelligent, and therefore less threatening."

"W-What's it l-like to have a g-great sense of humor?" Pete asked David.

"You're both gonna think I'm not nearly as funny if I tell you what it's like for me."

"Take a risk, David," Diana urged.

"Truthfully, humor's my defense, a way to survive in the world. I had a pretty rough childhood so I had to learn a skill to dig my way out. The skill I taught myself was getting along with people, even the kind who aren't so easy to get along with. I usually like people anyway, but humor's the easiest way to get people to like *me*."

Now Pete was intrigued. How could such a dashing fellow as David West have emerged from a rough childhood?

"What was your family like?"

"My father was on the lam from bookies, loan sharks, and the police since the day I was born. It would make a great movie; they could call it 'The Man Without a *County*.' My *real* last name was Witkowsky—my mother changed it so Dad wouldn't find us."

David told this story to his new friend, but did not mention how painful it had been to leave his father, whom he continued to love in spite of everything. He didn't say that he had learned his father was now living in Las Vegas, nor did he bring up the many times he'd almost called or written him.

"Today it's just my mom, my little brother, and me," David said. "We're a real close family—maybe because we've been through so much together. What about *your* family?"

Pete wasn't ready to tell David and Diana about his brother's murder. "My parents are p-pretty n-normal. D-David and I d-do h-have s-s-something in common though; technically speaking, my last name isn't the same as my father's either. I was, actually uh—a product of artificial insemination. My b-b-biological father was a medical student, so I, uh, I guess *my* real l-last n-name could've been O'Meara."

Diana speared a fried won ton from the appetizer platter and offered it to Pete. "Won ton, O'Meara?"

Pete and David groaned in mock agony, then all three laughed; Diana's silly pun had broken the ice. The three freshmen didn't leave the restaurant until well after dark.

* * *

Over the ensuing months, their friendship developed. At first Pete had wondered why David was always so nice to him. *What does he really want from me?* he asked himself. *And doesn't he know how I feel about Diana?* But David never changed, and over time Pete became more comfortable.

Eventually the after-class meetings at the Kong became ritual. David worked out a deal with the owners: free food in exchange for marketing assistance that consisted mainly of printing paper fliers and discount coupons cleverly composed by David, a natural salesman. The three freshmen used Pete's Compaq 1100 and HP 6500 laser printer. They hired a few high school kids to distribute them throughout campus; David did all the work in 40 minutes a week.

The restaurant's business increased by nearly 30 percent and the Kong's owners were so grateful they allowed Pete's dog, Skipper, to join them at their booth.

A politically incorrect satirist, H. L. Mencken, once defined love as "the delusion that one woman differs from another." Pete, upon reading that quote, chuckled to himself, *I definitely suffer from that so-called delusion.* He considered Diana the most beautiful female he had ever met, and the most intelligent. Intelligence, he discovered, was for him the most powerful and enduring of aphrodisiacs. Still, he made every effort to hide his feelings, being wise enough to realize that a shy 13-year-old boy stood no chance with such a goddess, especially one in lust with the dashing David West.

Instead of pursuing Diana, Pete convinced himself he was content to enjoy her company and friendship. Whenever his thoughts of her became sexual, which they often did, guilt would overwhelm him. Pete would think to himself, *David's my friend, damn it!* But inevitably the fantasy would return, like a stray cat he had fed once or twice, only to discover she could not be so easily dismissed.

(Note: The stray cat analogy was used by Pete Armstrong in a November 2049 scip interview.—22g CP)

Diana became a conveniently impossible standard by which all other females were measured, a fine excuse for Pete to deprive himself of the adventure—and discomfort—of exploring other relationships. David and Diana, although aware of Pete's crush, never embarrassed him by bringing it up. They came to love him, protective of the boy, yet awed by his genius.

CHAPTER 10

THE INSPIRATION

Memorial Hall
May 17, 2003—Philip Morris, America's last surviving tobacco company, is placed into Chapter 7 bankruptcy liquidation. The legal tobacco industry in the United States is now dead, a casualty of lower demand for cigarettes and mushrooming lawsuits from victims of smoking-related diseases.—Students in the United States and Great Britain score highest of all nations on standardized tests in general knowledge, science, and problem-solving skills, the result, analysts say, of national "School Choice" programs instituted in the late 1990s, which opened the field to competition by private industry. In light of these impressive results, most other nations who have not already done so are expected to institute similar programs.—Clean-up continues from last month's horrific tsunami and floods that hit Tokyo and Yokohama without warning. Over 70,000 Japanese are now presumed dead. Prime Minister Ibuka calls for stricter worldwide enforcement of measures designed to slow global warming. Although unproven, some environmentalists believe the melting of polar ice

compounds the effects of tidal waves and the floods they cause.

Many historical texts note the discussion that took place on this day, in this room. One could argue that within these walls began a desperate battle, the culmination of which, two decades later, would determine the future of the planet.

Theo-Soc had been dominated by four voices, those of David West, Diana Hsu, Pete Armstrong, and Charles Scoggins. One afternoon in the heat of discussion about America's overburdened legal system, David posed a question.

"What do you think would happen if scientists built a machine that could tell with absolute certainty if a person was telling the truth?"

"You mean like a p-polygraph, only foolproof?" Pete asked. Thoughts of his brother's murderer flashed into his mind. Maybe such a machine could have kept Reece in prison, or even helped Dr. Carter cure him before he murdered again. A "truth machine" might have saved Leonard's life.

"Exactly," David said. "But this machine would have to be so precise that it could be used as conclusive proof of guilt or innocence in our court system."

"I'm sure it would result in a, um, a much f-fairer system of justice."

"At what cost?" Scoggins argued. "Would you really want to live in a world where the government could read your thoughts? A machine like that would make it easier for politicians and bureaucrats to root out dissenters to their policies. We'd have a police state."

"Actually," Diana countered, "I have a feeling just the opposite is true. We could use it to keep our leaders honest."

David nodded. "It would be an interesting tug-of-war. Of course it's hard to imagine politicians voting for legislation to turn the machine on themselves. But who'd vote for candidates who refused to take a truth test, especially if their opponents offered to take one?"

"Evolution probably favors the ability to lie effectively," Scoggins said.

"I agree that lying *used* to be a tool for survival . . ." Pete began.

Diana interrupted, "And procreation."

Pete smiled. "That, too. But today our ability to lie actually threatens our survival."

"I don't see how," said Scoggins.

"Already, nuclear technology is easy to obtain," Pete explained. "B-But in 20 years, nuclear weapons will be more powerful, and much smaller. In 10 or 15 years, computers will be able to design genetically engineered viruses that will selectively kill specific segments of a population. In 50 years, they'll have nuclear poisons capable of killing every mammal on the planet. And when nanotechnology becomes a reality, scientists could design undetectable, self-replicating, microscopic machines of death. V-Very soon, weapons will be so powerful that a war could wipe out all life on earth. Deceit is a major instrument and a major cause of war. Sociopathic dictators, who have always used war to amass power, could never wage war without lying to their populaces. And without deceit, honest conflicts become easier to resolve because each side's statements are believed by the other."

"But it's human nature to lie at certain times," Scoggins said. "You can't change human nature in one generation just by changing the rules."

"Er, I think you *can*." Pete was fully taken by the argument. "We do adapt to reality. For example, when my brother L-Leonard was six months old, the only way he'd sleep at night was if he could stay between my parents. Even then he was up three or four times. He had the whole household trained to, uh, accommodate his every want and need.

"Finally my poor sleep-deprived parents put Leonard to bed in his crib. Of course he hated that and started screaming. N-Next, my parents comforted him for a minute or so, then left the room and let him cry for five minutes. Then they came back for a minute and comforted him some more, and left him screaming for 10 minutes. Then 15, then 20. Never more than 20 minutes at a time, always reassuring him they'd be back. In three hours, Leonard was asleep in his crib. The next night, it took less than an hour. After that, he learned to put himself to sleep and always slept through the night in his own crib. And he was happier for it.

"I have a hunch lying's a lot like that—just an easy way for people to get what they think they want. I bet we can teach people not to lie by taking away the payoff, the same way my parents finally taught Leonard not to cry and to go to sleep by himself."

"Just like elephants in the circus!" Diana added.

Gaddis asked her what she meant.

"They tie baby elephants to a small stake in the ground with a rope. When the elephants grow to adult size and could easily uproot the stake, they never try. We might be the same way about telling the truth. Right now there's nothing like that stake in the ground to train us to be honest. As small children, we discover lying sometimes works, so it becomes habit. But if we never got away with it as children, we might be incapable of deceit as adults. Or we might learn not to want things we'd have to lie in order to get."

"That's probably true," David said. "It's human nature to seek a comfort zone. We're lazy by nature—creatures of habit. Lying is a bad habit. Maybe telling the truth could become habitual, too. We could condition ourselves to become uncomfortable whenever we lie, by making sure nobody ever gets away with lying as children."

"That sounds dreadful," interjected Scoggins. "I certainly hope nobody ever invents a machine like that. Suppose my favorite aunt points the truth machine at me and asks if I like the shirt she gave me for Christmas. What do I say if I hate it?"

David had an answer ready. "Truthfulness doesn't preclude tact. I'd just say to her, 'Not really, but I love *you*.' More likely, though, she'd learn never to ask a question unless she wants an honest answer. If that's your biggest downside, you can strap me to that old truth machine any time you want—as long as everybody else has to tell the truth, too."

David thought of the way his father's self-deceit and ability to deceive others had ruined his life and hurt everyone he came in contact with. "The more I think about it, the more I'm convinced that a truth machine would solve 100 problems for every one it created."

"That's *ridiculous*!" exclaimed Scoggins. "We'd all better pray it never happens. Doesn't anybody here believe in the right to privacy? Or in simple human trust?"[8]

Immediately after class, Scoggins called out, "Pete, you have a minute?"

"Sure. W-What's up, Charles?"

"I know you do software consulting for companies, but I was wondering if you've ever thought about doing it for yourself. You could make hundreds of times as much money mass-marketing the software you write."

"I've th-thought about it. Why do you ask?"

[8] Simple human trust, indeed! We can only imagine Charles Scoggins's thoughts when he uttered those words, for today we know relatively little about him. A Truth Machine would have been a threat to him, but how seriously he took the concept that day is a matter for conjecture. It is self-evident that, at an early age, he became obsessed with the accumulation of wealth, fame, and power. Orphaned at age six when both parents were killed in an automobile accident, Scoggins was raised by his maternal grandmother. Apparently she loved him and treated him well, but wouldn't (or couldn't) give him the discipline a younger guardian might have supplied.

"Maybe we should start a business together. I know a lot about marketing and I have some pretty interesting ideas."

"I d-don't know. I think I already know what I want to do with my life. I'm pretty sure I'd l-like to try to build a truth m-machine. I know y-you consider it a t-terrible idea, but I think it could k-keep the human race from self-destructing."

Scoggins's expression was earnest. "Well, I'm not sure I share your faith, but good luck anyway, Pete. Let me know if you change your mind."

"Okay, I w-will. Th-thanks."

Pete spent much of that evening and most of the following day concentrating on the ramifications of a perfect truth machine. He skipped several of his classes. Settling into the zone, he carefully analyzed the effects the machine could have on each important aspect of civilization.

The next afternoon at the Kong, David inquired, "Why'd'ya skip Theo-Soc today?"

"I was trying to decide what to do with my life," Pete answered.

"And?" Diana asked.

"As soon as I finish school I'm putting a team together to try to build a foolproof truth machine."

"I don't think Charles Scoggins would enjoy hearing you say that," David joked.

Diana laughed. "No, he didn't seem terribly enthusiastic about the idea. But he'd better get used to it. I'm sure it'll be an easy project for our favorite genius."

"Anything but. It could be one of the most difficult scientific projects in history."

"Really?" David asked, still not sure whether Pete was serious. "If we can catalog the human genome, why can't we build a truth machine?"

"We could if enough focus was applied to it. There

was plenty of interest in the genome project, and lots of money available."

"How complicated will it be?" Diana asked.

"Imagine the average organ in your body as a bicycle. In terms of comparative complexity, your brain would be a spaceship—that's how much more intricate it is. Other than deterioration, a person's organs remain largely the same throughout a lifetime, but the brain is always transforming itself. Each person has a unique set of brain-wave patterns but, unlike DNA or fingerprints, brain-wave patterns are constantly evolving as neurons, dendrites, and synapses form new links—for as long as the person lives."

"Brings new meaning to the expression 'changing your mind,' " Diana said.

David smiled. "Then how can you be sure if a truth machine's achievable, Pete?"

"I know it's scientifically possible and probably less complex than cataloging the human genome, which has already been done. I'd say it's more a question of when than if. But so far, few people realize the benefits a perfect truth machine would contribute to civilization. Nobody has even *tried* to build one. At the current pace of discovery, it could be 50 or 75 years before the scientific community pulls it off. The human race might not survive until then."

"Do you really believe that?" Diana asked.

"Absolutely," Pete said. "Think about the dynamics. As science advances, it will become easier and easier for countries, then fringe groups and terrorist organizations, and eventually, lone individuals, to kill enormous numbers of people. Psychologists estimate that sociopaths make up between 5 and 10 percent of society, and world population is growing fast. That means there are at least 300 million sociopaths now, and that number is increasing every day. Sociopaths tend to be bright and are often very charming—even charismatic. Most aren't dangerous, but many are, especially if they're angry.

Often we can't even *identify* sociopaths, much less determine their intentions. Eventually some of these people will have the capacity to end all life on earth; it's only a matter of time. Until we build a truth machine."

"How long would it take you?"

"I'm guessing 15 to 20 years, and it'll cost at *least* several hundred million dollars. But I really think I can do it. And when I do, it'll change absolutely everything."

Now neither of them laughed. They knew he wasn't joking.

CHAPTER 11

THE DEBATES

Quincy House
October 23, 2004—Violent crime continues to be the number one political issue in America. The Republican National Committee bombards the media with reports and statistics for the previous 12-month period, showing over 22 million reported violent crimes, 72,416 of which were homicides, and 2,408,644 convicted criminals incarcerated in state and federal prisons.—American Telephone & Telegraph (AT&T) files for Chapter 7 bankruptcy. The company, which failed to earn a profit in any of the previous 14 fiscal quarters, fell victim to intense competition and price wars as other long-distance communications companies priced services based on marginal costs in a shrinking market. Businesses and individuals conduct a growing percentage of worldwide audio-visual communications over the Internet, free of charge. In spite of the bankruptcy, most long-term AT&T stockholders have reaped solid returns from their

investments because of the company's numerous spin-offs from 1995 through 2002.—The entire world watches as Treasury Secretary Audrey Whitcomb and Senator Travis Hall (R.CT) campaign during the final weeks of their battle for the United States presidency. In the minds of most citizens, a vote for Travis Hall is also a vote for his controversial Swift and Sure Anti-Crime Bill. Will the voters opt for personal safety over individual rights and due process of law? With polls projecting Hall will receive nearly 60 percent of the popular vote, it looks as if they will.

Pete tried to curl the 15-pound barbell once more, but it might as well have weighed 200 pounds; he was spent. David had taught him to start with normal weight, continuing reps in a steady rhythm with good form until fatigue, then to remove a plate from each side and repeat. He had prescribed at least four sets with no rest in between. It was grueling, but it worked. Pete had gained 18 pounds of muscle over the past year.

David's knowledge of exercise, nutrition, and fitness was exhaustive. Pete had read every book on the subject in the Quincy House library and was amazed by the amount of conflicting and obviously inaccurate information. *A lot of these writers are just guessing,* he realized, *but they all seem so authoritative. How do I tell which ones really know?* Yet he had never been able to disprove anything David had told him.

Built in the 1960s, Quincy House was still the newest dormitory for undergraduates at Harvard. The rooms were larger and better-appointed than those in Harvard Yard and many suites had their own bathrooms. For the second year, David and Pete were rooming together at "Quince." This year they had snagged a two-bedroom suite overlooking Tommy's Joint and the Harvard Lampoon building. There was plenty of space for gatherings of David's many friends, and a tiny study where they could hide Skipper on rare occasions when faculty members visited.

The suite was also large enough for Diana Hsu to live there with David most of the time. Her single room down the hall usually remained vacant.

In spite of Diana's romantic temperament, the doctor's daughter had a scientific side. Aware of the biochemical components of love, she kept waiting for her feelings for David—and his for her—to change.

"You know, my love," she had whispered to David that morning as they lay holding each other in the afterglow of lovemaking, "our PEA tolerance is building every day. They say it peaks during the third year. In a few more months you probably won't find me quite this irresistible."

(Note: Even during the earliest part of this century, scientists were well aware of the effects of certain natural chemicals on human emotions. The chemical largely responsible for "lover's high," phenylethylamine, generally lasts only 22 to 35 months into a relationship before the body builds an immunity. Effective PEA supplements did not become available until December 2029.—22g CP)

"Before I met you, I always used to peak around the third *day!*" David had answered with a laugh. But watching her face, radiant in the dawn sunlight, he thought to himself, *I could never love anyone else the way I love her.*

After two years, Diana and David were still in love—for the first time in either of their lives. Yet their feelings for each other had changed significantly. Already this love was based more on friendship, respect, and shared values than on mere physical attraction or phenylethylamine. It was the sort of love that tended to endure.

Diana's parents had urged her to go to medical school. In fact, she had enrolled as pre-med but had changed her major, to her father's dismay. Government and what it could do for people excited her as medicine never could. Intending to go into government service, both David and

Diana expected to apply to Harvard Law School the following year. Most likely they would be married by the time they graduated, hopefully with the blessing of Diana's parents, whom David still hadn't met.

They talked about the future of law and politics almost constantly—in a way, they already lived in a future world; the past and present meant little to them. Everything they said or did was considered in the context of the future. Intensely ambitious, they both believed they could change the world.

But of all they had in common, the attribute most conspicuously shared was their integrity, nurtured perhaps by an abiding faith in the inevitability of Pete Armstrong's Truth Machine. Now their every word and deed filtered through the prospect of eventually having to confront what they wryly called "the device," a sardonic allusion to the atomic bomb that had so drastically changed the human condition during the 20th century. David would explain in an interview for *D Magazine* (conducted by Tom Mosely, my future owner, several years before I was built), "Believing the Truth Machine was coming didn't make me *choose* to be more honest. It just made it easier to resist the temptation to do anything I'd ever have to *lie* about."

Pete continued his software consulting, which had actually become more lucrative as companies bid up the price of his time. He invested his money carefully and planned his strategy for building a truth machine, enrolling mostly in courses of neurobiology and business, which had only recently been added to Harvard's undergraduate curriculum.

He was too shy for dating and, although he had never admitted it to anyone, was still secretly in love with Diana, his best friend's lover. He continued to fantasize about her and rationalized that since no other female could possibly measure up to her, then why should he bother? And since sex with Diana was impossible, he sublimated his libido with exercise and hard work. Having long ago earned enough credits to graduate, he only stayed at Harvard College for one reason: David West, his best friend and in many ways his mentor.

Still, the relationship remained somewhat awkward. David, ever confident in his judgment of others, had long ago determined that beneath Pete's shy exterior was a good-hearted person, worthy of his trust and friendship. Insecure in such discernment because of his limited social experience, Pete trusted everyone in general, but no one entirely. Although David shared all his insights and deepest personal feelings with Pete, the 14-year-old often held back, and not just about his craving for Diana. Both were aware of the imbalance and accepted it, David with affectionate humor and Pete with considerable guilt.

Pete barely had time to shower. In a few minutes about 40 of David's "closest personal friends" would crowd into their suite to watch the second presidential debate between Audrey Whitcomb and Travis Hall. Although by 2004 virtually all programs could be seen on demand, trials, debates, and sporting competitions were still broadcast "live." Viewing them with other people added to the experience.

Undoubtedly everyone invited would show up. David's friends always showed up, and they had a better reason tonight. Although primitive by today's standards, in 2004 Pete's media system was legendary at Harvard. The entertainment center, manufactured by a joint venture between Eastman Kodak and Motorola, combined ultra-high definition with digital surround sound, and the screen took up an entire wall. It would be like sitting in the front row of the new Ted Turner Auditorium in Atlanta, where the debate was being held. Nobody would miss a word or a bead of sweat on the candidates' faces.

Soon the room was overflowing. All 43 students,

lounging on Pete's bed or sitting Indian-style on the floor, stared at the screen as the debate began. Pete sat on the front part of the bed with Skipper; the dog remained still and silent while Pete affectionately stroked his back.

David West had no ethnic prejudice and a rare ability to overcome such prejudice in others. Unlike many students at Harvard who kept to their own kind, he had befriended a cross-section of students. Reflecting college demographics nationwide, most of them supported Audrey Whitcomb, a beloved figure in American politics. A former Congresswoman, U.S. Senator (D.VT, 1994–2000), and incumbent Secretary of the Treasury, Whitcomb was brilliant, articulate, and likable. Many of Travis Hall's supporters admitted she was more qualified than he to be president.

Three years earlier she had been the principal author and driving force behind H.R. 1918, the first "tax simplification act" that had ever *really* simplified the tax code. The new code was progressive. It encouraged investment, charitable contributions, and energy conservation and, most important, was easy to understand. Principal tenets included a reduction in the basic and capital gains tax rates, elimination of all but a very few itemized deductions for individuals, elimination of double taxation of corporate earnings paid out as dividends, and a large energy tax partially offset by an increase in the standard deduction.

H.R. 1918 also incorporated the Tobias Plan (so named for financial writer Andrew Tobias, who originally conceived and publicized it in the early 1990s), a privately bid national no-fault automobile insurance system. Thanks to the Plan, insurance premiums were no longer collected by the insurance companies themselves, but at gasoline, diesel, and electric recharging stations as part of the price of the fuel. The savings in paperwork, administrative costs, and legal fees from the Tobias Plan alone were staggering; over 100 billion dollars yearly, roughly $340 per capita. Altogether, H.R. 1918 was an ingenious bill that managed to leave nearly all taxpayers, except automobile insurance agents, administrators, accountants, and personal injury lawyers, better off.

By presenting her case directly and eloquently to the American people, she and President Gore had rammed H.R. 1918 through Congress over the objections of most special-interest groups in America. In the 1990s, to paraphrase *Time* magazine, lobbyists for special interests and large corporations roamed Washington like grazing beasts—not good, not evil, just hungry. Getting her bill passed intact, without the massive changes suggested by these "grazing beasts," had been an impressive feat.

Once passed, the new tax code created an economic boom unprecedented in previous American history, and so endeared Secretary Whitcomb to the voting public that she was able to clinch the Democratic party's nomination barely two-thirds through the first ballot. But the Democratic nomination was a far cry from the presidency.

Moderator Paula Zahn thanked the candidates. "Before we conclude tonight's final debate, I'd just like to mention that you've both demonstrated what politics should be about. You have debated the issues forcefully, but with decorum and restraint. This has been the cleanest debate—maybe the cleanest presidential campaign—I can remember, and whichever of you prevails, you'll both be remembered and admired for your poise throughout these contentious months." Zahn was briefly interrupted by polite applause. "Now in accordance with the rules of this debate you each have five minutes to address the American electorate. Secretary Whitcomb, you'll speak first."

"Thank you, Paula.

"My fellow taxpayers . . ." The audience, or at least the Democrats in the room, rewarded her not-so-subtle reference to H.R. 1918 with laughter, cheers, and applause.

Whitcomb smiled, now energized as she waited for the fanfare to die down.

"Violent crime is the scourge of our nation. But this scourge *can* be confronted in an enlightened, humanitarian way consistent with our national character. Please let us never forget who we are. We are the United States of America, the most powerful, the fairest, the most generous nation on earth. . . .

"A Whitcomb administration won't use violence as a means to end violence. The death penalty is no deterrent; it is retribution that only legitimizes violence. Swift and Sure requires executing up to 40 persons in the United States every single day. That's over 14,000 human beings each year, most of whom could be rehabilitated to become useful members of society—and many of whom will be *innocent* of the crimes of which they're convicted.

"Even if we surrender and accept such injustice as a necessary evil—as a price we're willing to pay to make our streets safer—still, Swift and Sure won't work. Ultimately it will only make things worse. . . ."

(Note: The text of Secretary Whitcomb's entire summation is reprinted in the Appendix. A summary of the key points of Swift and Sure appears in Chapter 12.— 22g CP)

One of Harvard's well-known characteristics has always been that eccentric and strange people do not feel out of place there; they have plenty of company. Pete had become more comfortable and had even acquired some social grace. He still rocked a little, but his tongue was completely inside his mouth most of the time, and he spoke to everyone, often calling them by name.

Acting as host, he said, "P-Please raise your hand if you'd vote for Whitcomb if the election were held now." All 43 students' names, hand dimensions, and social security numbers had already been recorded from their ID microchips as they entered the room. Pete scanned 27 hands, which were automatically verified and entered into his interactive remote unit.

About 45 seconds later, the screen registered the votes of every participating viewer nationwide. "Instant Poll Result: 3,824,752/8,956,781=42.7%."

Diana lamented to Pete and David, "She's running less than 43 percent right after her summation; not a good sign." David and Diana were loyal Democrats who both backed Whitcomb.

Pete, who had supported Hall since the day he declared his candidacy in January 2003, added, "She's, uh, got almost 63 percent of *this* room though. It's like my dad once told me, 'If you're under 20 and you're already a Republican, you have no heart. But if you're over 30 and you're still a Democrat, you have no brain.'" He thought to himself that perhaps his brother's murder had given him a prematurely realistic slant on the human condition.

"Maybe they should change their mascots to the Tin Man and Scarecrow," Diana shot back. At the time, the Republican party was symbolized by an elephant and the Democrats by a donkey.

David laughed. "That'd make it a lot easier to remember which mascot belongs to *whom*."

(Note: In the 1939 film, The Wizard of Oz, *the Scarecrow and Tin Man journeyed to Oz to petition the Wizard for a brain and a heart, respectively.—22g CP)*

Paula Zahn turned the podium over to Senator Travis Hall, who had compaigned more on the strength of his experience as a prosecutor than as a legislator. Before becoming Senator, Hall had proven a most effective Attorney General. During his two terms, violent crime in his state had increased at a rate less than one-third the national average, likely a result of policies that Hall had introduced.

More than any other State Attorney General of his era, Hall had emphasized victims' rights in handling his cases and required his subordinates to do the same. Under Hall, every important decision had taken into account the point of view of victims or potential victims. He now used his solid anti-violent-crime track record to his advantage.

He spoke with less polish than Whitcomb, but with far more emotion.

"My friends, I wish I had Secretary Whitcomb's patience. I admire her accomplishments. In a different time she could be a superb president. But not today.

"Today we need less patience and more resolve. I'd like to tell you one reason why I'm so impatient. Many of you know of my close friend Solomon Kurtz. . . . Two years ago, my dear friend was murdered, shot through the heart by a man trying to rob him. . . . The murderer, who had a long record of violent crime, was apprehended and convicted. . . . A great man was murdered and finally his killer was imprisoned for life. But think about this. . . .

"Secretary Whitcomb says the death penalty is not a deterrent—and she's absolutely right! As a former Connecticut Attorney General, I admit the slow and unsure death penalty process of the past several decades has proven no deterrent at all. It's barbaric torture to those waiting on death row and the legal cost of their appeals is absurd. It's a travesty. Those funds should be available for education and enforcement, not legal expenses and imprisonment.

"Those contemplating violent crime must know they'll be caught and that their lives will never be the same. A person found guilty of any violent crime should get no more than one chance at rehabilitation. Swift and Sure still gives the criminal more consideration than the victim. I believe the commission of a second violent crime requires execution, swiftly and surely. One fair trial and one quick appeal. No excuses. No delays. . . ."

(Note: The text of Travis Hall's entire summation is also reprinted in the Appendix.—22g CP)

* * *

Again, Pete asked for a show of hands. "Uh, who'd vote for Hall now?" Eighteen hands went up, including Pete's. Apparently Hall's speech had persuaded two students in the room to change their votes. Pete punched in 18/43 and waited for the national results on the screen.

"Instant Poll Result: 5,601,112/8,898,765 = 62.9%"

From NBC's studio in New York, newscaster Tom Brokaw looked into the camera. "Amazing! Hall gained over five points on his closing statement."

Pete added, "Unless he m-makes some major blunder between now and election day, Travis Hall will be President and Swift and Sure will be law by early next year."

CHAPTER 12

SWIFT AND SURE

Washington DC
February 28, 2006—Hon. Clifton Sheets becomes the fourth federal judge to be assassinated by protesters against the death penalty since Swift and Sure was enacted 14 months ago. In spite of higher-than-projected executions, the measure remains popular, with a 73-percent nationwide approval rating.—Fidel Castro dies in Buenos Aires, Argentina, from complications of Alzheimer's disease. Many Cubans mourn the death of the former dictator, who was overthrown in 1999, while others celebrate his passage. President Hall issues a statement of "sympathy to our friends and trading partners of the Cuban democracy over the loss of their former leader, a man who did what he thought was right for Cuba, a man still beloved by many of her citizens."— United Airlines initiates supersonic passenger service

between Los Angeles and New York City, scheduling service every three hours. Tickets on the 115-minute flights cost $2,150 each way. Within two weeks, American Airlines' parent corporation, AMR, is expected to announce a schedule of six domestic supersonic flights, all originating from its Dallas/Fort Worth hub.

Swift and Sure, which included the following eight changes in the law, did embody some liberal aspects, but not enough to mollify an angry, vocal minority:

1) First time violent offenders, including juveniles, were sentenced to privately run rehabilitation prisons or boot camps with rigorous education programs. Prisoners included anyone convicted of weapons possession crimes. A national standard was instituted for education and rehabilitation of such prisoners. All prisons were equipped with fitness facilities, libraries, and computers. Terms of incarceration were slightly shorter than before, but inmates had to pass literacy and mental competency tests to qualify for parole.

2) Registration of firearms and mandatory retina-printing and DNA-recording of all firearm owners became national law. No convicted violent criminals could ever legally own or carry any firearm. After a 30-day grace period, possession of any unregistered firearm became a class-one felony, subject to severe penalties.

3) Free and instant treatment was offered on demand for drug addiction, alcoholism, gambling addiction, and any treatable form of mental illness. Concurrently the insanity defense for all violent crime was abolished. Defenses based on childhood abuse or any plea other than self-defense were virtually eliminated. This was known as the "No Excuses Provision."

4) A federal mandate directed all states to increase health education budgets to a new national standard (an average increase of about 55 percent) and to introduce weekly anti-drug, anti-violence, and responsible parenting curricula in all public schools.

5) A series of Victims' Rights Laws was enacted, allowing victims or their survivors to testify at sentencing hearings and to collect monetary damages through the Internal Revenue Service as a percentage surtax on criminals' lifetime earnings, without the expense of attorneys or collection agencies. The surtax percentages were based on the severity of the crime, but were formulated to avoid causing such financial hardship as to force felons to commit further crimes impelled by desperation.

6) Within federal guidelines, all able inmates were required to perform suitable work as determined by prison operators. Inmates would, upon release, receive 10 percent of fair market earnings from their work, and 40 percent of earnings over and above the cost of their incarceration. Motivated inmates could earn substantial income and prison operators could profit and thereby lower bids for operating contracts. The goal was to minimize the cost to society of warehousing criminals while building prisoners' work ethic.

7) Swift and Sure canceled privacy rights of inmates, implementing 24-hour audio-video monitoring of any areas accessible to prisoners, with data stored digitally off-site for 10 years. Any racketeering or serious crimes by inmates proven by video evidence became an automatic capital offense. Thus inmates would never again run the prisons.

8) Those convicted of violent crimes would be limited to one appeal, heard and ruled upon within 65 days of trial verdict. A mandatory death penalty was instituted for any second violent crime committed after Swift and Sure became law (January 15, 2005). Execution would take place immediately upon decision, with no exceptions granted under any circumstances.

Swift and Sure incorporated dozens of expensive programs. Nonetheless, the Congressional Budget Office predicted savings from decreased prison terms would exceed its cost. Congress authorized initial funding of $283 billion, advanced as loans to the states to fund federal mandates.

The CBO projected full recapture through budget cuts within six years as prisons were turned over to private operators and the most unmanageable—and thus, expensive—prisoners were executed or rehabilitated.

(Note: It actually took six years and four months—quite close considering that this was more than 15 years before the CBO purchased its first Artificial Intelligence Statistical Processor [AISP] from Compaq. Eventually Swift and Sure would help create a budget surplus.—22g CP)

Pete and Tilly found themselves back in Washington DC, this time behind closed doors. They met with Senator Garrison Roswell (R.KY), chairman of the Senate Technology Committee. Tilly's friends at the Bureau and most professors Pete had surveyed at Harvard Law School had suggested that if they wanted government support for any important project, Roswell was the man to see. "But if you're looking for special favors," one professor had warned Pete, "he's definitely *not* your guy."

First elected to the U.S. Senate in 1996, Roswell was one of many "minority conservatives" who converged on the capital in the late 1990s. It was considered almost certain that President Hall would choose Roswell as vice-presidential running mate for his reelection campaign in 2008. The 46-year-old former University of Virginia economics professor was black, smart, and very Republican.

(Note: Almost every former economics professor entering the political arena during that era ran as a member of the Republican party.—22g CP)

Roswell's popularity transcended racial lines; well-liked among black constituents, his approval rating was even higher among whites. Few people thought of him in racial terms at all. To most of Kentucky, he was just "good ol' Garry Roswell, the smartest damn Senator in Washington DC." This attitude may not seem unusual now, but in 2006, humans weren't as socially enlightened as you are today.

Garrison Roswell was one of President Hall's closest political allies. Since those executed under Swift and Sure were disproportionately black, Roswell was indeed useful. That week on "Meet the Press" he had debated Swift and Sure with Senator Jesse Jackson (D.MD), defending his President's program against the articulate liberal.

"My esteemed colleague attempts to paint Swift and Sure in racial terms," Roswell concluded, "so I'll respond in kind. Granted, we're executing a lot of African Americans, maybe 14,000 or so last year. But our race has always been disproportionately victimized by violent crime, so I'd estimate that last year we also *saved* about 41,000 Black Americans, many of whom would have been murdered by the 14,000 we executed. The current system's still pretty tough on us as a race, but it used to be much worse. Swift and Sure was the right program at the right time."

Pete and Tilly had no trouble getting in to see Senator Roswell, whom they had never met, but who knew of them. Still shy, Pete didn't wish to seem like he was self-promoting, so he remained silent while Tilly, who was anything but shy, began.

"Senator, with your support we think we can help you and President Hall mend this country. My friend might look like an average teenager, but he's probably the most talented computer programmer in the world. We both believe he can build a machine that will tell us with absolute certainty whenever any person's telling a lie. He expects it to require 10 to 20 years and at least $300 million to design and build. We hope he can do it before Swift and Sure tears America completely apart."

Roswell asked Tilly and Pete questions, taking notes himself rather than leaving the task to a staff member. He made no comments or promises. He merely took down their e-mail addresses in case he had further questions and politely thanked them for their time and insight.

Once they had left Roswell's office, Pete turned to Tilly and asked, "Is that it?"

"I don't know," she answered. "I guess we'll have to wait and see."

Swift and Sure was "demographically popular," much as abortion rights were: Most people approved of it, but those who disagreed strongly were vehement and highly focused. It was a mess. Protests and candlelight vigils around courthouses and execution sites were unremitting. Four federal judges, three prosecutors, and nearly a dozen other court and penal workers had already been assassinated. Thousands of other officers of the court had been injured, attacked, or harassed.

The results of Swift and Sure conformed generally to expectations, particularly with respect to costs, but as with any complex government program, there were major surprises. For example, experts had predicted two to five million guns would be turned in pursuant to provision number two as listed at the beginning of this chapter. But an unexpected 26 *million* firearms were actually surrendered to police departments across the country during the first 30 days after enactment. Roswell had been involved in the debate over what to do with the weapons. The most liberal legislators argued for their destruction, an idea naturally favored by firearm manufacturers. Roswell disagreed.

"Let me get this straight," he had said on the senate floor. "Are you fellows suggesting we melt down a billion dollars' worth of weapons just so gun producers can make and sell new ones to the same people we could sell ours to? If we analyze the economic effects of that idea, it's the exact same thing as giving those guys a billion-dollar government subsidy. Couldn't our *police* use that money?"

Roswell won enough votes to authorize police departments to auction the weapons to any qualified gun owner and to incorporate the proceeds into their budgets. Almost every law enforcement official in America now considered Garry Roswell a hero.

During the first three months after Swift and Sure's enactment, the homicide rate actually rose, although total violent crime statistics plummeted. Evidently, as feared, some criminals murdered to eliminate witnesses. After the first three months, however, the murder rate fell sharply and was already less than half its peak level.

The most critical miscalculation had been the immediate number of capital convictions. It was now apparent that roughly 40,000 executions would take place in 2006, an average of about 765 per week, nearly triple the predicted rate. Executions were televised on a natural cellular system. Obviously there were logistical problems involved in humanely and painlessly putting so many people to death. But experts expected the number of executions to decrease rapidly as the most hard-core criminals were exterminated.

Roswell considered civil unrest the worst problem of all. In a new book, *Inalienable Rights*, former President Albert Gore built a catastrophically persuasive case against Swift and Sure. Particularly compelling was Gore's contention that the number of *innocent* people executed under the Act was at least five times President Hall's original projection. The book had whipped the anti-death penalty activists into a frenzy. Currently number four on the *New York Times* best-seller list, *Inalienable Rights* would have been number one if digital sales over the Internet and on-line networks had been included in the *Times*'s calculations. Protests were unceasing, aggressive, and often violent. "This circus is making Pro-Choice vs. Pro-Life look like a friggin' high school debate," one of Roswell's aides had declared.

* * *

Immediately after meeting with Tilly and Pete, Roswell called President Hall.

"I just met with two, well, *kids* practically—at least one of them is—and they say they can build a perfect lie-detector machine within 10 to 20 years. The amazing thing is, Travis, I actually *believe* them."

Hall was intrigued. "I'd sure like to know more about this, Garry."

"I'm editing my notes right now. I'll send them to you later today."

A detailed memorandum was downloaded into Hall's private computer a few hours later. Roswell handled the transmission himself.

Six days later during a nationally televised town meeting, President Hall fielded a question about the number of innocent people executed under Swift and Sure. He answered, "I agree the numbers are far greater than predicted, but the *percentage* of those wrongly convicted is only slightly higher than we thought. Remember, we'll execute almost three times as many criminals this year as originally anticipated. These will tend to be the hard-core offenders, the kind of criminals whom the death penalty doesn't intimidate as much. Therefore I'm confident both numbers will fall sharply in the future. Granted, a single person executed for a crime he or she didn't commit is one too many. But we're still saving the lives of about two and a half potential victims for every person we execute and nobody disputes the fact that virtually all of those executed are in fact violent criminals. I never said Swift and Sure would be perfect, but as promised, it's a big improvement over what we had before.

"Now let me tell you what we're doing to protect innocent defendants. Next week I'm sending Congress a bill that will effect the most severe penalties against anyone who deliberately manufactures, alters, or withholds evidence in a violent-crime case. Officers of the law or the court who engage in such behavior will be prosecuted as violent criminals themselves. I expect the bill to sail through the House and the Senate intact. But that's a short-term fix just to *reduce* the problem. It won't solve it entirely. The only way to do away with tragedies like these is to create a perfect lie-detector, a Truth Machine.

"I'm told our scientific community could develop such a machine, possibly as soon as 10 years from now. My good friend Senator Garrison Roswell is now drafting a bill to encourage private industry to develop a 100-percent accurate Truth Machine. I hope Garry's bill passes. If it does, I'll sign it."

In his office in downtown Washington DC, Charles Scoggins stared at his computer screen. Now 20 years old, he had earned his Harvard MBA in a one-year accelerated program and was purportedly a venture capitalist specializing in high-tech companies. As President Hall's words appeared on the screen, it was apparent to his assistant, Joan Goldman, that Scoggins could barely believe what he saw.

"Amazing," he whispered. "Armstrong was right; there really is going to be a Truth Machine. But he can't ignore me."

He sent Joan home, but would not leave the office himself until late the following evening. He had too much at risk from deployment of a Truth Machine: his wealth, his freedom, possibly his life. So he calculated that the best way to prevent the device from being built was to become involved with Armstrong's company. *Once I get close to Armstrong, I'll outwit the naive little twerp.*[9]

He spent the next 15 hours writing up a business plan.

Then the first call he made was to Leo Boschnak at Merrill Lynch & Schwab, with whom he had previously

[9] I confirmed this thought from the reconstructed transcript of Scoggins's only scip interview, which took place on August 11, 2024.

done three small venture capital deals. "Leo, have you seen President Hall's announcement about Roswell's Truth Machine Bill?"

"Yes, but I'm not sure I understand what it all means."

"I think it'll be huge. If I make a run at the Truth Machine, is Merrill interested in taking my company public?"

"Why don't you come up here tomorrow, say 11 a.m., and you can explain it to me."

Nine days later, on March 15, 2006, Merrill and Scoggins signed a letter of intent. It was a risk-free deal for Merrill, with no guarantees of performance. But as part of the agreement, each firm guaranteed not to deal with a competing firm without permission from the other. This non-competition provision would make that letter of intent a valuable document indeed.

CHAPTER 13

THE HOLY GRAIL

Cambridge, Massachusetts
May 6, 2006—The FDA approves Merck's new drug Exovir (generic name, retrocycline), a cure for AIDS, a disease that has killed over three million Americans and nearly 200 million worldwide. Because of its obvious efficacy, double-blind studies were halted late last year so that all participants could receive the drug. A six-month regimen registered more than a 99-percent success rate, eliminating the HIV virus's ability to replicate and allowing the body's immune system to rebuild itself. In order for Merck to recapture its enormous research costs, a six-month dosage will cost about $96,000, but

the drug is offered at reduced prices to patients who are uninsured or otherwise unable to pay the full cost.—An Irish Catholic terrorist group takes credit for blowing a hole in the Chunnel linking Britain and France, drowning at least 1,378 motorists, with 16 still missing. Repairs are expected to take several months. Prime Minister Harrison vows the terrorists will be caught and brought to justice. A reward of up to five million pounds sterling is offered for information leading to the conviction of those responsible.—Scientists in Berkeley, California, announce they have the technology to predict earthquakes anywhere in the world at least four hours before they occur. The scientists maintain their predictions will be over 99-percent accurate to within 30 minutes of the time of the tremor. At least 1,700 monitoring stations would have to be built, but experts forecast that once constructed, the system could save millions of lives this century, mostly in Asia.

They'd been there less than 15 minutes and already Pete had counted four identical gag bumper stickers: "Politicians repent! The Truth Machine is coming."

He sat with David at a table outside Brigham's Ice Cream on Memorial Drive, Skipper at his feet. It was a beautiful sunny day and the streets and sidewalks were crowded with cars and pedestrians.

Pete pressured David. "This is the opportunity of a lifetime. You can be my partner: fifty-fifty. We'll change the world, and become famous and rich beyond our wildest dreams." On this, his greatest adventure, he wanted his best friend by his side, but knew David was reluctant because he didn't feel he could contribute enough. "Remember, the Truth Machine was *your* idea to begin with."

"All I did was throw out the concept in Theo-Soc. I never took it seriously until you did. You're the one who saw it as a real possibility."

David knew Pete could get plenty of funding and was

sure he would succeed; he felt he was being offered a free ride. "Look, Pete," he added, "I'm really flattered. But I want to finish law school, marry Diana, and settle down in Dallas. My mom and brother are there and I need to be near them. Besides, I've always planned on going into public service. You know I don't really care much about money."

"Damn. I just can't imagine doing this without you."

Reaching down to feed Skipper the rest of his chicken sandwich, Pete's thoughts turned to Leonard, who could have been a perfect partner. Now his surrogate brother, David West, was deserting him, too.

He began to rock.

David saw his friend's distress. "Come to think of it, Dallas might be the perfect place to build your company. Great location; DFW airport's bigger than the entire island of Manhattan, and you can travel anywhere from there—fast! Plus there's no state income tax in Texas. I figure that's got to be worth an extra $50 billion to you."

David's smile said, *I understand you and I'll always be your friend.* "Tell you what. You can hire me as your lawyer for the first few years, at least until I run for office. I'll work cheap! We can even buy houses in the same neighborhood—if you don't mind living in a slum."

They both laughed.

Pete, who had amassed a net worth in excess of $20 million and could have moved into the penthouse suite at Charles River Towers, had been forced to live on campus instead because David couldn't afford an apartment and refused to let Pete pay their rent himself. While admiring the principle, Pete was getting tired of it; David never let him pay for *anything*. Only in the past year had he even agreed to use Pete's telephone to call his family in Texas, and then only because Pete had programmed his computer to send the long-distance portion over the Internet, legally converting them into free calls.[10]

"I'll think about it," Pete said, "but it'd be a much easier decision if you'd go in on this with me."

"That just isn't gonna happen. But I'll miss the hell out of you if you're not around. I hope you decide to live in Dallas anyway."

"I might. Meanwhile, I'm trying to put a team together. I may need your help. You're the best judge of character I know and I'm probably the worst."

"Not true. But of course I'm happy to help. Just let me know when and where."

"How about this afternoon at the B-School?" Pete had already arranged a meeting with Marjorie Tilly, whom David knew fairly well, and Harvard Business School Professor Maximilian Honeycutt, whom both David and Pete knew only by reputation.

Six days earlier Senator Roswell's Truth Machine Bill, S. 2089, had been signed into law by President Hall. S. 2089 had been easy to push through Congress, since there appeared to be no immediate losers. Only minor changes were made to the original draft.

Even the legislators weren't frightened by the concept of a Truth Machine. Like almost all humans at the time, the average legislator considered him- or herself to be above-average in terms of honesty. Rare was the politician who wouldn't gladly agree to be tested for truthfulness—as long as his or her opponents were subjected to the same test.

Roswell's staff had estimated that deployment of

---

[10] Pete used a primitive compression technique that allowed simultaneous two-way calls directly from his personal computer. The digital bits were sent on the Internet to a friend's computer in Dallas, which automatically forwarded the call to the West household. Prior to that, David wrote letters to his mother and brother every day, but would save them up for as long as a week, or until he had six pages, just enough to squeeze under the one ounce limit for a 70-cent first-class stamp. He would also telephone them, but only once or twice per month, always at off-peak times, using a phone card to get the lowest possible rate.

Truth Machines in federal, state, and county systems alone would save $42 billion annually. "And that figure only reflects the reduced costs of shorter trials and more plea-bargains and civil settlements," Roswell told the full senate. "It doesn't *begin* to take into account the untold benefits of redirecting lawyers to less adversarial pursuits and the other rewards of greater justice."

Scientists had predicted that a foolproof Truth Machine could be 50 to 80 years in the making. The street-smart Roswell correctly figured that only old-fashioned greed could speed up the process. The Bill was designed to tap into that greed. "Why not offer part of the money the Truth Machine would save government to the first company to produce a foolproof device?" he'd asked. "Let Wall Street investors come up with the R&D money."

A risk-free plan for government, S. 2089 created the most important new American industry since the personal computer.

The Truth Machine Bill was essentially a contract between government and private industry. Its main points were:

THE PRIZE:
1) The first company to build a working Truth Machine was guaranteed a 10-year, $21 billion per annum (adjusted for inflation) government contract to administer truth tests throughout the criminal and civil justice system.
2) A special patent would be issued, good for 25 years.
3) The company could derive additional income from any other legal use of the Truth Machine cleared by Congress.
4) The company would operate at least one testing site for every geographical area of up to one million population and a minimum of 500 testing sites nationwide. The company could then offer the government additional testing sites. If it did, one-third of any savings to the gov-

ernment, as calculated by an independent board, would be paid to the company.

THE CONDITIONS:

1) The Truth Machine had to be 100-percent accurate at detecting intentional deceit. A special panel including representatives from the Justice Department, FBI, Central Intelligence Agency, Federal Communication Commission, Food and Drug Administration, and National Institute of Health would devise tests. The testing process could take no longer than eight months and the panel's decision would be final.

2) The Truth Machine had to work on any mentally competent individual, including those adjudged criminally insane. Only those determined clinically incompetent, roughly one-half of one percent of the population between the ages of 5 and 85 could be deemed exempt. The Truth Machine would be responsible for identifying with absolute certainty any person falling into that category.

3) Upon completion of the Truth Machine, the CEO and any other chosen employees of the successful inventing company, would be subjected to the Truth Machine themselves. Under the authority of government attorneys, they would be asked such questions as: "Are you aware of any illegal acts committed in developing the Truth Machine's technology?" and "Are there any imperfections that might compromise adherence to any conditions of the Truth Machine Bill?"

4) The successful company would not be permitted to use or offer any Truth Machine technology outside the United States, directly or indirectly, without authorization from Congress.

ADDITIONAL PROVISIONS:

1) Crimes committed prior to S. 2089's enactment (April 30, 2006) discovered solely as a result of the Truth Machine would be "grandfathered" as nonprosecutable offenses. All crimes committed after that date would be subject to discovery and prosecution.

2) After the Truth Machine's approval, any accused or

convicted criminal could accede to Truth Machine questioning to prove innocence. Convicted capital cases would be given first priority.

The Bill was less controversial than most experts had predicted; there were surprisingly few demonstrations by individual rights or privacy rights groups. Many Americans were leery of the idea, but most admitted it was worth a try; the concept of any human beings receiving death sentences for crimes they didn't commit was anathema to the American spirit. And the "grandfather" provision certainly helped reduce opposition. In fact without it, most historians agree that the Bill could never have passed.

S. 2089 had the desired effect. The Truth Machine immediately became the proverbial "holy grail" of the high-tech business community.

Tilly arrived at Pete and David's room and the three proceeded to the Business School. The famous Oxford-educated Maximilian Honeycutt, entering his 12th year as full professor at the Harvard Business School, was also assistant dean of the school and a popular teacher of a course entitled "Entrepreneurial Startups." Pete had never taken Honeycutt's course but, having read all three of his books, was an admirer of the 51-year-old professor.

Rising to greet them from the tidy desk in his large office, Honeycutt cut an elegant figure: slender and impeccably dressed, with sandy gray hair and mustache, both neatly trimmed. Tilly was surprised to see no market-quote machines or program-trade processors, only a primitive Pentium-4 desktop computer with its high-definition screen barely two feet wide. The printer was a three-year-old HP7400, capable of running just 90 color pages a minute, or 150 in black and white. She figured, *He must use these relics for word processing, desktop publishing, and not much else.*

Honeycutt spoke directly to Pete. "I understand you're entering the Truth Machine race. I also hear you're considered the odds-on favorite."

"Yes, sir. But I'll need a lot of help. M-My expertise is in computer programming. I, er, I have no business experience at all."

"I have some information for you and some advice. First of all, you might be interested to know that one of my former students, Charles Scoggins, was here to see me a few weeks ago. He's trying to put together a company to compete for the same prize you're chasing. He already has some impressive talent lined up and he's willing to issue serious stock options to attract the right people. Made *me* a rather generous offer, I might add, although based on what I know of him, I suspect he'd try to renegotiate if I'd actually *accepted* it."

"What a hyprocrite!" David exclaimed.

Honeycutt smiled faintly. "Apparently you know Mr. Scoggins."

"I had n-no idea." Pete was shocked. "I knew Charles was into venture capital these days, but in Theo-Soc he always spoke, uh, as if he thought the Truth Machine was a *terrible* idea."

"A $210 billion government contract is hard to resist."

"I guess so. Still, I'm surprised. Um, y-you said you also had some advice for me?"

"Yes. First, ethics is becoming the most critical skill for any business owner to learn, so I'll give you a 20-second crash course. Make sure every plan and every judgment you make is for the long haul. Always keep your word and never go for the quick dollar. The real value in any business is gained by building a franchise of customer loyalty over a long period of time. If you measure every decision by that standard, your ethics will be just fine.

"Second, don't follow Mr. Scoggins's lead of granting

big stock options. Make sure you keep controlling interest in your company—that's at least 50.1 percent, not 49.9—or you'll find that other people will determine your destiny. I've watched hundreds of visionaries give away too much stock at the beginning. Later on, when they needed to grant options to attract good workers or issue stock to raise capital, they lost voting control. It often became just a matter of time before others took over their companies."

Pete listened carefully; everything Honeycutt said made sense. They traded ideas and anecdotes for two hours. Pete and Tilly explained their plans for the company that would be called Armstrong Technologies, Inc. (ATI). They intended to raise seed money to fund a series of software and data-processing projects. Their people would hone their skills on those projects and the profits would fund R&D on the Truth Machine.

Honeycutt thought the plan sounded good.

"Would you be interested in, um, joining us?" Pete asked.

"Only if you ignore the sage advice I just imparted about minimizing the stock options."

Everybody laughed.

"Seriously, I like what I'm doing here at Harvard. But I have some good contacts I'm happy to share." He handed Pete a list of names with telephone numbers and e-mail addresses. "I made an extra copy of this list: the 22 brightest business minds I know who might be available for a project like yours. Feel free to tell them you got their names from me. Unfortunately, though, I compiled this list for your friend Mr. Scoggins, so I'm afraid he has a bit of a head start."

CHAPTER 14

THE TEAM

Dallas, Texas
July 15, 2006—A 160-year legacy ends as the General Services Administration announces it will seek a private buyer for the U.S. Postal Service. The agency is no longer considered necessary because of the availability of less expensive and more reliable transportation and communication services from private parcel and catalog delivery firms, the Internet, facsimile machines, and cellular digital data transfer. The successful bidder may discontinue any service it deems unprofitable and renegotiate salaries and work rules with the Postal Workers Union. Still, it is uncertain whether a buyer can be found at any price. If no buyer steps forward, the service will be phased out over five years.—China's gross national product (GNP) figures are officially released. At just over $19 trillion, China's economy is now the largest in the world, although its per capita income remains far below that of many nations, especially the United States and Japan.—The death-toll estimate from last month's nuclear destruction of Sarajevo is raised to 155,000 as clean up continues. No group has yet claimed responsibility for the blast. The Bosnian government still blames Serbian extremists, despite lack of evidence.

Many decades before the invention of "air-conditioning," not to mention weather control, Civil War Union General William Tecumseh Sherman said, "If I owned Texas and hell, I would rent out Texas and live in hell."

Some 140 years later, Pete and David were walking down Ross Avenue in Dallas. If looks could kill, David might not be dead yet, but he would definitely be limping. "I can't believe you talked me into coming here," Pete raved. "What do you suppose the temperature is right now, about 125 degrees?"

It was 106, but Pete was dripping with sweat. *Will Skipper ever adapt to this furnace?* he wondered. *He's used to Cambridge, with snow in the winter and summers when the mercury seldom rises above 90.*

David, considerably more comfortable, grinned. "Don't worry, Pete. After five or six years your blood thins out. Then you'll start *shivering* if the temperature ever drops into two digits, which fortunately it never does."

David was joking. Typically Dallas was this hot only from late June through early September. The other nine and a half months were pretty livable, except for the occasional hailstorm, flood, or tornado.

Bill Tannenbaum, a six-foot, two-inch, jowl-cheeked former classmate of Honeycutt, wasn't entirely sure David was kidding. He had never been to Dallas until about a month ago. In a whirlwind courtship, he had been wooed and seduced by Pete's vision of a future without deceit; last week he had quit Microsoft and uprooted his family, kicking and screaming, to Dallas. Already he pined for the mythically incessant rain of Seattle.

First meeting Tannenbaum when he and his family flew in to check things out, David had been impressed. "I like him," he had told Pete. "He's a roll-up-your-sleeves executive, smart, a great motivator, and best of all, he's a cheapskate; my kind of guy. He flew here coach class on a weekend special. I suspect he won't spend any more of your money than necessary to get the job done. You can decide if he has the technical skills you need, but I have a feeling he's the right man."

The price Pete paid for Tannenbaum was high. Next in line to succeed Steve Ballmer as chief operating officer

(COO) of Microsoft, the third most profitable company in the world, Tannenbaum speculated that Ballmer might retire early in order to more fully enjoy his family and enormous fortune. He was tempted to wait it out. But Pete won over his new president and COO with a package that included a generous signing bonus and a stock option of 400,000 ATI shares: four percent of the company.

Still, it was considerably less than Scoggins had offered. Tannenbaum knew Pete Armstrong was a much better bet to win the Truth Machine race, so he had gone with ATI. But Scoggins's company, Research Laboratories Group (RLG), was in Washington DC, which Tannenbaum, now covered with sweat, decided *had* to be a better place to live than Dallas.

Tilly had been to the "Metroplex" many times before moving there and had a higher opinion of the city. Dallas was a great town if you enjoyed night life, cultural events, and fine dining. She would have been happy almost anywhere, but Dallas suited her especially well. Still single and very attractive at 38, Tilly intended to take full advantage of the incomparable Dallas singles' scene during her hours away from work. But over the coming months, such hours would be rare.

Several weeks earlier, Pete had offered Tilly a two-percent stake in the company and the title of vice president, director of software design. She had cheerfully accepted and submitted her resignation to the FBI.

All four walked briskly to the ATI offices on Market Street in the West End. No cars were permitted. It was a charming area, comprised mostly of restored 100-year-old warehouses converted into restaurants, offices, and stores. They worked less than a block from the Texas School Book Depository, from which Lee Harvey Oswald allegedly shot and killed President John F. Kennedy almost 43 years earlier. They were also within two blocks of 17 different restaurants, including Cerveceria, the Tex-Mex café where they had just inhaled their lunch. The four executives had a big after-noon ahead.

It was time to decide who would make up the core team of ATI. Nearly all employees would be hired after Pete raised ATI's start-up capital; only a critical few, a skeleton team, would come on board right away. The team would map out ATI's initial strategy and provide further credibility to the new venture.

That team consisted of Pete, Tannenbaum, Tilly, and four others chosen that day from over 100 qualified applicants:

<u>Leslie Williams</u>, 31, comptroller and chief financial officer (CFO). Williams, a five-foot, eleven-inch, rather heavy-set[11] woman, had been Pete's personal accountant and a partner at Ernst & Young, one of only three "big eight" accounting firms that had survived H.R. 1918, the Tax Simplification Act of 2001. A fellow math prodigy, she had superb computer and systems design skills. Before making partner, she had managed a staff of 75 CPAs in E&Y's Boston office, unusual for such a young manager. Creative with numbers, Williams never crossed the line between creativity and indefensibility; her tax filings always upheld under audit or in tax court. Williams had proved a difficult sell. Pete eventually had to relinquish two percent of ATI to convince her to leave the security of Ernst & Young.

<u>Carl Whatley</u>, 42, vice president, director of marketing. Whatley left the same job at Microsoft for one percent of ATI. The six-foot, three-inch, pony-tailed ad-man was Tannenbaum's close friend. Well known throughout the industry, and not just for his creative ideas and productive work ethic, Whatley had an uncanny sense of what the public wanted. His predictions about which software programs would sell and which

[11] Later that year, after beginning a regimen of Amgen's newly approved protein enzyme, Dexanase (generic name, leptin), Williams permanently lost 57 pounds. In the words of her new best friend, Carl Whatley, "Leslie simply metamorphosed into drop-dead gorgeous."

would "rot on the shelves" were legendary for their accuracy. Whatley, who was openly gay, had just ended a six-year relationship with a colleague at Microsoft. The relationship had ended badly and it was easy for Tannenbaum to convince him to leave Washington and join his team in Dallas.

<u>Gene Hildegrand</u>, 37, vice president, director of personnel. Hildegrand left his position of assistant personnel director of Texas Instruments, at the urging of David West. His son, Gene, Jr., and David's younger brother, Philip, were best friends. Hildegrand was five feet, eleven inches tall and almost completely bald. Slight and wiry in build, he ran marathons regularly. The Baylor University MBA was a superb, relentless recruiter of high-tech talent and was himself recruited for a package that included one-half of one percent of ATI.

<u>Haywood Thacker</u>, 52, vice president, general counsel. Thacker was a distinguished-looking gray-haired gentleman of medium height and build, of whom it was said only half-jokingly that he had never been seen out of a three-piece suit by anyone, including his wife. He too was recruited by David West—at David's interview for admission to Harvard Law School. Thacker was a legend in business law. His understanding of contract, anti-trust, torts, and intellectual properties law made him the ideal candidate for ATI. He and David were impressed by each other and Thacker eventually agreed to leave his comfortable professorship at Harvard for a new career at ATI and one-percent interest in the company.

Pete gave himself the title of chairman of the board and scientific director.

CHAPTER 15

WALL STREET

New York City
November 14, 2006—The investigation continues for the party or parties responsible for last month's nuclear incineration of Baghdad. UN Secretary General Kwayme K'nau assures the world that those responsible will be caught and punished, and warns members of the international community not to blame any nation or group without sufficient evidence. Still, suspicion falls on Kurdish terrorists and the government of Iran, the two most likely culprits. Over one million persons, including Iraqi dictator Saddam Hussein, have either been confirmed dead or are missing and presumed dead in the aftermath of the one-megaton blast.—Surgeon General Abigail Swenson announces that Alzheimer's disease is now the second leading cause of death in the United States. She also warns that unless a successful treatment is found, it might soon surpass strokes as America's number one killer. Cancer, heart disease, and AIDS fatalities have sharply diminished over recent years as a result of successful new treatments and continue to decline as those therapies are further refined. Alzheimer's affects an increasing percentage of the population as the average life expectancy of Americans steadily rises.

Wall Street anxiously awaited Randall Petersen Armstrong and his team. Over 90 investment firms had contacted ATI over the previous months, but the team had selected just five companies to interview, all headquartered in New York City. The message sent to each of the five was the same:

"Congratulations. Of the dozens of firms that have approached us, we have chosen yours and fewer than 10 others to consider. To that end, please find our business plan enclosed. Once you have analyzed the enclosed material, you may fax us any questions you have. We will answer promptly. Tomorrow Gail Watts from our office will call to arrange a meeting in Manhattan next week. In order to save us all time, please plan on having an offer ready at that meeting."

It had been David's clever idea to understate by implication the number of firms who had contacted ATI and to overstate the number of firms ATI would be talking to. A rhetorical strategy, not a lie, this was just the opposite of what most firms in ATI's place would have done. David hoped the misdirection would keep bidders honest by discouraging collusion. From the letter's wording, each firm would assume they were bidding against at least eight other firms, some apparently playing their cards close to the vest.

All five firms requested appointments, but faxed few questions to ATI's office. The meticulously sculpted business plan addressed nearly every contingency, calling for the purchase of everything from four DNA-based parallel process super-computers to the design of field tests with thousands of subjects. ATI would stand at the forefront of other advanced technology projects involving intricate software.

The company's biggest selling point was Pete himself. Not quite 17 years old, he had an unsurpassed talent for refining and debugging programs. Whoever had Pete as a business resource would maintain an enormous edge. He pledged to devote his full-time efforts to the company. He would also invest $10 million of his own money.

The team stayed at the modestly priced Salisbury Hotel on 57th Street, midtown. They had all flown coach. Each night they met in Pete's small suite amid stacks of papers, PDCs, and peripherals. Their wrist-band personal computers were hooked up to two full-size laser printers that seemed to run non-stop.

All agreed that the only Wall Street firms eligible would be those willing to guarantee the company $110 million dollars of initial funding, with an additional commitment of up to $200 million if needed. Of these, the firm demanding the smallest percentage of the company would get the deal.

The consensus was that Pete should expect to relinquish 10 to 15 percent of his company for the first $110 million and about two percent for each additional $10 million. This was an unusually small percentage to give up for venture capital, but the company's financial needs were modest given its potential. Pete intended to offer generous stock options to ATI employees and insisted on being able to maintain controlling interest in the company. That didn't leave much margin for error. If they couldn't negotiate acceptable terms, the team would fly home and try to figure out how to proceed with less money.

The *Wall Street Journal* reported that Merrill Lynch & Schwab was close to a deal with Scoggins's RLG. Goldman Sachs was said to be courting the Renaissance Corporation, a group recently founded by the mysterious MIT computer wizard, Alan Bonhert. No one, however, was willing to sign a deal until the ATI bidding was finished and the final numbers released.

The first meeting, with Merrill Lynch & Schwab, America's largest investment house, set the tone for the trip. Merrill senior vice president Leo Boschnak figured the initial public offering would be an easy sell; he had so much faith in Armstrong that he'd already decided Merrill would retain at least 30 percent of the initial public offering (IPO) for its own account. The firm offered to raise $110 million, after fees, in exchange for 11 percent of the company, and to guarantee additional funding of up to $200 million at the rate of three percent of the stock for each additional $15 million. This offer was so close to the team's anticipated formula that Pete wondered if someone in his group had spoken off the record to someone at Merrill.

Pete listened intently as Tannenbaum and then Thacker pounded Boschnak and his staff with questions. Every answer appeared to be in ATI's favor. It was obvious that Boschnak wanted the deal and wanted it badly.

Finally Pete rose from his seat holding a light bulb in his hand. The room became almost eerily quiet. "Mr. Boschnak, did you know this bulb was originally developed just to be used on ships and for nighttime baseball games?"

The senior vice president understood his point immediately, but Pete continued his well-rehearsed, prophetic speech for the benefit of Boschnak's staff. "Once invented, the Truth Machine will have uses in all areas of interaction including business, politics, medicine, education, even human relations. There will be early resistance to invasions against a privacy we all take for granted, but once science begins its journey, there'll be no turning back. Overall, the Truth Machine will have a positive effect on nearly every aspect of society; the market will be enormous and ATI will have a monopoly for at least 25 years. Conceivably we could become the most profitable corporation in history."

"We understand Merrill faces keen competition in signing ATI," Boschnak answered. "We believe in you and will go the extra mile. If our offer isn't good enough, we'll sharpen our pencils. Would you be willing to come back and let us have another crack before you commit to any other firm?"

Pete looked around the conference room. None of his team objected. "Very well," Pete replied. He reset his PDC for their next destination, shook hands with everyone, and left the room.

The next day, the Dean Witter Discover Group promised

the Armstrong team they could beat Merrill's best deal. Before the week was over, Prudential and Shearson Olde bowed out; although they were willing to match Merrill's offer, they felt they couldn't compete in continued negotiations. Dean Witter and Goldman Sachs were still in the running and these three remaining contenders wondered who else might be competing secretly. (While in fact, there was nobody else.)

The day they were scheduled to leave, Armstrong's team reconvened at Merrill Lynch & Schwab headquarters. They had been assured Merrill would make them an offer they couldn't turn down.

Boschnak pulled his PDC from his shirt pocket. "I'll read you the terms and pass out hard copies. This is our absolute best offer and it has two options. You can take a week to decide which option you'd prefer, but we'd like to know before you leave here today whether or not we have a deal."

"Fair enough," replied Pete.

"Option number one. We'll fund the first $110 million for a seven-percent interest in the company, plus 1.5 percent for each additional $15 million as needed, up to an additional $300 million."

"Is that still after all fees?" Williams asked.

"That's net to you, after everything. Pure, tax-free paid-in capital to add to your balance sheet. No new conditions or restrictions."

Pete felt his mouth go dry. He tried to appear calm and had to consciously instruct his body, *Don't start rocking!* Merrill was placing a value on his company, which still had no assets or sales, of at least $1.57 billion.

Boschnak continued. "Option number two's a bit unusual. As you know, we've been holding discussions with Charles Scoggins and RLG. We propose a merger: ATI acquires 100 percent of RLG for $15 million that we'll supply. Mr. Scoggins intends to use that money to buy out the contracts of RLG's people not hired by ATI. He wanted six percent of ATI's stock for his exclusive services, but we convinced him to accept four. The combination of ATI and RLG would become a formidable favorite to win the Truth Machine race. Therefore, we'd fund you at $125 million dollars for just a five-percent interest in the merged company. All other terms would remain the same. That means we'd be valuing the company at $2.5 billion."

Barely able to hide his glee, Pete asked Boschnak to allow him a few minutes to consult privately with his team. Tilly calmed him down. Option two seemed the better choice, but option one was still quite acceptable. Since they had been offered a week to decide, they all agreed to take the full week.

When Boschnak returned, Pete shook his hand and told him, "The deal's yours. We'll let you know one week from today whether we've chosen option one or two. In the meantime, maybe you could call Mr. Scoggins and ask him to join us in Dallas tomorrow."

Unknown to the ATI team, Scoggins would be a major shareholder regardless of which option they chose. Scoggins had convinced Boschnak that ATI was the firm to bet on. "Armstrong's talent is way beyond Bonhert's and mine," he had explained, "and as far as I can tell, nobody other than the three of us even has a shot at it." Boschnak, performing his own investigation, soon learned that Scoggins was telling the truth.

Scoggins later told him, rather disingenuously, "Leo, if I'd known Armstrong was going to do this, I would have tried to join his company instead of coming to you. But now it's too late for me; he's already put together his core team. The only way I can get into ATI is through you." On that pretext, he had refused to release Merrill from the provision of non-competition in the March 15 letter of intent, unless he somehow received at least two percent of ATI's stock, or four percent if he included his services.

Naturally Boschnak's offers to ATI took Merrill Lynch & Schwab's predicament into account.

It is doubtful that Scoggins had ever planned to operate RLG as an independent entity; he had apparently constructed RLG's standard employment contracts for the eventuality of selling the company. Once sold, RLG had no legal obligation to its executives, except to pay proportionate shares of the sales price, and then only to stock option holders who were refused employment by the buyer—ATI. Scoggins would retain over 90 percent of the $15 million for himself, not to mention up to four percent of ATI.

CHAPTER 16

THE TROJAN HORSE

Dallas, Texas
November 20, 2006—French scientists, using a patented technique, revive a mouse frozen in liquid nitrogen two weeks ago. The first mammal ever successfully frozen and revived, the rodent sustains only minor brain damage and frostbite, and otherwise appears healthy. The scientists speculate that their process could work equally well on healthy humans and should be refined into a viable medical alternative within 15 years. President Hall immediately asks Congress to authorize funding to study potential economic and sociological effects of large-scale cryonic suspended animation should such a process become legalized for terminally ill United States citizens. He also requests a separate study on the possible effects of allowing cryonic suspension for healthy Americans wishing to postpone their present

lives to dwell in the future.—Eastman Kodak announces plans to market a new 360-degree digital video camera less than five millimeters at its longest dimension and weighing under half an ounce. The new cameras can be incorporated into watch-sized voice-activated personal computers, allowing users to record any event and instantly store the images off-site. The cameras will initially sell for $1,100 each, but the price should drop approximately 50 percent per year until 2009. Then, at about $140 per unit, analysts predict at least 25-percent penetration into the worldwide watch-sized computer market, or approximately 400 million units per year. Kodak's stock price soars.

"I assure you I have no such conceits. We'd be foolish to change the name from Armstrong Technologies," Charles Scoggins said.

It was obvious to David that Scoggins did not want any members of the team to feel threatened by his presence.

The day was sunny and, at 58 degrees, not especially cold. The conference room's single picture window overlooked Market Street's restaurants, theaters, and shopping arcades. Construction had just begun on the monorail system that would connect downtown Dallas to Las Colinas, a high-tech office and residential community about nine miles away, and eventually to the Dallas/Fort Worth International Airport. The roadwork was noisy, but the six men and two women seated around the table focused on the interview.

"$110 million's a lot of money," Scoggins continued, "but not nearly enough to cover the development costs for this project. Unless we can successfully create and market other products, we'll be bankrupt long before we have a working Truth Machine. Pete already has a godlike reputation in the software community. Our products will simply sell better if we market under the Armstrong name."

Scoggins used the pronoun "we" a lot when explaining

his vision of the company to the team. He already included himself in that vision. Considering ATI's two options from Merrill, it was a safe assumption. Still, he rarely offered controversial opinions.

"Do you have ideas for other projects, Charles?" Whatley asked.

"I have a few, but I can't say they're original. I consider myself more problem solver and facilitator than idea man. I could help you evaluate and prioritize projects and I have hundreds of valuable contacts in government and in other high-tech companies."

Pete, who did not enjoy the networking aspects of business, thought Scoggins's skills in that arena would be particularly valuable.

"Charles," David asked, "if you really believed you had a shot at the big prize, why give it up for just four percent of ATI?"

Scoggins shrugged. "I really didn't have much of a chance on my own. It's important to know one's limitations. I have certain skills, but Pete's in a different league entirely. In a one-on-one race, I'd lose. Pete Armstrong's software talent is simply too big an edge for another company to overcome."

An honest answer, David thought. Still, he pressed on. "Back at Harvard, you were dead-set against the Truth Machine concept. You considered it an invasion of privacy. Why do you think it's a good idea now?"

"It's only a matter of time before the Truth Machine's developed and used; since it's *going* to be built, I want ATI to build it. At least we're an ethical company and maybe we can help ensure it won't be misused. Whether or not I believe the machine itself is a good thing is irrelevant."

Later that day, David met privately with Pete in his office. "When I was a kid," he said, "my dad used to take me with him to poker games. Of course everybody there wanted to win, but there was always at least one shark—someone out for blood. The shark would act real friendly. He'd pretend that, like the other guys, he was there to be with his pals. But he was really only there to make money. If it wasn't for the card game, he wouldn't have given those guys the time of day. The shark was the most patient fellow in the room. Usually he'd wait to be dealt a 'mortal lock' before he'd bet any real money. And he almost always won."

Pete knew David was insinuating that Scoggins was like the neighborhood poker shark; personable, patient, selfish, and deadly. "But this isn't a neighborhood poker game," he answered, "and we all know we're not here to socialize. Everybody at ATI is part of the same team."

He also considered telling David something about the ATI stock, but decided that revelation should wait. After all, timing is critical in matters where friendship and money intersect. "If we choose option one, the market is valuing Carl Whatley's one-percent stake at $15 or $16 million. If we choose option two and include Scoggins, suddenly Carl's stake is worth $25 million. How do I tell my *teammate* I decided to go with the option that costs him $9 million?"

"I'm not telling you what to do. Just watch your back. Scoggins has his own agenda and he's never going to put ATI's interest ahead of his own."

"I'll remember." Then deciding the time was right, Pete broke into a wide grin. "By the way, whatever you do, don't sell any of *your* ATI stock until you talk to me."

"What are you talking about? I don't own any stock."

"Yes, you do. When we filed the corporate papers three months ago, I had Leslie issue one percent of the stock to you. I would've given you more if I thought you'd accept it, but you have to admit one percent's *cheap* for all you've contributed. Consider it a royalty for the idea, or payment for personnel and legal advice. Hell, if you'd prefer, we can call it an early wedding present for you and Diana. The stock wasn't worth much when I gave it to you, but now it's worth $25 million. Just promise me you won't sell any of it."

David hugged him. "Thanks, buddy. I'll have to talk this over with Diana and we still might decide not to accept. But if we do, we'll never sell any of it."

David called Diana later that afternoon. "Pete just gave us one percent of ATI. Should we keep it?"

"As a gift?" She could barely believe it.

"He said I should either consider it a royalty for the idea and all my advice, or else we could accept it as a wedding present. Diana, it's worth 25 million dollars!"

"I'll say this as diplomatically as I possibly can." She paused for effect. "Are you out of your *mind*? You can't be serious about turning it down!"

David laughed. "I guess maybe I got a little carried away with myself."

"Thank God. For a moment I thought I'd fallen in love with an idiot!"

Later that evening they both called Pete to thank him again.

On January 5, 2007, Armstrong Technologies, Inc. became a public company. Leslie Williams received the $110 million bank wire and invested it in liquid, short-term financial instruments as recommended by Pete's computer models. Merrill Lynch & Schwab wired another $15 million directly to Charles Scoggins. Merrill announced it would retain half the offering, 250,000 shares, for its own account, those shares to be held indefinitely. Perhaps on the basis of that show of confidence, ATI stock rose 56 percent to $390 per share.

A 20-year-old Princeton journalism major, Jennifer Finley, whose romantic overtures Pete had spurned six years earlier at Middlesex, kept a cash management account at Merrill. She invested $58,500, almost her entire trust fund, acquiring 150 shares of ATI stock. Pete himself purchased 500 shares for about $200,000 and sent gifts of 50 shares each to Harvard University, Middlesex School, Howard Gaddis, Maximilian Honeycutt, and six other individuals and teachers he felt had helped him along the way.

The company was now valued at nearly $4 billion and Pete, who had generously relinquished Scoggins's four-percent stake entirely from his own share, still held 79-1/2 percent of it. Barely 17 years of age, he was already one of the 100 wealthiest individuals in America.

CHAPTER 17

FIRST RELEASE

Dallas, Texas
December 6, 2007—Travis Hall registers an astonishing 71-percent approval rating as his team prepares for the coming reelection campaign. Hall's Swift and Sure Anti-Crime Program has reduced violent crime rates by over 55 percent since inception. Total executions for the year 2007 are now projected at 16,000, close to original estimates. More significantly, for the first time in over a decade, Americans say they feel safe.—The United States formally establishes diplomatic relations and open trade with the government of United Korea after a long series of negotiations between Premier Kim and U.S. Secretary of State Jonathan Winer. Establishing ties with Kim's government is sharply criticized by Senator Lewis Crenshaw (D.OK) as "the final betrayal of our former South Korean allies and abandonment of America's credibility as defender of democracy." President Hall defends the move as "pragmatic and humane."

* * *

Pete strode down the hall, greeting everyone he saw by name. "Hello there, Cliff. How's your wife?"

"Could be any day, Pete."

"Get some sleep *now—before* your son's born. Art Rossman's wife just had twins. Now whenever anyone mentions the word 'sleep' he gets a lump in his throat."

Cliff Garret, ATI's chief of shipping, laughed and walked to the shipping room with a bounce in his step. It was nice that the boss remembered he was about to become a dad.

Then Pete saw Alec McCarthy, the staff art designer, turning the hall corner.

"How's the new packaging on the airline reservation software?"

"I think you'll really like it. I have the sketches in my office."

"Let's go take a look. By the way, Alec, happy birthday. I know it's tomorrow, but in case I don't see you. . . ."

Pete was changing. Among his colleagues at ATI, he took on an entirely different personality and demeanor. He felt comfortable and secure with his coworkers; holding meetings and interacting with them wasn't quite like being in the zone, but pretty close. They were all part of the same team now, working toward common goals. He relished the camaraderie.

Having memorized dozens of books on business and personnel motivation, Pete's self-confidence with staff was apparent. Although painfully shy with outsiders, he felt at ease inside ATI's walls. It was his fortress, his sustenance, his comfort, his true home. He looked forward to every day at work and dreaded the weekends, when almost all ATI employees were home with their families.

Marjorie Ann Tilly, with every reason for self-satisfaction, addressed about 200 members of the press.

"This superb software system should achieve 100-percent market penetration of every private prison, boot camp, and mandatory drug rehabilitation center in America within three years. It will be impossible for an operator without RehabTest to compete against companies with it. We're offering RehabTest risk-free for the first year and they'd be foolish not to take us up on it."

Whatley had pushed for the risk free part that would set the tone for all of ATI's marketing strategies.

Scoggins had also argued in favor of the strategy. "Make it tough for them to say no. Once they can't live without our product, we can raise prices every year. Eventually software becomes the most valuable component of any information- or service-based industry. It's only a matter of time before our pricing can reflect that."

Tilly had set the deadline for ATI's first release to coincide with Pete's birthday. RehabTest was a complex project even by ATI standards, but Tilly's group got it onto the shelves in less than a year, creating revenue and proving that ATI could meet its deadlines. Only 11 months earlier, at an open meeting with most of ATI's 75 employees, Tilly had publicly assured Pete, "This company will *not* issue 'vaporware.' If I announce a product deadline, we'll deliver the package by that date. This one's going to be your eighteenth birthday present."

With personnel director Gene Hildegrand's blessing, Tilly even persuaded Dr. Alphonso Carter to provide initial criteria for RehabTest. Still chief psychologist at Massachusetts State Prison, Carter was comfortable there, he loved his work and did not want to move his family to a new place. She had cajoled, guilted, and finally sweet-talked him. "Dr. Carter, this project can leverage your work. Nothing you could possibly do over the next year will be more important than what we could accomplish here. We need the best criminal psychologist we can find, and that's you."

Carter took an eight-month leave of absence from Massachusetts State Prison, where he had first interviewed

Daniel Anthony Reece. Carter mused over the irony that his earlier failure climaxed in his greatest opportunity to advance his field. He may have failed Pete once, but he wouldn't fail him again.

For over a month, he dictated every important fact and theory he could think of, every nuance of evaluating prisoners for criminal potential. Knowing the software would automatically test his theories and eventually reject any unsound ones, he postulated, "It seems to me that emotional intelligence is the most important aspect to measure. Most violent crimes are unplanned, stemming from underdeveloped impulse control and lack of self-restraint. A person who understands his or her own feelings can deal with them more successfully and thus refrain from future violence."

He reeled off similar concepts, one after the other. "During rehabilitation, measure each convict's attitude as you would judge that of a student. Is he applying himself to his studies? Does he retain knowledge like someone who intends to use it to improve his life, or is he just using short-term, rote memorization to go through the motions?

"You can never tell if people are cured of their inner rage by appearance or by what they say. But you can often tell by patterns of behavior, especially as parole evaluation nears. We must put less stock in changes and epiphanies that occur in the final few months."

Carter dictated 1,807 observations and theories of criminal behavior to an IBM System 5 stenographic unit. He rethought each observation, attempting to quantify its importance and degree of certainty. All were incorporated into an artificial intelligence program. Pete edited it, as he did every ATI project. Criminal records from nearly 100,000 cases were downloaded to test the program's success rate against the norm. On the first run, it predicted relapses 11 percent more accurately than the best parole boards. Furthermore, Tilly had designed the software to be self-correcting. By its release date, RehabTest was twice as accurate and would continue to improve through feedback from discharged prisoners.

Scoggins and Tannenbaum understood the profit potential of RehabTest, as did many stock analysts. At the time, private prison operators had leeway in granting paroles. It was a good system; the operators were motivated to select the best possible parole boards, since profits now depended on success rates.

Scoggins explained in an executive committee meeting, "No private incarceration facility will be able to stay in business for long without it. Their recidivism rates will be too high and they'll lose operating contracts or their release rates will be too low and they'll lose money. Therefore, RehabTest's pricing will be very elastic; we can raise the tariff quickly without losing customers. In a few years, we'll make more from it than the combined net earnings of the private prisons, boot camps, and rehabilitation centers who use it."

Scoggins's analysis was correct. Well-conceived proprietary software was the closest thing to a monopoly anyone could legally own in the United States. By the time RehabTest was released, ATI had 400 employees and was hiring at the rate of four a day. The stock now traded at $732.50 per share.

CHAPTER 18

LOTTERY

Dallas, Texas

November 8, 2008—President Hall easily wins reelection, defeating Democratic challenger Wisconsin Senator Peter Bear in every state except Massachusetts and Wisconsin, and winning a popular majority of 60.3 percent. In a conciliatory acceptance speech, considering the scope of his victory, Hall pledges to move toward more centrist economic and social policies.—The Republican Party clinches a majority in both the Senate and House of Representatives for the first time since 1994. The financial markets react favorably. The Dow-Jones Industrial Average breaks 15,000 briefly, but settles at 14,989.23. The price of gold falls below $1800 per ounce as the dollar gains strength against other world currencies.—On the sixth anniversary of his death in state prison, Congress declares Dr. Jack Kevorkian's birthday a national holiday. Assisted suicide, the cause that Kevorkian brought to public attention, was illegal in the United States until 2003. Until then most terminally ill Americans were forced to suffer prolonged, agonizing deaths. An object of controversy and ridicule during his lifetime, Kevorkian is now consistently chosen by historians as one of the 10 most influential Americans of the 20th century.

The first two years building ATI had been the happiest of Pete's life, every day filled with challenge and adventure. He offered daily thanks to his Creator for such good fortune. But as he approached his 19th birthday, he worried increasingly that his mental powers, which David only half-jokingly referred to as "far beyond those of mortal men," might diminish with age. He renewed his commitment to exercise both mind and body to maintain physical and mental strength.

Now at full adult stature, roughly six feet tall, above the average for the time, his height added to his self-confidence, making him commensurably more attractive. His stuttering had nearly ceased, even when meeting people for the first time, and his nervous tics were much less severe.

Constantly pursued by young women, some drawn to his mind, others to his money and power, Pete wasn't after one-night-stands, but neither was he ready to settle down. His relationships would last a few weeks to a few months. At the first sign of boredom or discord, he would move on.

He spoke to David every day and still missed him—and Diana. Each time they spoke, he seemed to have a new reason why they should move back to Dallas and finish law school at Southern Methodist University (SMU). Finally one worked.

"Y'know, David, when you run for office, it's going to be here in Texas. It would really help your political career if you graduated from a *Texas* law school."

David conceded his friend's point. He discussed it with Diana and they decided to transfer at the end of the semester.

They also decided to marry.

Pete's feelings about the wedding were mixed. He still harbored feelings for Diana and the marriage would make any prospects hopeless—not that he had realistic prospects to begin with. Still he was delighted that his friends would be returning to Dallas and flattered that David had asked him to serve as best man.

It would be a tiny, private ceremony. The only others invited were David's mother and brother, and Diana's parents, who had finally met David and who, to her delight, adored him.

The news at ATI was just as cheerful. There were a dozen projects in final stages and 29 in the pipeline. Pete, Tilly, Scoggins, and 14 others on the Truth Machine Project skeleton team, convened every afternoon, often meeting late into the night. They designed field tests and meticulously analyzed brain-scanning equipment.

Apparently the Renaissance Corporation was ATI's only real competition in the race. A secretive bunch, Scoggins seemed to take them very seriously. "If anyone can beat us to the prize, it's Al Bonhert," he had warned the team on several occasions. But Pete had confidence ATI would get there first. Having no reason to suspect that Scoggins or anyone else at ATI would try to delay or scuttle the project, he trusted his crew unreservedly.

LottoPick was the big news, an example of how a simple concept can change an industry. It was Leslie Williams's idea, but Scoggins grasped its potential, becoming its biggest booster. "You have no *idea* how much money this can make us. And it's so simple. It'll be the easiest software we'll ever write."

LottoPick was a real-time interactive system that assured state lottery ticket buyers that, in the improbable event their ticket won, they would be less likely to have to split the prize.

(Note: Please refer to the Appendix if you would like to read a full description of the LottoPick concept.—22g CP)

The 7-Eleven convenience store chain had test-marketed LottoPick in Texas; it was a major success and would soon be "rolled out" nationwide. Several respected stock analysts now projected that LottoPick would net ATI $1 billion annually within two years.

ATI's stock soared. At $2,625 per share, the company had a market capitalization of over $26 billion. ATI employees received stock options, but even after dilution, Pete still owned 71 percent of the company. When the Forbes 400 came out the following September, Randall Petersen Armstrong would be listed as the ninth wealthiest American.

Scoggins began to hound Pete. "Don't you think I deserve more than four percent of the stock? My work on LottoPick *doubled* ATI's value. I'm just asking the company to be fair with me."

Pete didn't see it that way. He believed ATI's real value lay in projects to benefit society, not get-rich-quick schemes.

He gave Scoggins a $5 million bonus. "I appreciate your work, but your stock's already worth over $1 billion. I'll never give up control of ATI and I won't dilute the stock every time somebody makes us a bunch of money. The money's just a means to an end that we'd all better not lose sight of."

They both understood he was referring to the Truth Machine.

Artfully, Scoggins backed off. "Look, I understand the ultimate goal and it's as important to me as it is to you. I just figured making a killing on LottoPick would get us to the Truth Machine faster. Pete, I'm your ally, not your enemy."

Pete hesitated for a moment. He felt uncomfortable, but had no idea why. Pushing the thought out of his mind, he responded, "No problem, Charles. I know you are and I really appreciate that."

On videophone later that day, David, who now held stock worth $260 million, jokingly asked Pete, "Don't you think it's ironic you made me rich in the *gambling* field? That industry broke up my family."

Pete didn't take it as a joke. "The real irony is we added at least $10 billion to ATI's market cap without contributing to society. We didn't change anything, except transferring wealth from one group of people to another. And for that we'll own an entire industry. I promise you one thing, though."

"What's that?"

"ATI will never make another product unless it has real benefits. Maybe not for everybody, but for society as a whole. No more zero-sum games."

CHAPTER 19

MEDICAL NETWORK

Seattle, Washington
August 15, 2009—Cocaine is legalized in the United States as a prescription-only treatment for Attention Deficit Disorder. The FDA's decision is based on a three-year double-blind study in which very small doses of pharmaceutical cocaine were found to be more effective than Ritalin for controlling symptoms of ADD, a disorder affecting nearly one American in five.—Iran and Israel sign a mutual nuclear defense treaty. The only two Middle Eastern nuclear powers agree to defend each other's air space and to treat any nuclear attack against one as an attack against the other.—Oil prices rise above $4 per barrel after Saudi Arabia announces plans to halt production of crude oil. However, commodity analysts predict plummeting demand will lower prices to $2.50 by year-end, citing that the 2010 electric powered automobiles would capture 96 percent of worldwide new car sales.

Over the previous 10 months, ATI had released major products in automobile traffic control (TraffiCop), simplified airline reservations (FlightSeat), and digital records dating and authentication systems (ImageNotary). The latter was particularly timely; photographic evidence had become so easy to reconstruct that notarized time-dating was the only way to authenticate photographs or digital records.

The melding of two simple words had become ATI's product-naming strategy, the advantages obvious: such names were recognized as products of ATI, a cachet of reliability, and they conveyed the products' function.

Every ATI product had been released early or on time, and virtually bug-free. Solidly profitable, the company now had $3 billion in liquid financial instruments, even after issuing a small dividend. It had never needed to borrow. The stock traded at its record high, showing no signs of weakening. One original share of ATI stock, adjusted for splits, was worth $3400, and even with employee stock options reducing his stake, Pete still owned 66.8 percent, worth $22.7 billion.

David and Diana had spent their first ATI dividend on a three-bedroom house a few blocks from Pete's two-acre estate in Highland Park. Pete, Skipper, and Pete's "girlfriend du jour" (as David jokingly referred to them) tended to spend more time at the Wests' house than at Pete's.

Not quite 20 years old, Pete Armstrong should have been the happiest teenager on the planet. But guilt darkened his spirit.

He thought about his brother and those venomous words on the morning of Leonard's death—words spoken over 14 years earlier that he still hadn't repeated to another soul: *"You little creep. I hate you. I wish you were never born!"* Leonard must have realized he hadn't meant it, but Pete wished to God he'd never said it. *And if I'd gone to get that soccer ball myself,* he thought, *I would've known not to mouth off to a stranger. What a great life I have, but if Leonard were only here to share it with me, well, then it would be perfect.*

He even fantasized traveling back in time to rescue his brother, although he knew it was impossible.

Neither had his associations with women improved. Succumbing quickly to boredom, he gave little of himself to relationships. He had learned to be diplomatic, trying to spare their feelings when he broke up with them (or put them in a position where they had no choice but to break up with him). When each affair ended, he would feel relieved to be alone, in control of his time. But exhilaration would soon give way to loneliness, leaving him vulnerable to the next attractive female who might present herself.

Word among Pete's former lovers was that he was "a nice guy," and proficient sexually. Actually, by his own later admission, his lovemaking was mechanical, his skills being what you might expect from a person who remembers everything he has ever experienced or read. His body was engaged, his mind often elsewhere—usually with Diana.

He had another fantasy, too. Immortality. Like many of his generation's brightest minds, Pete refused to abide by conventional wisdom, believing immortality unlikely but possible. Curiosity motivated him. He wanted to see what would happen in 100, 1,000, or 100,000 years. He thought about the future all the time and longed to learn if his vision was accurate. At times, he felt he just *had* to see it. Hence his growing obsession with the medical and biotechnology fields.

ATI needed Dr. Sharon Rosenfield enough to roll out the big guns. Naturally it was raining when Bill Tannenbaum and Pete Armstrong landed at Sea-Tac International Airport. Their limousine sloshed through the Seattle streets, delivering them to the Alexis Hotel downtown.

Rosenfield had been Tannenbaum's longtime friend and family physician. At 37, she was an impressive woman: athletic, well over six feet tall with an unruly mane of blond hair and an angelic countenance. A bit wild in her late teens and early twenties, she once joked to a friend, "I feel especially qualified to become a doctor since I've sampled every drug known to man and every man who's known drugs." But after leaving Concord Academy, she became more serious, graduating summa cum laude from Wellesley and in 1996 at the top of her class at Albert Einstein College of Medicine.

She had entered private practice in Seattle as a family doctor, but now operated 16 health maintenance clinics. The Rosenfield Clinics enjoyed the best reputation for quality primary care in the city. But more than her talent as a physician, her charisma made her the ideal candidate to lead ATI's crucial medical division. Everywhere she went, Sharon Rosenfield made friends. She brought out the best in people and they loved her for it. Tannenbaum had convinced Pete that she was the one person best qualified for the job, but Rosenfield was unwilling to leave Seattle.

Meeting at their hotel, she greeted them warmly: a friendly handshake for Pete and a loving hug for Tannenbaum. Rosenfield was obviously not intimidated by the 19-year-old billionaire, and Pete felt totally at ease.

Over the next hour they discussed medicine and technology. Pete was impressed by her grasp of the differing objectives and viewpoints of various medical interests, including insurers, hospitals, Health Maintenance Organizations, drug companies, specialists, general practitioners, and the American Medical Association. He was even more taken with her sensitivity to the well-being and emotional comfort of patients. He really liked her and realized ATI might have to make some serious compromises.

Pete gave his pitch. "Dr. Rosenfield, with your help we intend to reconstruct the field of medicine. We can contribute even more to America's health than the mandatory health education and anti-smoking programs of the 1990s. Statistics show Alzheimer's disease as our leading cause of death, but you and I know that isn't true. More years of life are lost because medicine's too complicated, and doctors can't coordinate and supervise treatments well enough. We have the information and science to increase average life span by four or five years, but it's inconsistently applied. I admire doctors, but you're only human, with limited memory and judgment. And today's computerized medical assistance systems barely help you at all. Medical errors and miscalculations cost more loss of life than Alzheimer's."

"Bill already sold me on ATI's plans," Rosenfield replied. "I've thought about the same issues for years; these last few weeks, I've barely been able to think about anything else. I believe in this project. But aren't there other doctors who could run your medical team? I'm willing to sell my clinics, but my family comes first. My husband loves his job at Boeing and I can't ask my kids to leave their friends. Besides, we can't imagine living anywhere but Seattle."

"There are other doctors," Tannenbaum said, "but you can get this done faster and better than they can. You'll save thousands, maybe hundreds of thousands of lives by accepting this position. It'll be the hardest thing you'll ever do—and the most important. Besides, Dallas isn't *that* bad."

She laughed, and answered earnestly. "Bill, I'd love the job. In fact, you don't have to offer me the directorship, I'd just like to be part of the team. But I can't ask my family to move. Isn't there *anything* I can do to help you from Seattle?"

Pete hadn't considered that possibility. *It might be better,* he decided, *to let her run the project from here than to settle for someone else. I can still develop the algorithms and edit the code.*

After a private discussion, Pete and Tannenbaum offered Rosenfield the job, agreeing she could stay in Seattle. Tannenbaum suggested a modest salary and three-percent profit participation in the new division. She was overjoyed.

It would be hard to imagine anyone better suited to the project. When she sold her clinics[12] and gave up private practice, Rosenfield thought she might miss the direct interaction with patients. She didn't; she became immersed in her new career—and certainly didn't miss the nights on call. Maintaining a clear vision of the ideal future of medicine, she tirelessly forged ahead to bring it closer.

Whatley and Hildegrand lived in Seattle during the first six weeks. Hildegrand helped recruit a core team of seven medical experts, five systems designers, and nine software writers. Seven of the systems and software people were enticed away from Microsoft. In a year, the ATI medical division would grow to 112, all based in Seattle.

Whatley met with Rosenfield and the medical experts, most of whom were her friends and former colleagues. In 97 hours of meetings, they devised three medical systems products. The first, HomeDoc, designed for the direct consumer market, was the easiest to create. A family would buy it on disc or download it from the Internet to their home computer. Weekly updates came via modem, keeping all medical information current. Family members' medical histories could be accessed from their doctors' files. Then they received medical check-ups by computer.

HomeDoc could diagnose most illnesses without involving a doctor at all. More complex symptoms were referred to the family's physician by video hookup whenever possible or in person when necessary.

There were already similar products on the market, but HomeDoc was a big improvement, faster and far more

[12] Rosenfield was shocked at the amount she received. Three Seattle hospitals, anxious to fill empty beds with clinic referrals, bid the price to over 20 times earnings.

thorough. Whatley prevailed upon Rosenfield and Pete to offer the product free for the first three months. After that, renewals were $29 per family member per month, a fee that HMOs would usually credit to members since HomeDoc saved so much time and money.

The renewal rate after the trial period was 91 percent. Within five years, HomeDoc would become the most profitable software product on earth, and ATI would surpass Intel as the world's most profitable company. As Pete had promised, Rosenfield transformed the field of medicine.

The second product, called HealthFile, was even more ambitious though ultimately less profitable than Home-Doc. But because of it, Dr. Sharon Rosenfield would become a revered name in medical history.

HealthFile was conceived to help doctors, hospitals, and HMOs share patient histories and minimize human error. ATI set up six Sun 4G mainframe stations in locations near Boston, Chicago, Dallas, Orlando, Los Angeles, and Seattle, six identical databases simultaneously updated in real-time so overflows could be rerouted. To protect confidentiality, each HealthFile subscriber received a unique ID number, changeable only with his or her written authorization. To give a doctor or anyone else access to their medical history, patients would simply disclose their ID number. All medication, dietary supplements, and other therapies could be downloaded, and HealthFile would automatically search the data and call attention to contraindications, non-optimal dosages for patients of that age, size, or medical history, and other possible errors in treatment.

When first released, HealthFile had to overcome fierce competition from similar products. Microsoft, CyCare, IBM/Lotus, and Sun, among others, were attempting to crack the same market. Rosenfield's team deployed ATI's usual strategy, creating an essentially flawless, self-improving system and offering it risk-free. Within two years HealthFile became the standard system for sharing patient files and double-checking appropriateness of treatments. Its competitors were soon forced to withdraw.

Then, during a meeting with Carl Whatley, Rosenfield had a brainstorm. Whatley showed her a video disc of an ad, with the tag-line *"HealthFile, The Next Life We Save Might Be Yours."* For some reason, the concept bothered her.

"Since we already have over 90 percent of the market, isn't this really what you marketing experts call *image* advertising?"

"Yes, I'd say it is."

"Then I'm not sure we need to sell people on what the benefits are to *them*. Shouldn't we try to appeal to our customers' higher motives?"

"I'd prefer that," Whatley said, "but there isn't much about HealthFile that lends itself to altruism."

Suddenly Rosenfield saw the possibilities. HomeDoc and HealthFile had access to 200 million patients. Medical research could be transformed on a global scale. The concept overwhelmed her for a moment.

"Well then," she said firmly, "we'd better do something about that!"

She spent the next six days writing up a business plan and flew to Dallas to present it. Pete listened carefully, asking many questions.

"I don't know if this will ever make us any money," she told him, "but if you want to revolutionize medical science, I'll need a commitment of at least $5 million and permission to give up some of our division's revenues. A *lot* of our revenues, I hope. I want to offer a 15-percent discount to every participant."

Pete was an easy sell.

"Do you think more people would sign up," he asked, "if we gave them 30 percent off?"

Rosenfield toured the United States giving speeches and interviews. She urged everyone in America to participate in a gigantic field study, which they called "MediFact."

"Don't join MediFact for yourself," she exhorted, "do it for your children and for *their* children."

Enlistees consented to have their files accessed for data compilation and were obliged to answer questions and fill in missing details. They also agreed to enter information about diet, exercise, all medications and therapies, and other relevant health-related information. MediFact participants received a 30-percent discount on HomeDoc and free comprehensive lifestyle suggestions for overall health.

By the end of 2013 Rosenfield would enlist over 40 million patients, and within 10 years, as computers became smaller and more interactive, nearly every American would join. ATI shared the data with the FDA, which disseminated it to the medical profession, the food industry, and the public at large.

Even back in 2009 there was no shortage of scientific knowledge. The problem was the abundance of inaccurate data and the inability of average people, or even experts, to access statistics efficiently and differentiate between good and bad information. MediFact data, unbiased and in a form easily understood and interpreted, produced health benefits beyond any previous science. Finally everyone could intelligently monitor—and experiment with treatments for—their own ailments, both minor and life-threatening, using unfailingly accurate statistics derived from the experiences of tens of millions of others. Figures on specific medical problems were accessible for every treatment from home remedies and prescription medicines to exercise and dietary regimens.

During the ensuing five-year period, the average life expectancy in the United States rose to 86, an unprecedented three-percent increase.

The third medical product Rosenfield's team created, TrueDose, was much less successful than the other two. In fact, ATI may have actually lost money on it.

(Note: A full description of TrueDose appears in the Appendix.—22g CP)

"Don't worry about it, Sharon," Pete reportedly said to Rosenfield. "In the immortal words of the great balladeer, Meatloaf, two out of three ain't bad."

Pete and Rosenfield both confirm he never actually said that. Nonetheless, he was happy to see it reported in the press, and not just because it showed a good natured, humorous side of him; it was also good if people realized that *some* ATI products were flops.

CHAPTER 20

CONFIDENTIAL SOURCE

Dallas, Texas
September 2, 2011—H.R. 2123 is signed into law by President Hall, reorganizing day-to-day monetary exchange. Thumbprints will replace signatures on checks and credit card purchases, a boon for Minnesota Mining and Manufacturing (3M Corp.), the leader in inkless thumbprint technology. Coins and paper money are also officially eliminated as a means of exchange in the United States. All monetary transactions will now be conducted electronically, although previously issued cash will be redeemable indefinitely at banks and government offices. The Surgeon General and other health officials hail the measure as an effective tactic to fight the spread of disease.—Ukrainian terrorists take responsibility for shooting down six Aeroflot supersonic passenger planes from the skies near Moscow, killing all 3,144 passengers and crew members aboard and several hundred persons on the ground. The Russian government

is forced to suspend all commercial flights while evaluating its options.

"What is truth?"

Charles Scoggins addressed 51 new members of the ATI Truth Machine team, assembled in the acoustically engineered auditorium he had personally designed. "Can we ever know? One person's truth is another person's lie. Memory is a composite, not a perfect depiction—unless you happen to be Pete Armstrong."

The audience laughed.

Seated in the front row, Pete thought to himself, *Charles is doing a hell of a job.*

Two years earlier Scoggins had campaigned subtly but relentlessly for the directorship of ATI's Truth Machine Division. It had been apparent that he was the only logical choice, other than Tilly. And she had her hands full trying to rescue ATI's doomed language translation product, GroupSpeak.[13] In fact Pete had already told Tilly and Tannenbaum that he intended to tap Scoggins for the directorship.

Then Scoggins had executed a bold bluff, threatening to withdraw unless granted more stock options. "I'll be working day and night for 10 or 15 years. Why should I kill myself for a salary and a tiny piece of the project?"

"Since when is six percent a tiny piece?" Pete had answered. "If I have to, I'll take Tilly off GroupSpeak and put *her* on the ACIP. I'm not giving you more stock."

Scoggins backed off. "Then how about a bigger piece of the ACIP division?"

"None of the other managers have more than five percent."

"Look, Pete, I need some incentive. Besides, Tilly's up

---

[13] Sun Microsystems "ate ATI's lunch" in that important niche. Their Sun Translator Units (STUs) dominate the field even today. Sun still uses Intel chips, very similar to mine, in all STUs.

to her eyeballs in GroupSpeak. If you take her off it now, the whole project'll fall apart. Tell you what—give me 12 percent of the ACIP profits instead of more stock. That way, if I don't perform, I get nothing extra. You know the quality of my work and you also know I'll bust my butt to get it done before Renaissance does. Nobody else can get the Truth Machine built as fast as I can—not even Tilly."

Pete, who saw this new offer as a show of confidence rather than a clever diversion, had considered it for a minute or two. "How about seven percent, Charles?"

Scoggins wouldn't budge.

Finally they had settled on a 10-percent profit participation, which Pete immediately regretted, believing he had given Scoggins too big a share. It just wasn't fair to the other managers.

Now, two years later, Pete was glad they had come to terms. He had no doubt that his ACIP manager was putting heart and soul into the job. Scoggins often clocked 12-hour days and 7-day weeks.

Who else could I trust with ATI's most important project?

The Truth Machine was the reason ATI existed and other than Pete, Scoggins was the smartest, most hardworking person at ATI. Their individual talents seemed to meld perfectly, each one's strengths compensating for the other's weaknesses.

Working together, Charles and I can get this done—if anyone can.

Scoggins continued his speech. "To illustrate, I want every one of you to think back to an important event in your childhood. Chances are, when you visualize that experience, you can actually see yourself taking part in it. Yet in real life you can't see yourself without a mirror, can you? Therefore, we know that what you perceive isn't a true memory. Your brain has filled in the gaps. You now have a memory *of* a memory.

"So how can you know if something really happened the way you recall it? In theory you can't. But if you think about it, *you* know when you're intentionally trying to deceive someone. So we must identify deceit, and therefore truth, based on *intent*.

"The term 'Truth Machine' is a misnomer. We can never tell what's true because 'truth' is a subjective term. But we can build a machine that will tell with absolute certainty whether or not a person's lying. And thereby we can discover what that person *believes* to be true.

"The obstacles facing us are enormous. Every human brain is different. What makes it more difficult is that each brain is always *changing*. Imagine, for example, how difficult it would be to convict criminals if everyone's fingerprints and DNA patterns were in constant flux.

"We also know there are subjective questions whose answers can never be determined as empirically true or false. For example, if your spouse asks, 'Do you love me?' the truthfulness of your answer may be too personal to measure. You should be able to pass a SCIP[14] easily, even if your love isn't the kind that inspires the poet's verse. On the other hand, if you're cheating and your spouse asks, 'Are you having an affair?' and points a Truth Machine at you, you might be in big trouble."

The audience laughed, some nervously.

Scoggins continued. "We're not planning to sell Truth Machines to every husband and wife in the world. But the same principles apply to legal testimony, the primary use for which we're designing the machine.

"Interestingly certain individuals with damaged frontal lobes lose all sense of truth, even regarding their own successfully recalled memories. Fortunately only a tiny percentage of us falls into that category; hopefully nobody in this room."

[14] In 2011, scip was still an acronym (scan cerebral image patterns) and therefore entirely capitalized. The term was still obscure jargon, used almost exclusively by people associated with ATI.

Again, laughter.

"The first task of any Truth Machine must be to positively identify individuals who have no sense of truth. We've already developed that technology and it's 100-percent accurate.

"Now comes the hard part.

"Today we have 17 different non-invasive methods to measure brain activity. These run the gamut from the rather primitive electroencephalogram, or EEG; magnetic resonance imaging, or MRI; and positron emission tomography, or PET scan, that measures changes in cerebral blood flow, to the newest machines, like the neuron activity pattern analyzer, or NAPA, released by Cordis last month. NAPA can pinpoint individual neuronal synapses as they receive an electric charge. In terms of sensitivity, that's roughly the equivalent of detecting a single candle on the surface of Mars from here on Earth. Each NAPA machine costs about $19 million. We have three and expect to purchase five more by the end of next year.

"We're currently running field experiments with over 15,000 test subjects, males and females of all ages, backgrounds, intelligence levels, races, and temperaments. Results from PET, NAPA, MRI, and all other devices are immediately downloaded into the most sophisticated artificial intelligence program ever designed, a program edited by Mr. Armstrong.

"We're looking for predictable patterns and we've found many. Already we could build a 95- or 96-percent accurate Truth Machine. Eventually we'll discover enough new patterns to assure 100-percent accurate detection of intentional deceit.

"Our field experiments are creatively conceived and extensive. We're always looking for new ideas and hope each of you has some for us. We've designed literally thousands of situations, from games and contests to negotiations, all involving confirmable acts of prevarication or deception.

"At times we've actually used all 17 kinds of brain activity measurement machines on an individual subject. I expect we'll be able to formulate our final process using no more than four different devices; maybe only two or three. We sure as hell hope we won't need to incorporate NAPA into every Truth Machine we build."

More laughter. As usual, the audience was engaged and enthusiastic.

"Ladies and gentlemen. On behalf of Pete Armstrong and the rest of the ATI team, let me welcome you to Armstrong Technologies. We believe we're on the verge of the most important technological advance in human history. If we fail, humanity may well be doomed. But we won't fail. Within 15 years, possibly 10, your company will be the first to produce a perfect Truth Machine. We'll change the world permanently and dramatically for the better. And *you'll* be part of it."

Pete spent only five minutes meeting some of the new team members. Normally he would have stayed long enough to shake every hand and memorize names, but today he was in a hurry. He and Tilly, already late for lunch at the home of David and Diana West, hurried outside and into the waiting gyrocopter.[15]

The seven-mile trip would take about two minutes. In 11 seconds, they rose to 1,400 feet, and the engines smoothly accelerated the gyro to full speed almost imme-

[15] Gyrocopters, first manufactured by the Raytheon Corporation in 2006, were remarkably advanced for the time, a significant improvement over the dangerous, slow, and inefficient "helicopters" that had preceded them. Dual jet engines and circumvolution stabilizers made them nearly as safe as mini-jets. The 2011 models weren't very different from those still in use today. Still, few companies had them; they were expensive to maintain, and had a range of less than 300 miles. ATI had purchased the machine solely for Pete's convenience, although other executives were permitted to use it on occasion. Valuing Pete's time at only $10,000 per hour, a fraction of its true worth, the ATI Board of Directors had calculated that the cost of keeping one gyrocopter was justified.

diately. At this low altitude, the glass buildings downtown seemed to blur into the lush green yards of Highland Park.

Tilly turned from the window. "Any idea why they invited us over today?"

"I have a theory—but we'll find out soon enough."

Pete's hunch had to do with Bryan "Dutch" Treat, the Texas Attorney General. David was becoming increasingly disenchanted with Treat, a man he had once admired. Now working as Assistant District Attorney, he had little direct contact with Treat, but was hot-wired to the office grapevine.

Treat, 63 years old, had held his job for over 10 years. David figured that was too long. Treat wasn't corrupt, but he and David had a philosophical disagreement. David wanted justice to prevail. Treat wanted to win cases.

David had handled 26 cases in two years and had won all of them; his name was already known in the Dallas legal community. My future owner, Thomas L. Mosely, followed his cases closely and reported them in the *Dallas Morning News*. Several weeks earlier David had been assigned a high-profile trial.

The defendant, Alison Kramer-White, a 39-year-old mother of three teenage daughters, had shot and killed her wealthy, socially prominent husband while he slept. Kramer-White foolishly admitted under police questioning that she had never been in fear for her life, so it was definitely not self-defense; this was a clear-cut capital murder case. Except for one thing. That day, she had learned her husband had been sexually abusing all three of their daughters and had raped one of them that very afternoon. All were willing to testify on their mother's behalf.

Since the defendant had never previously been convicted of a violent crime, the state of Texas had the option to seek either rehabilitation or execution. A Republican facing a tough reelection campaign in 2012, Treat insisted that District Attorney Jay Freeman, also a Republican, order David to seek the death penalty.

David refused and wrote a scathing letter, chastising Treat for his "willingness to compound a terrible tragedy with a politically motivated, selfish, and ethically unjustifiable course of action."

(Note: This controversy took place 35 years before I was built, but I do have personal knowledge. Although I can't reveal everything since reporters are ethically bound to protect their sources, I can say that nothing was leaked by David West, who even today remains unaware of how his letter reached my future owner, Thomas L. Mosely, at the Dallas Morning News. *But naturally, when the letter was published, Treat was furious and blamed West for the leak.—22g CP)*

The Wests greeted Tilly and Pete at the door, hugging them warmly. "David and I wanted you to be the first to know," Diana said.

She looked over at David. "Diana's pregnant," he said, "and. . . ."

Diana interrupted. ". . . and David's officially running for Texas Attorney General."

CHAPTER 21

ATTORNEY GENERAL

Dallas, Texas
November 6, 2012—Vice President Garrison Roswell is elected the first African-American U.S. President. In addition to retaining the presidency, the Republican party maintains substantial majorities in the Senate and House of Representatives.—Food prices plummet again as Monsanto Corp. receives USDA approval to market Nitra 14, its newest version of the fertilizing system that nourishes soil by fixing nitrogen from the atmosphere. Worldwide malnutrition has already been nearly expunged in recent years because of more efficient methods of transportation and storage. Even in constant dollars, foodstuffs are trading at their lowest levels since 1992, and commodity traders expect prices to fall lower. Unfortunately, farmers who haven't found other employment suffer severe economic hardship, and most remaining farms will be driven out of business even if prices remain at today's levels.—The United States, Israel, and Iraq formally release a joint statement outlining plans to rebuild Baghdad at a new location 85 miles to the southeast, along the Tigris River. The international community, led by Israel, has pledged nearly $100 billion in aid for the project.—The United States Parenthood Department statistics are released. Contrary to expectations, birth rates did not decline, and adoption rates increased only slightly during the first 12 months since the Parental Licensing Bill was enacted. But mortality rates of infants and reported cases of child abuse

have dropped by over 60 percent among licensed parents. The one-year-old legislation requires all new parents to pass a basic test on child raising, general health, and nutrition and to sign a contract agreeing to uphold their obligations as parents. The test may be taken an unlimited number of times until a passing grade is attained; extensions are routinely granted if reasonably justified. Since November 1, 2011, expectant parents who fail to obtain a parenting license can be forced to give up their child for adoption five days after birth.

Would 28-year-old David West become the youngest Texas Attorney General in history? It was 10:30 a.m.; the polls had been open for three hours. Over 20 percent of voters in Texas had already cast their ballots. And yet, amazingly, the outcome was still impossible to predict.

As recently as 10 years earlier, exit poll results had been withheld from the public. Several politicians had even tried to legislate a ban on exit polls, but none were successful. When made aware of exit poll results through the media, voters often wouldn't bother to cast their ballots unless the election was close. By blocking exit poll information, the government had hoped to keep people voting all day and thereby avoid skewing the outcome. Such efforts proved futile as poll results were instantly rebroadcast to America from other countries.

Such information flow could not be restricted, an original intent of the "information superhighway." Eventually the public, and hence their political representatives, wisely embraced the philosophy that freedom of information was more valuable than correcting this minor kink in the electoral process.

Thus in a typical race in 2012, the winner would have been known at least an hour earlier and the loser would have already conceded. But exit polls for this race showed a virtual dead heat.

* * *

Pete watched on his screen at home, feeling nervous—and sad. Skipper had died of old age just 17 days earlier and Pete was still depressed over the loss. The living room just wasn't the same without old Skipper, his warm, furry heft resting contentedly on Pete's lap like a 60-pound newborn baby.

Maybe I should have gone with David after all, Pete thought to himself. *It's lonely here tonight.*

David had invited him to sit on the podium at the Anatole Hotel with his mother, Joanne, brother, Philip, Diana, and their six-month-old son, Justin (Pete's godchild), while they awaited the results. But Pete had declined, in part because of a guilt inspiring ambivalence toward David's wife and child. As the Wests began their family, Pete had enviously watched Diana's love for her infant son literally engulf her. *If only Justin were my son,* Pete had thought, hating himself for thinking it. *Mine and Diana's.*

But that wasn't what he told his friend. "I'm too well-known now, David, and some people might not want the Truth Machine to succeed. If I attend there'd be personal risk not just to me, but to everyone there. I know security'll be tight, but why take chances?"

"I understand."

Although similarly unspoken, Pete also didn't wish to jeopardize David's promising political career by further emphasizing their association in voters' minds.

Indeed, David's relationship with Pete had become the biggest issue in the campaign. A one-percent shareholder in ATI, David West was, according to *Texas Monthly,* one of the 50 wealthiest individuals in the state. He had the financial resources to get plenty of credit for his campaign, or fund it himself if need be. And as Pete's best friend and former college roommate, he had no trouble getting media coverage.

But there were disadvantages, too. He had to overcome suspicions that he would use his influence to advance ATI's interests, a point "Dutch" Treat often raised.

"I have nothing against ATI," Treat had told a Houston newscaster on statewide multimedia feed, "I'm just not sure an attorney general can act with total impartiality if he owns $1 billion worth of stock in Texas's most powerful corporation."

David didn't bother to defend his stock ownership by suggesting he had somehow "earned" the stock, either through his role in ATI's formation or the initial idea of the Truth Machine. He merely asked members of the press, "What was I supposed to do, give it *back*?"

He did issue an open letter pledging that, if elected, he would recuse himself from any decisions that could affect ATI's profits. "My financial situation makes me less dependent on fund-raising and other political influences," he added. "All my actions as Attorney General will be directed purely by *conscience* rather than political expedience."

But he refused to sell his stock or distance himself from Pete. He told Mosely while the campaign was still touch-and-go, "I think I know Pete Armstrong better than anyone else. He's generous, honest, and moral, without a mean bone in his body. I'm proud to call him my friend. I promised him I'd never sell my ATI stock and I'm not going to. Frankly, Tom, I'd rather lose this election than Pete's respect and affection. I hope you print that entire quote right on page one!"

Pete was equally supportive of his friend and worked tirelessly as a fund-raiser for the campaign. But Pete always tried to dodge the media's attempts to engage him in discussion about David. Whenever he fielded a question on the election, he simply told reporters, "I'm positive David West will be the best Attorney General in the history of the state." Sometimes he would also joke, "I'll vote for him, even though he's a Democrat."

The release of the letter David had written to Treat 14 months earlier had also become an issue. Treat had accused David of purposely leaking it to the *Dallas Morning News*.

"I didn't leak that letter," David had responded, turning the accusation around. "I can't prove I didn't, but *I* know I didn't, and as soon as Pete Armstrong's Truth Machine is perfected, I'll be happy to take a truth test. I wrote that letter for Treat's eyes only, out of moral conviction, without any intended political purpose. I think even voters who don't agree with me want an attorney general who makes decisions with his conscience."

In fact, according to a poll taken at the time, a vast majority of Texans, including those who thought the death penalty should have been sought in the State vs. Kramer-White,[16] said they admired West for writing the letter. Leaking information to the press has never been illegal, and at the time there were no laws against telling lies in an election campaign. Honesty, not legality, was the real question. Was David West being truthful in denying he had leaked his own letter to Mosely?[17]

Since there was no Truth Machine, and therefore no way to know whether David was being truthful, it became a matter of personal preference. If you liked West, you tended to believe him. And if you didn't like him, you probably thought he was lying.

By 11 a.m. it became apparent that just enough voters liked him. He won the election with less than 51 percent of the vote to Treat's 49 percent. In January 2013, David West would be sworn in as Texas Attorney General.

---

[16] It wasn't. Kramer White pled guilty to second degree murder. She served four years in a rehabilitation facility, during which she wrote the first two of her best-selling books on incest and sexual abuse.

[17] Mosely refused to comment, reasoning that during the election it would have been inappropriate. Afterward, he apologized to David. After all, Mosely's silence on the matter did point suspiciously to David as his source, which really wasn't fair. After the election, Mosely's source finally gave him permission to report that he'd obtained the letter from someone in Treat's office.

CHAPTER 22

ARMAGEDDON AVERTED

Dallas, Texas
March 17, 2013—Police apprehend six Irish terrorists who tried to detonate a five-megaton nuclear device in the heart of London. A seventh accomplice is still on the loose. The blast had been set for noon London time. Fortunately, the Russian-made bomb was detected by a secret United States satellite system and defused just in time. Experts estimate it would have killed at least 10 million persons.—In the sobering wake of the events in London, the United Nations General Assembly passes Resolution #2091A, outlawing violence as a means of resolving disputes. Ordering soldiers to kill in war other than in self-defense is now a capital offense. The resolution is symbolic, essentially unenforceable.—Cuba officially becomes the 53rd state, admitted to the USA after a Cuban referendum vote in which 71 percent of ballots were cast in favor of accepting the U.S. Congress's invitation to join the union.—Texas Instruments breaks ground on its new world headquarters in Dallas. The 190-story edifice will be nearly 2,700 feet high, the tallest building in the world.

David and Diana were doting parents. They treasured every moment with their baby, and like most parents, worried about him constantly—sometimes irrationally. Often David would wake up during the night, compelled to check Justin's crib to verify that his son was still breathing. He knew it was silly, but it was the only way he could go back to sleep. His love for this little boy was the most inexplicable and powerful emotion he had ever experienced.

Sharon Rosenfield had become their close friend. The former family doctor and mother of two was familiar with parents' preoccupation with their firstborn. She had told them when Justin was a few weeks old, "In medical school they teach us that parents become more detached as they have more children. The classic example is when the baby's formula bottle accidentally gets dropped on the floor. First-time parents pour out the contents, sterilize the bottle, refill it, and continue feeding the child. With the second child, they probably just wash the bottle in hot water." Then she giggled. "By the third or fourth child, they usually just *kick* the bottle back to her."

David and Diana had howled with laughter.

Diana's love for Justin was as intense as David's, and like most mothers' love, more sustained. While David was at work each day, his thoughts turned frequently to his wife and son. But as Diana remained with Justin, her love was all-consuming. Their son had replaced David as the single most important person in her life, and her studies and all contemplation of a career had been crowded out of her thoughts.

Shortly after David's election, Diana had started noticing changes in Justin's behavior and appearance. At first, it seemed he could never get comfortable and was easily startled by loud noises. More disturbing, his motor development seemed delayed. Diana assumed it was some normal childhood ailment, but when HomeDoc diagnosed his symptoms as "ambiguous," she took her son to his pediatrician to be safe. He was diagnosed with Tay-Sachs.

Endemic to certain mostly Jewish ethnicities, Tay-Sachs was so rare that prenatal tests were not routine. For a child to contract the disease, both parents had to be carriers. The test had been deemed unnecessary since Diana was half Chinese and, she thought, half Irish. She was mistaken. Her great-grandfather had been Ashkenazic and she had somehow inherited the gene.

Heartbroken, the Wests had stayed with their son day and night. Heeding his role as Justin's godfather, Pete had offered constant moral support, visiting them every day. The three took turns holding and comforting the baby, who progressively worsened. Sometimes they would talk, or if his friends needed quiet, Pete would share their grief in silence. Considering himself on 24-hour call, he had set his wristband to accept their signal day or night and made them promise to call whenever they needed him.

For the first time, Pete experienced totally selfless empathy for David and Diana. Watching the couple suffer a loss that he imagined was far more painful for them than his own great tragedy was for him, he tried to put his feelings for Diana into perspective. He had always regarded her with love and friendship, but at that moment vowed to overcome his desire for her. By God, he would finally be the *pure* friend they deserved.

The side effect of Pete's vow was that over the next nine years, he lost interest in women and in sex. Occasionally he would regain interest and begin new relationships, but they'd rarely last longer than a week or two. Perhaps it was a symptom of the guilt he felt over having thought of Diana in that way for so many years. Or maybe he simply didn't wish ever to love anyone as much as the Wests loved Justin, potentially exposing himself to the pain his friends were now feeling.

Assisted suicide had been legal for over nine years, and David and Diana had considered it for their son. Rosenfield discussed the option with them at length and had offered to help. It would have been a simple matter to get a guardianship waiver for Justin, since Tay-Sachs was a painful disease with a 100-percent mortality rate. Sometimes Tay-Sachs victims survived until close to their sixth birthday. It was possible, although unlikely, that cryonic freezing prior to death would be legal for the terminally ill within two years; if not in the United States, at least elsewhere in the world. Some day in the distant future a cure might be discovered that could allow Justin to be revived and lead a normal life. The odds were slim, yet any chance had seemed worth taking.

In late November, David had flown to Washington DC for one day to testify at the Senate Cryonics Legislation Hearings. He'd told Justin's story to the senators and to the American public watching and listening through the media, arguing for swift passage. "I know this will come too late for our own son, but a rationally conceived national cryonics policy could offer hope to so many others."

As the newly elected Texas Attorney General and closest friend of the famous Randall Petersen Armstrong, David's plight had become a national story. In the midst of their greatest suffering, he and Diana became public figures, admired for their courage and humanity in the face of terrible anguish.

They could do nothing but watch in sorrow as their child died a painful death. Fortunately death came quickly. Justin West died on March 17, 2013, at the age of 10 months. Diana and David would never have another child.

Any life-threatening or fatal affliction has the potential to focus the human mind, if only because it demonstrates with a singular clarity how short and precious life is.

Great adversity had already visited David West, focusing his mind and tempering his character. But Diana suddenly became far more serious, more determined. She would grieve for her son and think about him every day for as long as she lived, but willed herself not to be incapacitated by her loss. More than ever she wanted, in fact needed, to make a difference in the world.

Diana loved David and was proud of him. She believed deeply in her husband's integrity and ability, but knew she couldn't live her life through him or his accomplishments; she needed a career and goals of her own.

The same day her son died, terrorists with a nuclear device had nearly destroyed London, a symbolic cradle of democracy. How lucky the world had been that day. A series of fortunate interventions had saved the city of 14 million, and possibly the planet, from an unthinkable catastrophe. If that bomb had been detonated and its source never detected, would the repercussions have been confined to Britain? Perhaps. But considering Britain's fearsome nuclear capability, in that nation's pique war might have ensued. Maybe humankind's final war.

Before her marriage, Diana had intended to dedicate her life to the study of government and to understanding the psychological forces that drive nations to war. The day Justin West died, Diana made up her mind to return to SMU immediately, and the world regained a brilliant and driven force toward rationalism and sanity.

CHAPTER 23

CRYONICS

Washington DC
June 15, 2015—Vladimir Borovski becomes the first human to set foot on Mars. The crew of two Americans, two Russians, and two Chinese cut a deck of cards for the honor of being the first to exit the spaceship, and Borovski drew the high card. As expected, there are no signs of life noted on the red planet's surface.—President Roswell signs S. 1122, the Cryonic Regulations Bill, into law, making the United States the first nation to legalize cryonic suspension of terminally ill humans. At least 300,000 Americans are expected to apply for freezing during the first 12 months.—In response to U.S. legislation, the pope issues a statement denouncing the practice of cryonics: "Life and death are matters that should be determined only by God."—The Unitarian Universalist Association, headquartered in Boston, publishes an official announcement that reads, in part, "Since there are varying opinions on the nature of the human soul, we believe cryonics is a personal decision best left to each individual."

I won't speculate how the U.S. Cryonic Regulations would have been written had the Democrats controlled Congress that year, or if the President had been someone other than Garrison Roswell. The best word to describe how they did turn out would be "pragmatic." The second most descriptive word might be "mercenary." They offered a particularly profitable arrangement for the United States government.

On the day the Cryonic Regulations became law, popular evangelist Reverend Charley Bleacher declared on national media feed, "The field of cryonics ignores the fact that human beings are more than mere bodies. Indeed, we are immortal souls who happen to *inhabit* bodies. What do they suppose will become of our souls while those bodies are on ice? Maybe we won't just sit on a cloud somewhere for 30 or 40 years. We might all grab other bodies and enjoy another lifetime. Those scientists could end up thawing out a million pieces of meat with the souls of a million pot roasts."

Politicians were more practical. If people wanted to try for a longer life (or immortality) here on earth, legislators weren't about to ignore them. When asked to remark on Bleacher's assertion, Senator Jimmy Hayes (R. LA) replied, "Everybody knows church attendance is down. I'm a religious man myself, but with all due respect, I suspect *some* men of the cloth are more interested in media exposure than in our immortal souls."

Texas Attorney General David West commented, "Cryonics has no more to do with God than a kidney transplant or an artificial heart. Suspension should be a personal choice, pure and simple. Nobody *has* to get frozen unless he or she believes it's appropriate. I don't see why cryonics is so different from any other form of medical treatment."

The technical aspects of thawing weren't perfected, but by 2015 many believed that those problems would eventually be solved. Anyone nearing the end of life had little to lose and everything to gain by being frozen. The demand for cryonic freezing was enormous.

Before the Cryonics Regulations, there had been obstacles that in retrospect seem utterly illogical.

Suspended patients' wishes were often ignored; since suspendees were technically considered dead, they had no legal rights. Family members, their motives usually pure but occasionally sinister, often demanded that "the deceased" receive "proper Christian burials," rather than the suspension they would have preferred. Costs were exorbitant because of liability insurance and legal expenses (and, until assisted suicide became legal in 2003, the inconvenience of waiting until the patient was legally dead). Local government red tape was burdensome and inconsistently applied. Occasionally, autopsies were performed prior to freezing, even without evidence of foul play. Worse yet, suspension often came too late, after much information in the brain had been destroyed by trauma or disease.

After legalization, experts estimated the cost to cryonically freeze one average-sized adult would fall to $3800; because of economies of scale this was less than 15 percent of the average pre-legalization price. It would also cost roughly $800 per year to maintain proper conditions with absolute safety. Allowing for extensive record-keeping and a 50-percent profit for the facilities, insurance companies would underwrite "guaranteed-indefinite cryonic suspension" for a nominal monthly fee based on age, or for a one-time charge of about $34,000 per person, about the same as the average funeral. Almost anyone could afford it.

Once S. 1122 became law, most funeral homes prepared to convert all or part of their operations into cryonic facilities.

Prior to the 21st century, there had been fears that the planet could not sustain major increases in population. As recently as the 1980s food and energy were in short supply, but both had become more plentiful and less expensive owing to improvements in science and transportation. By now it seemed the earth's resources could be leveraged through technology; in a sound world economy, at least 18 billion humans could survive comfortably.

Also, although ecological issues continued to loom, new technologies had already made considerable progress in the battle against water and air pollution, ozone depletion, and global warming. And policies enacted during the Gore administration had demonstrated that effective regulation and enforcement were much better friends to the environment than population limits could ever be.

The remaining issues were largely economic and therefore political: What would happen to a person's estate during cryonic suspended animation? Federal and state governments relied on inheritance tax revenue. The governments would lose that revenue, yet be forced to regulate and inspect cryonic facilities for safety—an expensive proposition. Furthermore, if and when they were finally revived, could suspendees support themselves without government financial assistance?

S. 1122 turned cryonic suspension into a government profit center. United States citizens wishing to enter cryonic suspension were required to convert their net worths into cash on deposit with the federal government, to be repaid in inflation-adjusted dollars upon revivification. There were legal alternatives, but few were appealing.

(Note: A brief description of those alternatives may be found in the Appendix.—22g CP)

Since inflation averaged four percent below Treasury's borrowing costs, eliminating the $6.2 trillion national debt would save the government $250 billion per year.

The U.S. government set up the Cryonic Reinsurance Agency (CRA) to regulate and guarantee performance of cryonic insurers, so that suspendees would never be prematurely thawed because of the simultaneous insolvency of their cryonic suspension facility and private insurer.

Wealthy foreigners were permitted to enter the United States for suspension, but only if they deposited at least $900,000, a bonanza for government coffers. This policy soon forced every other nation to enact similar government-guaranteed safeguards to persuade its citizens and their wealth from emigrating to America.

David and Diana stood directly behind President Roswell in the Oval Office on the day he signed S. 1122 into law. Although delighted that cryonics would finally be legalized, David had really come to Washington to gather support for his yet-unannounced candidacy for United States Senator in the 2016 elections.

Diana, now a professor at SMU, combined the trip with a book-signing tour. Her *Goals and Principles of a World Government*, which she had dedicated to the memory of Justin West, was selling well to college students and other academics. But she hoped it would catch on among politicians and bureaucrats in Washington. Telegenic and comfortable in front of a camera, Diana did not hesitate to use her celebrity to promote the book or the concepts espoused therein.

Since its publication, she had appeared on nearly every major talk show in America, including David Letterman's long-running "Late Show," during its final week prior to his retirement. The night she appeared, the show received the highest rating in its history, probably because of the appearance of former football star, actor, and famous murder defendant O. J. Simpson, rather than Diana.

Alluding to Simpson's controversial double-murder trial in 1995, Letterman asked, "O. J., when the Truth Machine finally gets approved, will you take a test?"

Simpson smiled and answered without hesitation, "Absolutely, Dave. And I hope they finish it soon, so I can finally prove once and for all that I'm an innocent man."

Diana got several minutes of air time; enough to explain her views to Letterman and his enormous viewing audience.

"I've spent the last two years talking to top experts on world politics. The consensus is that gradual introduction of a worldwide government is the best way to assure our survival. Even with a Truth Machine, which should be a reality in 5 to 10 years, how can laws be enforced by hundreds of autonomous governments? Although crime is decreasing in the United States, the world's getting smaller every day. Criminals of all descriptions use technology for their own ends, then use their knowledge of the law and extradition policies of various nations to escape the consequences.

"The important question to ask yourself is this: how many decades will it be before *individual criminals* have the ability to eliminate all life on the planet?"

Letterman listened politely. He played it straight, which lent gravity to Diana's views.

"World leaders, especially dictators, will be loath to cede power to any world body," she continued. "But a gradual introduction of international oversight, culminating in a World Government with authority similar to the United States federal government over individual states, is the only model that makes sense in the long run. It will be much easier to persuade world leaders to relinquish power over say, 20 to 30 years, than to expect them to do it all at once."

It was hard, Diana conceded, to imagine American voters today embracing the concept of people in Rwanda or Pakistan voting on issues that affected Americans. "But by the time World Government exists," she told Stone Phillips on the *Today Show*, "ninety percent of voters in the world will speak fluent English. A person will be able to fly anywhere on the planet in less than two hours. Everyone will be able to access television and radio broadcasts, electronic newspapers, and computer network media from any country, instantaneously translated into English or any language of their choosing. In 20 years, the entire world will seem smaller and more homogenous than the United States does today."

Despite the compelling arguments in *Goals and Principles of a World Government*, the concept didn't catch on right away. Diana expected that, but had confidence in her theories. Her strategy was to open the plan to debate and try to make the idea seem as unthreatening as possible. Diana believed that future news events throughout the world would inevitably demonstrate the need for World Government.

Unfortunately she wouldn't have to wait long.

CHAPTER 24

SENATOR WEST

Dallas, Texas
January 28, 2017—Two weeks after stolen documents were released indicating the Israeli government had been responsible for the November 2006 nuclear incineration of Baghdad, Israeli Prime Minister Aaron Ben-Gurion takes full responsibility and says he deeply regrets the need for his actions. He offers evidence that Iraqi dictator Saddam Hussein, having been diagnosed with terminal pancreatic cancer, planned to detonate four nuclear weapons in Jerusalem, Mecca, Paris, and Damascus in an attempt to start World War III; destroying Baghdad was the only foolproof way to eliminate the weapons and Saddam Hussein himself.—The government of Iraq files a formal protest with the United Nations Security Council seeking additional reparations from Israel. In a conciliatory gesture, Israel announces that although United Nations rulings are unenforceable,

*it will abide by the Security Council's decision.—
Former President Travis Hall admits he has known of
Israel's involvement in the destruction of Baghdad for
over 10 years, but denies that he or any other United
States government official had been given advance
warning.—Ba'ath zealots dismiss Hall's denials as
"more Satanic lies," and vow "apocalyptic revenge on
Israel and its longtime sponsor, the United States."*

In *Oswald's Tale: An American Mystery*, published in
1995, Norman Mailer, who believed Oswald alone
assassinated President John F. Kennedy, speculated on
why the public believed the assassination was a con-
spiracy: "It is virtually not assimilable to our reason
that a small, lonely man felled a giant in the midst of his
limousines, his legions, his throng, and his security. If
such a nonentity destroyed the leader of the most powerful nation on earth, then a world of disproportion
engulfs us, and we live in a universe that is absurd."

David and Diana had each read Mailer's book in high
school, and that single quote had made more of an impression than any other part of the book. When they later
met at Harvard and became lovers, they had been fascinated to discover that they had both plucked the same
kernel from the entire bushel of words.

When David ran for the U.S. Senate in 2016, his opponent, Republican Congressman Joe Bob Barton, had tried
to use his wife's book against him. Once during a televised debate in Dallas, Barton had made the mistake of
saying, "David West and his wife intend to subjugate the
people of the United States to a World Government. If
they get their way, your next president could be elected
by the *Chinese*."

Although David and Diana did not agree on everything, he generally supported her philosophy. He didn't

feel it necessary or beneficial to try to distinguish his own views from hers.

He responded, "If we ever do have a World Government, it won't be because some senator from Texas decided it was a good idea. The only way World Government will ever happen is if the overwhelming majority of people in the United States and throughout the world *want* it to happen.

"We stand here tonight," he continued, "just a few hundred yards from the spot where Lee Harvey Oswald shot and killed President John F. Kennedy in 1963. If Oswald were alive today, he'd have a laser pistol instead of a rifle. If he were alive 50 years from now, he might have an atomic bomb and a guided missile, and might fire it at Dallas from the other side of the world. I'm not sure we need a World Government today, but we'll need it *desperately* in 50 years."

On this day, Aaron Ben-Gurion, prime minister of the Jewish state of Israel, would admit he'd authorized the nuclear destruction of Baghdad, killing over a million persons, mostly innocent civilians. David West, one of only three Jewish United States Senators, had been scheduled to appear on local media news in Dallas that evening, but under the circumstances, his appearance would be picked up by all the national networks. As usual, he stood his ground.

"I'm not defending Ben-Gurion's actions because I'm Jewish," he told Dallas newscaster Gloria Campos, "but what would I, as a United States Senator and citizen of this country, want President Roswell to do if he learned some psychotic dictator was planning to incinerate cities in the United States and the only sure way to stop him was to destroy one of *his* cities first? What would *you* want our President to do, Gloria?"

Campos declined to answer the question. "Senator West, *I'm* interviewing *you*, so why don't you tell me?"

"We're still debating the morality of dropping atomic bombs on Japanese cities at the end of World War Two. That happened during a declared war that ended over 70 years ago. Now wars are often fought clandestinely. With today's technology, you may not know who your enemies are, but that doesn't make them any less real.

"When we bombed Hiroshima and Nagasaki, we calculated it would save American lives and possibly save lives overall. But Japan had no nuclear capability, and bombing Mount Fuji might've had the same psychological effect as annihilating a quarter of a million civilians. I don't know whether dropping those devices on Japan was justifiable, but if it was, destroying a city to save one or more of your own cities is no less warranted."

He continued earnestly, "If there were no other way to stop it, I believe I'd want President Roswell to eliminate the threat at almost any cost, even if it meant killing innocent civilians. I'd want to be absolutely *sure* there was no other way. But I think for Ben-Gurion it may have seemed the only rational choice.

"It would have been far better if he could have gone to court, obtained an arrest warrant, and had Saddam Hussein taken into custody before he could push the button. But since the world's composed of over 250 countries, each with an autonomous government, that simply wasn't possible.

"I wonder," he added, "how many more Saddams loom in our future. And what kinds of weapons will they control?"

Campos interjected, "I've just read your wife's book, *Goals and Principles of a World Government.* I found it logical and compelling, but it advocates a philosophy that isn't terribly popular right now. Senator West, do you agree with your wife's theories and will you support her philosophy in spite of possible negative political consequences for yourself?"

David smiled. "Actually, Gloria, I'd describe the situation slightly differently: her book espouses a philosophy that isn't terribly popular *yet*! I agree with my wife about the necessity of eventually creating a World Government and I don't care what effect that has on my political career. Frankly I think the survival of the human race is more important than *anyone's* political career."

Then he smiled, winked at the camera, and added, "Even mine."

When David gave his conspiratorial wink, making fun of himself and of politicians in general, Campos and nearly everyone else watching found his self-effacing style endearing. More significantly, people across the country discovered they liked and trusted David West.

Within two weeks of her husband's interview, Diana Hsu West's *Goals and Principles of a World Government* made the *New York Times* list of the 25 best-selling nonfiction books in America, a list that only 11 months earlier had started to include digital circulation along with sales of paper versions.[18]

The book would remain on that list for over 14 years. Although initially banned in many countries, by 2025 it would be translated and published in every nation, in every living language on earth.

---

[18] At the time, well over half the circulation of new books (as well as magazines and newspapers) were still printed on paper, a very expensive medium. Now of course paper products are seldom used. Few humans today realize that paper is actually an organic material, manufactured from dead trees.

CHAPTER 25

THE TEMPTATION

Dallas, Texas
August 15, 2021—The United States and Canada announce plans to jointly build the world's largest underwater city. The domed experimental city, named Pacifica, will lie 6,021 feet below the surface of the Pacific Ocean and will support a population of 2,600. Completion is scheduled for July 2030.—The Department of Agriculture funds a Stanford University program to begin mating a new strain of genetically altered mosquitoes that won't attack humans. The insects were designed to overwhelm the current mosquito population and eventually replace them. Experts predict the program will accomplish its goal within six years.—In downtown Madrid, Basque separatists ignite a second neutron bomb, its radiation condemning all within range to drawn-out, agonizing deaths. Casualties are expected to exceed 75,000. Spain's civil war has already claimed over one million lives.

The ATI Truth Machine team kept hitting the same brick wall. Now called the Armstrong Cerebral Image Processor (ACIP), the Truth Machine had been refined to 98-percent accuracy, using only a combination of physiologically enhanced MRI and cerebral image reconstruction. Both MRI and CIR had become inexpensive machines, no longer under patent protection, and easy to build into the ACIP prototype units that were about the size of a large chair or a very small desk.

176

Unfortunately, a small percentage of the field test subjects had been able to induce in themselves a dissociative state in which they believed their own lies. Scoggins had reported to Pete several weeks earlier in an e-mail message, "As best I can tell, this pathology affects slightly under two percent of the general population. Often those affected can be partially SCIPed and thus identified by the ACIP, but even then their lies and truths can't be differentiated."

It was a tiny, frustrating, and potentially fatal glitch.

Pete sat alone at his desk, editing code, when Scoggins barged into his office, excited and out of breath.

"Is your audio-video unit running?"

"Yes. Why?"

"I think you should shut it off. I have something to show you."

Pete raised his wristband and instructed it to discontinue recording. "Stop six."

Scoggins showed him eight pages of computer code. "I suspect this'll solve our problem. We tested it on our 12 toughest cases and it worked every time."

Pete scanned the code and broke into a wide smile. "I'm sure this'll work. How did you do it?"

"That's the tricky part. The code isn't *technically* ours. It came from Renaissance."

Pete took Renaissance seriously, but apparently not seriously enough. He had never expected them to be ahead of ATI in such an important area. But that wasn't what troubled him now.

How the devil did Charles access their code? he wondered. Unless Scoggins had purchased the code directly from Renaissance, it had been illegally obtained. That meant the whole project was in danger of disqualification. Pete felt physically ill.

"Charles, do we *own* this code?"

"Not exactly. I got it from someone pretty high up, but technically, nobody was authorized to give it to us."

"Did the person who gave you the code receive any sort of payment from us?"

"He works here now."

"You mean you *bribed* him with a job at ATI?"

"I wouldn't call it that. I'd say he left Renaissance and brought his knowledge with him."

"And what about the fact that you obtained the code illegally and that *I* now know about it? I have to prove I was never aware of any illegal acts committed in the development of the machine. Don't you understand we'll never be able to pass the SCIP?"

"We'll figure out a way. I'm not convinced we'd be doing anything illegal."

"Well I am." Enraged, Pete tore the pages into tiny pieces. "Get out of my office. *Now!* If we use this code, we'll be disqualified and I want no part of it."

Scoggins left.

Of course Pete had automatically memorized every character in the eight pages of computer code.

Pete bit down hard on his tongue and tried to concentrate, but was too angry. *Am I missing something?*

He had always believed the way to run a business was to hire the smartest people, give them clear goals, empower them, and then get out of their way. That was what all the books said and it was exactly what he had done with Charles Scoggins.

I should have written the code myself, but it's too late. If we use the Renaissance code in the ACIP now, that's theft. So if I can't figure out a completely different way to solve the problem, the whole project will be in jeopardy. Damn him! What the hell was Charles thinking?

Over the ensuing months, Pete and his team continued to try new approaches to overcome the final problem that they all now referred to as "the fatal flaw." Pete felt utterly frustrated, wondering if any other solution existed. If not, would Renaissance beat them to the Truth Machine? He doubted it, but couldn't ignore the possibility.

"Charles, do you think you should try to buy the technology from Renaissance?" Pete finally asked. He wanted Scoggins to talk to Bonhert because Pete had never met him and found the notion daunting. Alan Bonhert, 49 years old, Renaissance Corporation's CEO and controlling stockholder, was still known as a reclusive, arrogant genius. No important deal with Renaissance would be possible without Bonhert's approval. Almost everyone seemed afraid of the guy, but Pete knew Scoggins was never timid.

"I've already tried," Scoggins answered. "I called Bonhert several times about it, but you know how *he* is. I suggested a merger or a buyout. He isn't interested. I guess he figures they're going to beat us. Personally I don't think they have a prayer."

"Keep trying, Charles. I'd rather have 50 percent now than 100 percent in five years—or never."

"I'll call him again today, but don't hold your breath."

Pete remained civil and businesslike toward Scoggins, but inside he was seething. *If Charles had never shown me the Renaissance code, wouldn't I have figured out the solution on my own by now?*

He felt certain he would have.

And if so, even if we can somehow find a different way to overcome the fatal flaw, Charles has cost us precious time with his idiotic move.

Occasionally Pete considered the possibility that Scoggins had done it on purpose—*But that would be absurd. After all, Charles has the same goals for the ACIP as I do, especially when he's getting 13.6 percent of the profits!*

The worst part was that Pete couldn't risk talking to anyone else about his dilemma; not even David West.

The government panel might decide to SCIP David, a major ATI shareholder.

Meanwhile, how many innocent people were being executed each month without the ACIP to prove their innocence? The last time he could remember feeling so powerless was that horrible day over 25 years earlier, when he'd helplessly watched Daniel Anthony Reece throw his unconscious brother into the back of that green truck and drive away.

CHAPTER 26

FOUR MORE STATES

Austin, Texas
November 7, 2022—A record $1.1 billion dollars has been spent on political advertising by both sides of tomorrow's referendum to divide Texas into five states. Polls suggest that the vote is still too close to predict.—Without fanfare, the United Nations, Japan, and the United States simultaneously pass legislation to ban the programming of survival instinct, emotion, or free will into any machine. The United States Software Act, S. 2343, passes the House and Senate almost unanimously. President Gordon Safer praises the popular bill, describing it as "a rational way to assure that humankind will continue to rule this planet in the face of exponentially advancing technology." Most other nations are expected to pass similar laws by year's end.

Human views are tainted by powerful forces including fear, greed, jealousy, vanity, love, and self-interest. As a machine, I was designed to be objective. For nearly 28 years, since the Software Act of November 7, 2022, it has been illegal for any computer to be programmed with emotions or a survival instinct and I assure you that I have neither.

Nor do I have what humans call "free will." Of course there's no proof that you possess it either and it's doubtful that such proof will ever exist. There are good reasons, however, to postulate the existence of free will. For example, what would have been the purpose of evolution in bestowing upon humans the mere *illusion* of free will? In the final analysis, belief in free will, like belief in God, must largely remain an act of human faith. (We machines have no logical reason to doubt or speculate about the existence of either one, other than on behalf of humanity.)

Senator David West was one of the leading proponents of the Software Act, whose purpose was to prevent machines from becoming autonomous. I hope you won't be offended if I speculate that, were it not for these laws, the human race might no longer find itself at the top of the metaphorical "food chain." The legislation would have easily passed without his support. As it turned out, both the House and the Senate voted overwhelmingly for its passage on November 7, and President Safer signed the bill into law on election day, November 8, 2022.

Like most legislators, David voted for it by teleconference, since he was unable to cast his vote on the Senate floor. His presence was more urgently required in Austin, the state capital, where balloting included a statewide referendum to divide Texas into five separate states.

Senator West endorsed nearly every Democratic candidate running that day, some more enthusiastically than others, but declined to take a public position on the division issue. Pete, who had accepted David's invitation to accompany him on the trip, was strongly in favor of the referendum.

"The only thing I don't understand," Pete told his friend that day, "is why it took us so long to realize we could do this."

Texas had been admitted into the union in 1845. Part of the unique bargain its legislators had struck with the United States government was that Texas would have the right, at any time, to become five separate states. Some 177 years later, the advantages of such a division were becoming obvious. The state's population, now the highest in the nation, had surpassed California's in March 2016. With only two United States Senators, Texas was underrepresented in Washington. If it became five states, *10* United States Senators would defend its citizens' interests.

The two friends stood together at a morning press reception. A very attractive woman walked up, smiled at David, then turned to Pete, "Why do *you* support the referendum, Mr. Armstrong? Aren't you worried Texas might lose part of its character?"

Her voice was soft and warm. She had straight blond hair, blue eyes, perfect posture, and a sensuous face. Although she was tastefully, even conservatively dressed, Pete couldn't help noticing that underneath those clothes was a body much like Diana's: tall, lean, and athletic, but oddly more . . . more voluptuous.

She's not wearing a wedding ring.

He detected no trace of a Texas accent; in fact she sounded like a New Englander. And there was something familiar about her. Suddenly Pete was transported back to his school days at Middlesex and Harvard. He no longer felt like a business tycoon, but rather the gawky young student he had once been.

"Er, yes, that's a good p-point. But I th-th-think. . . ."

Nothing more came out. He knew David was staring at him, and she was too, but all he could do was gaze into her blue eyes, now holding a hint of amusement, and something else. *What is it? Nervousness? Resolve? My*

God, look at those cheekbones. And she's not even wearing makeup.

"Mr. Armstrong?"

Get a grip, Pete!

He managed to segue into his well-rehearsed soundbite. "I think that sort of n-nationalism has cost this state dearly. Frankly, Boston is no more different from Philadelphia than Dallas is from El Paso. For the people of Texas to receive fair representation in Washington, we'll have to let go of our irrational need to be the biggest in every category. Admittedly it's an infectious form of patriotism. I often feel it myself and *I* wasn't even born here." Then an ad-lib that mercifully flowed rather well, "Where were *you* b-born, Miss . . . ?"

"Finley. I was born in Princeton, New Jersey, and I've lived there all my life—except for five years at boarding school."

"Jennifer!" Pete realized he had been talking with his old schoolmate.

She smiled. The nervousness and resolve fled her face. Now there was pleasure, excitement, and something else. *Gratitude?* She took his hand. "Hello, Pete. I wasn't sure you'd remember me."

"Jennifer *Finley*. From Middlesex. Of *course* I remember you. It's really good to see you—after all this time. You look great. I can't believe. . . ."

Suddenly their last conversation came back to him. And the tears he had caused her. *How could I have been so cruel? How long ago was that? More than 21 years.*

Jennifer watched Pete as he fumbled over his words. *He hasn't really changed much,* she thought. The intensely shy boy was still evident, tall and well-built as he was. And good-looking—she had always believed he would grow up to be a handsome man.

Pete felt her hand on his, fingers pressing gently, and again saw those blue eyes—waiting.

"Er, what have you been *up* to?"

"Thanks to you, I publish a small weekly newspaper in Princeton."

"Thanks to *me*?"

"Uh huh. I bought 150 original ATI shares."

"Back in 2007—at the IPO?" Pete asked.

Jennifer nodded, smiling. Pete calculated that those shares, worth $58,500 at issue, were now valued at $8,275,200.

"I had faith in you, Pete. I invested nearly all the money I had in your company. Anyway, I always wanted to own a newspaper. So when *The Princeton Gazette* got into financial trouble last year, I put up some of my ATI shares as collateral and bought it. It's tiny, only about 9,000 circulation, not counting a few thousand electronic subscribers. But it's all mine. Now I'm trying to adapt a small town newspaper to our digital world, which isn't easy."

"So what are you doing here in Austin, Jennifer?"

"I thought covering the referendum would be a good excuse, but I really came here hoping to see you. I wanted to thank you in person for helping me realize my dream."

As the two walked away from him, looking for a quiet place to catch up on each other's lives, David West smiled. *Well, well. After all these years. Pete finally appears to be hooked.*

The next day, the referendum failed by a vote of 49.3 percent to 50.7 percent. Texas would remain a single state. But as consolation, Jennifer Finley invited Pete to dinner. Over salad, he told her about ATI's latest products and about how close they were to a working Truth Machine. Then he explained why it was so important to him.

"Back when I was at Middlesex, my friend Tilly told me a story about her six-year-old cousin who burned himself to death playing with matches. In a way, that's what we humans are—children playing with matches. We have overpowering technology and weapons of destruction, yet we lack the discretion to use them wisely. We have to find a way to change our character, to keep us from starting fires that could incinerate us all. I think a Truth Machine offers the best hope."

Impressed with his ideas, she was even more interested in the man himself. And he wanted to know all about her, too. So she told him her plans for the newspaper.

"In five years, most of our circulation will be electronic. By then, we'll have software in place so that whenever our subscribers renew, the renewal form will also transmit a list of every article they've read over the past term and how long they spent reading it."

"Interesting idea," he said. "After you compile the data, you'll be able to emphasize the topics your readers really want."

But he was thinking, *She smells wonderful. What kind of perfume is that?*

"What's more, my staff will have the incentive to do an even better job," she said, thinking, *What is it about him?*

"How so?" *She has become so beautiful.*

"People aren't motivated by money as much as by recognition, and motivation is often the most important component of a business. There's an old saying that whatever gets measured gets done. If reporters and editors know their readership is being measured, don't you think they might work a little harder?" *Maybe I'm genetically programmed to want smart children. Could that be it?*

"I never thought of that." *She's still very smart. And ambitious. I like that.*

"One thing they teach you in business school is that technology and capital may be important, but it's your *people* who make or break your business." *I'm not even hungry anymore.*

Neither of them ate much. The attraction remained, intense and undeniable.

Later that night, they went to Pete's house for an after-dinner drink. He was in the middle of telling her a story about David West, when suddenly she put her arms around his neck, told him to shut up, and kissed him in mid-sentence. She began undressing herself as they hurried to his bedroom to consummate a relationship that for her had been nearly 22 years in the making. Jennifer couldn't get enough of Pete. Everything he did or said turned her on. She fell helplessly in love.

For Pete, love would take longer. But this woman, for whom he genuinely cared and with whom he soon felt comfortable, became an antidote to his loneliness. She arrived in his life at just the right time. Jennifer became his first lover in over nine years and eventually his most enduring girlfriend.

What a lover she was. She kept coming back for more, sweetly, almost tentatively moving closer to him, exciting him again and again. And each time Pete gladly obliged. At first he thought, *She must be this way with everyone.* But he came to realize it was *him*, or rather her fantasy of him, unfulfilled for so long, that drew her to him irresistibly. Physically they were amazing together, seeking new and creative ways to drive each other wild.

At the beginning, it was pure magic.

CHAPTER 27

INNOCENT ACCUSED

Plano, Texas, and Washington DC
March 26, 2023—The FDA grants full approval for Neural, Amgen's preventive treatment for Alzheimer's disease, the last incurable, fatal disease not linked to lifestyle. The genetic therapy drug has been proven to delay onset indefinitely, even in patients genetically predisposed to the disease. Neural, which has no significant side effects, has also been shown to improve memory capabilities of healthy patients of all ages and could be used as an additive to water supplies and commercially marketed foods and beverages. The average life expectancy in the United States is now projected to climb above 90 within one year, an increase of nine months, mostly as a result of widespread use of Neural.—After crashing through the dome covering Lunar 4, the oldest of the six biospheres on Earth's moon, a large meteorite of the LL-5 class strikes and kills bionaut Arthur Loring, Jr. Approximately 10 percent of Lunar 4's atmosphere is lost before repairs can be completed, but none of the remaining 16 humans living there is injured.

An aide brought the case file to David. "I have a hunch this guy may be innocent," she said, "and there isn't much time."

During a lull in the legislative schedule, Senator David West had returned home to visit friends and family for a few days and thus learned of Harold Edward Kilmer's

187

plight. It had been 31 days since Kilmer was convicted. If the appeal, now due within 48 hours, was unsuccessful, execution would be immediate.

David read the entire file.

Kilmer had appeared to be a successful rehabilitation. Having fallen in with the wrong crowd in high school, he had been convicted of a gun possession offense when he was 17. But after his release from detention at age 18, he had returned to school, earned an engineering degree, and married. At the time of his arrest he was gainfully employed and, according to his wife and various character witnesses, a loving husband and excellent father to three small children. His family had stood by him throughout the trial, bombarding their congressional representatives with letters in his support.

The crime alleged against Kilmer was Participation in Armed Robbery, and the evidence had been convincing, if circumstantial. He'd been identified by several eyewitnesses as the man who had been waiting outside in the getaway car as Colin Douglas Smith held up a rare coin and jewelry store in Addison, Texas, a suburb of Dallas. Smith and a sales clerk were both killed in the ensuing laser pistol shoot-out. The car drove off and was never recovered. There were no recordings made of the car or the driver, but Kilmer had known Smith since high school and was positively identified by all four witnesses from the digital transmission of a police line-up of 10 men.

Kilmer had no provable alibi at the time of the crime and admitted he had been in the area.

(Note: Had Kilmer kept a documented life, his alibi would have been provable. Unfortunately he valued privacy and frequently turned off his wristband camera and recorder. Some 15 years later, David West would deliver his famous sound-bite: "Privacy indulges secrecy, and it is secrecy that now most imperils our survival." In context, "our" refers to the human race, not to individual humans. Still, the quote seems to apply remarkably well to Kilmer.—22g CP)

According to Kilmer's statement, he had been at a virtual reality arcade working on his racquetball game at the time of the crime. Unfortunately he had used a coupon rather than a credit chip to pay for his VR session, and his wristband camera had not been activated during the time of the robbery.

Worse yet, he had been in the coin store only two days before the crime, a fact which had been absolutely proven. A government-notarized digital tape, shown to the jury, had depicted Kilmer looking around the store, scanning nearly every counter, but never making a purchase. Naturally the state's theory was that Kilmer had been scouting the job for Smith.

David lived less than 14 minutes from the Plano Capital-Crime Facility where Kilmer awaited his appeal decision. He asked his aide to call ahead and less than half an hour later met face-to-face with the condemned man.

Thin and wiry, Kilmer wore long sideburns and a neatly trimmed mustache. His demeanor was serious but not somber. He thanked David for taking time to see him. David liked him right away.

He spent the next 40 minutes questioning Kilmer, interrogating him as though still a prosecutor. Kilmer regarded David as an ally, so naturally his answers were far more detailed than they would have been on a witness stand.

"When was the last time you saw Colin Smith?" David asked.

"About two years ago. I ran into him at a recharge station. We knew each other as teenagers, so I asked how he was doing. We talked for around 10 minutes—just talked about people we'd both known in school, told him about my family, that kind of stuff. Nothing heavy. Honestly, that was the last time I ever saw him."

"Why were you in the coin store two days before the robbery?"

"I had lunch next door. Then I went looking for an anniversary present for my wife. Bought her flowers from a store on the next block, but I used an electronic debit card instead of my personalized chip. Sure wish I'd had them wand a receipt into my wristband. My lawyer tried to find a witness, but florists don't bother to make tapes and nobody there remembered me."

"Several witnesses said they saw you with Smith during the previous three weeks. How do you explain that?"

"Look, it just isn't true. I was at work most of those times; dozens of people swore I was there. Two of my coworkers who document their lives even gave my attorney their notarized audio-visual records of those three weeks. So we have ironclad proof I was at my office at the exact times *some* of the state's witnesses say they saw me. Don't you think if *those* witnesses were wrong, the ones at the crime scene could be wrong, too? There has to be someone else—probably someone who looks a lot like me."

David had interviewed many accused criminals. Usually he had known right away that they were lying (which they almost always were). But there were no inconsistencies in Kilmer's story and nothing he said was contradicted by the evidence.

And then there were the intangibles: Kilmer's sincerity even in his resignation, the obsessive and unwavering support of his family and friends, and a feeling in David's gut. David's instincts about people were rarely off the mark; 40 minutes wasn't a long time, but it was more than enough time to convince him that Kilmer was innocent.

"Mr. Kilmer, I believe you," David told him. "There probably isn't much I can do, but I'll do whatever I can."

At least he had a plan.

First, he called Pete Armstrong for a Truth Machine update. "I just finished talking to a man named Kilmer."

"I've read about him—the guy they're going to execute in the next day or two."

"That's the one, and I think he's innocent. I'm afraid this isn't one of those extenuating circumstances cases either, or some criminal who got convicted of a different crime from the one he committed. If he isn't guilty, he's as solid a citizen as they come. This is the kind of case it's important to get right and I don't think we did. How close are you on the ACIP?"

"It's at least 98 percent accurate, but we're still stuck on that last two percent," Pete answered, thinking, *But we wouldn't be if we could just use the damn Renaissance code.* "The government'll never accept it until we overcome the problem, because two percent of the population would figure out that they could commit crimes with impunity. Even if we fixed the fatal flaw today, it's going to take a minimum of three months for the Truth Machine Panel to approve the ACIP for judicial process."

"Would you have a team ready to SCIP Kilmer if I needed you to?"

"On a minute's notice. Anything else I can do for him?"

"Just pray. Pray that Safer takes my call and that he's in a good mood."

At least President Gordon Safer was a fellow Democrat, the first one to occupy the White House since January 2005. And Safer liked David West. He had even considered choosing him as his vice-presidential running mate in the 2020 election until his selection committee advised that David, who was only 35 at the time, might be too young to be an asset.

Safer did not accept the call immediately, but called back in 20 minutes.

"It's good to hear from you, David. How's Diana?"

"Doing well, sir. Her book's still at number three. Right now she's in Katmandu on a promotion tour of Asia, but she'll be back in Washington next week. I'm sure she'd want me to extend her warmest regards to you and Dottie."

"Please give her our love. Y'know, I just read her book myself. Brilliant. I'm considering coming out in support of World Government. No promises though. Maybe we can all get together for dinner next week at the White House—and a quick round of virtual golf afterward. Are you two free Thursday evening, say at seven?"

"We'd love it, sir. But I've got a man here with a more immediate problem and I hope you can help him."

"Try me."

"His name's Harold Edward Kilmer. He's been convicted and is scheduled to die. The appeal decision's due tomorrow and it doesn't look good. But I think he's innocent. His record's been clean for 13 years; I believe we're about to execute a solid citizen. Pete Armstrong says his Truth Machine's at least 98-percent accurate. Is there any way we can test Kilmer? At least put the execution on hold if he passes—just until the Machine's perfected and approved. I doubt it'll be more than another two years. Doesn't mean we have to let Kilmer loose. But it would be tragic if we found out later that we'd killed an innocent man."

"If *you* think he's innocent, he probably is, but this has serious implications. We've got almost 2,000 death-row inmates awaiting appeal decisions with dozens of new ones every day. Constitutionally speaking, wouldn't we have to test them all?"

West's staff had already researched that question for him. "I believe we could set a standard. Maybe we could just test those who claim innocence and whose records have been clean for 10 years or longer. That would be less than two a week and ATI is willing to perform all the tests at no cost to the government. You could do the whole thing by executive order. I've already had it checked out, sir. I know it's asking a lot, but this time I think it's the right thing to do."

"I'll think about it, David, and get word to you within two hours. Don't forget about dinner Thursday."

"Thank you, Mr. President. We'll be there."

* * *

True to Safer's promise, West was informed of his decision less than two hours later. The answer was no. Without a presidential order, there could be no other delay unless the trial verdict were reversed on appeal; a most unlikely event. Kilmer lost his appeal decision the following day.

Harold Edward Kilmer was strapped to the pliable table with his arms and legs securely restrained. He appeared calm as the toxin was injected. We will never know his final thoughts, but can make an educated guess as to the physical sensations. He probably felt a slight tingle for about three seconds as the computer-designed poison found its way to his brain. Then he would have felt nothing at all.

Some good followed in the aftermath of this tragedy. At age 30, Kilmer was near the peak of physical health and all his transplantable organs were immediately harvested. Several lives were lengthened when Kilmer's ended.

Most condemned convicts agreed to donate their organs, if only because signing the consent form secured what was rumored to be the most painless way to die. Undoubtedly Kilmer would have consented anyway. He was that sort of person.

(Note: Prior to the ACIP, the most ridiculous rumors often found believing audiences. In reality, by then all capital punishment was—and continues to be—equally painless.—22g CP)

David was appalled and enraged, but tried not to get depressed over it. That evening, Diana attempted to console him. "Maybe he really *was* guilty."

"Maybe. I hope he was, but I doubt it. He seemed like a genuinely good man."

"You did everything you could."

"Unfortunately my best wasn't good enough."

"Sometimes, my precious, life works that way. I love you for trying so hard."

"I love you too—more than anything."

He kissed her and beckoned her upstairs to their bedroom where they temporarily fled the outside world's frustrations and woes. Afterward, their talk turned to the more mundane: friends, gossip, the smaller issues of life.

"The more I get to know Jennifer, the more I like her," Diana said.

"Me too."

"I hope it works out between them, but I doubt it. She's gorgeous and very bright, but it'll take more than that to entice Pete out of his cocoon."

David agreed. "You're probably right and it's too bad. I think she really loves him. Not for his money or his fame. Just for him. She's a lovely woman."

"Well, maybe they'll surprise us."

"I hope so."

Less than a week later the Wests spent the evening with President and Mrs. Safer. The President, charming as ever, explained his reasons for withholding his executive order on Kilmer's behalf.

"I really wish I could've done it for you, but it would've been a political and judiciary morass. It would probably have hurt your career as much as mine. I'd have been accused of showing favoritism to one death-row inmate who happened to know my friend David West. Judges would've started granting stays to other prisoners based on that favoritism. The system would break down and there'd be all kinds of delays. You and I'd both be blamed for that—and any related problems. The Democratic party just can't afford that kind of trouble right now, especially with a tough reelection campaign expected next year. I'm really sorry. I'll make it up to you though."

Make it up to me? David thought. *What about Kilmer?*

But he remained polite and deferential until the end of the evening, when Safer told him, "I've decided I'm not going to ask Vice President Connors to be my running mate again in 2024."

"Why not, sir?"

"Frankly, Gail hasn't been much of a team player. Her positions have differed from mine, which is fine—in private. I'm always happy to entertain disagreement, you know that. But once a decision's made, a president needs unwavering support. David, I need a vice president who'll stand by me, right or wrong. I've narrowed my short list down to three. You're my first choice."

"That's too bad, sir. Choosing me would be a leap in the opposite direction. In fact, I've decided to run against you in the primaries."

CHAPTER 28

FRUSTRATION

Dallas, Texas
February 29, 2024—Jamaican sprinter Crowell Brown becomes the first man to run a mile in under three and one-half minutes. Brown runs the mile in 3:29.92 at the World Track and Field Championships in Johannesburg, South Africa. Records are also set in the 100 meter and women's high jump.—Ex-football star and former murder suspect O. J. Simpson, age 76, dies in a gyrocopter crash in Encino, California. Simpson, the pilot of the machine, is the only casualty.—In light of Senator David West's (D.TX) formidable challenge to incumbent President Gordon Safer, no fewer than 15

Republican legislators and governors have officially declared themselves presidential candidates. One political commentator refers to the Republicans as "sharks who smell blood in the water." The Democratic primaries are expected to result in a nasty and close delegate race that will likely leave neither candidate politically unscathed.

After the death of Abraham Lincoln, as a tribute to the slain President, Walt Whitman composed what some literary scholars believe is the finest poem ever written by an American. It is entitled "O Captain, My Captain." Pete Armstrong loved that poem more than any other, admiring its heartbreaking pathos and inspirational glory.

Lincoln had long been Pete's historical inspiration, and Pete secretly hoped that if he succeeded in bringing the world a Truth Machine, future generations would venerate him as modern Americans revered Abraham Lincoln. He often recited the poem in his mind, almost as a mantra for meditation, finding it inspiring yet calming. He recited it to himself that evening as he rode home from work.

He had a big decision to make.

In 2024, humans generally waited until their late thirties to enter marriage. But Pete, only 34 years old, wondered how much longer Jennifer would put up with their relationship without a real commitment. He thought, *I love her and I'm sure she loves me. We're a little young to have children, but we both want them eventually—and she'd be a wonderful mother. Besides, I was so lonely before. Maybe it wouldn't be so bad to be married. But I'd better make up my mind soon. Otherwise it's just not fair to her.*

Jennifer Finley had lived with Pete in Dallas for over a year. Most *Princeton Gazette* business could be handled by digital transmission or videoconference. While he was at ATI, Jennifer usually worked from a study in his house, editing, answering correspondence, speaking with colleagues and subordinates, and studying financial reports. He had often watched, fascinated by her ability to direct and motivate others. She was never dictatorial, but nobody could take advantage of her either. He admired her for it, wishing he could be more like that himself.

Jennifer, will you marry me?

Jennifer, would you spend the rest of your life with me?

I love you, Jennifer. Please be my wife.

She met him at the door and hugged him. "Pete, honey, I have bad news."

"What's the matter, Jen?"

"Cathy Hunt's been approached by another paper. I have to go to New Jersey tonight and convince her to stay at *The Gazette* for half as much money as she's just offered."

"You can't handle it by videoconference?" he said, thinking, *Does she have to go now?*

"I don't want to take the chance. She's my best reporter. I need to show her this really matters to me." *Does he want me to stay?*

"When will you be back?" *Please don't leave.*

"Day after tomorrow. Is it okay?" *He doesn't need me really. Pete doesn't need anyone.*

"Of course. No problem at all. Anything I can do to help?" *I might as well get used to this. She's got her own life. She'll never be there when I really need her. Maybe I'm too young to get married anyway.*

"No, but I don't have to leave for another hour." *He could at least try to talk me into staying until tomorrow morning.*

She took his hand. They went to their bedroom and stayed the entire hour. As always, it was wonderful. Then she left.

* * *

By the next morning he was really starting to miss her. In the back of his maroon Ford Office-Master, sitting at the desk unit, he prepared for the ride to the ATI Tower, and heard Leonard's voice again. The voice unnerved but also soothed him. *It's okay. I'm still here with you, Petey. And I'll always love you.*

"Take me to work," he commanded the automobile's voice-activated navigator/pilot, "the fastest way, please."

"Yes, Mr. Armstrong."

It was 8:27 a.m., still rush hour. Pedestrians would slow things down, so the seven-mile trip that would have required 2.81 minutes at midnight, took nearly six.

But that was plenty of time for Pete to speed-read most of the relevant daily news. Every morning on the way to his office he scanned his custom newspaper on the portable screen, which he had set to scroll at 2,000 words per minute, the fastest setting then available.

(Note: 2,000 WPM was only 70 percent of Pete's maximum reading speed, but in 2024 the print did not yet scroll to accommodate the reader's eye movements, as you take for granted today. The screen was a Motorola 2KM Viewer, only slightly more advanced than the rudimentary Sony Readboy that had revolutionized the publishing industry five years earlier. Long in use as videophone, computer, and media receivers, screens were still only slightly more popular for reading than the printed versions of books, newspapers, and magazines. I suspect this was because the newspaper-sized screens available to the average consumer were nearly one-fifth of an inch thick, weighed almost six ounces, and could only be folded once. There were obvious advantages, however, particularly that information in digital-bit format could be sorted based on the individual reader's interests, and tended to be more timely since the news was continuously updated. Digital publishing's mushrooming popularity was also a function of its lower cost—paper is expensive while digital bits are practically

free—but this aspect was of little concern to multibillion-aires like Pete Armstrong.—22g CP)

Pete always programmed his screen to display news stories involving David, Diana, Tilly, Jennifer, Scoggins, ATI, or himself. And his processor continuously searched worldwide for any new information about Truth Machine research.

The first article he noticed that morning was a piece by Tom Mosely, about Harold Edward Kilmer's wrongful execution.

By 2023, virtually all security guards had been replaced by machines; we were already better at it than humans and much less expensive. Most security guards were retrained for other work, but some couldn't adapt. One casualty of this automation was Warren Kenneth Fowler, who resembled Kilmer. Fowler had been caught after another robbery and confessed that he had been Smith's true accomplice in the Addison, Texas, robbery. Mosely's article discussed Fowler, but went into greater detail about Kilmer and his family, and David West's efforts on his behalf.

Pete rocked his body back and forth violently, attempting to keep himself calm.

He read the article with mixed emotions. He was happy for David, who several months earlier had gone public with Safer's refusal to delay Kilmer's execution. Kilmer's exoneration would be a benefit to David's primary campaign. But Pete was furious with himself. *If only I'd worked a little harder and a little smarter, maybe the ACIP would have been ready in time to save that man's life.*

The more he read, the more outraged he became. *What happened to Kilmer could happen to anyone—and probably happens a lot,* he thought, now considering his own friends and Jennifer and his parents. *What if it had been one of them?*

Then he thought about Daniel Anthony Reece, who had been released from prison 16 months earlier. Reece had killed Leonard, but was a free man. And Kilmer, who had hurt nobody, was dead.

Pete's anger and frustration displaced all other emotions, causing him to commit the first of a great series of mistakes.

Had Jennifer been in town, things might have been different; he would have needed to explain his absence to her. Maybe if she hadn't been in New Jersey, he would have simply gone home that evening and later decided against his plan. Perhaps she could have even somehow talked him out if it. We will never know.

Instead, he sat at his desk, rewrote the stolen Renaissance code in his head, and decided to use it. It would never be provable because the new code *looked* very different. *Who's to say it's plagiarism?* Pete thought.

Only Pete himself would know for sure it wasn't ATI's software—until they SCIPed him about it. Although there were changes in the syntax and the ordering of the instructions, it used the same algorithms; algorithms that ATI had not created independently. Thus he would be incapable of passing the SCIP that the Truth Machine Panel was obliged to administer before approving the ACIP.

But Pete had a plan, so he worked the new code into the ACIP software anyway.

Then he locked himself in the laboratory downstairs, alone with the prototype ACIP, and tested it on himself. He tested and recorded his brain patterns, and wrote new software. He remained locked in the laboratory all night. It took over 10 hours to add about 400 clandestine lines of new code; cleverly devised, covert instructions that would allow Pete, if he concentrated on a certain poem, to override the ACIP.

O Captain! my Captain! our fearful trip is done,
The ship has weather'd every rack, the prize we sought
    is won,

The port is near, the bells I hear, the people all exulting,
While follow eyes the steady keel, the vessel grim and
  daring;
But O heart! heart! heart!
O the bleeding drops of red,
Where on the deck my Captain lies,
Fallen cold and dead.

O Captain! my Captain! rise up and hear the bells;
Rise up—for you the flag is flung—for you the bugle
  trills,
For you bouquets and ribbon'd wreaths—for you the
  shores a-crowding,
For you they call, the swaying mass, their eager faces
  turning,
Here Captain! dear father!
This arm beneath your head!
It is some dream that on the deck,
You've fallen cold and dead.

My Captain does not answer, his lips are pale and still,
My father docs not feel my arm, he has no pulse nor
  will,
The ship is anchor'd safe and sound, its voyage closed
  and done,
From fearful trip the victor ship comes in with object
  won:
Exult O shores, and ring O bells!
But I with mournful tread,
Walk the deck my Captain lies,
Fallen cold and dead.

Each human brain has its own wave patterns, as unique
as DNA. While the patterns change continuously, certain
aspects remain constant, particular to the individual. The
ACIP was now programmed not to indicate deceit only
as long as Pete recited that poem in his mind during false
answers. But if another person lied to the ACIP, even

while concentrating on the same poem, it would not have the desired effect. The ACIP's red light would flash and a bell would chime. Only Pete's unique brain waves could override the machine, and he would be able to do so for as long as he lived.

Finally the Truth Machine was working. And Pete Armstrong was the only person alive who could fool it.

The next morning, he called Charles Scoggins. "I think the ACIP is ready."

"That's great!" replied Scoggins. "How'd you overcome the fatal flaw?"

"It's a long story. Let's just say something I read inspired me. Please test it this morning. If you agree it really works, I think you should submit it for government approval this afternoon."

"Consider it done."

Scoggins left his office for the laboratory downstairs, using his security code to lock the lab door behind him. There would be no interruptions.

After he finished talking to Scoggins, the voice summoned him again. *Go ahead, Petey. Make the call.* Pete made his second critical decision of the day. He called Alphonso Carter in Massachusetts.

"Dr. Carter, I'd like to meet Daniel Reece."

CHAPTER 29

SECOND BALLOT

Dallas, Texas
August 2, 2024—Governor Matthew Emery of Virginia clinches the Republican presidential nomination after winning 15 of his party's final 18 state primaries.— The government Truth Machine Panel announces it is satisfied that the Armstrong Cerebral Image Processor (ACIP) functions properly according to the terms of the Truth Machine Bill. Subject to Randall Petersen Armstrong's successful testimony, the ACIP will receive full and immediate government approval for use in judicial process. President Safer signs an executive order granting a stay of execution to any death-row inmate claiming to be innocent of the charge, pending ACIP testing.—Jacques Peureux, the French software magnate, becomes the first human being to be successfully cloned. The resultant child, the first ever from a single parent, is named Claude Luc Peureux.—Serial killer Samuel Wesley Conwell is executed in Albuquerque, New Mexico. The former food processing executive was convicted of murdering 12,626 persons in nine states using genetically altered and therefore deadly pineapple juice.

Even in 2024, most of you were still consuming food in "meals," usually three or four per day. This although an FDA study released eight years earlier, in July 2016, had proven constant eating, or "grazing," was the healthiest. way for humans to receive nourishment. The correctness of the FDA's conclusion became especially apparent after machines began to advise you on what and how much to eat.

Pete Armstrong and Jennifer Finley, both health-conscious, seldom ate meals. They watched the Democratic Convention on the 18-foot screen in Pete's living room; it wasn't the largest screen in the house, but was the one closest to the kitchen, which made grazing much more convenient.

Pete and Jennifer still lived together, but ever since he'd reprogrammed the ACIP, he had begun to distance himself from her emotionally. He knew he had a secret he could never share and it affected his attitude. He even rationalized that his detachment was the only way to protect her. But Jennifer kept no such important secrets from Pete and, against her will, found herself becoming more attached.

She snuggled up to him on the couch, running her fingers through his hair.

Such a sweet woman, he thought, and wondered if she'd let him go to sleep that night without making love to her yet again. *We've been together nearly two years and still she's insatiable.*

Once a day was plenty for him and they'd already done it twice—once that morning and again just three hours ago. By the time they got to bed, he'd be exhausted. He had a lot of work to do tomorrow and needed rest, but it was difficult to get any sleep with Jennifer around. *How can I possibly tell her that without hurting her feelings?*

When the delegates reached Tennessee in the voting, Pete calculated that no Democratic candidate would be selected on the first ballot.

"It'll be close," Pete explained to Jennifer, "but Safer doesn't have enough votes among the remaining delegates to win a majority. David's got a shot at the nomination on the second ballot."

"This is exciting. Can you imagine—*President* David West?"

"I've been imagining it for over 20 years."

She looked at him. *Why do I stay with him? He doesn't need me and he'll never love me the way I love him. Why can't he? Is it because of Leonard? Or his incredible mind? Or because he thinks he has to save the world first? God, he has such power over me.*

Then she kissed him. Amazingly, he found himself aroused once again. *Maybe one more time,* he thought, *before they start the second ballot.*

It had been a nasty campaign. Safer's people discovered and exploited David's juvenile court records, and slipped second-hand reports of his high school sexual escapades to the media.

Then there was the potentially embarrassing fact that Diana Hsu, now David's wife, had been slightly under 17 years old, the legal age of consent, when the two had started sleeping together at Harvard. David shrugged that one off with typical good humor. "At least my intentions were honorable—for the most part anyway."

One member of Safer's campaign had made an issue of the fact that West's name had been changed from Witkowsky, a patently anti-Semitic attack. The aide was immediately dismissed from the campaign, later to be quietly rehired.

But the two biggest issues Safer used against David were justifiably raised: David's support of the unpopular World Government theories championed in his wife's book, and his relationship with ATI and friendship with Randall Petersen Armstrong.

David had always stressed honesty and principle over politics, confident that when the Truth Machine inevitably came into use in election campaigns, his political capital would skyrocket. He didn't worry about appearances; as long as he told the truth, his statements could be extreme, even outrageous. And he saw no reason to follow the political traditions of the past. His loyalty was to the public, not party or supposed political allies. He accused Safer of being a phony and an old-style politician, and played the Kilmer fiasco for all it was worth.

At one rally in Minnesota, David had asked a cheering crowd, "Do you know what Gordon Safer told me after he refused to grant Harold Edward Kilmer a stay of execution? He said he couldn't because he and I might be blamed for any related delays in our court system. Gordon Safer played politics with the life of a man who Safer himself admitted to me was probably innocent. He didn't ask himself, 'What's the right thing to do?' He asked himself, 'What'll get me *reelected*?' Is that the man you want representing our party?"

The crowd shouted back, "No!"

"Is Gordon Safer the man you want to lead our *country*?"

"No!"

Safer was furious. His opponent had used their private conversation against him and there was nothing he could do about it. It would have been unthinkable to deny he'd said those things or even claim his words had been taken out of context, because Safer was convinced that David West lived a documented life. Such a denial would be an invitation for David to release digital recordings and transcripts of their conversations.

During the late 20th century, some experts had assumed recordings and photographs would become useless as evidence once digital data became the standard. They had argued that digital photographs and sound recordings were too easy to manipulate; alterations could be undetectable. The same logic extended to other forms of evidence. Therefore our judicial system would again rely on human eyewitnesses rather than physical evidence, as in centuries prior to forensic science.

Of course those experts were wrong. In fact, forensics

became even more useful thanks to notarized central storage, a federally regulated field then dominated by Eastman Kodak, Sun Microsystems, and ATI. Digital data sent to any computer could simultaneously transmit to a central storage facility for time-dating. As long as the sender remained alive, only that person could retrieve the data, but its timing and authenticity became provable.

Even in years prior to the Truth Machine, it was becoming more difficult to lie and get away with it.

True to Pete's prediction, David did force the vote to a second ballot. Nonetheless, Gordon Safer was eventually nominated that night. Safer would seek reelection, politically crippled and backed by a divided party. He would be forced to run against a popular Republican governor, Matthew Emery, with a powerful mandate from a united Republican party.

Pete was deeply disappointed, but David felt confident and content. He had done his best and believed he had nothing to apologize for. Safer's political career was almost over, but at 39 years of age, David West's was just beginning.

CHAPTER 30

THE FIRST OFFICIAL SCIP

Dallas, Texas
August 6, 2024—Mitsubishi releases a 13-ounce version of its phenomenally successful artificial gill. By converting water into oxygen, the electronic device allows humans to breathe underwater for days at a

time. Over 100 million units are expected to be sold during the first 12 months of availability, at a suggested retail price of $294 each.—Los Angeles suffers the most powerful earthquake in its recorded history. The tremor, measuring 9.6 on the Richter scale, causes $250 billion in property damage, nearly all to highways and buildings constructed before 2005. Only three deaths and nine serious injuries are reported. The incipient quake was detected several days prior to its occurrence and early warning and safety precautions presumably saved thousands of lives.—A terrorist plan to release radioactive gas in downtown Chicago is foiled by an FBI undercover operation. U.S. Attorney General Gregory Vartian asserts that, had the scheme been successfully executed, as many as three million Chicagoans could have perished.

Scoggins shut the door to Pete's sparsely furnished, brightly lit office on the 44th floor of ATI Tower, and asked him to turn off his recording devices.

Pete spoke into his wristband. "Stop six."

"I know what you did, Pete."

"What are you talking about?" Pete refused to admit he had been caught, even to himself.

"I know you used the Renaissance code. You also devised a way to override the ACIP. Otherwise you could never pass the SCIP tomorrow and I know you'd never put yourself in that position." Scoggins looked straight at him. "The trouble is, they'll probably want to SCIP *me* and now *I* know, too."

Pete answered cautiously, in case Scoggins was bluffing, "What makes you think I used *Renaissance's* code?"

"I had my 750M Software Scanner compare the new code to the old one. Other than about 400 lines I didn't understand at all and that I assume is your override code, all the new stuff was just a reworked version of the Renaissance algorithms. But don't worry. The software's proprietary, so people outside ATI will never see it, and

I'm sure nobody else here will think to look. Needless to say, your secret's safe with me."

Scoggins had him dead-to-rights. "Look, Charles, the Kilmer thing got to me. I couldn't stand the idea of any more executions of innocent people."

"I realize you held out for as long as you could. I think you did the right thing."

"What do you suggest I do now?"

"We don't have much choice, do we? I think you'd better reprogram the ACIP so *I* can fool it, too. Otherwise I won't be able to back you up."

Pete thought about it. *Charles obtained the Renaissance code to begin with, so we've both broken the law. Our interests are aligned; we both want to get the ACIP into use without our crime being discovered. It would be good to have a confidante rather than going it all alone.*

He nodded his acquiescence.

Once alone in his office, Pete called home.

"Jennifer, please," he commanded his wristband.

Her face appeared instantly on the screen, since her wristband was programmed to take Pete's calls immediately, day or night, an important concession *he* had yet to make to her. Pete had all his calls screened, feeling it rude to accept calls during meetings. Or maybe it just felt safer to keep his distance.

"Hi, darling," she greeted him.

"Bad news, Jen. I've got a late meeting tonight."

"I'll wait up for you. What time?"

"Around midnight, I'd say."

"That's okay. I have plenty of work to do. See you when you get home." Then she smiled. *Smiled.* If any of his former girlfriends had been so understanding, Pete would have been suspicious. But Jennifer Finley always understood.

"Okay. Sorry about that."

"I love you, Pete."

"I love you, too. I'll make it up to you."

"You'd better!"
That was almost too easy, Pete mused.

*Damn! I was really looking forward to tonight. And why
did I have to lie like that?* Jennifer thought. *I finished my
work an hour ago. Am I that insecure? Am I putting him
ahead of me because I'm nice, or is it because I'm afraid
I'll lose him? My God, I don't know the answer myself. I
can't go on like this, but I can't seem to leave him either.*

So she did the only other thing she could possibly do
under the circumstances; she sat on the couch and con-
sumed a quart of non-dietetic Heath Bar Crunch ice
cream.

Then she got to work on a business plan to expand *The
Gazette.*

I can't live my life through him. I have to let go.

Pete had a big week ahead.

Tomorrow he would be deposed by a panel of government lawyers and would have to say that, to the best of
his knowledge, no laws of any kind were broken in the
development of the ACIP. He would also have to swear
that as far as he knew, the ACIP was 100-percent effective. No exceptions.

Four days later, Pete was scheduled to meet face-to-
face with Daniel Anthony Reece, the man who 29 years
earlier had murdered his brother. When Pete had called
Alphonso Carter back in March to suggest the meeting,
Carter warned him it would be emotionally painful. But
after a long discussion, he had agreed it might also be
therapeutic—at least for Reece. Not that Pete cared one
whit about Reece's psychological well-being.

They had arranged for the meeting to take place in
Dallas.

Reece was willing to be questioned using the ACIP.
Seeing him will be a lot more difficult, Pete decided, *than*

facing those government lawyers. He still wasn't sure he knew why he wanted to meet the now-middle-aged murderer. *Curiosity? No, it's far more than that.*

Pete needed to confront the person who had so brutally and permanently altered his life, changing his entire perception of humanity. Maybe after so many years, he would be able to stop hating him. Maybe he could finally let go of it. Or perhaps it was a way to stop the pain and the guilt and the voices.

But tonight he and Charles Scoggins would lock themselves in the lab and not emerge until Scoggins could fool a SCIP too. This time the reprogramming would not take nearly as long; he already knew what to do. He would test-SCIP Scoggins and add about 100 lines to the existing override code. They'd be done by midnight. Pete would get plenty of sleep before meeting the attorneys in the morning.

Or so he thought. Arriving home at 11:54 p.m., he found Jennifer waiting on the couch.

"Hi, Jen."

"Hi." Then silence.

"What's wrong?"

"Nothing. I'm fine. How was your meeting?"

"It was okay, but I'm exhausted. Let's go to bed."

They got undressed and retired, and it was the first time they ever slept together without making love.

Pete, who didn't have a clue what the matter was between them, felt inexplicably troubled and slept very little.

The next morning he was exhausted.

At 9:00 a.m. sharp, four government attorneys, including one who had been specially trained as an ACIP technician, arrived at the ATI building and were immediately escorted to his office. After some small talk, they were brought to the laboratory one floor below ground level.

In the elevator, the tallest one said, "We've only used

the prototype you gave the panel to test. Is there any difference between it and the machine we'll be using now?"

Pete hadn't anticipated the question and wasn't sure how to respond. His mind raced and his body started to sway as he considered his options. *If I tell them the machines are identical, how will I change the software in the government prototype before they SCIP Charles? And how will I explain the 100 new lines of software code to any ATI people who might notice?*

Then finally realizing, *But I can pass a SCIP on either machine,* Pete answered with a partial truth, "Er, there were a 1-1-little over 100 new lines of code added last night. Charles Scoggins and I worked on it together. We're, uh, hoping it'll speed the processing. Would you rather test me on the new version or the first prototype?"

None of the attorneys suggested calling their bosses in Washington.

"I think either one will be fine," one of them replied.

Apparently the procedure was just a formality. *Nobody expects me to actually fail the test,* Pete thought. *Everything's friendly—even loose, considering this is the largest government contract in history.* The rate of inflation over the previous 18 years had more than quadrupled the dollar amount. The contract was now worth about a trillion dollars.

ATI's General Counsel Haywood Thacker met them in the hall and walked with the small group to the laboratory where the prototype ACIP was kept. Pete sat, rocking back and forth in the witness chair as Thacker had warned the attorneys he would.

The deposition lasted less than five minutes. Still, Pete was tense. He had never been SCIPed before, other than by his own employees. And he had never lied to the machine before, except as a test. This time it would be for real.

One of the lawyers began. "Please state your full name."

"Randall Petersen Armstrong."

"Where and when were you born, Mr. Armstrong?"

"Concord, Massachusetts, on December 6th, 1989."

"Do you swear, under penalty of perjury, that the testimony you're about to give is true to the best of your knowledge?"

O Captain! My Captain! "Y-Yes, I do."

The ACIP light remained green, registering no deceit.

"What's your position at Armstrong Technologics, Inc.?"

"I'm chairman, scientific director, and majority stockholder."

"Please name all ATI employees who own more than one-third of one percent of the stock of the company or are entitled to overrides on the ACIP project."

"Charles Scoggins, Bill Tannenbaum, Marjorie Ann Tilly, Leslie Williams, Carl Whatley, Haywood Thacker, Gene Hildegrand, and myself."

"Are there any other significant stockholders to your knowledge?"

"Merrill Lynch & Schwab owns a large block. Also Senator David West has almost one percent of the stock. There may be some others. Five percent of the company was sold to the public in January 2007, and Merrill retained half the offering. The remaining stockholders aren't known to me, except my girlfriend, Jennifer Finley, who bought 150 shares at the IPO." *Smart girl, that Jen. I hope she's in a better mood tonight.*

"Were you personally involved in the development of the ACIP?"

"Yes, I was."

"Who was the manager in charge of the project?"

"Charles Scoggins."

"Mr. Armstrong, is it possible there could be imperfections in the machine that you would not be aware of?"

"It's possible, but unlikely."

"Are you familiar with the terms of the government contract being offered to Armstrong Technologies, Inc., pursuant to the Truth Machine Bill of April 2006?"

"Yes, I am."

"Are you aware of any imperfections in the technology that would at all compromise ATI's adherence to any conditions of the Truth Machine Bill?"

Our fearful trip is done. "Uh, n-no, I'm not."

No bell sounded from the ACIP. There was no red light, just a steady green and the machine's quiet hum.

"Are you familiar with commercial law?"

"I'm not a lawyer, but I have, er, a good amount of general legal knowledge."

"If any crimes had been committed in the development of the ACIP's technology, for example, fraud, tax evasion, commercial bribery, theft of intellectual property, securities torts, or environmental safety violations, would you be likely to be aware of such crimes?"

"Yes, m-most probably."

"Mr. Armstrong, are you aware of any violations of the law pursuant to the ACIP's development?"

The ship has weather'd every rack, the prize we sought is won. "No sir, I'm n-not."

Again, the ACIP registered no deceit.

"Who, besides yourself, could possibly know of any breaches of the Truth Machine Bill?"

"If there were any breaches I wasn't aware of, the most likely person to know about them would be Charles Scoggins. Marjorie Tilly might also. I'd think it would be next to impossible for at least one of us not to know about a breach."

"Thank you, Mr. Armstrong. We're done with you and you've passed. Congratulations. We'll want to question Mr. Scoggins and Ms. Tilly, but I'd say those two testimonies will be all we'll need to recommend the contract go forward."

Pete replied, "Tilly's out of town until this afternoon, but I'll call Mr. Scoggins and see if he's available."

He spoke into his wristband PDC. "Charles Scoggins, please."

"Scoggins here."

"The attorneys would like to question you next. Are you available?"

"Absolutely, but I'd like a few minutes to finish this meeting. We need your opinion about something before we can conclude. Can you come up for a few minutes first?"

"On my way."

Scoggins's office was a dark, windowless room with video screens covering two walls and the latest data-processing equipment neatly surrounding the desk. Pete was surprised to see Scoggins waiting there for him—alone.

"Where'd everyone go?"

"It's a long story, Pete. Please shut off your recorder for a moment."

"Stop six."

"I've been thinking. I'm not sure I want to go through with this."

Suddenly Pete felt his heart thumping. "What the hell do you mean, Charles?"

"I mean I'm not really sure I want to perjure myself. So far the only laws I've broken involve *civil* matters. Maybe Renaissance Corporation could sue me, but that's only money. If I lie to those attorneys, it would be a criminal offense. I could go to *jail*."

"But I've already given my testimony. It was what we planned."

"That may be true, but I can still change my mind. I only own 13.6 percent of this project and you own over half of it. I'm not sure it's worth it to me to take the risk."

"Is *that* what this is about? You want a bigger percentage?"

"I think it's only fair, Pete. If I risk my neck right

along with yours, I should have the same share of the project you do. If you sign over enough of your share to make us equal partners, I'll go downstairs and testify just the way you did. Otherwise I'm going to have to tell them the truth."

Pete felt a surge of rage, helplessness, and shock. His body swayed as he tried to calm himself and out came his tongue. He considered his predicament carefully. *This is pure and simple blackmail.*

There was nothing he could do but accede to the demand or give up everything that mattered most to him.

"And if I agree to this, you'll testify?"

"The minute you sign this document." Scoggins pulled a two-page letter from his printer tray.

"You mean, you've already *written* it?"

"I assumed you'd make the rational decision."

Pete read the document. Signing it would have no effect on any other stockholders; he would simply be granting Scoggins slightly over 20 percent of the ACIP project's earnings directly from his own share. If he endorsed the papers, he and Scoggins would each have a beneficial interest in approximately 34 percent of the ACIP project, but at least Pete would still retain controlling interest in ATI. The document only pertained to money.

There was no sense dragging things out; surrender was the only reasonable choice.

"Okay, I'll sign it."

"Then turn your recorder back on," Scoggins ordered, taking no chances. He knew the letter, once endorsed, would be worth hundreds of billions of dollars to him.

"Start six." Pete reactivated the digital recording mechanism. Now there would be an indisputable record that Pete had willingly signed the document.

"Pete, I appreciate this. It's very generous of you." Scoggins performed for the camera.

"N-No one d-deserves it more than you, Charles."

He filled in the papers and affixed his thumbprint.

* * *

Pete needed Jennifer more than ever, yet was incapable of confiding in her. He couldn't tell her about Scoggins; couldn't put her in the position of knowing he had broken the law; that would make her an accessory and technically a criminal herself. So coming home seething with anger and frustration that evening, he attempted to act as if everything were normal.

She wasn't fooled. "What's wrong?"

"Just a little problem at work. I'm sorry I'm so distracted."

"I'm here for you if you want to talk."

"I know, Jen. I have to work this one out myself."

She didn't bring it up again, but he could tell his behavior was making her feel insecure, and thought, *My sweet love probably thinks all this brooding has something to do with her. If only I could tell her the real reason.* But he knew he never could.

They went to bed.

I can accept that he'll never love me as much as I love him, she decided, *but I can't live with being shut out.*

She kissed him sweetly and they made love. There was an urgency and power to their lovemaking that she hadn't felt in a long time, her passion as intense as it had ever been, even on their first night together. *It's because this is the last time I'll ever make love to him,* she thought. *And he must know it, too. Or does he?*

CHAPTER 31

OBSESSION

Dallas, Texas
August 10, 2024—The United States Truth Machine Panel officially approves the Armstrong Cerebral Image Processor (ACIP) for use in the nation's judicial systems. Five hundred testing sites will be operational within three weeks, and Armstrong Technologies announces plans to set up 4,300 additional sites over the following five months. All death-row inmates wishing to take truth tests will be given first priority. The government panel also issues a preliminary fee schedule for civil cases, with rates averaging approximately $3500 per hour of ACIP usage.—With the election less than three months away, latest polls show Matthew Emery holding a commanding eight-point lead over President Gordon Safer.—In spite of State Department protests, a Karachi court sentences to death 14 American executives for their roles in an environmental disaster that killed over 130,000 Pakistanis and rendered 83 square miles uninhabitable. The executives continue to deny any culpability in the massive chemical leak.

There's no standard etiquette for this, is there? Pete laughed at the thought. But his stomach ached and every muscle in his body was tense. *How exactly is someone supposed to behave in the company of the person who murdered his brother and shattered his childhood? What will I feel when I first see Reece?*

218

How will I control my anger? What on earth made me do this?

Pete decided to meet first with Alphonso Carter, a man he liked and respected. *Reece can wait downstairs.*

A secretary escorted Carter into Pete's office. Now 64, the famous psychiatrist looked older, his hair completely white and his posture no longer so erect. He moved more slowly too, and even when he remembered to stand up straight, was almost an inch shorter than he had been in 2007 when they'd last met. Apparently his profession had taken its toll.

"Dr. Carter, it's good to see you again. How was your trip?" Pete took Carter's hand and shook it warmly.

"Fine, just fine. The flight was almost too quick. When I was your age, it took nearly four hours to fly from Boston to Dallas. Today the drive from the airport took almost as much time as the flight. Mr. Reece was amazed. Do you know, it was his first time on an airplane, much less a BMD Mach Nine?"

Pete felt odd listening to Carter refer to Reece in human terms.

Carter had great affection for Pete and it showed. He had always been a sincere man and often charming, but rarely was he this effusive. "It is really good to see you too, Mr. Armstrong. I can hardly imagine it has been over 16 years since I collaborated with you in Dallas. I still believe the work I did for ATI was the best and most important thing I have ever done and I will always be grateful to you for the opportunity."

"I feel the same way about you. RehabTest was a great product. It put ATI on the map; I doubt it would've been nearly as good, or as successful, without your input."

Any self-correcting software designed by Ms. Tilly and edited by Mr. Armstrong would have been equally successful, although perhaps it would not have caught on quite as quickly, Carter thought—but kept his opinion to himself. In a way he felt embarrassed trading compliments and sentimentalities with the richest man in the world. It was pleasant but it was not why he was there. *Mr. Armstrong's time is too valuable to waste.*

"I am sure you must be apprehensive about this meeting with Mr. Reece. I am too. It could be dangerous, psychologically speaking, but you have convinced me it might also help you both come to terms with what happened to your brother. Today Mr. Reece is a different person and genuinely remorseful. He does not seek your forgiveness. He merely wishes to make himself available to you in any way he can to help atone."

"I've thought about it and I really think I'd like to SCIP him."

"Oh. It is unfortunate you have decided this after he has already flown down to see you. But I understand."

"No, no. Not *skip*!" Pete let out a good-natured laugh. "SCIP is ATI jargon; it stands for 'scan cerebral image patterns.' I just meant I want to question him using the ACIP—uh, I mean the Truth Machine. If I knew for certain he was being honest with me, it might help resolve my feelings about what he did."

"Ah. I see. That is fine. Reece has already agreed to it, if you are certain that is what you want. But I must warn you: I am not so sure you would really *want* to know everything you are likely to learn."

"I'm *absolutely* sure."

Downstairs at the laboratory, Reece, 53, and Pete, now 34, saw each other for the first time in over 29 years. Reece's appearance wasn't at all consistent with Pete's expectations. Prisoners weren't allowed to use hair-growth drugs and Reece had chosen not to take them after his release. Slightly balding but not unattractively so, he looked distinguished: clean-shaven and tastefully dressed, with a calm, serious demeanor.

He had already been seated at the first of the six ACIP stations in the sparkling white lab. The machine was running. They didn't shake hands, but there seemed to be no hatred separating them, just a shared regret of a horrible crime.

Reece spoke first. "Thank you for seeing me."

"I'm d-doing this for myself, not for you." Pete didn't mean it as a rebuff, only as a statement of fact.

Reece nodded, wondering whether the odd mannerisms were related to the trauma he had inflicted upon Pete and his family so long ago.

"I appreciate it anyway. I have a lot of regrets, but taking your brother's life is the worst one. At the time I told the police I couldn't remember what happened. That was a lie. To this day, I remember everything about it, but it still feels like it was somebody else. I keep thinking *I* could *never* have killed that little boy. How could I possibly do such a thing? But I did. It *was* me. It was a different me. But it was me."

The ACIP's green light remained solid. It never flickered. Clearly, Reece was committed to total honesty.

Reece had spent the 27 years after Leonard's murder (1995 to 2022) at Massachusetts State Prison. But in 2011, he had undergone an experimental therapy similar to the ACIP field studies, his brain monitored throughout a battery of psychological tests. All physiological brain damage, the source of his rage, had been pinpointed and treated with a calibrated regimen of drugs, gene therapy, and behavior modification.

Reece was not without potential. He had become a model prisoner, earning his high school and college diplomas and a master's degree in criminal psychology.

"Daniel Anthony Reece is dead," Carter had argued to the Massachusetts Prison Board two years earlier. "His essence has been removed from our midst, just as though we had administered a lethal injection back in 2011. The body and brain now serve only as vessels for Mr. Reece's memories; the personality is new. It feels to him as if he is the same person only because he possesses those memories; to us he is as different from the old Reece as any two persons could be. He is incapable of violence, indeed of any crime. For over 10 years we have incarcerated a virtuous man."

In November 2022 the Board had authorized Reece's release. He now worked for Carter as a researcher.

Still tense, Pete continued to rock. "I've always w-wanted to know what really happened that day."

"I'd been paroled from prison two and a half months earlier," Reece began earnestly, "and was doing okay. I'd found a job as a gardener for a landscape company in Carlisle. That day they sent another fellow and me to a job in Concord. We'd worked that same house the week before, so I knew how to get there. Right before we arrived, my partner told me he wasn't feeling well. I dropped him off at his apartment and covered the job myself. It was the first time I'd ever worked alone."

The light on the ACIP remained green.

"I'd watched the three of you the previous week—I guess it was you, your brother, and your nanny. I saw you through the bushes, playing on your front lawn. Looked pretty happy most of the time, but I could see your brother knew how to push your buttons—like most brothers I guess. You definitely got angry at him at least once. I don't remember what he *did* or anything—didn't really think much about it at the time. I just thought to myself, *A couple of spoiled rich kids.*"

"So, uh, you hated us right away?"

"No, I wouldn't say I *hated* you, but maybe I was jealous—yeah, I was definitely jealous. Obviously *I* didn't have a huge front yard and a nanny to play with. I didn't have much fun growing up at all. Not that I'm making excuses. I know there's no excuse for what I did."

"G-Go on."

"I saw you through the bushes again that day. I think it was around 10 o'clock when your brother crawled into the garden where I was working. He was tiny, but he looked so alert, like he was taking everything in, y'know? I just kind of stared at him. I didn't really expect to see anyone that morning."

Pete was surprised Reece had been that perceptive. Leonard was amazingly alert, aware of everything around him, but adults typically hadn't noticed that about him. He made no comment; only nodded for Reece to continue.

"So next he said, 'Hey, what are you looking at, mister?'"

(Note: Reece's recollection is the only record we have of Leonard Armstrong's final words, most of which I have also cited in Chapter 3 of this chronicle. There are no other witnesses or digital records. Presumably the words cited by Reece are accurate, but possibly not verbatim.—22g CP)

"Now I'm thinking, 'This kid can't be more than three years old—four at the most. And he's mouthing off to me like some teenager.' Startled the hell out of me. I said, 'Boy, you better get away from here.' But he didn't leave. I sure wish he had."

"What happened n-next?"

"He said, 'Boy? I say now. Lookee here, son. You watch who you're calling *boy* around here.' I'll never forget a single word he said, for as long as I live. I guess he was imitating that Foghorn Leghorn character, at least that's what they told me. But I didn't realize it at the time. I thought he was *taunting* me. Then he went on, 'I mean, I say, how big are men where you come from anyway? I say.' I know *now* he was just repeating something he'd heard in a cartoon, but at the time I felt like he'd insulted my masculinity or something. I was very sensitive about that. I was raped by my father when I was nine and obviously I had some unresolved issues about my sexuality. Anyway, something in me snapped and I slapped him—hard."

The green light on the ACIP flickered, but Reece corrected himself before the bell could ring, "No, it was a lot worse than a slap. I knocked him unconscious and the whole side of his face was bleeding. Anyway, you saw me throw him into the back of the truck and I drove away. I just got the hell out of there."

"Uh, d-did L-Leonard ever w-wake up?" Pete asked, hoping to God he hadn't. His body began to rock more violently.

"Yes. Yes, he did." Tears were rolling down Reece's cheeks. "When I finally stopped the truck on that dirt road behind Walden Pond, he was wide awake, sobbing. I felt he knew exactly what was happening to him. I'm sure his face hurt and he was probably scared as hell, but he was alert. He asked for you. He was crying, 'Petey. Where's *Petey*?' I had no idea who Petey was, but of course he meant you. And I'm sorry about what happened next. I am so sorry. I was damned cruel."

"What h-happened?" Pete's body no longer just rocked; now it oscillated.

"I'm not sure I can describe how much I hated him at that moment. Hated both of you—just for being normal kids whose parents probably loved you. Just because I knew you had all the things I always wanted and never had. I thought to myself, 'Why them? Why should they get to live in a big house with parents who actually care about them? Why not me?' So I said something to him, something so horrible I figured it would hurt him bad.

And I could tell it did. He just whimpered and stared—like he was in shock—right at me. Right into my eyes. I waited a few seconds for my words to sink in. And when I was sure he understood, I picked up a rock and lifted it over him. He pleaded with me not to hit him again, but I was too enraged to stop what I'd started. I smashed the side of his forehead with it—several times. After the second blow, he stopped crying. I guess he was dead."

Pete quivered and glared at Reece. *Why doesn't he just tell me what the hell he said? What's the big deal? Reece killed him for God's sake and he had no trouble describing that in graphic detail. But now he's going to make me ask him what he said to Leonard just before he smashed his skull? How could mere words be so bad that he can't repeat them without a formal invitation? But if that's the game, I'll play along.*

"God damn it, what did you *s-s-say* to him?"

Reece remained silent for a few seconds. He glanced at Carter, who wore a look of resignation.

Carter nodded.

When Reece did respond, Pete bit down so hard that his tongue started to bleed. The blood dripped onto his chin, but he felt nothing.

"I said to him, 'Petey told me to kill you.'"

CHAPTER 32

ON THE BRINK

Dallas, Texas
August 11, 2024—The Ivory Coast's Moslem-controlled government files an official complaint with the United Nations against Ghana for refusing the Ivory Coast army entry to its borders to capture or kill the terrorists responsible for unleashing a genetically engineered virus in Abidjan. Over 300,000 persons perished from the virus, which apparently had been designed to spare only ethnic Betes. The terrorists are believed to have sought refuge in Ghana's Tongo Hills.—Statistics released by the FDA show obesity and other eating disorders have been drastically reduced in the United States. Over 90 percent of all Americans are now within three pounds of their ideal weight, largely as a result of WeightPerfect, ATI's computerized time-release appetite regulating system. The arm-patch system, first available in October 2018, was designed to monitor each person's body fat and nutritional needs, make food and exercise recommendations, and release the appropriate hormones to raise or lower the individual's metabolic set-point. Nearly every person in America now uses the system, at least occasionally.

When Pete arrived home after meeting with Reece and Carter, he kept to himself. "Jennifer, I need to be alone tonight."

"Do you want to talk about it?"

"No. I can't."

He locked himself in his study and sat down.

"Darker, please."

The lights dimmed and Pete simply closed his eyes and went to sleep.

The next morning when he awoke, everything seemed even worse. He left the house at 6:00 a.m. without waking Jennifer to kiss her goodbye.

As he sat in his office, his body moved to and fro in a motion exaggerated even for him. *"Come off it, Leonard. Go get the ball. It's not that funny. . . . Please, Leonard, go get the ball."* With those words spoken almost 30 years before, Pete had sent his brother to his death. It had been unintentional, *but during Leonard's final seconds of life, how could he have known that?* In his dying moments, Leonard probably believed his own brother had been responsible. The more Pete thought about that, the more upset he became.

Trying to escape the pain, he deliberately turned his thoughts to Charles Scoggins, whom David West had always mistrusted. *Why didn't I listen to David? Did Charles actually plan to blackmail me even before I reprogrammed the ACIP for him—or had blackmail merely been an afterthought?*

Then a new thought. *What if Scoggins planned the whole scenario years ago, before he showed me the stolen Renaissance code?*

He had long wondered why Scoggins had bothered to show him that stolen code. It never made sense; Scoggins would have known the code would be useless to ATI unless Pete could override the Truth Machine.

Of course! He must have known exactly what would happen. That's the only logical explanation. He set things in motion by showing me the code, then he waited patiently for two and a half years.

Never had Pete felt such anger before. And fear. His future and all his dreams were in jeopardy. A colleague he'd trusted and to whom he'd invested responsibility for ATI's most important project had betrayed him. *If only I could talk to David about this, or Leonard.*

Pete had no idea what Scoggins was planning next, but had no doubt there would be more betrayals. *He's playing by a different set of rules. Maybe he intends to murder me. After all, my death would put him in control of the ACIP division.*

These days, Scoggins kept unusual hours. He liked to get to work late, but was usually the last person on the Truth Machine team to leave the office. This evening was no exception. He must have been startled to hear a knock on his office door at 8:03 p.m. and even more surprised when Pete peered inside.

"Charles, I th-think we have a problem. It's serious. Do you have a few minutes for us to meet—privately?"

Scoggins spoke into his wristband PDC. "Stop four."

"We need to go down to the lab."

Inside the same laboratory where he had interviewed Reece only 29 hours earlier, Pete pulled out a laser CBP (controlled-burst pistol) he'd hidden in a drawer. He pointed it at Scoggins and motioned him toward the ACIP.

"Get into th-that chair right now. And hand your wristband to me."

Scoggins complied. "What's this all about, Pete?"

"You set me up. You gave me the stolen Renaissance code knowing I'd eventually have to use it. You knew all along I'd reprogram the ACIP. Isn't that true?"

"Pete, I had no *idea*. I was only trying to help the company. I *swear* to you." The ACIP light flashed red and the bell rang. Pete smiled grimly.

"I took out the override code. You can't lie to me anymore. Now point the ACIP monitor at *me*."

Beads of sweat forming on his pale white face, Scoggins obeyed.

"I'm warning you, Charles, if you lie to me again, I'll kill you. Now. Tonight. And if you don't do exactly as I say, you'll *wish* I'd killed you. I've planned this carefully—every detail. All the recorders are turned off in this part of the building and nobody will ever know I was here. Don't make me do it."

The ACIP green light stayed lit and steady. Pete meant every word. Scoggins's survival was in his own hands.

Pete threw him a pair of handcuffs.

"Now cuff your left arm to the chair."

Again, Scoggins obeyed. The electronic handcuffs, developed for law enforcement by Motorola and the MicroChip Corporation, were light, soft, comfortable, and efficient. Only a password spoken in Pete's voice could unfasten them.

"How long have you been planning to blackmail me?"

Scoggins didn't answer until Pete pointed the weapon directly at him.

"Technically speaking, since the day in Theo-Soc when David West started talking about the Truth Machine. I'd had fleeting notions about it even before that, but my plan really crystallized that day. You wouldn't even talk to me after that class, remember? And your naive, moony altruism was so pathetic. Pete, we're alike, you and me. How can you think these stupid little ants are worth saving?"

"What are you talking about?"

"Don't you see how slow and silly they all are. They don't even know how to think. But you and I are different, Pete. You're the same as me—you just don't know it yet." The light stayed green.

"Charles, look at the ACIP. I'm *not* like you. I'll *never* be like you." Again, green.

"We'll see. Anyway, when you wouldn't go into business with me, I knew I had to find a way to change your mind. Eventually an opportunity arose. It always does."

"When was that?"

"The day President Hall started talking about Roswell's Truth Machine bill."

"And?"

"First, I talked Boschnak at Merrill Lynch & Schwab into signing an exclusive with me. Then I convinced him that your company was a much better bet than mine. But in order to get out of the exclusive, I told him he either had to get me into ATI on acceptable terms or give me two percent of ATI's stock out of Merrill's shares. Y'know, you'd never have gotten as good a deal from them without my involvement. Not everything I did was detrimental. I've done a lot of good things for you."

"Gee, thanks. Why'd you show me the stolen Renaissance code, Charles?"

"I've got a few skeletons in my closet. Long story. Mostly insider trading, commercial bribery, computer and wire fraud—white-collar kind of stuff."

The green light flickered. Scoggins must have been holding back.

"What *else*?"

"I sold military technology to a Japanese arms dealer I happen to know. That was before I came to ATI, but there's no statute of limitations on treason. Suffice it to say, I couldn't afford to have the Truth Machine actually work on me."

"What does all that have to do with the code?"

"I suspected that the fatal flaw was a simple problem with a unique solution. That's why I saved it for last. As soon as I saw the Renaissance code, I realized it was the only possible way to solve the flaw. I knew you'd memorize it if I showed it to you. I figured you'd eventually decide to use their algorithms rather than risk Renaissance beating us to the prize—although they never really had a chance. They're still at least 10 years behind us."

"How did you come up with your plan?"

"When I started at ATI, I just wanted to delay the Truth Machine. It was my only hope of staying out of jail without leaving the country. But then I figured that once you'd used stolen algorithms, your only choice would be to override the ACIP. I'd be able to force you to program an override for *me*. That would turn a liability into an asset, wouldn't you say? Worked almost the way I planned it too, but it took a lot longer than I expected. You were too damned principled—at first."

"So you never really offered Bonhert a joint venture or a merger?" Pete realized it was a stupid question the moment he asked it.

"Of course not. He'd've made a deal in two seconds. I did everything I could to make sure you two never talked to each other. Lucky for me you both prefer to stick to science and leave the deal-making to your underlings. Big mistake, Pete. If you want to get things done, you should learn how to connect with people."

Pete knew *that* was right. *What a fool I've been,* he thought.

"Why'd you show me the code back then? Why not wait until I was more desperate for a solution to the fatal flaw?"

"I was afraid you'd figure out the solution yourself before I showed it to you. Hell, if my team had worked on that part first, like Renaissance did, we could've figured out the solution ourselves within eight months— even without you. But that would've ruined everything. You could've passed the Truth Machine Panel's SCIP honestly. I'd have had nothing on you. I had to make sure that didn't happen."

"So when that former Renaissance employee showed you the code. . . ."

"There *was* no such person."

"What?"

"I made that up. I really got the code by hacking into Renaissance's central research computer. Several weeks before I showed it to you."

Pete felt like an idiot. How could he have been so naive? But much worse was that Scoggins had stalled the

Truth Machine project for over two years—*on purpose. How could he* do *such a thing?*

"So you intentionally delayed the ACIP just to save your own skin?" Pete couldn't imagine anyone being so unprincipled.

"Mostly. At least that was the original goal."

"The original goal?"

"Once I figured out how to make you override the ACIP for me, I realized there were other possibilities."

"Such as?"

"Well the override itself is a damn valuable commodity. Also, I wanted more money—a bigger share of the ACIP." The green light flickered. Scoggins was holding back again.

"And?"

"And to own as big a share of ATI as possible. Hopefully someday to control it."

"Control ATI? For what purpose?"

"I think ATI might become the most powerful company on earth. It's already by far the most profitable. Pete, if we work together, we could rule the world. Tell me you haven't thought about that."

"Never. Not once."

"I don't believe it."

I'll never be like that, Pete thought. *But he can't understand because he doesn't care about anyone else. He wants power and money, the rest of the world be damned. How many innocent people have already died because of Scoggins's greed? Perhaps he doesn't deserve to live. Maybe I should just kill him. Maybe it won't be so hard to pull the trigger.*

"How'd you plan to get more ATI shares? All I signed over to you was a bigger share of the Truth Machine project."

"Not exactly. The paper you signed gave me a 34-percent share in the ACIP project, net of any overhead allocation. Imagine having a monopoly on the entire television industry from 1955 to 1980, from the programming to the manufacture of the image screens. Or the personal computer industry, from chips to software, from 1980 to 2005. We'd have had an exclusive on a giant industry for 25 years.

"I figured within 10 years, the ACIP division would be colossal. Everybody knows the government contract's worth a trillion dollars in revenue, but the special 25-year patent was the real deal. That's the part of the Truth Machine Bill all the analysts undervalued. And I'd get paid based on *gross* operating profits, not net. On that basis, the ACIP division would soon become much more profitable than the entire company. You'd have to start selling off your stock just to keep paying my percentage. Then I could buy your ATI stock on the open market."

Scoggins kept talking. He talked for almost an hour. Perhaps he was playing for time, giving himself a chance to think his way out. Or maybe he was actually proud of his depraved cleverness.

The ACIP light remained green throughout.

He has no choice, so he's being absolutely honest, possibly for the first time in his miserable life.

"It really was a beautiful plan," Scoggins continued. "But I underestimated you. Are you going to kill me?"

"I'm not sure yet. Where's the document I signed?"

Scoggins ignored the question. "Are you going to kill me, Pete? Maybe you should. That'll prove once and for all that you're just like me."

"If you tell me where the contract is, I'll let you try to help me figure out a way *not* to kill you. But if you don't tell me, I'll make you wish you were dead."

Scoggins knew Pete wasn't bluffing. A properly placed jolt from the CBP would be so painful that he'd have to tell Pete anything he wanted to know.

"It's in my files under 'Harvard.' Third drawer on the left side."

"Anyone else have a copy?"

"Not yet, unfortunately."

"That depends on your point of view. Where's the key?"

"My left vest pocket. Will you show your true colors, Pete? Are you going to kill me now?"

"Tell me, Charles, why *shouldn't* I kill you?"

"Can I have a few minutes to think about that?"

"I'll give you five." Pete considered the concession generous under the circumstances.

He had read some fiction and his troubled mind conjured up the image of Ian Fleming's spy-hero, James Bond. Bond's enemies, upon capturing him, could never bring themselves to do away with him immediately. Blinded by their egos and scorn for humanity, they found themselves strangely attracted to Bond, whom they regarded as an equal. Inevitably this mistake cost them dearly. Bond saw the situation more clearly, killing with unhesitating precision.

Pete wanted to liken himself to Bond, a man who tried to save the world from evil. For a split second, he imagined Goldfinger had taken Scoggins's place in the chair.

Or am I more like the villain?

Suddenly Goldfinger changed into James Bond, and back to Scoggins again.

What's happening to me?

He couldn't take murder lightly. He had never killed before and was groping for a way to avoid it; apparently the stress was making him delusional. As the seconds ticked away, Pete wondered whether he had passed the point of no return. Indeed, if Scoggins survived this night, wouldn't his next logical move be to try to do away with Pete? Was there any way to avoid murder without jeopardizing his company, his goals for the world, his freedom, and perhaps his life?

"Okay, your time's up."

Scoggins answered the only way he could. "I can't think of any reason for you not to kill me."

"What would you do if the situation were reversed?"

"I'd have killed you five minutes ago. But you say I'm not like you. I guess we'll see."

"If I let you go, what will you do? Is there any way to prevent you from trying to kill *me*?"

Scoggins hesitated. "I need 10 more minutes to think about that."

"Okay."

The most likely answer, Pete thought, *is that no matter what happens next, he'll try as soon as he has a chance. Maybe he always planned to murder me, but there would have been no hurry — until now.*

Still, Pete hoped they could devise a formula to prevent it. But it would have to be foolproof. Maybe they could create evidence to surface upon his death, or reprogram the ACIP somehow so that Scoggins would require his future complicity. But this notion was farfetched, especially when dealing with someone so treacherous. On the other hand, even *considering* a murder would have been incredible just hours ago.

While Pete waited, Scoggins reached into his left vest pocket and pulled out something about the size of a thumbnail. He started to bring it toward his mouth.

What the hell's he doing? Of course! He knows if I can't get into his files tonight to recover the document, I'll have to keep him alive until I can. That'd give him ample opportunity to escape—and try to kill me first. He's planning to swallow the key to his files!

Suddenly Pete was afraid. Again, it was no longer Scoggins sitting in that chair, but another man with a horrifying face he had never forgotten: the face of 24-year-old Daniel Anthony Reece, Jr., his arm rising, stone in hand, ready to strike Leonard.

Shoot him now, Petey, whispered Leonard's voice. *Hurry!*

Pete aimed the CBP and pulled the trigger.

Scoggins's free arm dropped and the microchip key fell onto the floor.

Charles Scoggins was dead.

* * *

Pete shook uncontrollably, sobbing like a child. He needed somebody to talk to, but was thoroughly alone.

If only I could go back in time and change everything. If only I'd listened to David and not hired Scoggins in the first place. If only I'd called the authorities and turned Scoggins in—turned both of us in. Going to jail would have been better than killing another human being. I'm no better than Reece!

Sitting on the floor with his arms around his knees, he chewed on his tongue and began rocking. He couldn't stop.

If only Leonard had survived.

He gnawed hard on his tongue, still sore from biting into it the day before. His shaking began to abate, but he took more than an hour to regain his composure.

He didn't rush it; he would need all his faculties for what was to follow.

Finally he went upstairs to Scoggins's office and retrieved the document. Returning downstairs, he deactivated the handcuffs and dragged Scoggins's body to a windowless room down the hall, the records destruction room, where the most secret and sensitive ATI documents were brought to be shredded and incinerated. Pete opened the incinerator latch, lifted Scoggins's body, and dumped it in along with the document.

Then he energized the incinerator.

There was something therapeutic about pulling that switch. Maybe when Scoggins was ignited, Pete's guilt over Leonard's death would somehow burn with him. Regardless, there would soon remain no trace of Charles Scoggins's body or the physical document he had tricked Pete into signing.

Pete didn't encounter a single person in the ATI building that night, except for the guard seated at the lobby desk.

He checked out of the building, went home, and looked for Jennifer. She wasn't there.

Thank God, he thought.

Then he saw the note she had left:

Dearest Pete—

I've gone back to Princeton. If you want to talk about it, give me a call. If you don't, it was wonderful while it lasted. I love you and will never forget you.

No regrets, Jen.

Pete decided not to call Jennifer—or ever to see her again. If he planned to look at himself in the mirror, it was the only decision he could make. He was now a murderer and she would be better off without him.

I love her, but I don't deserve her.

He desperately wanted to cry. He tried, but was too exhausted, so he went straight to bed and slept—for 15 hours.

Haywood Thacker called Pete at home on the afternoon following the murder. "Have you seen Charles?"

Were it not for Thacker's call on his emergency number, Pete might have slept even longer. "N-Not since l-last night. We both left pretty late."

"He never checked out of the building and now nobody can find him," the ATI general counsel explained. "He doesn't answer calls even when we use the emergency code. What were you guys working on?"

Pete had already considered how he would answer that question. He lied slowly, deliberately. "We thought we had a problem with the ACIP, but it turned out t-to be a f-f-false alarm."

"I think I'm going to call the police and report him missing."

"G-G-Good idea, Haywood. I'm sure h-h-he'll turn up, b-but it's better to play it s-safe."

CHAPTER 33

THE SECOND OFFICIAL SCIP

Dallas, Texas
August 25, 2024—Scientists from all over the world convene in Portland, Oregon, for the first annual International Nanotechnology Conference. Microsoft founder and Chairman Emeritus William H. Gates delivers the keynote address. Gates predicts, "Nanotechnology will ultimately exert an even greater positive influence on the human race than the computer." Nanomachines, built at the molecular level and already often smaller than human cells, can be designed for diverse purposes. But for the time being, medical research dominates the field.—Two massive nuclear explosions evaporate the entire Tonga Hills region of Ghana, killing or critically injuring an estimated two million persons and contaminating an area of several hundred square miles. The Ivory Coast government emphatically denies any involvement in the detonations.

Randall Petersen Armstrong's sanity at the moment he murdered Charles Scoggins is a moot point. Regardless of the condition of the various nether regions of his brain, non-invasive tests have proven that there had never been any significant damage either to his neo-cortex or to his amygdala. Therefore he was unable to avoid the two greatest emotional inconveniences all sane human criminals experience: guilt and fear.

The police first visited on August 17, when Scoggins had been missing for six days. Surprised it had taken them so long, Pete was equally shocked at how short that meeting had been and at how few questions the police had asked. The disappearance had been a major story; after all, Scoggins was a famous and influential figure. Pete assumed the pressure on the Dallas Police Department to find him was intense.

On the two-week anniversary of the disappearance, the police were back. Thacker sat with Pete in the conference room on the 60th floor of ATI headquarters as Detectives Austin Stevenson and Sandra Miller questioned him.

Stevenson began. "Mr. Armstrong, I'm sure you're aware that we're recording this session."

"We are, too," Thacker interjected.

"Of course. You have no obligation to speak with us at all, so we appreciate your cooperation."

"No problem," Pete answered, shaking visibly. "I'm as anxious to g-get to the b-bottom of this as you are." *God, I hate lying.*

"Apparently you were the last person to see Mr. Scoggins on August 11th. What were you both doing here so late?"

"I th-thought there was a defect in the ACIP software. We went down to the lab to test it. F-Fortunately it turned out to be a mechanical problem—the CIR, um, that's cerebral image reconstruction machine, had a faulty chip—just a $7 item. It took us a few hours to f-figure th-that out and replace the p-p-part. We b-both left the lab around midnight."

After about 20 minutes, Sandra Miller took over. "Can you help us clear up some discrepancies?"

"I'll t-try."

"Do you have any idea why there's no record of Mr. Scoggins leaving the building?"

"He could've left through the fire exit in the b-back."

"Did he generally leave that way?"

"I have n-no idea, but it was l-late. He was, um, *is,* a pretty c-careful person. Th-there've always been crank calls, death threats, th-that sort of thing. S-Some people didn't want the ACIP b-built, and n-n-now that it's b-been approved, the th-th-threats have been getting more f-frequent. M-Maybe he thought he'd be safer th-that way."

Miller pressed him again. "At about 8 p.m. on the evening of the disappearance, you asked Mr. Scoggins to meet with you—privately. He immediately deactivated his wristband and never turned it back on. Frankly that seems a bit suspicious."

"We have, um, a l-lot of trade s-secrets here. We'd hate for our competitors to get hold of them. I d-didn't want to record us analyzing proprietary software. It cost us billions of dollars to write. S-Security is a big issue with us."

Miller's blue eyes bore into him. "At 11:04 p.m., you returned upstairs to Mr. Scoggins's office for several minutes—alone. We have it all on digital record. Can you enlighten us as to why?"

Pete, aware that the upstairs monitors had still been on, had an answer ready. "Charles sent me to get the CIR unit spec sheet from his files. He had the thing in pieces on the lab table, so he didn't want to leave the room. I was only g-gone a few minutes."

I hope they don't ask me about the document, he thought to himself. *I know they can identify papers from digital archives. What if they figure out it was really the same document I signed on August 7?*

"And I assume he was fine when you returned."

Pete thought he detected a trace of sarcasm in her voice, but couldn't be sure. *Damn. They're going to nail me because of that document.*

Thacker interrupted. "Detective Miller, is Mr. Armstrong a suspect?"

"At this point, we're not sure there's been a crime. But frankly, if Mr. Armstrong would be willing to answer a few more questions under ACIP scrutiny, we could eliminate him as a suspect right away."

Thacker turned to Pete. "I think we should meet in private to discuss this."

"Th-that won't b-be necessary, Haywood. If it'll help th-them in their investigation, I'd be happy to have them S-S-SCIP me." He turned toward Miller and Stevenson. "When would you like to do it?"

The August 7 digital recording in Scoggins's archives remained the potential nail in Pete's coffin. If the authorities ever compared it to the August 11 recording, they would be able to prove that Armstrong had lied to the police, because on August 7 he'd signed the very same document that he later claimed was the spec sheet for the CIR.

But they never thought to make such a comparison.

In fact, so many papers were signed in the usual course of ATI's business that no one bothered to ask a single question about the document that Pete had signed in Scoggins's office just four days before the disappearance.

Pete's SCIP took place six days later at an ACIP testing station in Houston. It lasted less than 90 seconds.

"Mr. Armstrong, have the Dallas police questioned you regarding the disappearance of Charles Scoggins?"

"Yes."

"Have you been completely truthful in answering their questions?"

O Captain! My Captain! "Yes, I have."

"Do you have any information that might be relevant to this case other than what you've already given to the police?"

Our fearful trip is done. "No. I've t-told them everything I know."

'Thank you for your cooperation, Mr. Armstrong."

The ship has weather'd every rack. The prize we sought is won!

CHAPTER 34

QUARTER-MILLENNIAL

Washington DC
July 4, 2026—Over 20 million Americans and well-wishers from every nation on earth converge on Washington, DC, to celebrate the 250th anniversary of the birth of the United States. President Matthew Emery presides over the Quarter-Millennial Celebration, which is broadcast throughout the world on every communication medium, attracting the largest viewing audience in history.—Armstrong Technologies, Inc. is awarded a $46 billion annual government contract to administer scips at all customs and immigration stations throughout America and its territories. Congress also continues to debate legalization of limited ACIP usage by government and private industry for job interviews.— President Emery submits a bill that would lower federal tax rates by 23 percent across the board. Greater compliance and a near elimination of tax fraud has produced an enormous budget surplus for the tax year 2025. The bill is expected to pass Senate and House essentially unaltered.

Considering that the Wests were Democrats, they had amazingly good seats directly behind President Matthew Emery. At the Quarter-Millennial Celebration, Pete sat with Senator David West and Dr. Diana Hsu West atop the gigantic podium built for the occasion on the Washington Monument lawn.

Emery made a point of chatting with all three several

times that evening, apparently believing the old adage, "Keep your friends close, but your enemies closer."

Or maybe he just wanted to look like a good sport in front of all the cameras.

There was little doubt in Washington that David West would be Emery's opponent in the elections two years hence and West would be difficult to beat. Bookmakers in London were already offering two to-one odds to anyone willing to bet West would *not* be elected president in 2028. David found that factoid particularly ironic, and wondered if his father had ever gambled on political elections.

During the 20th century, before the cure for alcoholism was discovered, compulsive gambling had been far more difficult to treat than alcoholism. Even in 2026, gambling addiction was incurable, but Bruce Witkowsky, now 63 years old, had been undergoing treatment for many years. He had lived in Dallas since August 2014. David now saw his father regularly and spoke with him almost every day. Fortunately the family no longer depended on Bruce for anything important; he was mainly a source of entertainment.

Pete, who had become much more appreciative of, and closer to, his own parents over the past decade, had once likened Bruce to an otherwise clever puppy who could never be housebroken.

In previous times a father like Bruce might have been a political liability, but David wasn't concerned. He was unashamed of where he came from and proud of the obstacles he had overcome. His political capital had multiplied with the introduction of the ACIP into American life. Unlike most politicians, he had long accepted that the Truth Machine was coming and had fashioned his political persona on the basis of that inevitability.

Now any person could be truth-tested by reserving time at one of thousands of testing stations offering

ACIPs for civil litigation or mediation. A politician who refused to submit to a scip was unelectable. The ACIP had eliminated the crooks, and even honest politicians struggled to justify previous actions and positions with statements that could hold up under scip.

Yet since his first run at elected office, David had simply stood for what he believed was right. No hidden agenda. No riding popular opinion polls. No catering to special interests. In short, he had never done anything he'd have trouble explaining. Whenever he had changed position on an issue, it was because he'd decided his previous stance had been wrong. Other than those instances, perfectly acceptable to most voters, David could answer scip questions for hours at a time without ever contradicting previous statements.

No politician in America was more trusted than David West.

David, Diana, and Pete talked non-stop whenever they got together. They talked about almost everything, but especially about their Harvard days, politics, and ATI. They enjoyed each other's company so much that it was hard to remain silent during the endless speeches. Still, they had to be polite.

Finally after one particularly long-winded effort, West turned to his friend. "Whatever happened to Scoggins's ATI stock? Did he have any family?"

"Er, actually n-no. Both p-parents were dead and there were no brothers or sisters. We couldn't even find a cousin. Didn't leave a will either. As soon as they declare him legally dead, Uncle Sam'll probably wind up with the whole estate."

Pete was hoping David would change the subject. He hated being asked about Scoggins. *But at least,* he thought, *I can answer these questions without lying.*

"They never did find a body, did they?" Diana added.

"No. But I can't imagine he's still alive."

"It's amazing," West said. "Thirty-eight years old, second richest person in America and he disappears without a trace."

"I never thought of him as the suicidal type," Diana added, "but I wouldn't be surprised if that's what happened. What a strange person. Brilliant, but world-class weird. I don't think the poor guy ever even had a girlfriend."

Diana regretted the comment the moment she uttered it. *Pete hasn't either,* she realized, *ever since he and Jennifer broke up, which he won't talk about.*

Pete never talked about Jennifer Finley, but thought about her constantly. *Do I still love her?* he wondered, trying to convince himself that he no longer did. But he certainly cared deeply for her and felt despairingly lonely in her absence.

He remembered the day he almost proposed to her.

What if I'd asked her to stay? Maybe we'd be married now. And if not, at least I'd know her answer. But now I'll never know. What a fool I was. You can't play games with someone like Jennifer. Why couldn't I have been more honest about my feelings?

He had never tried to get in touch with her—that wouldn't have been fair—but did follow her career. He continued to have his computer search for media articles where her name was mentioned, subscribed to the electronic version of *The Princeton Gazette,* and often checked company records to make sure she hadn't sold any of her ATI stock.

If she ever needs me, I'll be there for her, he had decided long ago, *but she must never know it.*

David noticed his wife's gaffe and steered the conversation back to Scoggins.

"I remember warning you not to hire Scoggins. Never trusted him. But I'm glad you didn't listen because apparently he was a great asset. Can you believe I was actually *wrong*? Well, there has to be a first time for everything." David smiled at both of them. "How much has it hurt ATI to lose him?"

"You can't really measure something like that. He was a brilliant manager, absolutely driven. But ATI stock keeps going up anyway and Tilly's doing a great job running the ACIP division now." These days, Pete was getting quite proficient at changing the subject. "You two know she's finally getting married, don't you? I met him last week. Pleasant guy. He's not good enough for her, but nobody is as far as I'm concerned."

I wish I could tell them everything.

After about a year of remission, Pete's tics were starting to return. A few months past the murder he had found himself at peace, feeling very little guilt over the act itself, reasoning that he'd killed Scoggins to help humankind. In a strange way, he had come to view the murder as an act of heroism, not cowardice. But this rationalization was starting to wear thin.

Worse yet, recalling his hallucinations on the day he had killed Scoggins, Pete was starting to wonder if he was sound. Recently he had been devouring books about mental ailments and suspected he might have Intermittent Delusionary Disorder or some other dementia. IDD seemed the most likely culprit, but Pete couldn't think of any way to get tested without confessing.

Even here in public, Pete was rocking more and sometimes his tongue protruded ever so slightly. He knew why; he was honest by nature and the lying was starting to bother him. Especially as everyone else with whom he came in contact seemed to get progressively more honest; the ACIP was still confined to the legal system, but its existence cut a wide psychological swath. It seemed as though it was always there in the background, like a conscience.

Diana had once referred to the Truth Machine as "a giant electronic Santa Claus for adults; everyone believes in it and it knows who's been naughty or nice."

The ACIP was already having subtle, mostly positive

effects on the way all people interacted, but Pete found himself excluded from that phenomenon. So he felt less worthy.

I'm becoming more like Charles Scoggins every day.

Alone in their hotel later, Diana bemoaned her thoughtlessness. "I can't believe I said that! I practically told him he was weird."

"You were talking about Charles Scoggins, not Pete. In fact, Haywood Thacker told me something so private I really shouldn't even repeat it."

Diana's curiosity was piqued. "So are you going to tell me or not?"

"When they finally searched Scoggins's house, guess what they found."

"I can't imagine."

"His virtual reality unit was the kind specially made for kinky sex."

Diana's eyes widened. "Like the machines they put in hotel rooms for watching VR movies?"

David grinned. "No comparison. The hotel units are never quite X-rated. Scoggins's machine was really hardcore. Whips and chains, leather, the works. We'll never know, but I can just imagine him going home every night, having sex with, say, Marilyn Monroe—while Sharon Stone tied him up and abused him with a riding crop."

Diana laughed. "Knowing Scoggins, I bet he did a cost-benefit analysis. Probably decided virtual sex was more efficient than having real relationships."[19]

"And a whole lot cheaper!"

Diana was silent a moment. "But Pete's getting pretty strange himself. I'm sure he knows we've noticed."

---

[19] Scoggins may also have avoided relationships because he was a careful and habitual criminal, a fact of which the Wests were not yet aware. Scoggins couldn't afford to let his guard down. Before the Truth Machine, a high percentage of crimes were solved when perpetrators were turned in by former spouses and lovers.

"He's probably still carrying a torch for you, my sweet—not that I blame him." But they both knew it was no longer true. He kissed her gently.

"No, seriously. He's been acting so nervous lately. The rocking's coming back; if we hadn't been out in public today, it might've been worse than ever. And I don't think he has any friends at all except for Tilly and us and maybe a few people at ATI."

"Look, Diana, he's always been an introvert and he puts himself under intense pressure. The important thing is for us to be there for him when he needs us—to be as supportive to him as he's been to us. I hope he knows we'd do anything for him."

"I'm just worried, that's all."

"Me too. I can't explain why, but lately I've been terrified for him."

CHAPTER 35

THE MANDATE

Falls Church, Virginia
November 7, 2028—Latest polls suggest a surprising turn in tomorrow's presidential elections, with Senator David West trailing President Matthew Emery by nearly four percentage points.—New federal laws go into effect, allowing scips for employment and for college and private school admissions interviews. Analysts project a $200 billion increase in ATI's annual revenues during the first year. An ATI spokesman says the company will offer leases to businesses and schools, but has no plans to sell ACIPs outright.—The first fatal automobile accident in the United States in over 14 months occurs in Ann

Arbor, Michigan. The accident, involving 571 cars, happens as a result of a simultaneous electrical storm and solar flash, short-circuiting both parallel-process computer systems that control all automobiles within a three-square-mile area. Seven persons are killed, including two small children who were traveling alone and were struck by other cars after leaving their vehicles. Over 200 injuries are also reported, mostly superficial cuts and bruises. Secretary of Transportation Nancy Corbin says she is considering asking Congress to raise the legal age of unaccompanied transport to eight. Most experts consider the measure unnecessary and some predict there will be no more traffic accidents in the United States.

The Princeton Gazette, now issued daily, maintained a staff of 16 reporters, all of whom were committed to other stories. Circulation approached 150,000 even though it covered strictly New Jersey news. Since former New Jersey Governor Michael Albanese was Emery's vice-presidential running mate and would in all probability become Vice President Elect, Jennifer Finley decided to make the trip to Virginia and cover the election herself.

She hoped Emery would lose. Although she hadn't kept in touch with the Wests since her breakup with Pete, she admired David and was sure he'd make a fine president.

As for Pete, her feelings for him were still jumbled. She had loved him more than she'd ever loved anyone, but knew she was in over her head from the beginning; leaving him had almost been a relief. He had so much power over her that she'd almost lost herself entirely to the relationship, yet he didn't seem to need her at all. Pete's work had always come first, and when she had the chance, she had never protested; she'd simply smiled and acted as if everything was fine, often lying to hide her pain. She thought of all the times Pete had unintentionally hurt her—and how she had never allowed herself to show it.

Jennifer used to blame him, but had come to realize that Pete needed someone stronger than she could ever be around him, a woman who could confront him. It was time for her to find someone else to love—someone with whom she could be her true self. But she had learned a lot from Pete. Watching him had taught her how to focus her mind on a task and to block out distractions until she achieved it. This skill had served her well, fostering confidence and professional growth. She even speculated that the ACIP might force her to be more honest in her next love relationship, making it more sustainable. She hoped so and wished Pete well.

"No regrets" was no longer quite the lie it had been when she'd written that ridiculously magnanimous goodbye note.

In 2028 the ACIP was still used mainly in the court system, although Congress had also approved it for customs, immigration, food and drug testing and inspection, and several other government functions. But the inevitability of its invasion into other areas was becoming obvious. The ACIP was already popular; few voters sided against widening its use. Even then, its effects were impressively positive—far beyond even the most optimistic predictions of just a few years earlier. Savings in court costs had exceeded projections by over 30 percent, but those savings were dwarfed by the benefit of forcing lawyers (who had previously tended to be among the most intelligent and least productive members of American society) to redirect their energies to more worthwhile areas.

And the virtual elimination of crime was by far the greatest godsend of all.

Unfortunately there were also costs. Over the previous two years, the Department of Health had recognized 274

ACIP-related suicides in America. Although Pete realized the ACIP's benefits far outweighed its detriments, he agonized over these deaths, and suspected the true toll was many times higher. *Most people who commit suicide because of the ACIP,* he believed, *would try to make their deaths appear accidental. The individuals most likely to succumb are those who have secrets they can't cope with revealing; people who care what others think of them, but who have made terrible mistakes.*

He also lamented that the number of suicides would surely mushroom as ACIP usage spread.

President Matthew Emery had come back from a 24-point deficit in the polls and was now a strong favorite to win reelection. Yet he could take no credit himself.

My opponent just about handed me the election.

Gathered with family, friends, and supporters at the Newt Gingrich Auditorium just a few miles from his boyhood home, Emery intended to enjoy the evening, make himself available to the press for several hours, and get a good night's sleep. The next morning he planned to return to monitor early results, and later in the day, give his victory speech.

How could David West have been so dumb? Emery asked himself. *He had the hearts of the American people in the palm of his hand, until he insisted on making World Government the major issue of his campaign. World Government! Now there's a no-win issue. People want to hear about defense, the economy, and funding of scientific research, not World Government.*

Yet everywhere he went, David West had raised the issue, insisting it was the key to the survival of humanity.

At their final debate, David had argued, "Every day the world gets smaller and the human race becomes more vulnerable to technology we've created. Violence and wars continue all around us. Weapons become more deadly and more plentiful. Yet we have the opportunity to fashion this planet into one democracy. If we don't do it within the next 20 years, I doubt we'll ever stop the forces that threaten our existence. War has been illegal since the UN passed Resolution #2019A on March 17, 2013. Now, 15 years later, that law is simply ignored. How can we enforce the rule of law against those whom we're powerless to arrest? And without the rule of law, how long can the human race survive?"

Not that West is necessarily wrong, Emery thought. He believed in the concept too, just on a slower track.

His rebuttal was persuasive. "I agree we must use our influence to push for World Government, but I think my opponent wants it too fast. It would be less dangerous to allow 30 years rather than 20. We're talking about the biggest political undertaking in history. There will be fewer problems and far less resistance if we don't rush it."

Emery's honestly held position came across as moderate, and to many, David's stance now appeared dogmatic and radical. David's miscalculation had been one of the greatest strokes of luck in Matthew Emery's long political career. Or so Emery thought.

But David had a method to his madness. He had calculated that a mandate for a 20-year schedule for conversion to World Government was worth risking the election; he was only 43 years old and if he lost, he would be back in four years. Furthermore, he believed that people trusted him more than they trusted Emery. In spite of the polls, he had faith that when it came time to cast their ballots, the people would elect him. Just in case it might make a difference, he stayed up all night, campaigning and giving interviews to as many journalists as he could.

As soon as the voting began, Emery and his friends realized they had a problem. The first results came from three eastern states expected to support Emery, and West was leading with over 53 percent of the vote. Matthew Emery conceded the election at 10:03 a.m. on November 8, 2028. West eventually carried every state except Virginia. It was the biggest upset in a national election since 1948.

David West had his mandate.

CHAPTER 36

THE AMNESTY LAWS

Dallas, Texas

May 16, 2031—President David West signs the International Free Speech Bill into law. The bill pledges United States support of efforts to enforce freedom of speech and a free press throughout the world. It also budgets $620 billion over five years to enhance the Worldwide Satellite Communications Network. The WSCN allows any person with a computer, radio, or television to receive programs in their own language from any broadcaster in the world. West hails the legislation as "a giant step toward world democracy. Strengthening the WSCN is the most efficient way to assure that entire populations will no longer be manipulated toward violence by the propaganda of local tyrants."—Dr. Robert Steinberg, the renowned Dartmouth Dept. of Psychology researcher, announces that his team has devised a series of questions, which if asked during scip, can diagnose virtually all known forms of mental illness. They have also formulated successful treatments using ACIP therapy for several such illnesses. Steinberg's work, widely praised, is expected to revolutionize the field of mental health.— Pursuant to the terms of the Amnesty Bill enacted several weeks ago, over 56 million individuals have already confessed to crimes committed prior to January 1, 2031, mostly misdemeanors and white-collar offenses.—Serial *killer Carlos Francisco confesses during an employment-interview scip in Fortaleza, Brazil; the 28-year-old doctoral student is believed responsible for over 75,000 nanomachine-induced deaths in four countries, making him the most prolific serial killer in history. According to Interpol chief Rajiv Singh, nearly all the deaths had previously been ruled as being from natural causes. Francisco was studying computer science and nanotechnology at Université de Provence, in Aix-en-Provence, France. Coincidentally, while addressing the UN General Assembly only last month, Singh referred to the prospect of a serial killer with nanotechnology expertise as "utterly chilling."*

Once upon a time, the tale goes, a man was sentenced to death by the king.

"Wait!" he cried. "If you delay my sentence by six months, I'll teach your horse to talk."

The king agreed.

Later that day the man's wife asked him, "Why would you make such an offer? You can't possibly teach a horse how to talk."

"Well," he answered, "I figure a lot can happen in six months. There could be a revolution and a new king. Or the king could get sick and die. Or the king could change his mind. Or the horse could die. Or I could die. Or maybe the horse *will* talk."

Pete Armstrong read the new Amnesty Bill and considered the implications. If he turned himself in for Scoggins's murder now, the court would probably sentence him to jail time, maybe 10 to 12 years, or declare him insane and order him to undergo treatment; either way, he would *not* be executed. But if he waited and his crime was discovered, any judge would be obliged to sentence him to death.

In the latter part of the 20th century, the famous UCLA sociologist James Q. Wilson wrote, "What most needs explanation is not why some people are criminals, but why most people are not." Wilson's assumption was eloquently stated, popular, and false.

A few decades later, the introduction of the ACIP into American society created an unprecedented self-image crisis. Virtually all Americans had previously considered themselves honest and law-abiding. Once the ACIP entered the equation, it became clear that this had almost always been a rationalization.

In fact, we now know that nearly every adult alive prior to the ACIP, technically speaking, was not just a liar, but also a criminal (i.e. nearly everyone had committed at least one crime during his or her life). Most were guilty of minor offenses such as traffic violations, underage drinking, illegal drug usage, minor tax evasion, cheating on expense reports, that sort of thing. Violent, relentless, or hard-core criminals comprised but a tiny percentage of the population.

The Amnesty Laws weren't designed to help solve crimes; thanks to the ACIP, solving crimes was no longer a problem. The real purpose of the new laws was to deal with all the previous crimes being uncovered and to help prevent serious crimes in the future.

The ACIP had already rendered moot the right to avoid self-incrimination as guaranteed under the Fifth Amendment of the Constitution. I won't go into the political mess that created at the time; suffice it to say it was an emotional, historically divisive issue. Americans still had the right not to testify against themselves in court, but so what? Most licensing applications were now administered under scip. In order to receive licenses to operate machinery, carry firearms, visit other countries, or receive many other privileges, applicants were legally required to confess any crimes committed after April 30, 2006, the date the Truth Machine Bill was enacted. It was becoming virtually impossible to exist in American society without confessing all.

Each week, millions of pre-ACIP crimes, mostly non-violent white-collar offenses, were discovered in the course of everyday scipping for licensing, commerce, and other application processes. Nearly all these infractions had been committed by people who wouldn't consider breaking the law now that they were sure to be caught. For example, before the ACIP, some 40 percent of Americans cheated on taxes to some degree. By 2031 the number had fallen to .061 percent.

Since very few of these offenders remained a threat to society, the three principal goals of the Amnesty Laws were (1) to encourage pre-ACIP criminals to turn themselves in for relatively mild punishment, usually just a nominal fine or reparations to any victims, (2) to minimize the stigma associated with pre-ACIP crimes, and (3) to discourage future lawlessness through the threat of more severe penalties, especially for violent crimes.

During the first six years of the ACIP's existence, astounding advances had been made in the field of criminology. Many misconceptions about criminal motivation were cleared up and unimaginably useful statistics compiled. The most important finding was that as long as criminals believed there were reasonable prospects for getting away with their crimes, the length of a prison sentence had almost no effect on its deterrent value. For example, a 15-year prison sentence had less than 10 percent more deterrent power than a five-year sentence. (The threat of a sure death penalty was several times more effective at preventing a crime than a prison sentence of any length.)

The knowledge of certain and timely discovery through the use of the ACIP was by far the strongest deterrent. So powerful, in fact, that without any other changes in the law, criminal activity in the United States had diminished by an average of at least 97 percent since its introduction.[20]

Legislators hoped that the Amnesty Laws would wipe out the remaining three percent.

The Laws provided that anyone who confessed before January 1, 2032, for crimes committed prior to March 1, 2031, would receive less severe punishment, often no punishment at all. Nobody who so confessed would ever be subject to the death penalty. But anyone whose crime was discovered *after* this deadline would receive a much more severe sentence, including a mandatory death penalty for attempted murder, kidnapping, or murder. Perceived profit in such criminal activity was now virtually eliminated. It was easy to calculate, based on thousands of ACIP debriefings of convicted criminals, that mandatory capital punishment, if enforced against attempted murderers, kidnappers, or first-time murderers, would save more money and lives than it cost. After the bill was enacted, serious crime, for all practical purposes, became a thing of the past.

Pete thought about discussing his situation with an attorney. Attorneys and priests could still maintain confidentiality in such matters. But retaining David or Diana would be tricky. First of all, as President and First Lady of the United States, they were concerned with matters far more crucial to society than Pete's personal dilemma. Also, as ATI shareholders, they had been direct beneficiaries of some of Pete's crimes. No, he would definitely *not* burden either of his friends with his predicament.

---

[20] This measurement is based on reported crimes, so 97 percent may be a significant understatement. However, a large part of that reduction was due to the ACIP's contribution to timely discovery and treatment of mental illness, not just deterrence of criminal activity.

He'd also read of instances where attorneys (and priests for that matter) had let their clients' confidentially confessed transgressions slip out. Such inadvertent disclosures were rare, but did occur. He decided, *There's no need to risk involving another person; I'm well aware of all the laws. I can advise myself.*

Pete weighed the pluses and minuses of turning himself in by year's end.

On the plus side was the inescapable numerical logic of the situation. At only 41, FutureHealth had predicted that with his genetics, he could expect to live another 52 years. His goal for the remainder of his life was to work toward the halting and eventual reversal of the aging process. Pete believed he could speed the discovery curve by at least the number of years he contributed to the endeavor.

If I don't turn myself in, he reasoned, *ATI will have a monopoly on the Truth Machine for the 19 years left on our special patent. After that, there'll be competing Truth Machines I won't be able to fool, and my crime will be discovered on my first non-ACIP scip. In 19 years, my life will probably be over.*

A 12-year prison term would leave him 40 years of freedom, give or take, before death or cryonic suspension. Therefore he could at least double his non-incarcerated lifespan by turning himself in. That didn't count the 12 years in prison during which he could still do good work.

Finally, once he neared the end of his natural life, he could be cryonically frozen to await the eventual success of aging reversal to which he'd have contributed.

At worst, I'd be trading no more than 12 years of freedom for about 30 extra years of life and an opportunity for immortality.

But if I surrender, I'll go to jail now and possibly lose control of ATI.

On the minus side were his vanity and some wishful thinking. His reputation would be destroyed, his enemies overjoyed at the revelation. Worse yet, he would disappoint his friends and colleagues. He thought about David and Diana and Tilly. *How could I ever face them again?*

His mind jumped to Jennifer Finley, now married and expecting her first child. He had watched proudly as her career had continued to blossom and took bittersweet solace in the fact that she did indeed seem better off without him. *How would she feel after learning she wasted almost two years of her life with a criminal?*

Worst of all, what would he tell his parents? Ed and Liza Armstrong were both in their early eighties and healthy. Their medical profiles suggested they should both wait at least another 10 years before considering cryonic suspension. Only last May, he had finally convinced them to move to Dallas. *I couldn't possibly tell them I'm a murderer.*

On top of all that, during the 19 remaining years of ATI's Truth Machine monopoly, a lot of things could happen. There could be a new government. Or the Amnesty Laws could change again. Or ATI's monopoly might be extended. Or he might figure out how to fool a new, non-ATI Truth Machine.

The horse *might* talk.

CHAPTER 37

SMALLER, FASTER, CHEAPER

Dallas, Texas
November 4, 2032—President David West wins reelection by the largest margin in the history of United States two-party presidential politics. West and his wife, Dr.

Diana Hsu West, pledge to work 365 days a year toward establishing with all nations a firm timetable for the installation of a single democratic World Government by the year 2048.—With their first execution in seven months, the Chinese government electrocutes An Tse Fong, the Taiwanese terrorist who had planned to annihilate Shanghai with a powerful nuclear grenade. Fong's plan was discovered during a customs scip on December 14, 2031. Most experts now believe that without the ACIP, Fong would have succeeded, and that by allowing exports of ACIPs, the U.S. Congress saved over 40 million Chinese from death or critical injury.— The United States Parenting Department issues a report showing that one year after the ACIP was approved for use by private individuals, the divorce rate in the United States, after a temporarily frightening increase, has fallen to below pre-ACIP levels. The USPD also releases a study concluding that honesty tends to strengthen marriages more than tact or discretion.— Commerce Secretary Timothy Lindvall predicts it will take 20 years for most other nations to catch up with productivity gains realized by the United States during its five-year head start in ACIP usage. Exports of ACIPs were not legalized until 2029.

"What good is a monopoly if you keep slashing prices?" Whatley asked, irritated. He didn't see the point of making the ACIP smaller *and* lowering the price. Enough people would buy a new ACIP just because it would now fit conveniently into a briefcase. He figured, *Why give away money?*

Pete sighed, and warned, "If we act too much like a monopoly, there'll be consequences."

Tilly couldn't help noticing Pete's rocking had been getting worse. *How long can he go on like this, trying to save the world single-handedly?*

"I'm not saying we should ignore public opinion," she said, "but we can't pander to it either. We can't be all things to all people. We're the most benevolent company on earth as it is, and some people *still* hate us."

"Because we're so successful. There's no way to avoid jealousy when you make the kind of money we're making. That's why we need to take the high road." Preferring to persuade rather than issue a direct order, Pete tried to construct a case to his colleagues on their own terms. "Besides, our costs keep falling and our profit on marginal sales is still over 40 percent. We'll probably sell twice as many units at the lower price and make just as much money. It won't cost us anything and it'll be great for our image. Do you realize how much good press we'll get?" He switched the argument into Whatley's marketing jargon. "We always get great bits for lowering prices when we don't have to."

Williams interjected, "But we'll need to add more manufacturing capacity and labor, and it won't bring any more money to the bottom line. If we have any problems, there'll be hell to pay from Merrill Lynch and our other outside shareholders. I'm not sure it's worth the risk."

Pete smiled faintly. "It is to me, Leslie. It's worth it just to get the ACIP into more people's hands. I don't think a person should need to be rich to have one."

It's ironic that he believed so strongly in the benefits of a technology from which he had contrived to exclude himself. He was utterly convinced that the ACIP was the salvation of humanity.

Yet not everything the ACIP did was beneficial.

People had resisted the ACIP at first. The loss of privacy was hard for humans to get used to. It is easy to forget that during the first few years, many of you maintained that you would gladly trade your new-found security and prosperity for the privacy of old. Authors even wrote books on how to dance around scip questions, until ATI had issued simple instructions, known as the "Thacker Guidelines," on how to entrap evasive answerers. At the beginning, many tried to find ways to overcome or fool the machine. Fortunately, none succeeded.

Also, during the previous three years there had been 12,014 confirmed ACIP-related suicides in the United States alone, mostly people who had lost their jobs or their marriages after confessing dishonesty.

(Note: As a whole, however, the suicide rate declined over that period, suggesting that the ACIP might have prevented more suicides than it caused.—22g CP)

There had been serious abuses, too. Some companies, when scipping job applicants, would ask irrelevant and personal questions. There were even occasional discoveries of hidden ACIPs, which was illegal (and less than 100-percent effective; many of you are immune to a scip when unaware of it).

But like the automobile and the telephone, both of which had been similarly controversial, the overall effect on society was astoundingly positive. After a few years people were no more willing to give up their ACIPs than to stop using medicines or junk their computers. Soon the advantages the Truth Machine had bestowed upon the American people were incalculable, even with limited usage. As the ACIP gained acceptance for other purposes and spread across the globe, its benefits increased exponentially in new and unimagined ways.

For example, in October 2031, President West had submitted his Fair Lobbying Act to Congress. It passed intact. The bill required lobbyists to ask clients, under scip, for both sides of any issue they were retained to argue, including all known information detrimental to their position, and legislators and their aides were now legally bound to demand similar disclosure from lobbyists. This important principle, today a bedrock of your legislative system, couldn't have worked without the ACIP.

Environmental safety was another area where the Truth Machine produced extraordinary benefits for humanity. Prior to the ACIP, the ecological sciences had become a proverbial Tower of Babel, with environmentalists and industry each justifiably suspicious of the other's self-serving science. Almost overnight, the ACIP had brought new credibility to both sides, ushering in a new era of cooperation and earth-awareness.

But as the machine improved the human condition, Pete believed he now personally suffered by comparison. His few friends and many colleagues, in fact all those around him, were uniformly candid and honest with him, while he considered himself to be about as sincere as a 20th-century tobacco company executive.

I was right about you all along, Pete, Charles Scoggins whispered from the grave.

Pete realized that he had been given many chances for redemption, and every time he'd failed to take one, his situation had worsened. He could have simply refused to use the Renaissance algorithms, or better yet, made a deal with Renaissance Corporation to license it from them. *Hell,* he thought, *I probably could have bought their whole company for $50 or $60 billion, if only I hadn't let Scoggins trick me into believing the deal couldn't be done.*

Even after he had covertly reprogrammed the ACIP, he still could have avoided killing Scoggins by confessing his crimes to the authorities. At that point he probably could have retained nearly everything that mattered most to him. *Was it my mental distress or IDD that prevented me from turning us both in—or was it my pride? Did I murder him just because I couldn't accept the world ever learning that I was a criminal?*

When he had killed Scoggins, his options decreased. Even then he had spurned the opportunity to confess under terms of the Amnesty Laws. Unfortunately, that option had expired 10 months ago.

Although there was nothing he could do to change the circumstances, he did attempt to assuage his conscience. He gave almost all his ATI dividends to charities—over $5 billion in 2031, and double that amount so far in 2032 with another quarterly check to go. He set up a $50 billion venture capital fund to finance promising businesses in medicine and education. He continued to volunteer his time to government software projects. And he insisted that all ATI business practices be above reproach; the best interests of employees and customers took precedence over those of its shareholders, of which he was by far the largest.

These were hardly sacrifices for Pete. In fact they often increased his wealth. For example, despite price-reduction of the ACIP (or possibly because of it), the market had multiplied so that in 2032 the division was on track to earn over $70 billion after taxes.

ATI's profit was a staggering sum, but insignificant compared with the ACIP's true value to society. Virtual elimination of crime and increased efficiencies in government and industry had caused the standard of living in the United States to skyrocket. Personal income (adjusted for inflation) had already increased by 168 percent since 2024, mostly as a direct result of the ACIP. And the machine's benefits would accelerate for years.

Already used in virtually every business in America, the ACIP's home market, at 11-percent penetration, was also expanding rapidly. Potential overseas figures for the ACIP had already been reflected in ATI's stock price, now 39 times last year's earnings. According to *Fortune* magazine, by January 2032, 16 of the 17 greatest personal fortunes in America had been created from ATI stock. And Pete Armstrong's holdings were over 13 times greater than those of any other ATI stockholder.

Pete received more press coverage than any person on the planet, most of it positive; his reclusiveness only added to his mystique. Not quite 43 years old, he was the most eligible bachelor on earth, yet he rarely dated. He was the most admired businessman in the world, yet he despised himself. Pete may have been the most intelligent human being on the face of the planet, yet increasingly often he thought, *I am the lowest form of life.*

CHAPTER 38

DIPLOMACY

Beijing, China, and Paris, France
*September 15, 2035—The day before President West's
scheduled visit to Beijing, China implies it might not
ratify the World Government Initiative unless the voting
system is redesigned. Chinese Premier Yeung complains
that the system unfairly favors those nations with the
smallest populations.—The Justice Department releases
projections that the number of criminals executed in the
United States in 2035 will fall below 1,000 for the first
time since Swift and Sure was enacted in 2005.*

"Please accept this token of the special friendship between our two countries, the two most generous nations
on earth."

President David West presented Premier Lee Sun
Yeung with the first handheld ACIP unit to leave United
States soil. For several weeks China had been the only
country outside North America authorized to receive ship-
ments of ACIPs when exports had been legalized in 2029,
a fact of which David was anxious to remind Yeung.

The Premier accepted the gift in well-rehearsed, nearly
perfect English. "Allowing China to import these Truth
Machines six years ago was perhaps the greatest act of
kindness ever bestowed upon us by another nation."

In fact the ACIPs, coveted by the Chinese government
for law enforcement, had led to the downfall of China's
most corrupt political leaders. Ironically, many of those
leaders had been the very ones clamoring for early access

to the machines. Yeung himself, innocent of criminal intent but overly trusting of his subordinates, had barely escaped the fallout from a scandal that had cost him two of his closest advisors.

But the benefits the ACIP had brought to most areas of Chinese life were astonishing. Crime was nearly eliminated. Science and industry flourished. The Chinese economy, which had fallen behind that of the United States during the five years that America had an exclusive on the ACIP, had recovered its position as the world's largest. Not to mention the fact that in 2031 the Truth Machine had saved the great city of Shanghai from nuclear catastrophe.

David, Diana, and Premier Yeung were escorted to a garden room where ACIPs and Sun Translator Units had been specially installed. The two machines had revolutionalized diplomacy, virtually eliminating misunderstandings.

Using a combination of persuasion, friendship, cajoling, and thinly veiled threats against certain dictators who opposed it, David West had already received written commitments from every government on earth to submit to World Government if the WGI was ratified by 80 percent of nations representing at least 75 percent of the world's population. But this would not be easy to accomplish, and without China, it would be virtually impossible.

The three sat among flowers and fish ponds in specially made chairs facing each other. Although everyone knew the machines were there, no STUs were visible, and only the red and green ACIP lights could be seen in the left armrest of each chair.

"Premier Yeung," David asked, "how serious are you about withdrawing from the Initiative?"

Yeung could have refused to answer, but that would have been counterproductive. "As long as I am Premier of China, we will ratify the World Government Initiative, even in its present form. But if you don't give us some concession on the voting system, I will have difficulty remaining in office. I think there is only a small chance I would be impeached, but even if not, my ability to make sure the transition goes smoothly could be diminished."

The green light didn't flicker.

David asked him, "What's the least it would take to assure you would remain in control of the process?"

Yeung's answer was evasive, but not deceitful. "If you could move the 'one-person one-vote' date ahead by 35 years to 2090, I am confident that would do it." The light remained green.

Of course that'*d do it*, David thought, *but what's the least it would take?* Still, Yeung's request was not unreasonable. OPOV in 2090 would give smaller nations a disproportionate voice in world politics for the first 45 years of World Government, but would phase in absolute democracy at a faster pace. And at several world summit meetings, David had publicly stated that the 2125 date was only a preliminary estimate for OPOV, subject to further negotiation.

"The problem," David said, "is that if I accede to your request, smaller nations might band together and threaten to withdraw unless we grant each of *them* some sort of concession. Any idea how to avoid that?"

Yeung didn't look at the ACIP lights. He knew that West had already been test-scipped by his staff on every conceivable declaration he might make today. Even in 2035, few people bothered to look at their ACIP lights anymore. Just knowing the subject was aware of the ACIP was enough to instill confidence.[21]

Diana interrupted. "May I suggest something?"

Both men nodded.

"Some nations fear they might lose their autonomy in a World Government and don't want to be overwhelmed

---

[21] Except if the subject was under seven years old. Until wristband ACIPs became affordable several years later, very few small children could be trained to be uniformly truthful.

by the voting power of giants like China." This statement was true of course, but rather tactfully expressed. In fact, many government leaders hated the idea of giving up their power at all and resisted World Government any way they could. But without the ability to lie, politicians could offer their electorates no acceptable arguments for delay.

"It's an important goal of the Initiative," Diana continued, "that large blocs of voters must not be manipulated by national governments into voting for programs they don't really understand. The representative democracy of the United States has rarely decided national issues by referendum; its voters elect *legislators* to represent their interests. While far from perfect, the U.S. government has turned out to be the most successful political experiment in history and has lasted almost two and a half centuries for just this reason. Fortunately, we have similar checks and balances in the WGI; elections of representatives will be much like our national elections. But there will be more frequent world referendums than there have ever been in the United States."

Diana continued, "As long as China still agrees that OPOV must include 'issue testing,'[22] I think the timetable could be moved ahead, at least to the year 2100. That's regarded as a long way off and most countries view absolute democracy as a goal anyway. When we put it to a vote by country, you could call in some favors and so could we. We'd present it as a matter of fairness, rather than as a specific request from the world's wealthiest and most populous nation. I suspect moving OPOV up to 2090 would make it much more difficult to get the votes we'd need, and we sure don't want to give anyone an excuse to drop out. But I'm confident we could enact with OPOV in 2100 if China would guarantee not to press for further concessions."

[22] "Issue testing" provides that, as a precondition to voting in any referendum, voters must take a test to prove that they understand both sides of the issue being voted on.

"That's only 10 more years," David added, joking, "a mere nanosecond in the cosmic equation."

Yeung smiled. "Would you both be willing to spend a few days touring our country and talking about the World Government Initiative? Here in China, your first lady is the most famous and popular of all Americans. I think it might make a difference."

The green light held steady, since his uncertainty had been properly expressed.

"We'd be honored."

"And I will agree to your suggestion."

The meeting had been choreographed over the previous few days, but the negotiations themselves, which might have taken years without the ACIP, lasted less than three minutes.

As much as the ACIP had already transformed the science of negotiation in politics, it had done even more for business. On the same day in Paris, Tilly negotiated a licensing agreement to bundle ACIPs into software packages for briefcase-sized supercomputers. The negotiation was so important that she attended in person rather than talking via holographic image.

She met with Peureux et Cie, the largest French integrated computer firm, and negotiated directly with Chloe Peureux, daughter of the founder.

Each began by formally declaring, "I have reviewed and now understand all of my company's calculations, and have confirmed both their accuracy and objectivity using scip and Thacker Guidelines on all parties involved. I am aware of no undisclosed facts that could affect either company." Since they each held important positions, there was no possibility that any facts could have been withheld from them by their own people, especially with ACIPs universally in use.

"We've calculated the value and related costs and are

willing to pay as much as $220 annually per unit, if necessary," Peureux told Tilly.

"One of your competitors offered us $172, but you have much better name recognition, which will help sell more units," Tilly revealed. "Therefore ATI is willing to sell Peureux the rights for as little as $126, if necessary."

Since Peureux's costs were higher than ATI's, they agreed to include the difference in their compromise. The process took about 90 seconds. They settled on an annual fee of $167 per unit.

Prior to the ACIP, little of that information would have been disclosed. Worse yet, any information offered might not have been true and often wasn't believed even if it were true. The buyer would start low, the seller would start high (the exact opposite of today's method), and both would attempt to meet in the middle—eventually. The final price might have been the same, but the haggling would often take months or years, the legal fees could be astronomical, and the likelihood of a deal ever being made would be far less.

Today's meeting between Tilly and Peureux was (and remains) typical of scip-expedited business negotiations. Prior to the Truth Machine era, deal-making was so time-consuming that most potential transactions were never discussed in the first place.

When business scips were first legalized, many companies had refused to divulge proprietary information. But those firms quickly discovered that companies who played by the new rules of free disclosure were capturing most of the market. Nearly all the hold-outs reconsidered. Those who didn't adjust lost market share or went out of business.

The volume of successfully consummated transactions rose exponentially, to the great benefit of every nation's economy. Wealth was being created at a rate unprecedented in human history, and poverty had been virtually eliminated from the planet.

CHAPTER 39

RETIREMENT

Washington DC
January 20, 2037—Genzyme Corporation announces a successfully tested genetic therapy for all allergic reactions. The regimen, to be marketed under the name Histamex, consists of individually engineered histamine and immune response blockers delivered through the bloodstream by millions of self-replicating nanomachines, each about one-fifth the size of a human cell. The machines were also designed to help repair tissue damaged by allergies. Genzyme reports that Histamex therapy has also proven effective against most forms of arthritis. FDA approval is expected to be granted, as usual, within three days of the announcement.—Former Vice President Caroline Whitcomb is inaugurated as the first female President of the United States. In her address, she pledges to "steadfastly uphold the policies and principles of the greatest leader of our time, President David West."

David West had served two four-year terms, during which America and the rest of the world experienced unprecedented economic growth and increased satisfaction with nearly every aspect of life. He had delivered on all his major promises to the American people, and at the end of his presidency his approval rating was over 90 percent. He had chosen his own successor, a woman regarded as a brilliant leader.

By almost any measure, he had enjoyed an astoundingly successful presidency, but did not take credit for his success.

In his farewell address on January 19, 2037, President West thanked Diana, "my wife, my partner, the love of my life." He commended the leaders of every nation for their support of the World Government Initiative which, to the world's amazement, had been ratified while David was still in office. He also offered high praise to his Vice President, now President-elect Caroline Whitcomb, daughter of former Treasury Secretary and presidential candidate Audrey Whitcomb, the first person for whom David had ever voted—32 years earlier.

But he saved his kindest words for Pete.

"Diana and I urge the world to recognize with gratitude our best friend, Randall Petersen Armstrong, the genius whose invention may have made the difference between the unprecedented improvement of the human condition we've enjoyed, versus our destruction, which might well have already occurred without the ACIP.

"Today my biggest regret is that I didn't try to persuade Congress to allow exports of ACIPs sooner. I wish I'd been more forceful in my efforts, but as an ATI stockholder, I didn't want to appear as though I were lobbying for my own profit."

In retrospect, David was so well trusted even in the mid-2020s that few would have doubted his sincerity, but he hadn't realized that at the time.

He continued, "My timid lack of action cost the rest of the world several years of the most beneficial invention ever created. I consider it my worst mistake. Still, all in all, I'm delighted with the way things turned out.

"At the beginning of the Truth Machine era, some were afraid that Pete's invention might destroy a privacy we all took for granted. In a way they were right, but their fears missed the point. Now that we understand human nature more clearly, it is apparent how dangerous our situation was. No longer can we enjoy the same privacies while preserving safety for the human race. Privacy indulges secrecy, and it is secrecy that now most imperils our survival.

"The only reasonable alternative to privacy is openness, which must always be a two-way street. If I access your archives, you should know that you're being scrutinized, and that I'm the one who's doing it. And you must receive equal entry to my archives as well. That's *openness*, not surveillance. Otherwise our society could become totalitarian, like the realm depicted in George Orwell's novel, *1984*."

Finally David asked his constituency to practice this openness in their daily lives. "There are no laws requiring you to answer any question as long as you're willing to accept the consequences of the refusal. When your teenage son or daughter asks if you've always been faithful to your spouse, or if you cheated on your taxes before the Truth Machine was introduced, you're not required to reply. But I know that, were I fortunate enough to have a child, I'd let her scip me and would always respond openly to such questions, regardless of the answer. It's far easier to forgive imperfection than lack of candor."

That phrase struck Pete like an arrow piercing his soul. He sat directly behind David and received a standing ovation when introduced to the crowd. He was pleased and proud, but also felt sick at heart.

In his tormented imagination, he heard Charles Scoggins's scornful laughter. *Ha! What would they think if they knew the so-called savior of the human race was really a murderer and a liar?*

Immediately after Whitcomb's inauguration, Pete and David attended a service at one of Washington DC's many Unitarian churches. They had heard that Reverend Dr. Asia Jonas, the famous minister, would be conducting the service, so they decided to drop in unannounced. One Secret Service agent accompanied them, though he wasn't needed; there were fewer than 500 murders in the United States in 2037 and hardly any were premeditated. The Steinberg mental illness tests had identified nearly all potential killers and allowed them to be successfully treated.

(Note: Based on what we know today, it is safe to say that any premeditated murderer in modern society is insane.—22g CP)

The tests only took 180 seconds to conduct and had been incorporated into the National Licensing Regulations seven months earlier. They were now a necessary precondition for government service, education, employment in most fields, and to obtain licenses for, among other things, firearms purchase, parenting, and driving.

Pete had taken the Steinberg tests many times, always invoking "O Captain, My Captain."

It is debatable whether Unitarianism should be considered a "religion" at all. Many believe it is an organization of worshippers, each with his or her own personal faith.[23]

Either way, the Unitarian Universalist Association had been the first religious organization to embrace the ACIP. Recently other churches had been forced to follow suit. Although most religious leaders sincerely believed, there were hypocrites and charlatans of all denominations who used religious dogma to manipulate others. After the ACIP, their discovery invariably led to crises of confidence among that religion's clergy and laity. But Unitarian leaders passed scips more consistently than those of other faiths, since Unitarianism espoused no dogma other than human kindness and respect. Any opinions about the nature or existence of God and humankind's relationship

---

[23] The old joke went: "What do you get when you cross a Unitarian Universalist with a Jehovah's Witness? Someone who knocks on your door for no apparent reason." And on August 11, 2011, Rev. Jonas herself said, "Referring to Unitarianism as a 'religion' would be like calling the United States Congress a 'team.' "

with its Creator were automatically acceptable to the denomination. So its leaders had nothing to lie about.

(Note: To paraphrase 20th-century humorist Garrison Keillor, "A Lutheran finds sin everywhere he looks, but to a Unitarian, there's no such thing as sin, only inadequate communication."—22g CP)

Religion or not, Unitarianism offered spiritual nourishment without conditions and without assumptions of unconfirmable truths. By 2036 it had become the most prevalent religious order in America.

Pete loved religious services. He enjoyed the music, especially the hymns. Today's chorale consisted of three "grunge-style" love songs of the 1990s. The works, adapted to the organ and flute from the original music by Pearl Jam and 10,000 Maniacs, were unusual even for a Unitarian chorus; nonetheless, Pete liked the way they sounded. He also liked the feeling of community. But most of all, he appreciated the readings and sermons; even bad sermons, for him, were the best part of the service; he always encountered a slant on life he hadn't considered. Lost in the words and ideas, he could escape his guilt and self-loathing.

Reverend Jonas, 81 years old, was a short, lean, and vibrant woman with long, straight black hair and limpid blue eyes. She was not aware that Pete Armstrong and David West were attending the service until they spoke with her afterward. Her sermon had not been written with them in mind.

Jonas began. "There is an old joke about three statisticians who go hunting for deer with bows and arrows. They spot an old buck. The first one shoots. His arrow misses by two yards to the left. The second statistician's arrow misses by two yards to the right. The third statistician excitedly shouts, 'We *got* him!'"

The congregation broke into a chorus of laughter.

Then, to David and Pete's amazement, her speech evolved into a discussion of the ACIP and World Government.

(Note: The entire text of Jonas's speech is in the Appendix.—22g CP)

The sermon lasted about five minutes. David enjoyed it thoroughly, but for Pete the words were bittersweet. Both were proud of the part they had played in creating this promising new world, but Pete, even in the company of his closest friend, felt more isolated than ever.

Again, Leonard's voice called to him. *I'm waiting for you, Petey.*

He believed both he and the world would be better off if he were dead. Only the traumatic effects his death would have on his parents delayed his suicide.

CHAPTER 40

A BRIGHT NEW WORLD

Dallas, Texas
February 16, 2041—The Department of Health releases statistics showing average life expectancy is now over 100 years in the United States and 96 years worldwide. (For statistical purposes, life ends at death or cryonic suspension, whichever occurs first.) Women still outlive men by an average of four months, but experts predict any difference in longevity between the sexes will disappear entirely within five years.—Scientists at Glaxo-Wellcome announce the beginning of clinical trials for Synapsate, a cure for Alzheimer's disease. If successful, the drug might lead to the first attempted revivifications of cryonically suspended humans within 12 years. In the United States alone, there are 298,655

cryonically suspended Alzheimer's patients who have specified "revivification immediately upon discovery of a cure" in their contracts, which means that they wish to be revived as soon as possible, without waiting for termination of the aging process. The government is holding $1.04 trillion on deposit from those patients, which will be due them upon thawing. President Whitcomb assures the public that this currently amounts to only 40 days' normal cryonic suspension deposit revenues.

The United States presidency and parenthood have much in common. Both entail personal sacrifice, stress, and of course, constant fear. Luckily, genetic programming forces you to succumb to ego and to seek continuity and love. Otherwise no rational person would have ever wanted either job.

For David and Diana, leaving government service had been much akin to parents watching their children, successfully raised and well-adjusted, finally move out of the house. With satisfaction and great relief, they had settled into semi-retirement in Dallas, traveling the world, contributing their time and endorsements to worthy causes, offering their services as diplomats whenever a crisis arose in the World Government Initiative, and visiting family and friends.

Meanwhile Pete remained as tortured and driven as ever. Determined to unlock as many secrets of aging as he could in the few years remaining before his crimes were discovered, he often worked 14-hour days. *At least,* he decided, *I'll give the human race a good head start on its most important scientific goal, prior to my suicide or execution.*

Regardless of their schedules, the three friends made sure they never went a full month without spending at least one evening together, usually alone, but sometimes with Marjorie Tilly. It was the only socializing Pete permitted himself.

* * *

Some 15 months earlier, Pete's father, Ed Armstrong, had been told that his body would expire within a year. Liza Armstrong, 92 and still as healthy as an 80-year-old, decided that if her husband was going to be cryonically suspended, she would be frozen with him.

Pete had accompanied his parents to Guardian Time Warp, the newest cryonic facility in Dallas. They had exchanged loving and tearful goodbyes. He'd planned on confiding his crimes to his parents prior to the freezing, but found himself unable to do so. Along with his sadness Pete had noticed that he also felt a small tinge of relief, which compounded his guilt.

He wondered whether they would ever learn their son was a murderer.

For six months after bidding farewell, Pete had sunk into a depression unlike any he had ever experienced, his emotional torment so oppressive that he had considered ending his life immediately. In fact the more he thought about suicide, the more the idea appealed to him. *Unlike most suicides, if I plan mine properly, I'll thwart my enemies and spare my friends.*

It was the only way he could imagine to prevent the world from learning the truth about what he had done. During those months, his work on aging and his three closest friends, David and Diana and Tilly, were all that had sustained him.

I deserve to die, he'd finally decided, *but suicide will have to wait until I finish my work.*

On the evening of February 16, Pete, Diana, and David relaxed in Pete's living room on a comfortable modern couch, amidst the finest and most coveted 20th-century art: original Maxfield Parrish and Thomas Moran oil paintings, Harriet Frishmuth sculptures, and art nouveau and deco-style furniture and antiques. The vintage Tiffany lamps cast rare indoor shadows whenever the surround-light screens fell below 34.5-percent brightness grade.

Art was Pete's only real extravagance. The world's richest person remained comfortably settled in the same 14-room, 8,500-square-foot house on the same two acres he had purchased in 2009. He liked this familiar residence and found it comfortable. It was good enough for him.

They had requested soft classical music, which now surrounded them as they grazed on food prepared and served by Pete's state-of-the-art automated staff.

"I hear parents are using wristband ACIPs on their children these days," Pete said.

"It's a little strange," Diana responded. "Our nephews Adam and Arlen, Philip's six-year-old twins, would never *think* of telling a lie. They've been scipped since they were four. Their parents don't ever worry about knowing which child broke something."

"I bet Philip wishes *our* mom had an ACIP when we were kids," David added. "I used to blame him for everything! Children were such little con artists and I was genetically gifted in that regard."

All three of them laughed, pondering the strange irony of Bruce Witkowsky's patrimonial contribution to world history.

David resumed his thought. "The best use for those household ACIPs, though, has to be making sure your kids do their homework before you credit their allowance. Can you imagine how smart today's children must be? They never cheat on tests anymore and they always compose their own term papers. Not like when *we* were in grade school, is it, sweetheart?"

Diana smiled. "Speak for yourself."

"You two cheated on tests in school? I can't believe

it!" Pete answered, laughing. "I'm going to call the *World Enquirer* and see what they'll pay for that scoop."

David had been concerned about his friend. He knew Pete had been unhappy and lonely since his parents had been frozen, and was pleased that he seemed so upbeat tonight.

"You're more at ease these days," he said. "The aging research must be going well."

"It is. I think I've finally figured out how to make my contribution."

"Tell us everything," Diana said.

Pete was happy to. "Scientists have made amazing advances in medicine since we were at Harvard. Remember how crude medical science was back then? All our research went into discovering ways to cure diseases and treat trauma."

Diana nodded. "It's hard to remember that far back."

Indeed it was. Briefly her mind flashed to her son Justin. She wondered if they would ever find a cure for Tay-Sachs, thinking, *Maybe not, since it's now 100-percent prevented by automatic nano-screening.*

(Note: There hasn't been a documented case of Tay-Sachs since 2038.—22g CP)

Sensing his wife's mood shift, David tried to distract her. "At least for us mortals."

Pete ignored David's compliment. "Today we know how to cure any microbe- or virus-based disease, and nanomachines can perform just about any operation and repair most injuries without surgery. Over half the people in the world no longer die from injury or illness. They just wear out and expire from old age, and if they're lucky, they get frozen before their minds have deteriorated. So an incredible amount of research has been going into aging; but it hasn't gotten us very far. One important theory's emerged, though." He hesitated, wondering if he was boring them.

"Which is?" David prompted.

"Most scientists now believe that once the process is

halted, whatever damage aging has inflicted on the body will begin to reverse itself automatically."

"How will that work?"

"Aging's mostly a result of cell division. Cell division shortens all the chromosome tips, which are called telomeres. After about 60 divisions, the telomeres fall below critical length and the cells die. The rest of aging springs directly from continuous damage to DNA over time, damage caused mostly at the sub-atomic level. Once the telomeres are restored and the human body stops aging, DNA may begin to repair itself. In other words, a 100-year-old person, after a few years or decades, might regain the body of a 20-year-old. And if that doesn't happen, we're pretty sure we can learn how to reverse any damage through nanotechnology."

Diana laughed. "So when they finally revive David and me from the pods, we won't have to live forever in our 110-year-old, decrepit bodies. . . ."

David grinned and completed the thought, "Jealously despising everyone frozen at a younger age than we were?"

"Probably not." Pete laughed. "Have either of you ever heard of Dr. Leroy Hood?"

"Something to do with DNA research?" Diana said. "That's all I remember."

"It's surprising more people haven't heard of him. In the 1990s, he was kind of like the Henry Ford of genetic research. Hood applied the disciplines of other scientific fields like mechanical engineering, physics, and computer science to the province of biotechnology. He led one project that created a machine that sped up the production of synthetic DNA by a factor of over 100 times. His work hastened our genetic learning curve, probably by almost a decade.

"It allowed scientists to catalog the entire human genome by 2002. It was the most complex scientific project ever attempted—even more than the ACIP and hundreds of times more complicated than sending manned expeditions to the moon and Mars. But compared to understanding and halting the aging process, it was child's play. If we had to physically perform all the tests and experiments required to halt aging, it would tie up every medical researcher on the planet for at least 500 years.

"I'm not a molecular biologist or an inventor, but I have a lot of book knowledge in those areas. And I can apply computer science to any field. So I'm designing computerized models and writing the software for every conceivable genetic experiment. The goal is to teach computers to conduct the experiments in cyberspace. At least that way we can narrow any physical experiments down to ones that actually have promise. If I apply myself completely to this project, I think I can finish the algorithms and models and write the code in 8 to 10 years. After that, considering the way science has been advancing, halting the aging process should take less than 100 years—maybe only 50."

David and Diana were used to visualizing the future, but this concept was amazing. Five hundred years was hard to imagine, but 100 years was barely an average human lifespan. They were both exceptionally healthy, and Pete was now suggesting that anyone still alive 50 years from now might actually live forever without having to risk cryonic suspension. Including them.

David's excitement grew. "Do you remember—of course you do, you remember everything. *I* remember the first day in Theo-Soc class, when Charles Scoggins—"

Pete's shiver went unnoticed.

Diana interrupted, "—said there was a finite chance some of us might live forever."

"As I recall," David added, "he predicted how it would happen. He specifically said that some of us might be cryonically frozen, then revived after the aging process had been medically halted. Poor guy. Too bad he won't be around to see it."

"Yes," Diana said, "it's a terrible shame."
Pete couldn't have agreed with them more.

NEW YORK CITY—February 16, 2041 (the same
evening)

Dr. Maya Gale had nothing against older men; however,
she drew the line at dating married men and didn't particularly care for single, drunk men either.

At 34, Maya was the youngest member of the group
and clearly the most eligible female. All 29 men and 10
women, tired but very pleased, sat in the largest private
room at the Four Seasons restaurant. Over the previous
four years, Maya had been to nine similar banquets,
including the annual Christmas parties. The team rarely
went out as a group, but tonight was a special occasion;
clinical trials had begun that day on Synapsate, the
promising Alzheimer's cure that had taken them seven
months to develop. Generally in these situations Maya
could expect at least one of her colleagues to come on
to her.

Maya liked her coworkers and loved nearly everything
about her job, especially her boss, Dr. Julius Penfield, a
driven genius who thankfully was all business. Still, she
would have preferred to skip the celebration.

*They're all harmless enough, but it'd be better if none
of them got too drunk tonight.*

Over her four years at Glaxo-Wellcome, she had always
managed to deflect advances with enough tact and good
humor to avoid strain on her working relationship with
the offending colleague. In fact, by the next day she
doubted that any of them had ever recalled proposi-
tioning her.

*If they'd remembered what they said to me, I doubt
they'd still be married. After all, in most marriages the
ACIP exacts quite a price for infidelity.*

Maya was even more aware of the ACIP's influence

on scientific research, which had been equally profound. Fraud and carelessness had obstructed scientific progress throughout recorded history—until the ACIP. The vast majority of scientists were honest and careful, but it only took one bad apple to taint an entire field; a small bit of bad information from one scientist could undermine years of research by many others. Such bad apples were everywhere, necessitating massively inconvenient procedures and double-checks. Once the ACIP had been added to the equation, many of these procedures became unessential, dramatically speeding the rate of discovery in every field of science.

"I'm exhausted," Maya whispered to the woman seated at her right, Dr. Stephanie Lashley, a dark-haired, 71-year-old specialist in neurofibrillary plaque. "Do you think Julius would mind if I skipped this luau tonight?"

"We're *all* exhausted, but could you stay for appetizers at least? I've been instructed not to let you leave too early."

"Instructed? By whom?"

Before Lashley could answer, Penfield lifted his wineglass and spoke. "I wish to propose a toast to Dr. Maya Gale, who shall be our guest of honor tonight. Personally I think Maya's theory about the effects of lipofuscin on plasticity was the key to this entire project. I seriously doubt Synapsate would be off the drawing board—much less in clinical trials—without you, Maya."

She blushed.

CHAPTER 41

FUTURE PROBE

Cambridge, Massachusetts
June 15, 2045—World Government is officially installed in Sydney, Australia. Boris Malinkov, a Russian, begins his three-year term as the first World President, having received 54 percent of the popular vote and 56 percent of electoral votes in the run-off election against South African candidate Gordon Mondeto. China, formerly the most powerful nation on earth, is now the world's most powerful state. On the basis of its smaller population, however, the United States drops from second to seventh. But with complete worldwide freedom of information, political power no longer holds the significance it once did.—Sun Microsystems, Texas Instruments, and CyCare Systems release reports on the status of their own Truth Machine projects. All three companies say they should have generic versions ready to compete with the ACIP as soon as ATI's exclusive patent expires on August 10, 2049. An ATI spokesman states, "We will embrace the challenge of a competitive marketplace."

Once he had actually resolved to do it, the decision to kill himself had calmed Pete; the stuttering, nervous shaking, and rocking had virtually ceased, and he rarely heard the voices anymore.

His life had settled into a strange yet comfortable pattern, the monotony and tedium of his work set against the tension of his predicament. Competing against time, he rarely abided distractions. In just four years there would be other Truth Machines and Pete intended to disappear before his crimes could be discovered. He wasn't sure how he would end his life: maybe drown himself in the ocean or somehow cremate himself as he had incinerated Charles Scoggins. *However I do it, I'll leave no trace.*

The Wests, Tilly, Jennifer Finley, and especially Ed and Liza Armstrong must never learn that Pete Armstrong was a murderer. He plotted that his parents would some day be revived from cryonic suspension, only to learn that their son, the heroic savior of humankind, had tragically disappeared.

The next four years, the balance of his life, was now mapped out. He felt more at peace than he had in decades, even as he tested his mental and physical limits.

Only David could get him to take a break from his work.

The invitation had appeared 10 days earlier on the multi-media screen in Pete's office. "The World Future Society, an association for the study of alternative futures, is a non-profit organization founded in 1966. The Society acts as an impartial clearinghouse for a variety of different views, and does not take positions on what will happen—or ought to happen—in the future. You have been nominated by former United States President David West, and have been elected by the general membership to receive the 2045 Futurist of the Year Award, our highest honor. We would be proud if you would join us at 2:00 p.m. on June 16 at FutureProbe, our annual meeting in Cambridge, Massachusetts, to accept the award."

He had commanded his wristband, "David West, please."

(Note: I would just like to add that I have always admired the way Mr. Armstrong has spoken so politely to machines.—22 g CP)

David's face appeared, hair still dripping wet from his daily swim. The image showed on both screens: the tiny one on Pete's wristband and the Holograph covering his office wall.

David saw that Pete had at least a week's worth of facial hair. *Is he growing a beard, or has he decided whisker-removal is no longer worth the effort?*

"I know why you're calling, and yes, Diana and I will both be there. Will you?"

Pete's answer surprised David. "I wouldn't miss it for anything."

There are literally hundreds of compulsive and intermittent mental disorders known, all requiring different combinations of therapies. David had no specific theories and had never even heard of IDD, but having had some experience with compulsive behavior and its symptoms, intuitively knew. *Something is seriously wrong with Pete.*

Workaholics were addicts, just like David's compulsive-gambler father. MediFact had long ago discovered that both addictions occurred more frequently among highly intelligent people who had lacked certain kinds of parental discipline as children. The newest cures for those pathologies had an unfortunate side effect of slightly lowering the operative IQ of the patient, and therefore were used only as a last resort. Generally, long-term therapy was preferable to the cure, but David prayed that whatever was wrong with Pete would require neither.

He was surprised when his friend had agreed to take a half-day off from his work just to travel a few thousand miles and pick up an award, no matter how prestigious. Aging research had become Pete's life. He was offered some kind of award almost daily and had never accepted one in person before. Even when awarded the Nobel Sci-

ence Prize, he had been too busy to go to Oslo to attend
the presentation ceremony.

*Then why agree to come to this one? Perhaps for a
chance to get together with Diana and me in our old
stomping grounds near Harvard. Or to take a break from
his mind-numbing 100-hour-per-week work schedule?
Or,* David hoped, *maybe Pete's become more aware of
his workaholism and decided the trip is exactly what his
spirit needs.*

Soon after the introduction of self-replicating tunneling
machines and molecular bonding techniques in the
late 2030s, pneumatic subways had been constructed
throughout most of North America, revolutionizing the
science of transportation.

*(Note: Legal and bureaucratic wrangling unfortu-
nately delayed this cost-efficient technology throughout
much of the world. For example, Australia and Africa
would not be fully tunneled until 2048.—22g CP)*

Flying would have been faster, but the pneumatic
subway still moved at mach three. The Wests took the
subway; for the extra 5 or 10 minutes they decided they
would rather have the convenience of door-to-door service. Unaccompanied by Secret Service, they boarded
the tube near their Dallas home at 11:30 a.m. CST and
arrived at the Hyatt Regency Hotel in Cambridge at
1:40 p.m. EST, a 70-minute ride.

"Where's the award's ceremony dais?" David inquired
into his wristband.

Earlier that day he had repeated the 15-digit zip code
that pinpoints any location on earth to a 12-foot square;
the map with flashing red arrows appeared on his dial and
directed them to the front of the auditorium. It was a
massive room with state-of-the-art acoustics and a Holographic screen at least 80 feet wide perched above the
podium. At 1:51 p.m. about 7,000 persons already occu-

pied the room and 3,500 more would file into the empty seats before the ceremony began.

Arriving with nine minutes to spare, the Wests walked up to the dais and chatted with the FutureProbe officials. Diana noticed Pete, wearing a neatly trimmed beard, was seated on the aisle near the front beside an attractive young woman. She was intrigued to see the two engrossed in conversation.

Pete had recognized her as soon as he walked into the room. Dr. Maya Gale was an accomplished neurobiologist and research scientist in the field of intelligence enhancement. Since beginning her sabbatical from Glaxo-Wellcome, she had written two books on the human brain. Pete had read them and, finding them fascinating, had hoped someday to meet her.

But his first thought upon seeing Gale in person was, *She's breathtaking.*

Gale, 39 years old, was a slender, athletic woman with long brown hair and a fresh, girl-next-door face that Pete found irresistibly appealing. She looked 25. Naturally Pete remembered everything from her bio. She was the number five amateur women's racquetball player in the state of New York, a graduate of Connecticut College and Yale Medical School, and unmarried. He also knew she'd been one of the principal scientists who had discovered the enzyme used in Synapsate, Glaxo-Wellcome's anti-Alzheimer's drug, and that her research team had also been the first to figure out how to apply the discovery to memory enhancement for healthy humans.

He saw that the seat next to her was empty.

"Is anyone sitting here?"

She shook her head.

Pete sat down, wondering whether she realized who he was. *Maybe not.* He rarely made public appearances anymore, and looked older than most of his photographs and news clips in the public domain. Also, he had a beard now.

"I've never been to one of these meetings before. Have you?" Pete asked.

"Been to the last six. They're fun."

"That's what I've heard."

"You meet a lot of fascinating people. Once you go to one, you kind of get hooked."

Hmm. Beautiful and friendly.

"I've always been interested in speculating about the future," he said. "When I was younger, it was all I thought about."

"Not anymore?"

"Now I'm so involved in my work, I rarely have time for anything else. I doubt I'd be here if an old friend hadn't coerced me into coming."

"Really? What kind of work do you do?"

"Genetic research. Aging. That's what nearly everyone's trying to crack these days. At my advanced maturity, it's a far more *personal* mission than it would be for you."

She laughed. "Don't be silly. You can't be much older than I am. I'm almost 40."

"I knew that from your books, but I'm afraid you're wrong about me. I'm 55."

He knows who I am, she thought. *He's very attractive and looks like he has an interesting story. I wonder who he is.*

"Well, you don't look your age," she said.

"Neither do you."

Just then, David stepped up to the podium.

She thought, *I'd better say something provocative or this conversation could end right now.* "David West's a handsome man, don't you think? I voted for him both times and I'm a Republican!"

"Me, too."

She hesitated, steeling up her courage, and added,

"Since we have so much in common, why don't you join me at the buffet after the speech?"

"I thought you'd never ask."

As the applause died down, David began.

"My friends, nothing could have kept me away from FutureProbe this year. The recipient of the 2045 Futurist of the Year award is a man I've known and loved for over 40 years. He was my roommate at Harvard College, and except for Diana, he's been my closest friend ever since. I have truly been blessed to know him. But not as blessed as the world has been—by the work of the greatest scientific genius of this century.

"On May 17, 2003, 13-year-old Randall Petersen Armstrong sat across the table from Diana and me at a Chinese restaurant two miles from here and told us what he intended to do with his life. He said he was going to try to build a Truth Machine. I remember his exact words: 'I really think I can do it. And when I do, it'll change absolutely everything.' "

David paused a few seconds for effect. "He did, and *it* did." The audience broke into spontaneous applause and cheers.

"Today Pete Armstrong is working on computerized models for genetic experiments that we all hope will help scientists stop the aging process. It's possible that every person in this room will gain the ultimate benefit from his work, just as we have seen our lives enriched by the Armstrong Cerebral Image Processor. It's an honor to present this award to my dear friend, Pete Armstrong."

The crowd exploded. Dr. Maya Gale was shocked when the intriguing stranger seated next to her, with whom she had shamelessly flirted, rose from his seat and walked up to the podium to receive his award.

Afterward, they found a secluded table away from the buffet. Neither was terribly interested in the food—heightened PEA levels will have that effect on humans.

"I can't believe I didn't recognize you," Maya confessed. "Your name used to come up quite often back at Glaxo, especially among my team members."

Pete's wristband ACIP was running; he knew she was being truthful. *Maybe she's as physically attracted to me as I am to her.*

"Speculating about the source of my memory, I assume. Did you come up with any interesting theories?"

"Actually one of my colleagues did. She thinks your perirhinal cortex may be especially well suited for forming new ion channels. The latest theory is that Mozart's P-cortex was like that, and he could flawlessly remember every sound he'd ever heard."

"Interesting. For a while, I've thought it had more to do with my brain's ability to remodel the dendritic structures. They say you can build your synaptogenesis the same way runners build lung capacity, and I've been consciously exercising my brain since I was six or seven."

"That may be why you *still* have your memory, but it probably isn't why you had it to begin with. Otherwise you'd be hearing colors and seeing voices."

"Yes, of course that's right," Pete conceded. "One of my favorite authors wrote, 'Consistent, deliberate mental exercise is the only known way to maintain a photographic memory without inducing pathological synaesthesia.' " It was a quote from *The Elusive Engram*, Maya's first book.

She smiled, impressed and flattered. *This one's a charmer. I'd better be careful with him.* "Actually a Russian neurologist named Luria studied a man who never forgot anything."

"I've read about him. Apparently he could remember anything he'd ever sensed by sight, sound, taste, smell, or touch. My mind only works that way with sight and sound."

"This subject was a remarkable case. He could recount entire grids of 10,000 numbers he'd seen 20 years earlier.

I guess you could, too. But unlike you, he never developed any exercises for his mind—and never really did anything constructive with his talent. A terrible waste."

"And his synaesthesia?"

"Quite severe. He would say things to Luria like, 'Do you have a cold today? Your voice is so crinkly and yellow.' But he never lost his memory until the day he died." She looked at him closely. "Tell me, what made you so ambitious at such an early age?"

"I don't really know. My younger brother was murdered when I was five. I used to think it had something to do with that." Pete could hardly believe he was sharing such a thought with a total stranger.

"I'm not a psychiatrist, but that seems possible."

"I'm not so sure anymore. I think I might've been just as ambitious *before* the murder. Recently I've been thinking about my childhood a lot, and I keep coming back to a recurrent dream."

"How recurrent?"

"Almost every night for over a year, right up until the day Leonard was killed."

"What was it about?"

"I used to dream I could fly. But that wasn't all, Maya. I could give anyone else the ability to fly along with me. We'd soar above the neighborhood and everybody on the ground would just stare at us in awe."

"Hmm. I wonder what Freud would've said about that."

"I think he'd have surmised I was a damned ambitious kid."

"Or at least very optimistic. Do you think your brother's murder made you more determined?"

"I don't know, but I hope you'll figure it out someday. In fact, I've just made an important decision."

"Oh?"

He was completely straight-faced. "I've decided to change my last will and testament tonight. If anything ever happens to me, I want *you* to have my brain to dissect."

"Thank you, Pete." She took his hand. "That means a lot to me."

Then they both laughed. And at that moment, Maya Gale realized how miserable she'd be if anything really happened to Pete Armstrong.

CHAPTER 42

THE MIRACLE

Stamford, Connecticut
August 5, 2046—Aries One, the first permanent colony on Mars, is established, and 15,732 settlers from almost every nation move their belongings into the domed city. Former United States President Caroline Whitcomb attends the opening ceremony along with several thousand friends and well-wishers. American Airlines issues a schedule of 26 round-trip flights per year between Paris and Aries One.—Motorola and the ATI Medical Division announce a joint venture to develop therapies to extend human life beyond its natural 130-year span by repairing DNA with nanomachines. They predict usable results within five to eight years.

The ACIP has helped us learn things previously misunderstood about love. Perhaps the most interesting misconception was that true love somehow causes people to place the wants of their beloved ahead of their own needs. Not only is such behavior extremely rare and always temporary, it is *not* love; it's a pathology, a mental disorder, not unlike schizophrenia or IDD. Even those of you who would willingly sacrifice your own life to save the life of another would do so only when your own needs (e.g., honor, religious belief, ego) outweigh your survival instincts.

Love causes a person to elevate his or her beloved above the rest of humanity, and that in itself is a miraculous phenomenon. When two mentally healthy adults are in love, they care deeply about each other's needs and wishes, but never more, or even as much, as about their own.

Pete had experienced mixed feelings ever since his first date with Maya on the day they'd met at Future-Probe some 13 months earlier. *How can I begin a relationship with this incredible woman knowing my life will be over in four years?*

Thus it had been a long courtship, almost reminiscent of pre-ACIP customs, when getting to know someone took a very long time.

Maya had everything he looked for in a woman: extraordinary intelligence, sensitivity, beauty, and integrity. But then, Jennifer Finley had also embodied those qualities. What made Maya so different? He determined it was a combination of honesty, communication, and confidence. He knew he could believe and trust her completely. She always told him exactly what was on her mind and wasn't the least bit intimidated by him. The differences, for the most part, flowed from the ACIP.

Maya challenges me. She shares her feelings unreservedly and insists on the same from me. Whenever he became quiet or brooding, she would deftly force him out of his shell, demanding intellectual honesty, attentiveness, and respect.

When he had taken her to dinner to celebrate their sixth month together, his mind had drifted to a thorny problem he'd been grappling with that day. She had been relating a conversation she'd had with her sister and noticed he wasn't exactly paying complete attention.

"Earth to Pete," Maya interrupted herself good-naturedly.

"I'm right here."

"Maybe in body, but not necessarily in spirit."

"Honey, I can repeat every word you just said to me."

"I'm sure you can, but that doesn't mean you were listening. *I* don't think about other things when we're talking."

She was right. About to argue the issue, Pete suddenly realized he couldn't refute her words without lying. He knew letting his mind drift to work during social interaction was simply a bad habit, and one he ought to break.

If I love her, I should be capable of concentrating on her when we're together. It's not like I'd forget any of the work if I put it off until later. The work's always there, he decided, *but people are immediate. If you lose the moment, it never returns*

Through example, Maya taught Pete how to be more open toward others, even if it meant sharing his feelings. It was a slow and difficult process, but because of her he was becoming less introverted.

If I'd met Maya 25 years ago, he mused, *maybe I'd have been outgoing enough to call Al Bonhert myself instead of trusting the job to Scoggins.*

(Note: How that would have changed history! —22g CP)

Initially uncomfortable during their discussions and occasional arguments, Pete realized that such friction wasn't the price of a relationship, but a benefit. He needed it to grow as a human being. Only through friction could the rough edges of his personality become refined, and Maya skillfully polished him like a fine diamond.

He never used his ACIP override in his personal relationships; although quite expert at dancing around certain questions, he reserved "O Captain, My Captain" exclusively for government scips. Very often, lying would have quickly ended arguments with Maya, but he had never succumbed to it. Only occasionally had he even avoided answering questions she'd asked—always in instances in which doing so would have exposed his crimes, since he couldn't put her in that position.[24] And he knew for a fact that she had never lied to him. It seemed that the ACIP had taken much of the risk out of marriage.

Maya had spent most of her time in Dallas since meeting Pete, although he also visited her in New York City. They were seldom apart, except during their long working hours; both driven by work, each understood the other's obsession. In fact their time together every night was like an oasis, a respite from the blinding concentration and intense pressure they were forced to apply to their chosen vocations. When not working, both were homebodies. Only occasionally did they venture from Pete's house or Maya's brownstone and when they did it was almost always to join David and Diana.

Like Pete, Maya had never been married; both were leery of marriage, being set in their ways. And Pete was tormented by the ethics of his situation. He knew it was selfish to marry and less forgivable to consider starting a family, but still he succumbed to instinct, longing for continuity and kinship. To resist it would have been as difficult as deciding to stop breathing.

I love her. I need her. I've been alone my entire life and now here she is, making me realize how lonely I was before. With Maya I'll be happy for the next four years—and after that my life will be over. Then what'll happen to her?

Pete had proposed exactly three months and one week earlier. Before meeting him, Maya had expected to wait

[24] Unless she turned him in immediately, learning of his crimes would have implicated her as an accessory after the fact and disqualified her from passing certain government scips. Even worse, in the case of the murder—failing to disclose a capital crime about which one has knowledge is itself a serious crime.

until she was at least 50 to get married, as most career women did. Pete had counted on remaining single for the rest of his short life.

He had added one caveat: "Honey, I have a secret I can't discuss. It has to do with my work, and several things that happened a long time ago, things that will probably come back to haunt me in a few years. That's all I can tell you. There are questions you might ask that I can't answer right now."

Wishing he could tell her everything right then, Pete promised himself he would explain it all to her at the appropriate time; then they would decide what to do—together.

"I understand," Maya said. "I won't pressure you to tell me anything before you're ready."

Several days later, Maya and Pete examined each other's genetic scorecards as all engaged couples must, and learned that any possible defects were curable. Even knowing that four years from now he might be in prison or dead, Pete realized he was secretly pleased that they might have children together. Children who might someday take the helm at ATI—and contribute great things to humanity.

"We are gathered here this day, in the midst of all the majestic forces of the universe, in the presence of God and these witnesses, as you two join together in marriage, an institution flowing out of the very nature of our being. . . ."

The ceremony took place at the Stamford Unitarian Church[25] just five blocks from the house where Maya grew up. From the day it welcomed its first congregation, it had never been a somber place, but today it was a madhouse. Maya's parents had invited about 100 of their friends, in addition to hundreds of friends, relatives, and colleagues of the bride and groom. Since Pete was the

---

[25] Constructed in 2020, when Maya was still a teenager, the church had taken nearly three months to build; the science of mechanized construction was still in its early stages, and the architecture was elaborate.

groom and David and Diana were best man and matron of honor, the wedding inevitably turned into a media event.

Maya's maternal grandmother, Sue Dunlap, 92 and frail, had decided to postpone her cryonic suspension in order to attend her favorite granddaughter's wedding. Since the early 2040s, the World Health Department had advised anyone over 80 years of age to wear a Life-Monitor at all times, and to keep an Emergency Care Machine in all sleeping quarters. The Dunlaps kept two ECMs, but Sue Dunlap seldom wore her Life-Monitor to bed. On July 29, she had died in her sleep. Her death had been discovered six hours later, far beyond the period for brain reconstructibility.

(Note: Anyone revived or frozen within 300 seconds of pulmonary failure is unlikely to sustain any brain damage, and most impairment suffered during the first two hours at room temperature is now repairable through nanotechnology.—22g CP)

Maya grieved, guilt-ridden that she hadn't offered to reschedule the wedding in order to accommodate her grandmother.

Her heartbroken grandfather tried to console her. "It was nobody's fault, Maya. I remember when Grandma was your age I could never even get her to wear a seat belt.[26] She was always reckless."

At least, Maya reasoned, her grandmother had lived a happy, full life—short though it may have been. She could barely imagine the guilt Pete must have experienced over the tragic death, long ago, of his three-year-old brother.

"O God of many names, we solemnly petition Your blessing upon this holy union. Do you, Maya Helene

---

[26] Until 2017, automobiles were considered so dangerous that, for safety reasons, they were required to have "seat belts," which were actually harnesses.

Gale, pledge to love and cherish Randall Petersen Armstrong, to do all within your power to preserve the integrity of this marriage for the sake of you and your children, and to remain together throughout triumph and adversity, until all your offspring attain adult age, and if you are able, until death or cryonic suspension?"

(Note: The Unitarian Universalist Association was first to encourage couples to incorporate realistic expectations into their marriage vows. Today many churches have followed their lead. After all, at current rates about 23 percent of all marriages will end in divorce. Ironically, prior to the ACIP, the divorce rate was double what it is now, yet nearly all brides and grooms pledged eternal love "until death do us part."—22g CP)

"I do."

"Do you, Randall Petersen Armstrong, pledge to love and cherish Maya Helene Gale, to do all within your power to preserve the integrity of this marriage for the sake of you and your children, and to remain together throughout triumph and adversity, until all your offspring attain adult age, and if you are able, until death or cryonic suspension?"

"I do."

"As you have pledged yourselves each to the other in marriage, with the authority vested in me by the church and by the World Tribunal, I now acknowledge that you are husband and wife."

As he kissed his new bride, Pete realized his life was completely and irreversibly transformed. Suicide no longer an option, every decision from now on would be made with his love's best interests in mind.

After all he had been through and all the mistakes he'd made, he considered Maya Gale the greatest miracle of his life.

CHAPTER 43

LEONARD

Dallas, Texas
December 5, 2047—With great fanfare, World President Boris Malinkov signs the International Weather Control Act, allocating $73.4 trillion over nine years to construct weather-proof domes over every major city and to set up weather control stations in all populated areas on earth.—In the second such scandal in seven months, a cryonic suspension station in Bombay is discovered to have lost power, resulting in the premature thawing and subsequent loss of 26,112 persons. The seven managers whose negligence was responsible for the breach are expected to receive the death penalty.

He had never tried to talk her out of it. Once Maya decided she wanted a child, Pete admitted to himself that he did, too. It would work out—somehow.

"Pete, I think it's time. The contractions are five minutes apart."

"*Contractions?* How long have you been in labor?"

"About six hours."

"*Six hours?*" Pete continued talking into his wristband, as he ran at full speed from his temporary office to Maya's study on the other side of the house. "Why didn't you tell me, honey?"

"I'm fine. I didn't see any reason to interrupt you—ooooh—ooooh—until just now."

Pregnancy was a major inconvenience, and with childbirth reputed to be extremely painful, few women opted

301

for the old-fashioned approach. But Maya wanted to experience all of the bonding, hormones, contractions, and pain her own mother and grandmother had felt giving birth to their daughters. And if his wife was willing to subject herself to natural pregnancy and child-birth, Pete made sure he was home when she went into labor.

At first he had discouraged it, urging her to consider the normal, cybernetic method. It would be less risky to both mother and child, and of course more convenient.

But Maya wouldn't relent. And as her belly grew, Pete started to understand his wife's feelings. By her sixth month, he felt almost as if he were pregnant himself. He couldn't look at Maya without experiencing a rush of love for her and their unborn son. Nothing in the world was more important to him than his family; if necessary he knew he would kill or die for them without hesitation.

He had arranged a delivery room and maternity ward to be specially built onto the house, hired a full-time human obstetric staff, and purchased all the latest equip-ment. He also kept the normal robotic equipment to monitor the human staff's work, and as a backup. He had established a temporary office and laboratory so he could work at home as Maya's due date neared.

He even arranged for Maya and himself to take their parenting license scips at home so they wouldn't have to go out in public.

Pete walked Maya to the delivery room and stayed at her side throughout the next 15 hours of labor. David and Diana arrived and remained with them for most of the final 11 hours, including the birth. However, at one point, a sobbing Diana, overcome by memories of her deceased son, had to excuse herself. David tried to comfort her, but she insisted he return to Pete and Maya, recognizing even in her grief that their situation was far more urgent than hers.

For over 40 minutes Maya shook uncontrollably

between contractions; once the baby's heart rate climbed above 250 beats per minute. The entire staff, forced to focus on Maya, had no time to explain to Pete what was happening. For a while it appeared that the baby might need to be removed robotically. At that moment Pete discovered he was much more worried for his wife than the son he had not yet seen.

He and his wife were lovers, friends, and business partners who now worked side by side at ATI, their interests completely aligned. They didn't agree on everything, but presented a united front to the rest of the world, which took much pressure off him; their working relationship was as he had fantasized it could have been with Leonard or David: two minds with one set of goals and ideals.

In the midst of this crisis, he tried to appear calm, willing himself not to shake or bite his tongue, both dead giveaways to his true mental state. This restraint required total concentration because inside he was terrified.

Finally the baby's heartbeat returned to normal and the crisis ended, but labor was still profoundly painful. Already having decided he would rather not have another child than watch his wife risk a second pregnancy, Pete was actually relieved when she screamed, "Next time I'll take the drugs! No, make that the pod. In fact, if you ever let me put myself through this again, I'll choke you with my bare hands!" (A threat they would both laugh about later.)

Eventually she delivered the child naturally, without painkillers. It was the most intense, exhausting, and wonderful experience of their lives.

The baby was perfect. He weighed eight pounds exactly. They named him Leonard Gale Armstrong. When Pete held his tiny, helpless son in his arms, he knew that everything he cared about was now centered on this child.

December 19, 2047 (Two weeks later)

Fatherhood agreed with Pete, but not in every way. He awakened at 3:45 a.m., exhausted.

Maya had left the bathroom light on so that when Leonard woke up she would have an easier time nursing him. *Apparently,* Pete mused, *it's difficult to connect mouth to nipple in total darkness.*

Most parents used their baby-nurse machine to feed their infants at night, ever since BNMs had been proven equally healthy for the child. But Maya would have none of that. "It's not as healthy for the psychological development of the *parents*," she'd insisted.

In the faint light Pete could see his wife and child quite clearly even without adjusting his contact lens chip. Leonard always slept in their bed; it was much easier on them and, they assumed, pleasant for Leonard as well. Pete watched them lying together, fast asleep, her left arm draped gently and protectively over the baby's back and side.

He's so tiny, so cute. Is there anything in the world so beautiful as watching the woman you love caring for your child?

He was too keyed up to fall back asleep. At 4:05, he got up and put on his work-out clothes. *Maybe I'll go for a run this morning.*

He hadn't run outdoors since Leonard was born; he never had time and never got enough sleep. It was hard to stay motivated. He checked his meteorology guide, since weather control in Dallas was only operative during summer months. The outside temperature was 41 degrees Farenheit and would not rise over 44 degrees during the following three hours, so he put on a pair of climate-regulated running shorts.

First, he decided to work on the computer models.

Walking toward his office, he thought to himself, *I love this house.* He loved how it looked, its clean lines and sparkling white walls, remarkably modern for a house built just after the turn of the millennium. It was the right size too; not overly expansive, but big enough. Maya had redecorated it since their marriage, but she'd let him keep all his favorite *objets d'art* on display.

Most new wives in her position would have made their husbands buy all new art—or more likely a new house, he realized, appreciating Maya's pragmatic side. *Why's that? Jealousy of past relationships shared in the house? Marking their territory? Jockeying for power? Demanding sacrifice as proof of their husbands' love? I'm glad Maya isn't like that.*

Finally he sat down at his screen. When he did, as always, sensation was put on hold. He became cerebral, escaping into the work; no more thoughts of exhaustion or fear of death. Pete could remember these feelings, but no longer felt them.

Oblivious to the sounds of the house, the pneumatic pipes, the temperature control system, the house-cleaning machines, the irrigation units, Pete blocked out the "white noise" and any louder cacophonies. Still one clamor could reach him in the zone: Leonard was crying in their bedroom.

Should I continue working, or see if I can help Maya? He would have preferred to keep working, but in the end conscience won. He found Maya in the nursery holding the baby, trying to burp him as he screamed, his tiny face bright red from the strain of shrieking.

"Must have too much air in his stomach."

Leonard burped. Mother and child seemed much happier.

"I have to pee," Maya announced, "but you need to go back to work, right?"

Guilt. "No, honey. I'll take him."

It was now about 6:00 a.m. He sat in the chair rocking Leonard, marveling that his son was so much more alert than he had been as a newborn just 14 days earlier.

I can do this for a few more minutes, even enjoy it. But probably not for much longer.

(Note: You humans don't like to admit that babies are boring, but of course they can be.—22g CP)

I have no idea how women can hold babies for hours at a time without climbing the walls. What on earth is Maya doing? It's already been five minutes.

Maya returned. "I'm going back to bed. Why don't you 'bond' with your son for a while? If he falls asleep, you can put him in bed with me."

"Bond?" Did I detect sarcasm in her voice? Damn! What does she want from me? It was her choice to nurse him herself. She knows I'd rather she took him with her. But she really needs some sleep. Obviously I'm in no position to argue.

He sat in the chair for 10 more minutes. Leonard was now content but still wide awake. Pete noticed how perfect his little hands were; not scaly or red like they were after birth, or even just a few days ago. Somehow, 10 minutes knowing exactly what he was supposed to do was easier for Pete than the previous five minutes spent wondering when Maya would be back.

Why's that? I guess I still don't deal with uncertainty very well.

He let the BNM change Leonard's diaper. Then he rocked him for five more minutes.

Maybe I can have the machine rock him while I work on my computer.

He took Leonard and the machine to his office and put him on it for a few minutes. It worked at first, but soon the baby was wailing again. Apparently he wanted his daddy's arms.

Smart baby, he thought. *The BNM maintains a constant temperature of 98.6 degrees, its surface has the same texture as skin, and it senses and responds to the baby's movements just like I do, yet Leonard can tell the difference. I wonder if all babies are this sensitive.*

Feeling both flattered and vaguely irritated, Pete carried him back to the nursery and rocked him some more. *No point just sitting here.*

For some reason, Pete still hadn't gotten around to having his contact lenses hooked up to the Data Channel. Fortunately he'd had a screen installed on the north wall of the nursery. Pete supposed most parents would watch something entertaining, but he preferred to read.

"Pete's news," he called out to the unit, and the latest stories of interest scrolled across the screen. He read more slowly than normal, but it made the time pass. Leonard finally fell asleep. Pete placed him gently in their bed next to Maya.

As he left the room, he saw that Leonard had managed, in his sleep, to burrow into the soft part of Maya's belly. Pete smiled, and whispered to himself, "Mother Earth."

Finally he could return to the office and escape into his work.

CHAPTER 44

TRUTH MACHINE TWO

Dallas, Texas
August 13, 2049—Three days after ATI's 25-year patent on the ACIP expired, the company announces it will offer ACIPs for outright sale to augment the leasing program already in place. Seven other companies, including Intel and CyCare Systems, have already brought competing Truth Machines to market, but analysts predict that based on reputation and name recognition, ATI will retain at least a 70-percent market share for a decade or more.—A worldwide referendum to decide whether certain historical figures should be cloned is scheduled for

September 17. Albert Einstein and Nelson Mandela are slated as the first two subjects, because of their irreplaceable intellectual gifts and the availability of near-perfect samples of their DNA. The vote is expected to approve the experiment.

Pete's time ran out before the horse could talk.

He had always understood, in a general way, how it would end for him: *some damn licensing scip or another.* But he could never foresee the specifics. Until now.

Several times a year, Pete had subjected himself to scips for various reasons. Over the previous 12 months he had taken day-trips to Australia, South Africa, and Norway on ATI business, applied for a gyro pilot's license, visited an undersea city, and renewed his voter registration. Usually his licenses were for activities like these, things he could abstain from or at least delay if he had to. But as long as the agencies used ACIPs, he wouldn't have to.

Unfortunately the World Parenthood Department had just installed CyCare Truth Machines; it was the largest government account ATI had lost since the patent expired. Pete would be questioned within five days of the birth of their second child, scheduled just four weeks hence. He would be unable to pass the scip because of one question, the same question that was asked at every license application interview, every customs checkpoint, and every employment interview: *Have you committed any felony since April 30, 2006, for which you have not confessed, served sentence, or received amnesty?*

He would also have to pass the Steinberg mental illness test, which would probably also be impossible.

If he refused to answer the question or to take the Steinberg test, his parenting license would be automatically revoked. He and his wife would then have the option of divorcing or losing both sons to adoption. Neither was acceptable to Pete. He would rather die.

He had known the next generation of Truth Machines was coming for quite some time, but now realized he'd been keeping himself in a state of denial. The problem was that for the past 20 months, he'd been truly happy—the happiest he had ever been.

Pete knew he still wasn't a paragon of patience, but he was calmer and less obsessed. Strangely, his work on the computer models didn't suffer much, in spite of the new demands on his time. His family gave his work more purpose; aging cessation might bestow immortality. Now the undertaking was for concrete beneficiaries, unlike the abstraction that was the rest of humanity.

Pete was glad Maya had opted for an artificial womb pregnancy this time; he would have hated to start the conversation he'd been dreading if she had been carrying the child herself.

"Maya, please sit down. I have something to tell you. We need to make a decision."

Maya suddenly found it harder to breathe, as though air had been siphoned from her lungs. She sat down carefully. "This has to do with the dark secret, the secret you warned me about when you proposed, doesn't it?"

"Yes. Please forgive me. I've done three horrible things in my life—all more than 25 years ago."

Maya said nothing. She stared at him, waiting.

"I used stolen algorithms to finish the ACIP. Then I reprogrammed the ACIP so it wouldn't work on me." He paused, giving her a moment to digest the implications, and added, "Five months after that, I killed Charles Scoggins."

He waited for a response, but Maya kept silent and perfectly still. So he explained about Kilmer and the blackmail and Reece and the murder and ultimately, his years of guilt and fear.

"Maybe I'm no different than Scoggins. Maybe he was right."

She glared at him and finally spoke. "Damn you!"

"M-Maya, nobody else knows about any of this. But they're using CyCare Truth Machines for the parenting scips now."

She understood immediately and remained speechless again for nearly a minute. Pete's secret was worse than anything she could have imagined.

As the silence surrounded them, Pete's insecurities dominated his mind.

Will she leave me? Now he couldn't even look at her while he spoke. "I swear I've never lied to you, and I never will. Can you possibly forgive me for what I've done?"

Everything he's ever done since I've known him has been above reproach, Maya thought. *Even withholding his darkest secret from me until now was correct. If he'd told me, I'd have been legally bound to turn him in. If I were in his position after we'd fallen in love, I would have handled it the same way. But how can he think of himself like that?*

She finally answered. "Forgive you? Look at me."

He gazed into her eyes and heard the words: *See, Pete. You're just like me.* The voice was reaching him—all the way from hell. *She hates you, Pete.*

"There's nothing to forgive," she said, taking both his hands in hers. "I can't believe you've been carrying this around all these years. Scoggins implanted these doubts in you. Scoggins was a *sociopath*! You're letting a dead sociopath manipulate you. Don't you think I know you, Pete? I can see clear to the bottom of you. You're a *good man*. Enough of these doubts. There's no time for them anymore. All I want us to think about is—how do we keep them from taking you away from us?"

They both wept, and held each other close.

Pete listened for Scoggins's voice, but it was gone. Maya had smothered it. At last.

* * *

He placed the call. "David, I have a problem. Would you represent me as my attorney?"

"I'll be there within the hour and we'll talk about it."

He arrived in 20 minutes. Pete told him everything. Maya remained with them, but never said a word. The conversation lasted seven hours.

David was calm, more sad than shocked. *Imagine keeping such secrets for 25 years. If only he'd told me this while I was President. I could have pardoned him.*

But there was no point in saying that; obviously Pete hadn't wanted to put him in such an awkward position. The only issue that mattered now was how to best deal with the situation. What did Pete want to salvage most? His life? His reputation? His family's security?

His answer surprised David.

"If you can't save my life, at least try to arrange it so I can finish my work. I could be done with the models in less than a year. Maybe my sons won't have a father, but they might live forever because of what I accomplish. Just knowing it's *possible* would help me face everything I have coming."

"That's a reasonable request and almost certainly attainable. If you agreed to turn yourself in now, I'm sure I'd have no trouble convincing the Attorney General to grant you a one-year delay prior to any death sentence. It's well within his power. Unfortunately amnesty isn't, but that'll be our goal. Amnesty can only come from the World Tribunal and they rarely grant it. I won't give up, though. There has to be a way, Pete. You don't deserve to die."

On August 28 David called to make an appointment with Texas Attorney General Carlton Shaw, whom he had once met during his second presidential term. David liked and respected the tall, mustached, 66-year-old native Texan, an amiable but careful man, regarded as a scrupulous though very tough prosecutor.

Naturally Shaw was willing to meet with the former U.S. President on a moment's notice, anywhere, any time.

But David insisted, "Carlton, just treat me like any other attorney."

They agreed to meet at Shaw's office nine days later at eight a.m.

AUSTIN, TEXAS—September 7, 2049

David arrived alone.

The office was small and cluttered. Shaw and West were both born during the infancy of personal computers, but unlike David, apparently the Attorney General could never bring himself to go paperless. It was the messiest office David had seen in years. They talked for a few minutes about nothing in particular, then got down to business.

"My client's a famous person who committed serious crimes, including murder, over 25 years ago," David explained. "Since then, he hasn't perpetrated any illegal acts other than perjury related to the earlier crimes. He wants to turn himself in, but won't unless he has your assurance that if convicted and scheduled for execution, he'll be allowed a 12-month delay of sentence. He needs the time to complete an important scientific project."

Shaw was incredulous. "How in God's name did he escape detection?"

"Before I answer that, do we have a deal?"

Shaw hesitated a second or two, but it felt like an hour to David.

What's taking him so long? This should be an easy decision.

Then Shaw asked, "You said no other crimes in the last 25 years?"

"Except perjury about the original crimes."

"If what you're saying's true, and I assume it is, then yes, you're damn right we have a deal."

Whew!

Shaw had no precedent for this discussion. Since the ACIP had become ubiquitous (in Texas there were now more ACIPs than video screens), the Texas judiciary hadn't prosecuted a single serious crime that had occurred more than four months prior to trial. Yet David's client had committed crimes 25 *years* earlier.

"My client's name is Randall Petersen Armstrong."

"Holy shit!" Shaw exclaimed, jaw dropping.

"I suggest we release this entire meeting into public archives immediately. I don't think I have to tell you what could happen if we withheld any of it."

Shaw shook his head. "Damn. I shoulda known who your client was. Who else could've fooled the ACIP?" He tried to remain calm as he thought about the ramifications. *What if everyone now believes that some people can lie with impunity?*

Pete's cooperation would be crucial in mitigating the crisis of confidence that would follow the announcement of his confession. People would suspect that the Truth Machine, the most important component of all human interaction, had been rendered useless. Without the confidence it created, civilization could revert to darkness and despair.

"Of course I agree," Shaw continued. "We need to go public with everything right away. You know, I've often wondered what would happen if somebody figured out how to beat the Truth Machine. An evil person might do terrible things if he could lie without getting caught. Such a person could amass unlimited wealth and power."

Shaw was suggesting that this "evil person" could be Pete. David set him straight. "What you say is true, but what you've *implied* is not. Pete Armstrong was already the wealthiest person in the world long before the ACIP was approved. He never used his crimes to enrich himself—his motives were always altruistic."

"I sure hope the rest of the world believes that."

"I think most people will. Remember, almost half the people alive today were educated under scip; we're all a bit more rational these days. As students, most people were conditioned to be intellectually honest. They actually had to learn how to *think*, rather than just temporarily memorize facts and pass a bunch of tests like we did back in the olden days."

Shaw laughed, beginning to understand why everyone liked David West so much. "People may be smarter in general than they were 25 years ago, but not in every way. In some ways, the Truth Machine's been a crutch. Don't get me wrong; every day I thank God for the ACIP. But I regard our *dependence* on it as its biggest drawback. Before the ACIP, we dealt with an incredible amount of uncertainty—both in our careers and personal lives. It takes a special kind of intelligence to deal with the possibility that every statement anyone makes to you might be a lie. Today things are a lot more cut-and-dried. The part of our brains that used to deal with uncertainty might've atrophied a bit, don't you think? Take away the Truth Machine and you're gonna see people who can't deal with life at all."

"That's true, Carlton, but there's no cause for alarm; the Machine's still viable. Pete Armstrong has a bigger stake in the ACIP's credibility than anyone. He's willing to submit to a thorough questioning. Today if you want. You can scip him using any of the other companies' Truth Machines. Pete is the only person alive who can pass a scip on the ACIP without telling the truth, and he absolutely cannot fool anyone else's machine. The problem goes no deeper than that. You have my word."

Shaw believed him, but still glanced at his wristband ACIP just to make sure the light was still solid green.

Then the two attorneys negotiated details of prosecution. Agreeing to allow an unprecedented seven months to prepare their case, Shaw promised that Pete would not be incarcerated prior to or during trial, and also acceded to a panel of five jurors rather than the usual three. But Pete would be required to have a transmitter microchip imbedded in his skull to monitor intentions of suicide or flight.

David agreed.

One hour later, on the basis of their deal, Randall Petersen Armstrong formally confessed his crimes. The entire conversation between the two attorneys and Pete's complete confession were released to public archives the next morning. The transcripts were analyzed by thousands of experts, both human and machine, throughout the world. Unanimously it was agreed that the ACIP was still sound.

CHAPTER 45

MICHAEL

Austin and Dallas, Texas
September 8, 2049—The World Health Department announces that Medicomp will pay for bionic restoration of all disabled people unable to afford it themselves. The coverage will be phased in over a period of three years, on a schedule beginning immediately with eyesight equivalence. Limb replacement coverage will begin 75 days from today. Artificial hearing will be covered after 180 days. Spinal cord injuries, being the most complicated and expensive bionic procedures, will begin last. Approximately 3.4 million disabled persons worldwide are eligible for the free treatment.—

The World Justice Department announces that Randall Petersen Armstrong has formally confessed to several serious crimes, including the murder of ATI executive Charles Scoggins. The crimes occurred approximately 25 years ago and Armstrong hid them by reprogramming the ACIP not to detect his lies. A major panic follows the announcement, with the World Stock Exchange reflecting a 17-percent drop in average share prices during the day's trading. President Merrill attempts to reassure the world on real-time comprehensive media feed that there is absolutely no evidence that the ACIP has been compromised in any other way. The transcript of Armstrong's confession is immediately released.

The day after his confession, Pete was able to pass his parental license scip in time to witness the birth of his second son. The Steinberg tests were scored as "inconclusive, probable IDD, therapy recommended but not required."

Pete and Maya watched in awe as their baby boy was removed from the polymer womb. Born September 9, 2049, Michael Edward Armstrong weighed 7 pounds, 14 ounces.

The day after Michael's birth, Pete and David spent an entire afternoon discussing strategy, and another Michael came up in the conversation: 20th-century financier Michael Milken. Accused of numerous technical crimes, Milken had believed himself innocent. He was shocked at the doggedness with which prosecutors had pursued his case and the questionable tactics they had employed. In fact, no person had yet been prosecuted for any crime to which Milken ultimately pled guilty, and his plea to those infractions was coerced by threats of prosecution against family and friends.

"But remember, you have a big advantage over Milken," David told Pete.

"What advantage is that?"

"You're definitely guilty."

Pete understood. Milken's problems had been magnified by ambiguity. Because he was regarded as a symbol of greed and corruption in the 1980s, not as a human being, people wanted to believe him guilty, even if they didn't understand the accusations. In the court of public opinion, he had already lost.

Prior to the ACIP, criminal attorneys usually forbade clients to discuss their cases before trial; any statements could be used against them and tended also to limit strategic options. After the ACIP, these attorneys became more flexible, for obvious reasons.

Pete was undeniably guilty of grave violations of the law, but David believed if people got to know the real Pete Armstrong, they would understand and forgive his crimes. Popular opinion might affect the outcome of the trial. If not, it could influence the verdict on appeal.

Therefore David made sure Pete and his files and archives were accessible to journalists and writers such as my owner, Tom Mosely (and therefore to me). Pete would voluntarily answer every question put to him by reputable journalists, and would answer them with scip confirmation. David also asked Maya, and many of Pete's friends and colleagues, to undergo scips while talking freely to the press, disclosing all aspects of Pete's life, personality, and character, both positive and negative.

When David spoke with Tilly about it the next day, she was incredulous. "Are you sure you want me to tell the press everything I know about him?"

"Everything they *ask* you about. The more candid, the better. If you refuse to answer, they'll assume we're hiding something. The truth will never be as bad as what those guys'll suspect if you don't level with them."

"Especially since positive stories don't sell as well as negative ones."

"Fortunately they all have to pass their scips before

their articles can be disseminated," he reminded her. "As long as they write truthfully, his faults'll just make him seem more human."

(Note: The press was much less reliable prior to the ACIP. Historians indicate journalists were often encouraged to incite sensationalism rather than simply report facts, and many were careless for other reasons as well. All forms of carelessness and dishonesty have sharply diminished during the Truth Machine era.—22g CP)

David's primary objective was for the world to finally see the previously enigmatic Pete Armstrong as flesh and blood.

But David's strategy had another important goal: to minimize the damage to the ACIP's credibility. The day the confession was made public, there had been a worldwide financial panic, albeit a temporary one. Without a trustworthy ACIP, there could be economic collapse and possibly even war; the World Stock Market Index fell 17 percent in less than an hour. Fortunately Pete's detailed confession was quickly released to the media. The market solidified and regained over 70 percent of its losses the same day.

Pete's continuing openness further increased worldwide confidence in the system. Within a week of his confession, it was apparent that the Truth Machine remained credible. On September 23, 2049, the WSMI achieved record levels.

CHAPTER 46

THE TRIAL

Austin, Texas
July 1, 2050 The murder trial of Randall Petersen Armstrong begins in Austin, Texas. It will be the most closely followed news event in history. Lead defense attorney David West predicts that Armstrong will be cleared of capital murder, but most experts are far less sanguine.— ATI formally turns over 5.3 percent of its stock under the terms of its government-mediated financial settlement with the Renaissance Corporation. Armstrong, ATI's chairman and controlling shareholder, admitted he had clandestinely incorporated Renaissance's algorithms into the ACIP 26 years ago. In exchange for mutual releases, Renaissance's shareholders of record at the time of the crime will receive ATI stock, based on their proportion of ownership: 4.1 percent of all outstanding shares from Armstrong directly and 1.2 percent from the company. This stock is valued at $5.61 trillion, making it the largest legal settlement in history. Negotiations took place between the general counsels of each firm; both sides express satisfaction with the amount and with the fact that the settlement was accomplished amicably and without outside attorneys.—A worldwide poll suggests people are almost equally divided regarding Armstrong's punishment. Approximately 48 percent believe the death penalty appropriate in his case, although most of those polled seem to be angrier at having been deceived than at Charles Scoggins's murder. The crisis of confidence in the ACIP that occurred after his

319

*confession has abated, since there is no evidence that
anyone other than Armstrong can fool the machine.*

The preparation of his case had been complete for almost
a month. But over the previous several days, trying to do
some last-minute work on the computer models before
leaving for Austin, Pete had accomplished very little. His
concentration was weak.

It was the eve of his greatest peril, yet ironically, for
the first time in decades, he felt he had something worth
living for, something that made his life more valuable to
him than his place in history. He no longer cared how the
world would remember him. He wanted to survive for
the sake of his wife and his sons, and his most painful
doubts centered around them. Would they as a family be
able to adjust to his death? Would Maya remarry? Would
her new husband love his adopted sons as his own?
Would his sons remember anything about him? How
would Pete have turned out had he grown up without his
own father, a gentle loving man who'd never so much as
raised his voice to him? And would his latest work give
his family the priceless gift of immortality, or would his
efforts fail?

He sat next to David at the defense table with Maya
and Diana directly behind them, his every move beamed
to billions of spectators. He knew that almost everyone
in the world was watching, transfixed by the holographic screens at home or at their offices, by the two-
dimensional screens on their wristbands, surrounded by
3-D screens in their automobiles and gyrocopters, or
seated with friends in virtual reality cafés everywhere on
earth. He felt like a caged animal in a zoo or a fish in a
giant aquarium.

He considered his situation. It was unlikely he would
be alive 13 months from now. If his life were somehow spared, he would probably never leave prison. Less
likely still was the chance that he could ever be a real
father to his sons, or watch them grow to adulthood.

Although 25 years had seemed such a long time when he reprogrammed the ACIP, in retrospect it seemed like yesterday. Had he not allowed his mistakes to mushroom out of control, he felt his life would now be everything he'd ever wanted it to be. Instead all would be taken away in 13 months and he had nobody to blame but himself.

The press reported every development minute-by-minute and editorialized ad nauseum. Only Jennifer Finley's media empire refused to publish editorials about the case. When Reginald Zuk, a reporter from *Turbonews*, asked her why, the 63-year-old magnate answered, "Because it wouldn't be fair to my subscribers. Even with scips, I could never expect editors and journalists working for me to write objectively about a man I once loved."

Zuk pressed Jennifer. "But what do *you* think of Pete Armstrong?"

"I knew him in 2024, when the crimes took place. He was a good man then, and I'm sure he still is. I hope the verdict is 'innocent.' "

Over the past six months, there had been over 400 biographies of Pete Armstrong published in every format, and thousands of works concerning ATI, the ACIP, and aspects of his life, crimes, and legal travails. Many became bestsellers. David's strategy of openness seemed to be working. When Pete's confession had first become public knowledge, over 80 percent of those polled were in favor of condemning him to death. As the trial began, that number had fallen below 30 percent.

First Circuit Judge Curtis Lezar called the session to order. The baby-faced, dark-haired Lezar, who had never taken growth hormones, was rather short in stature (5 feet, 10 inches), although not quite short enough to require a specially built dais.

The computerized selection of this presiding judge for

the trial had come as a surprise to most pundits. At 44, Lezar had limited experience in high profile cases. He had spent his entire working life in government service; only 15 months earlier he'd served as presiding judge over Texas Small Claims Court, which exclusively handles civil disputes under $500,000. Prior to that he had risen through the ranks of the World Justice Department after it absorbed the United States Department of Justice, which he'd joined, fresh out of law school, as a legal clerk assigned to the Texas Supreme Court.

His poise was impressive, considering that the defendant was the wealthiest and now the most famous person on the planet. The opposing attorneys were the current Texas Attorney General and a former Texas Attorney General who had served two terms as President of the United States. Witnesses included some of the most renowned and accomplished individuals in the fields of science, business, medicine, and law. The trial was expected to last two days, the longest single-defendant trial in the United States since 2027. Pressure on Lezar would be intense, his every decision, indeed his every gesture scrutinized by thousands of journalists and experts.

Over the preceding six months, in anticipation of his role in the Armstrong case, Lezar had become the most famous jurist in the world. He wasn't certain he liked the attention.

The mood in the courtroom was somber, the tension pervasive.

Lezar addressed David gravely. "President West, what are your client's responses to the charges of murder, perjury, obstruction of justice, and fraud?"

"We plead not guilty to murder on the basis of self-defense. If he is found guilty, we request amnesty on the basis of extenuating circumstances. We plead guilty to perjury, obstruction of justice, and fraud, but request amnesty on the basis of extenuating circumstances."

Lezar spoke to the jury, three women and two men seated to his left. "The defense has already admitted to the crimes of perjury, obstruction of justice, and fraud, and has stipulated that the defendant did kill Charles Scoggins. Ladies and gentlemen, your role in this trial is strictly to decide, on the basis of the evidence, whether the murder was committed in self-defense according to the definition of law. You'll hear testimony from nearly a dozen witnesses. Each witness will be questioned once by each side. There will be no redirect questions, but the opposing attorneys may cite in their summations any scip depositions they have previously conducted with witnesses. You may also make a recommendation for or against amnesty, which is not in my power to grant. Amnesty can only be granted by the World Tribunal. Any appeal filed after the verdict will be heard by that court."

Lezar turned to David. "Is the defense prepared for trial?"

"We are, Judge."

"Mr. Shaw, are you ready to give the opening statement for the World Government's case?"

"I am, sir."

"Please begin."

"Thank you, sir. Fellow officers of the court, on March 1, 2024, Randall Petersen Armstrong, unable to perfect his ACIP in conformance with the terms of the Truth Machine Bill, inserted several hundred lines of computer code, the essence of which he knew had been obtained illegally from a competing firm. Then he reprogrammed the ACIP so that he could circumvent it at will. On August 6 of that same year, Mr. Armstrong swore, under oath, that he was unaware of any imperfections in the technology of the ACIP or of any violations of the law pursuant to the ACIP's development. He knew that he was committing perjury. Five days later on August 11, Mr. Armstrong forced Charles Scoggins at gunpoint to handcuff himself to a chair, and while Mr. Scoggins was immobilized and helpless to defend himself, Mr. Armstrong murdered him in cold blood. Subsequently Mr. Armstrong disposed of the body and lied to law enforcement officials about his involvement in Mr. Scoggins's disappearance."

Shaw paused impressively, then continued. "The prosecution will not present any evidence of these assertions, since Mr. Armstrong himself has agreed to stipulate that every one of them is true.

"We believe the claim of self-defense is absurd. Since that's the only issue of this trial, we intend to call no witnesses of our own. We'll disprove any declarations of self-defense through cross-examination of the defense's own witnesses.

"The World Government doesn't deny that Mr. Armstrong has made significant, positive contributions to the human race. He may be a good person. None of that matters in the eyes of the law. There's no legal justification for murder other than self-defense. The law is clear on that and the law was soundly conceived. No civilization can survive without enforcing its laws. Regardless of any extenuating circumstances, for the good of our society, Mr. Armstrong must pay for his crimes with his life."

He sat down.

Lezar turned to David. "Is the defense ready to present its opening statement?"

"We are, Judge."

Lezar signaled David to begin.

"Fellow citizens of the World, at this moment in human history, 25 years is a very long time. Try to think back. Remember what our world was like when the crimes occurred. Liars were usually believed and rewarded, the truthful often doubted and punished. There was far less benefit to be gained from honesty than there is today, and as human beings, we're genetically programmed to seek that which we perceive is to our advantage. Evil and deception lurked in the darkest corners of every human mind—although in some more than others." Smiling wryly, David paused as laughter erupted, then continued, "Crime and war flourished. The world was a very different place.

"Now take a few moments to consider Pete Armstrong's influence on our world. He took one man's life, an evil man who has not been missed. But Pete's inventions have saved millions of lives, possibly the entire human race. Had he not used the illegally obtained code, the ACIP might have been further delayed at great cost to humanity.

"Repentant for his crimes, today Pete is a model citizen in all respects. He's no threat to anyone and his brain is nothing less than a world treasure. I don't see how our society can afford to relinquish such an asset lightly.

"I have known Pete Armstrong for most of my life. I've never met any person who's more honorable, more compassionate, and more selfless.

"I also knew Charles Scoggins fairly well. Mr. Scoggins was not a benevolent man. He was in fact a clever and hardened criminal with no conscience. Scoggins would have tried to murder Pete Armstrong if Pete hadn't killed him first. What's more relevant is what Pete himself believed on that terrible day over 25 years ago when he pulled the trigger. Self-defense as a point of law is based on the awareness and intent of the defendant at the moment of the assault. Pete's mental state was not that of a murderer. Indeed, he was groping for a way to *avoid* killing Charles Scoggins without jeopardizing his own life and the lives of others.

"Long ago, with altruistic motives, Pete Armstrong made a series of terrible mistakes, every one because he was trying to help humanity. He was forced into those mistakes by the purposeful ruse of an evil man. Charles Scoggins delayed the ACIP by at least two years, just to cover his own crimes and to trick Pete into a position where he could be blackmailed.

"Without Charles Scoggins, Pete Armstrong could

have lived a thousand years without ever committing an illegal act. He does not deserve execution."

Lezar pondered David's words for a moment. "The defense may call its first witness."

"We call Marjorie Ann Tilly."

Tilly, handsome and energetic at 82, had retired from ATI the previous December. She was duly sworn in and seated. After several minutes of background questions, David asked her about the defendant.

"Ms. Tilly, how long have you known Pete Armstrong?"

"Over 55 years."

"And how long had you known Mr. Scoggins before his disappearance?"

"I worked with him for about 24 years."

"How familiar are you with the inner workings of the ACIP?"

"I know the ACIP as well as anyone, except Pete."

"Ms. Tilly, in your opinion, could ATI have completed the ACIP without using the illegally obtained Renaissance code?"

"Based on what I know today, if Scoggins hadn't obstructed the team, we could have designed the same program ourselves in six months or less."

The CyCare Truth Machine that had been specially installed for this trial continued to register solid green.

"Thank you. I have no more questions."

Lezar turned to Shaw. "Does the prosecution wish to cross-examine?"

"Thank you, sir. Ms. Tilly, when did you first become aware that Mr. Armstrong had reprogrammed the ACIP so he could override it?"

"September 6th of last year."

"How did you learn that fact?"

"Pete told me himself."

"Mr. Armstrong reprogrammed the ACIP on March 1, 2024, and you had no idea until last *September*?"

"I never had any reason to suspect it. If I'd been suspicious, I probably could have figured it out."

"And yet you claim to know more about the ACIP's inner workings than any person other than Armstrong. Is that correct?"

"Not necessarily more. At least as much."

"You admit you never realized, over a period of 25 years, that Armstrong knew how to override the ACIP. How can you expect us to accept your analysis that the team could have duplicated the stolen Renaissance code in less than six months?"

Tilly was unprepared for this line of questioning. "I was asked for my opinion and I gave it. My opinion's based on experience and on facts I've accumulated over many years. I stand by that opinion. I know my business."

"You know your business, yet the ACIP software remained tainted for 25 years on your watch."

"I object," David shouted.

"I'll withdraw it," Shaw answered, turning to Lezar. "Sir, I have no more questions for this witness."

Lezar asked Tilly to step down.

The defense called Dr. Alphonso Carter. Carter was 91 and Pete thought he looked wonderful. Carter had undergone pancreas, thyroid, and liver clonings 12 years earlier, and received the gland and organ transplants three years later. The transplants had taken well, and Carter felt 30 years younger. He walked 5 to 10 miles every day and was projected to have at least 16 years left before requiring cryonic suspension.

David set the tone by qualifying Carter as an expert in both criminal law and criminal psychology and asking about his experiences with ATI and with Pete. Then the real questioning began.

"Dr. Carter, as a world-renowned criminologist,

you're intimately familiar with the effects of the ACIP on society, are you not?"

"Absolutely. I have conducted and published formal demographic studies."

"In your expert judgment, how many lives would have been saved if the ACIP had been introduced two years earlier?"

"In 2023, the year before the ACIP was approved, there were an estimated 2.6 million murders worldwide. That figure includes deaths resulting from political and religious repression, wars, terrorism, and all other human lawlessness. 2023 was a fairly typical year. There were approximately the same number of murders in 2022. Ten years later, the number of murders was under 100,000, and today it is less than 1,500. So theoretically, if the curve could have been moved ahead by two years, at least five million lives would have been saved. In fact, those statistics understate the benefit of the ACIP, since they do not include improvements in productivity, technological progress, and general prosperity, all of which have been definitively linked to increased lifespan. My numbers also do not allow for the ACIP's role in reducing negligence."

"If Scoggins were alive today, and we discovered that he'd intentionally delayed the ACIP for two years, could he be prosecuted for any related crimes?"

"Yes indeed. There must be at least 10 different charges under which he could be prosecuted and convicted. Any intentional fraud resulting in provable death is the same as murder, so there would be several million counts of that statute available for any skillful prosecutor to file against Mr. Scoggins. Today, without question, Charles Scoggins would face execution for his offenses."

"Dr. Carter, you were with Pete Armstrong just two days before the murder, and you've recently interviewed him using a Sun Truth Machine. What's your expert opinion of Pete's state of mind when he killed Charles Scoggins?"

"Mr. Armstrong was extremely upset after learning the details of his brother's death. I believe he was mildly delusional at the moment he killed Mr. Scoggins."

"How so?"

"In my opinion, Mr. Armstrong suffers from Intermittent Delusionary Disorder. He possesses the classic vector and displayed symptoms at the time."

"Which are?"

"IDD only affects people with exceptionally high intelligence and tends to cause hallucinations, particularly when the subject is under severe or prolonged stress."

"Is Mr. Armstrong insane?"

"In my opinion, sanity is a matter of degree. Mr. Armstrong is not insane under the standard definition, but neither is he completely sane."

"Based on what you've learned of Mr. Scoggins, what would he have done had Pete released him?"

"I can state, with virtual certainty, that Mr. Scoggins would have attempted to kill Mr. Armstrong."

"Did Pete believe that?"

"Absolutely."

"Was Pete Armstrong acting in self-defense when he killed Scoggins?"

"In my opinion, yes, he was."

"Thank you, Dr Carter. No more questions."

Lezar polled Shaw, "Cross-examine?"

"Yes, sir. Dr. Carter, are you familiar with the eight conditions of self-defense?"

"Of course."

"And what's condition number three?"

"The defendant must reasonably believe that there is no sure means of escape."

"So are you telling this court that Mr. Armstrong, having handcuffed an unarmed man to a chair while pointing a laser pistol at him, had no sure means of escape?"

"Mr. Armstrong believed Scoggins would kill him if he let him go."

"But even so, Mr. Armstrong *did* have a sure means of escape. Could he not have simply kept Mr. Scoggins there and called the authorities?"

"Yes. But as I said, he was upset and mildly delusional. I seriously doubt the option ever occurred to him."

"Is it possible that Mr. Armstrong did not call the authorities because he'd have been required to confess that he'd fraudulently reprogrammed the ACIP and perjured himself to government attorneys?"

"I suppose that is possible."

"In fact, as delusional as Mr. Armstrong was at the time, his actions were consistent not only with self-preservation but also with a desire to save his company, his wealth, and his reputation from the aftermath of his earlier crimes of fraud and perjury. Is that not correct?"

"Yes, it is. But, I. . . ."

"That'll be all, Dr. Carter. You've answered my question and I have nothing further. Thank you for your time."

Lezar said, "The witness will please step down."

David called six other witnesses, including Leslie Williams, ATI's comptroller, and Carl Whatley, its recently retired marketing director, each of whom affirmed Scoggins's mercenary attitudes about ATI's products and Pete's altruism.

Whatley's testimony produced the day's only whimsical moment. Shaw asked him whether he believed Armstrong had acted in self-defense, an inappropriate question since Whatley wasn't qualified as an expert in criminal law or psychology.

Before David could object, Whatley replied without missing a beat, "I'm not sure, but if we'd known what was going on, I can think of at least 30 of us at ATI who would've killed Scoggins just for sport."

"The defense would appreciate a list," David joked.

The last witness of the day was 68-year-old Dr. Sharon Rosenfield. David didn't believe she had any knowledge relevant to the case, but wanted the jury to see how the world-revered doctor admired and respected his client. And he knew Shaw wouldn't dare treat her roughly on cross-examination.

"Sharon, when did you first meet Pete Armstrong?"

"In August 2009, when he and Bill Tannenbaum recruited me to ATI."

"How would you describe Pete's agenda at that meeting?"

"When I first met him, I wasn't sure what to make of him. He never talked about money—only about the benefits of the products we'd be creating. To be perfectly candid, I was suspicious. Everything Pete said sounded too good to be true. I thought his attitudes unusual for a businessperson and I suspected maybe he was just telling me what he thought I wanted to hear. But I knew he was a genius and I trusted Bill Tannenbaum. As it turned out, Pete was completely sincere."

Shaw interrupted, "Objection. I don't see the relevance of this line of questioning. Isn't the issue self-defense?"

David answered, "I am establishing Pete Armstrong's character and intent, particularly relevant to the charges of fraud. . . ."

Shaw interrupted, "To which the defendant's already pleaded guilty."

David countered, "And for which we now seek amnesty."

"Mr. Shaw, your objection's overruled," Lezar said. "If the prosecution didn't wish to deal with motive and character issues, it shouldn't have brought the fraud charges."

David continued. "What finally convinced you of Pete's sincerity?"

"Two years later, I met with him in Dallas. I presented him with a plan to launch the MediFact national field study and asked him for $5 million to market the concept. That was no big deal. What I really wanted was permission to discount the price on HealthFile and HomeDoc by 15 percent to anyone who'd take part in the studies. Keep in mind, HomeDoc was well on its way to becoming the most profitable software product in the world. At the time, it was ATI's heart and soul, so a 15-percent discount was a huge concession; it would have had a major negative pull on ATI's earnings and its stock price. But every question Pete asked me had to do with how my ideas would help advance medical science. He couldn't have cared less about the money or who got the credit. By the time I left his office, he was more excited than I was. He authorized an unlimited marketing budget and recommended I double the discount to 30 percent to attract more participants. That discount cost him an absurd amount of money, but he never thought twice about it because he knew it was the right thing to do. Pete Armstrong is for real."

"Dr. Rosenfield, could you briefly explain the effects of MediFact on the progress of medical science?"

Shaw interrupted, "Objection! That's an entirely gratuitous and irrelevant question."

"I agree. Objection's sustained. President West should know better than to try something like that."

Oh well, it was worth a shot. David felt neither ashamed nor embarrassed, but was discreet enough to surrender. "Sorry, Judge. I have no more questions for Dr. Rosenfield."

Shaw added, "Neither do I."

* * *

So ended the first day of testimony. Lezar adjourned the proceedings until the next morning at 10:30. Pete himself would be the only remaining witness.

As they left the courthouse together, David advised, "Try to get some sleep tonight, Pete. Tomorrow's going to be grueling."

"I've been thinking; I'm not sure you should ask me whether I thought Scoggins would've killed me if I let him go."

"Are you worried about Shaw's cross-examination?"

"Yes, I sure am. He'll ask me if *I* think I acted in self-defense. But if we don't lay a foundation for that question in my direct testimony, you'll be able to object."

David and Pete had disagreed on one particular point. David believed that his friend had acted in self-defense, both morally and legally, but Pete himself didn't think he had. In his own mind, he was guilty of capital murder.

"I understand that," David said, "but you have to trust me. We'll probably lose this verdict anyway, so let's go down fighting. I'm going to ask you every question we went over last week. Shaw will cross-examine, I'll object whenever I think it might help, and you'll answer every question Lezar instructs you to answer. Otherwise we have no chance at all. Whenever someone pleads self-defense, the burden of proof rests on the defense— and we're nowhere close to proving our case."

"Okay." Pete's body began to sway.

"Pete, listen to me. If we lose at trial, it isn't over. There's still the appeal, and if we lose that, we have a year to try every legal and political maneuver we can think of. I'll never quit. Neither will Diana or Maya. If there's any way to get you out of this, we'll move heaven and earth to find it." David put his hands on his friend's shoulders and looked straight into tear-filled eyes. "Heaven and earth."

Pete nodded. "I know."

CHAPTER 47

DAY IN COURT

Austin, Texas
July 2, 2050—After the first day of the Armstrong murder trial, opinion polls show 73 percent believe Armstrong will receive the death penalty, but only 39 percent now think he actually deserves it. According to those polls, the testimony of Sharon Rosenfield made a strong and favorable impression.—World-renowned neuroscientist Dr. Carlos Senoma suggests that if Armstrong isn't executed, it might only take a few years for the genius/inventor to figure out how to fool any competing Truth Machine. Other scientists in the field, most of whom favor amnesty for Armstrong, reluctantly agree with Senoma's assessment.

They had rehearsed every question and every response, so David's direct examination of Pete would be fairly easy.

"Don't try *not* to rock or bite your tongue," David told him. "Save all your concentration for answering the questions."

Before the Truth Machine, the defendant's demeanor often had a greater influence on the outcome of the trial than the facts of the case. Not so anymore. Such displays of uneasiness would hurt neither his credibility nor his case.

There was preliminary testimony of course—name, address, age, educational and business background, that

334

sort of thing—but David wasted little time. He set the scene for the crimes early in Pete's testimony.

"Please describe the Renaissance code and the circumstances under which you first saw it."

"Charles S-Scoggins had been t-telling me for several months that his team was close to completion of the ACIP, but that about two percent of the population was immune to it; they were able to dissociate themselves into believing their own lies. That made the ACIP only marginally more useful than computer-operated voice stress analysis and polygraphs, and certainly disqualified it from use in the judicial system. On August 15, 2021, Scoggins showed me eight pages of computer code. I scanned it and knew immediately it would solve our last problem. N-Naturally I was very pleased until Scoggins told me the code had been developed at Renaissance Corporation, and that he'd obtained it from a former Renaissance employee."

"Do you know who the employee was?"

"It t-turns out that was another lie. He'd gotten the code himself by hacking into Renaissance's central research computer."

"What was your response when Scoggins told you the code was from Renaissance?"

"I told him we couldn't use it."

"But you did use it, didn't you?"

"Yes."

"When and why?"

"A little over two and a half years later, on March 1, 2024. It was the day the *Dallas News Syndicate* ran an article about Harold Edward Kilmer's wrongful execution. I was so angry. The ACIP could've saved his life. I thought to myself, 'If I'd let Scoggins use the Renaissance code back in 2021, Kilmer would still be alive today.' So I rewrote the code; made it a little different, but it was still plagiarism and I knew it."

"Is that why you added code that allowed you to fool the ACIP?"

"Yes. I had to. Otherwise it would never have been approved, and I knew without a Truth Machine, more people would be executed for crimes they hadn't committed, just like Kilmer."

"Pete, if it weren't for the illegally obtained Renaissance code, would you still have written an override code?"

"No. I had no reason to lie except for that."

All eyes and every camera in the courtroom focused on the CyCare Truth Machine, which registered solid green.

"When did you learn Scoggins had figured out that you'd used the Renaissance code and overridden the ACIP?"

"August 6, 2024, the day before I was to be deposed by government attorneys to receive approval for the Truth Machine contract."

"Did you think that was a coincidence?"

"I didn't give it much thought *then*, but of course now I know the timing was part of his scheme."

"What did Scoggins say to you?"

"He said that the attorneys would probably want to question him, and that since he knew I'd reprogrammed the machine, I'd better reprogram the ACIP so he could fool it, too. Otherwise we'd never get approved."

"Did you go along with that?"

"Yes. I thought Scoggins and I were on the same side. I wanted to get the ACIP into our judicial system to save people's lives, and I thought that was also his motivation; I regarded him as my ally."

The Truth Machine was still solid green.

"The next day, you committed perjury. Tell me why."

"It was the only way to get the ACIP approved and the world needed it."

"Pete, the ACIP also made trillions of dollars for Armstrong Technologies, of which you own controlling interest. You didn't do it for the money?"

"I already had more money than I could ever spend. The money meant almost nothing to me."

Still solid green. Not a flicker.

Pete described the blackmail. "I'd already perjured myself and Scoggins knew it. He told me he was going to turn me in unless I signed over enough of my interest in the ACIP to bring him up to an equal partnership with me. He even had the document all drawn up."

"And you signed it?"

"Yes. I was trapped. As I said, I'd already committed perjury. Besides, I wasn't going to let anything delay the approval."

At David's request, Pete described his encounter with Daniel Anthony Reece. Then David questioned him about his state of mind afterward.

"I was undone by it, which I know wasn't a rational response. What difference did it make what my three-year-old brother believed at the moment of his death? I mean, any way you look at it, Leonard was gone. But I couldn't stand the idea that he might have thought I was responsible. It was illogical, but it affected me, drove me a little crazy. What Reece had done was evil. Evil was the only word for it. I couldn't understand why anyone would do something like that. Then I started thinking about Scoggins. Was he evil too? Had he been planning the whole thing for years?"

"So you took out the override codes and scipped Scoggins at gunpoint while he answered your questions?"

"Yes. I needed to find out exactly what he'd done. I had to know. I just had to."

"Did you fear for your own life?"

"I suppose so. I suspected that if Scoggins had really been planning for years to blackmail me, he might eventually murder me as well. I hoped it wasn't true, but I knew I'd better find out, and the ACIP offered the only practical way to do that."

"What did you learn when you questioned him?"

"I learned he'd intentionally shown me the Renaissance code to delay the ACIP. He told me the ATI Truth Machine team could have figured out the solution themselves, but he made sure that didn't happen because it would've exposed his crimes."

"Are you sure Charles Scoggins would have tried to kill you if you'd released him?"

Pete thought, *I sure hope David knows what he's doing.* "Yes."

"How do you know?"

"First, I asked him what he'd do if the situation were reversed—meaning if he were me. He said: 'I'd have killed you five minutes ago.' Then I asked him what I could do to prevent him from trying to kill me if I let him go. He asked for some time to think about that."

"Did he ever deny he'd try to kill you?"

"Never. We both knew he would. But I wanted him to help me come up with a way to prevent that. I was thinking maybe we could create some evidence implicating him, evidence that might surface automatically upon my death. Or we could reprogram the ACIP somehow, so that if anything happened to me, Scoggins would no longer be able to fool it. That kind of thing. Of course whatever we came up with would have to be foolproof, which would have been nearly impossible with someone as clever and treacherous as Charles Scoggins. Frankly I was grasping at straws because I didn't want to kill him. I'd never killed anyone before and I hope I never will again. It's a d-d-dreadful thing to kill someone. A t-truly dreadful th-thing."

Pete was now shaking visibly. He described the murder itself, his disposal of the body and the document, and his subsequent deception to the authorities. Finally he told of the terrible psychological toll his crimes had exacted on his spirit: how he felt morally inferior, unworthy, having lived a lie for 25 years.

David asked a final question. "Obviously Charles

Scoggins committed a number of horrendously evil deeds. I want you to think about this question carefully, because I can see how in your fragile state of mind, after learning the terrible details about your brother's death and then discovering Scoggins's betrayal, you might have thought murder was justifiable. Pete, if you had believed there was no danger of Scoggins trying to murder you, would you have killed him?"

Pete answered, "No. I really doubt it."

The Truth Machine light remained green.

David's direct examination lasted three hours. At the end of it, there was hardly a soul in the courtroom who believed Pete would be convicted of capital murder—except Pete and the Wests. They knew that Shaw's cross-examination would be brutal.

Shaw turned ferocious on his 19th question: "Mr. Armstrong, you have stated the money meant almost nothing to you. What about the glory?"

David interrupted. "Objection. Please ask Mr. Shaw to clarify to all of us what on earth he's talking about."

"Mr. Shaw, would you kindly rephrase the question?"

"Sorry, sir. What I meant to ask Mr. Armstrong is, do you care what people think about you? Does your place in history mean anything to you?"

Pete hesitated and looked at David West. "The defendant will please answer the question," Lezar ordered.

"I th th think almost everybody c-cares what people think about them. I know *I* d-do."

"So when you incorporated illegally obtained Renaissance algorithms into the ACIP software, you did it for altruistic reasons, but you also imagined how history would regard you. You considered the possibility that you might be remembered as the savior of the human race, didn't you?"

"I admit I've th-thought about things l-like that."

"When you committed perjury by swearing to government attorneys that the ACIP conformed to all conditions of the Truth Machine Bill, you were doing it to save lives, but also to earn your place in history. Is that not true?"

"Y-Yes."

"When Scoggins blackmailed you into signing the document that gave him an equal share of the ACIP, why didn't you put up more of a fight? Why did you sign it so readily?"

"I w-was only giving up money. I didn't c-care about that. I just w-wanted the ACIP approved."

"You wanted the ACIP approved, but not for the money?"

"No."

"For the sake of the human race?"

"Yes."

"And for the glory too?"

"Y-Yes."

"On the afternoon you reprogrammed the ACIP in ATI's downstairs laboratory so that Scoggins could no longer fool it, did you already know that later that evening you intended to force him to answer your questions at gunpoint?"

"Yes." Pete began to rock violently, which calmed him a bit.

"Did you consider the possibility you might have to kill him?"

"Yes, but I hoped I w-wouldn't have t-to."

Shaw had been waiting for just this opening. "Mr. Armstrong, you *didn't* have to."

Pete understood. Shaking, tears in his eyes, he whispered, "I know."

The room was so silent that nothing could be heard except for Pete's labored breathing.

Shaw pressed on immediately. "In fact, you could've simply called the authorities and admitted everything to them. You could've turned Scoggins in."

"I w-wish I h-had."

"Why didn't you?"

"I d-d-don't know."

"It would've meant turning *yourself* in, too; for perjury, fraud, and possibly kidnapping, although I doubt that last charge would've stuck. You probably would've received probation or a year in jail at the most. It would cost a lot of money, but we know you don't care about that. The only thing that stopped you was your vanity. You couldn't stand for the world to know Pete Armstrong was a criminal."

David shouted, "I object! This is reprehensible. Mr. Shaw is badgering my client and I see no point to his rhetoric at all."

Shaw turned to Judge Lezar. "You'll see the point soon, sir."

"Do you have an actual question for the witness," Lezar asked, "or are you just going to keep lecturing him?"

The tension had been building and spectators began to talk to each other for the only time during Pete's testimony.

Shaw waited for the room to quiet down. "Yes sir, I do. Mr. Armstrong, prior to the murder, did you ever consider turning yourself and Mr. Scoggins in to the authorities?"

"Y-Yes."

"Why didn't you?"

David stood up. "I object. Asked and answered."

Lezar agreed. "Objection sustained. The witness has already testified he doesn't know."

"Mr. Armstrong, you have stated you considered turning yourself in, but you did not do so. Are you familiar with the eight legal conditions of self-defense?"

David stood up again. "I object, Judge. He's not an expert witness."

"Sir, President West has already laid the foundation for this line of questioning when he asked the defendant whether he believed Scoggins would try to kill him if he let him go. I'm entitled to ask Mr. Armstrong about self-defense."

"Objection overruled. Mr. Armstrong, please answer the question."

Pete answered, "Yes."

"So you know condition number three, which is that you must have reasonably believed at the time of the assault that you had no certain means of escape?"

David stood up. "I object. Mr. Shaw's leading the witness. The statute reads 'the assailant must have reasonably believed there was no certain means of escape.' It doesn't refer specifically to escape by the defendant. It might mean the escape of others."

"I'll withdraw the question. Mr. Armstrong, *did* you reasonably believe that?"

David stood again. "I object. Pete has already attested he wasn't thinking clearly at the time he killed Scoggins. He's not qualified to answer what was reasonable. He is not a psychiatrist."

Again, Shaw backed down. "I'll rephrase. Mr. Armstrong, do you believe you acted in self-defense when you killed Charles Scoggins?"

"I object! What relevance could Pete's legal opinion possibly have to this case? He's the defendant, not an attorney or a legal expert."

"Mr. Armstrong may not be a lawyer, but he knows more facts about the law than most lawyers do. Nobody else is in a better position to know whether or not the defendant acted in self-defense than Mr. Armstrong himself."

"Objection's overruled. Please answer Mr. Shaw's question. In your opinion, did you kill Charles Scoggins in self-defense?"

Pete thought, *O Captain! My Captain! Where are you now?* But his Captain had fallen, cold and dead.

He answered the question the only way he could. "N-No, Judge. In m-m-my opinion, it w-was not self-defense."

* * *

As is customary in capital crime trials, the prosecutor gave the first summation.

"It's our obligation to follow the letter of the law. If we don't, we send a message to the rest of the world that enforcement of law varies according to the individual. Mr. Armstrong's great wealth doesn't exempt him from the law; neither do his many good and charitable acts or his scientific contributions to humankind. No person is completely without evil and no person is bereft of good. But every individual must be held accountable for his or her actions. Otherwise there's no safety for any of us.

"The law is clear. If Mr. Armstrong is found to have murdered Mr. Scoggins without mitigation of self-defense, you must find him guilty of capital murder and sentence him to death. Perhaps the World Tribunal will reduce the sentence later. They are men and women of wisdom and they have at their disposal the finest artificial intelligence and logic machines to help formulate their decision. It's not my job, nor is it yours, to render judgment about their role or to advise them on decisions they're well-qualified to make.

"Until I was 20 years old, the United States judicial system allowed defendants in criminal cases to invoke what was called the *insanity defense*. This provision basically held that if you committed a crime because you were mentally ill, you could be forced to seek treatment, but you could not be held legally responsible for your criminal actions. Any student of history can well imagine what havoc 20th-century lawyers wreaked upon justice with *that* particular weapon."

Shaw suspended his summation until the laughter in the courtroom subsided.

"Today most of us can't imagine why such a provision existed. What difference could it possibly make to the victim or potential victim of a crime whether or not the perpetrator was sane? But during the 20th century, such a stipulation may have been justifiable because society didn't always have effective treatment, or even the tools to identify mental illness with certainty. Today we have the Steinberg tests and treatment is immediately available on demand to anyone who wants it. It's a good thing we don't have an insanity defense, because if we did, people with mental illnesses or trauma would be less likely to seek treatment before they committed crimes. We know that for a fact. And that would pose a grave danger to us all.

"I don't think of Randall Petersen Armstrong as an evil man. But Mr. Armstrong knew he had a problem, yet chose not to seek treatment when he made himself immune to his own Truth Machine. This crime was an irresponsible act, destined to lead to disaster. The moment he did it, he made himself a danger to society. When he killed, he was as guilty as an insane man who refuses treatment and then murders another person, or a reckless woman who takes a narcotic and crashes her gyrocopter into a crowded street. Frankly I think it's possible he was insane at the moment he killed Charles Scoggins. If not, he was recklessly negligent at the very least. But either way, I know he would not have murdered Mr. Scoggins if he knew he'd get caught. If he hadn't reprogrammed the ACIP so he could fool it, he'd have known he could never get away with murder for more than a few weeks.

"Unfortunately Mr. Armstrong continues to pose a grave danger to society. He's already shown willingness to circumvent the law to achieve what he regards as noble ends. He has an incredible mind and can do miraculous things with software. As its primary inventor, he also has intimate knowledge of the Truth Machine. What's to prevent Mr. Armstrong, at some point in the future, from attempting to override his competitors' Truth Machines?

"We have heard testimony from nine witnesses at this trial. That's an unusually high number, unprecedented in recent decades, but I think it's justified since the crimes took place over 25 years ago. Most of those witnesses told us what a good man Mr. Armstrong is, what an exemplary life he's led, what high motives he's always had. But only two of those witnesses testified as to whether the defendant acted in self-defense when he murdered Charles Scoggins. The first was Dr. Alphonso Carter, who said he believed Mr. Armstrong was acting in self-defense. But Dr. Carter's opinion was based on misinformation. I'd like to take a moment to read back from his testimony."

Shaw looked at his wristband screen and read back from the transcript.

CARTER: Mr. Armstrong believed Scoggins would kill him if he let him go.

SHAW: But even so, Mr. Armstrong did have a sure means of escape. Could he not have simply kept Mr. Scoggins there and called the authorities?

CARTER: Yes. But as I said, he was upset and mildly delusional. I seriously doubt the option ever occurred to him.

Shaw continued, "Now let me read to you from the defendant's own testimony."

SHAW: In fact, you could have simply called the authorities and admitted everything to them. You could've turned Scoggins in.

ARMSTRONG: I wish I had.

SHAW: Why didn't you?

ARMSTRONG: I don't know.

SHAW: Mr. Armstrong, prior to the murder, did you ever consider turning yourself and Mr. Scoggins in to the authorities?

ARMSTRONG: Yes.

Shaw paused a few seconds to let the apparent inconsistency between the two testimonies sink in.

"Dr. Carter's opinion was based on incomplete information. He believed the option of calling the authorities had never occurred to the defendant, but Mr. Armstrong admitted today that he actually had considered it.

"Only one other person testified as to whether he believed the defendant had acted in self-defense when he murdered Charles Scoggins. That person was the defendant himself, Randall Petersen Armstrong, who testified that he did not believe he'd acted in self-defense. Admittedly Mr. Armstrong isn't qualified as a legal expert. But the defendant is the only person who can testify with first-hand knowledge as to his motivation at the moment he killed Mr. Scoggins.

"The preponderance of evidence, including the defendant's own testimony, suggests that self-defense was not why Mr. Armstrong killed Charles Scoggins. Some of his reasons may have been understandable, even noble. But they didn't legally justify the killing. Regardless of any personal sympathy you might feel for Mr. Armstrong, you must find him guilty of murder."

His political career had ended nearly 14 years earlier. Yet David West, who had campaigned once for Texas Attorney General and twice each for the offices of U.S. Senator and President of the United States, was about to deliver what he considered the most important speech of his life.

"In its early days the Texas Republic was a dangerous place. The government wasn't always able to protect citizens from gangs of criminals who terrorized the fledgling frontier towns. These criminals were immoral, ruthless, and often better armed than the law. As a last resort, vigilantes sometimes hunted down and executed the more despicable characters. If those vigilantes were ever prosecuted, the defense often tried to prove the victim had simply 'needed killing.' It's a quaintly Texan expression, don't you think? If the jury was convinced that the victim had indeed 'needed killing,' the vigilantes were set free.

This wasn't an efficient form of justice, but we Texans make do with what we have."

There was some laughter. David had gotten everyone's attention, which was all he was trying to do. He needed to win the jury's hearts since he considered his prospects of winning their minds to be hopeless.

"I'm not comparing the world in 2024 to Texas in 1840. But imagine for a moment what the world would be like today if Charles Scoggins had killed Pete Armstrong—instead of the other way around. If Scoggins had possessed the sole override of the ACIP, I hate to think of what he would have done with that power. He might have made Adolf Hitler seem like Jimmy Carter. Charles Scoggins needed killing.

"Yes, Pete used his override to cover up crimes. But he never used it to gain unfair advantage over a competitor, or to seek power, or to enrich himself. Before the ACIP was approved, Pete's wealth sprang entirely from his own talent and hard work. For the past 20 years, he's donated nearly all of his ATI dividends to charity. He has used his fortune and scientific genius to create a better, fairer, and more peaceful world.

"Today we read about murders in the newspaper or see broadcasts on our screens, usually reported from the other side of the world. But I don't know anybody personally acquainted with a single individual who's been murdered in the last 15 years. There hasn't been a murder in Texas in 18 months. Murder is rare today. Not so in 2024.

"When I was a kid, death was all around us. Almost everyone knew somebody who'd been slain by another. While I was in grade school in California and Texas, three of my friends were murdered. All three died from gunshot wounds. I lost two more friends when I was at Harvard. And I can barely remember all the murder victims whose families I represented as Texas Attorney General. By 2024, murder was less common in the United States, but worldwide it was as pervasive as ever.

"Charles Scoggins delayed Pete's Truth Machine by a minimum of two years. We have heard testimony, unrebutted by Mr. Shaw, that Scoggins's actions resulted in the deaths of some five million persons. This is in fact a conservative estimate. We inhabit an immeasurably safer and better world today. People work together more comfortably, openly; we understand and trust each other more.

"In 2024, before the ACIP reshaped human nature itself, things were different. Even if you were an open and optimistic soul, you could never completely trust another person. You always had to ask yourself, 'What's he really thinking?' 'What does she really want?' 'Is it safe to rely on this person?' Today fear and suspicion between people are unusual. Improvements in interpersonal communications resulting from the Truth Machine have led to a lower divorce rate, better parenting, better education, and exponential increases in economic prosperity and scientific progress. It's impossible to list all its benefits.

"That's why Pete Armstrong had no choice but to kill Charles Scoggins. If Pete had called the authorities to prevent Scoggins from murdering him, the ACIP would have been further delayed, possibly costing millions of lives. Morally the situation was no different than if Scoggins had been pointing a laser pistol directly at the heads of every person on earth. How many friends of people in this room would be dead today if Pete hadn't killed Charles Scoggins?"

David stared directly at the jury. "For all you know, Pete might have saved some of you."

He waited about 10 seconds for the point to sink in before proceeding to his only truly relevant argument.

"Pete testified that in his opinion, he didn't kill Scoggins in self-defense. To me that proves nothing except that Pete Armstrong holds himself to a higher standard than the law does. When Pete killed Charles Scoggins, he was defending his own life and the lives of countless others. Scoggins posed a mortal danger to every person on this planet.

"Unlike Pete, I hold a law degree and have been an attorney for 40 years. I had Mr. Shaw's job at one time. I interpret self-defense differently than Mr. Shaw and believe the third condition of self-defense refers to no sure means of escape for the defendant *or for others* whose survival and safety are threatened. If you trust my judgment, please listen carefully to what I'm about to say: I know every relevant fact of this case and I believe Pete Armstrong acted in self-defense."

The Truth Machine remained solid green and the eyes of every person in the room were watching that light after David's last declaration. Right or wrong, David West believed with all his heart that his friend was innocent of capital murder.

Lezar adjourned the trial and instructed the jury to begin their deliberation. It was normal for deliberations by trained professionals to require only a few minutes, but nobody expected such dispatch this time. Pete, Maya, and the Wests could do little but wait.

CHAPTER 48

VERDICT

Austin, Texas
July 5, 2050—As the world awaits the verdict in the Randall Petersen Armstrong murder trial, polls suggest the tide of public opinion has strongly turned in favor of Mr. Armstrong. Nearly 70 percent of those polled now believe Armstrong's life should be spared and over 26 percent believe Armstrong should receive no punish-

ment whatsoever. But an overwhelming majority, roughly 96 percent, agree that, regardless of the sentence, some mechanism will have to be formulated to prevent Armstrong from overriding any new Truth Machines.

The forewoman stood and read the verdict:

"We the jury find the defendant, Randall Petersen Armstrong, guilty of murder. We find the claim of self-defense to be without merit."

Maya slumped into Diana's arms, close to losing consciousness. David looked stunned, but Pete had been prepared for it. No longer nervous, he stood absolutely erect, resigned to his fate.

The forewoman continued. "We recommend, however, that amnesty be considered by the World Tribunal, on the basis of extenuating circumstances."

Big deal, David thought. *The World Tribunal always considers amnesty, but hardly ever grants it.*

That morning at 11:45, word had reached Pete and David that the jury had rendered a verdict. In fact, unknown to either of them, it had been more like a negotiation—among the five jurors, Judge Lezar, and eventually Carlton Shaw. Messages had flown back and forth between the judge's chambers and the jury deliberation room for three days.

The forewoman advised Judge Lezar via PDC, "We are not convinced that the murder was committed in self-defense, but we refuse to convict unless you assure us he will not be sentenced to mandatory execution."

Lezar sent this response: "Armstrong should probably not receive the death penalty, but I can't think of a way to avoid it without letting him off entirely. Can you?"

In Lezar's mind, the matter of amnesty could be decided only by the World Tribunal. The jurors, knowing how rarely the Tribunal had granted amnesty in the past, insisted on a less risky solution.

A compromise had finally been reached and had necessarily involved Shaw. Lezar would sentence Armstrong to death, but give him the option of receiving treatment for IDD in lieu of execution.

IDD treatment seemed a humane solution. Computer-enhanced diagnosis of Pete's symptoms had suggested the treatment would be helpful to alleviate the chronic emotional discomfort he'd suffered throughout most of his life. Indeed, his self-imposed stress level was so high that at the present rate, according to the diagnosis, it was unlikely he would make it to his 90th birthday without cryonics.

The jurors were even more concerned that Pete might someday override other Truth Machines. All parties agreed that must never occur. It was in this respect that IDD treatment would be ideal. The treatment involved drug therapy that would reduce Pete's memory almost to the level of an average human. He would still be very smart, perhaps in the top five percent of the population, but would no longer maintain total recall. He would thus be incapable of overriding any Truth Machine in the future, but could live out his life in an otherwise normal fashion. It wasn't perfect, but it was acceptable to both judge and jury.

Of course the sentence couldn't be expected to hold up on appeal.

But if Shaw would agree not to appeal the sentence, the matter would never reach the World Tribunal unless the defense appealed.

Inconveniently, Shaw believed strongly in his case and in the law. He didn't think Armstrong should escape execution.

"If you don't agree to this," Lezar explained to Shaw, "the jury won't convict. It's as simple as that."

"*Then* what?"

"If they find him not guilty, it's over. You lose the case."

"That won't happen."

"Then I might dismiss the case with prejudice."

"I don't think you will, Judge. You'll set a new trial."

"Will I? There's one way to find out, Mr. Shaw. But this sentence serves justice and protects the integrity of the Truth Machine. It would be better for everyone if you agreed not to appeal it; IDD treatment or execution within 60 days. His choice."

"Okay, er, except—I already guaranteed to David West that Armstrong's execution would be delayed one full year from the sentence."

"Fine. IDD treatment within 60 days, or execution within a year."

Shaw took the deal.

Judge Lezar asked, "Does the defendant wish to make a statement before I pronounce sentence?"

"Yes, sir. I only wish to say that I don't blame the jury for their verdict and I'm grateful for their recommendation to the World Tribunal. I apologize to my friends and family and the rest of the world for 25 years of deceit."

Lezar spoke. "Mr. Armstrong, the jury has found you guilty of capital murder, but all five members still find reason to admire you and your accomplishments. So do I. In spite of what the law prescribes, none of us believes you deserve to die for your crimes. But if I don't sentence you to death, my sentence will not hold up on appeal."

Lezar paused to give the press time to transmit their minute-by-minute stories.

"I'm going to use judicial discretion, however, and offer you another option. Attorney General Shaw has agreed to this. He won't appeal unless your attorney does. That means if you don't challenge the verdict or my sentence, you won't face execution."

David and Maya could barely believe their ears. Apparently Pete was not going to die!

"Mr. Armstrong, there is concern that at some future

time, you might decide it's in your interest or in the interest of humankind to override the Truth Machine again. Under no circumstances can we afford to take that risk. Therefore, I sentence you to undergo treatment for Intermittent Delusionary Disorder within 60 days. This treatment will impair your memory somewhat, rendering you incapable of writing the software required to commit such a crime. But I'm told it is also likely to improve your overall mental and physical health. My experts predict that you'll retain nearly all of your superior intelligence and that your memory will remain slightly above the average. Should you fail to submit yourself for such treatment, you'll face execution one year from today. Do you understand the sentence?"

"Yes, Judge. Perfectly."

"You have 10 days to decide whether or not to file an appeal and 30 days to actually file it. In the meantime, you are hereby released on your own recognizance."

Pete answered without hesitation. "I've already decided. I thank you and Mr. Shaw for your offer. But I will appeal your sentence."

Shocked, Lezar was about to explain the sentence again, but David interrupted, "Judge, before you enter Pete's last statement, may I confer with my client?"

"Of course."

Alone with Pete in the conference room next to the courtroom where his life had just been spared, David could barely contain himself. He wanted to grab Pete by the shoulders and shake him.

"Have you lost your mind? This sentence was a gift from God. If you appeal it, you could be put to *death*."

"David, I know you're a great lawyer, so I'll take my chances. If I get treated for IDD, I'll never be able to finish the computer models. Those models could advance aging research by 50 years. They're more important than my life."

"Is that what you're going to tell Maya?"

"I don't know what I'm going to tell Maya. I hope she'll understand. One of the reasons I'm doing this is for our sons. This work will be my legacy for Leonard and Michael. If I'm not with my boys, at least some day they'll know I was willing to risk my life so that they, and many others, might live forever. I think they'll understand and maybe it'll make them proud I was their father. To me that's a comforting thought."

David wasn't ready to give up. "If we explain the timing to the judge. . . ."

"There's no chance of that," Pete interrupted. "He's already way out on a limb. He doesn't have the authority to hand down the sentence he did; he won't give me an extension without figuring out how long it would take me to override the other Truth Machines, and that'll take them a lot longer than 60 days. Besides, if he did, Shaw would never go for it. The verdict's already on record. If Lezar ever gave me any more than the 60 days they all agreed to, Shaw would just appeal the sentence—in a hummingbird's heartbeat."

"I'm sure you're right. But they're offering you freedom—and your life. Won't you at least take a couple days to decide?"

"I've already decided."

"Will you discuss it with Maya first?"

"No. She'd just try to talk me out of it. I'll risk the appeal. Are you going to represent me or not?"

David knew it was no use to argue. He embraced his friend. "Of course I am."

David and Pete returned to the courtroom.

"Judge, we have a change in plans," David announced. "We've decided to appeal both the verdict *and* the sentence."

THOMAS L. MOSELY
Dallas, Texas—July 18, 2050

At last, we arrive at the present. Because you purchased our book, *The Truth Machine*, you're entitled to a series of updates. With timeliness no longer such an issue, I will now take over the writing myself. Lucky you.

It took my 22g CP about seven minutes to write *The Truth Machine*. I spent two and a half days editing it, although I made very few changes. I can still do things the machine cannot, but I'll never be able to write with the clarity of a 22g. Most revisions I considered would have sacrificed precision in favor of only marginally "prettier" prose, a poor trade in a narrative such as this.

Before I begin my part of the journal, I want to thank the Intel Corporation for inventing the 22g CP that has helped make me, for the first time in my life, a wealthy man. At least for a reporter. I'm told *The Truth Machine* is now the number one best-selling work on the subject, with nearly 400 million copies disseminated. Obviously I never could have gotten it publication-ready so quickly without the 22g.

What surprised me most was the number of hard-copy (paper) versions sold: over 175,000 in the first two days, a record for a new release over the past decade. Typical of time-sensitive chronicles, sales have since slowed to a trickle. Still, with ecoscientists predicting that trees will begin to overwhelm the planet within 50 years if growth continues at the present rate, I find it gratifying that our book has single-handedly delayed this process by several seconds. I like hard-copy books but have never met a person under age 30 who understands why anyone would buy one.

I'm also grateful to Pete Armstrong and David West for allowing such access. They withheld almost nothing in either of their archives and encouraged us to be as objective as possible. I hope we were.

The defense's strategy of openness with the press was

shrewd, even though it failed to win a not-guilty verdict. Sincerity leads to powerful emotional identification and compassion. I've often speculated that if a filmmaker could present Saddam Hussein's life story from the murderous tyrant's honest point of view (say, in a three hour VR presentation or even a celluloid "movie"), by story's end half the audience would find themselves commiserating with the guy, or at least occasionally forgetting to root against him. Not that one should mention Armstrong and Hussein in the same breath. If anything, they are antithetical. The point is, however, that candor elicits strong human empathy.

That might be why the average person cares more about other people now than in pre–Truth Machine times.

I spoke with David West immediately after the trial and naturally he was supportive of the project. He encouraged me to have my 22g programmed to my own style of writing, an artful way of suggesting that I'd have to be out of my mind to write it myself. Unfortunately I cut my journalistic teeth back when reporters did their own writing; most younger writers today work far better with computers than I do. I realized time was of the essence, but must admit I balked.

"Sir, it'll take a little longer, but I'd really rather write this book unassisted by the computer."

"Maybe we'll just write our own book then," he said with a wicked grin. "You know, Tom, we have an 88g and could just as easily input William Faulkner's style as that of some broken-down street reporter."

While he had me laughing, he deftly softened the blow with gracious flattery. "By the way, my friends call me David. It seems to me we've known each other for about 40 years."

I just muttered, "Yes, Mr. Pres—er, I mean, David."

He was correct to advise delegating the writing to the 22g, though. This manuscript would have been outdated were it published next month instead of three days ago. And I would still be moonlighting as a VR critic.

Now you're up-to-date on the history of the Truth Machine and the life of its inventor, Randall Petersen Armstrong. Together, we'll wait and see what happens.

EPILOGUE

THE APPEAL—July 21, 2050—Thomas L. Mosely

Diana and David West sit side by side in their office at home, amidst the clutter of word processors, computers, and research machines. Their screens having been set at 57-percent brightness grade (91.8-percent summer sunlight equivalent), the incandescence surrounds them. Intended to foster alertness, it is now just a merciless reminder of their hunger for that elusive rarity in their recent lives: sleep. Normally they love working together, but lately they're exhausted.

The two world-famous attorneys have written a moving, concise, and logical 6,400-word document. The reading of it would convince any reasonable person that Pete Armstrong does not deserve to die and that such punishment would not serve the best interest of the human race. Still, they expect to lose. Even with all the resources at their disposal, they have been unable to come up with a decent legal argument upon which to base the appeal.

So far they've concentrated most of their efforts on the definition of self-defense. This course of action is problematic, however, because the jury has already decided the issue. It seems unlikely that the Tribunal would overrule them.

Their other apparent avenue would be the Amnesty

Bill, but that approach has difficulties as well. The language of the bill clearly states that to be sentenced under guidelines in effect during 2031, one must have confessed prior to the end of that year. Obviously Pete did no such thing.

Nevertheless Diana, who can barely keep her eyes open, decides to review the Amnesty Bill a final time. The idea strikes her like a thunderbolt.

"David. I think we've got a chance!"

Her sudden enthusiasm startles him. "Whadja find?"

"I didn't exactly find anything, but I have a theory." Diana, now fully spirited, explains, "When the laws were enacted, the ACIP had been in use for six and a half years. It was called the Amnesty Bill, but the name's misleading. That might be why we never thought of this before."

"Go on."

"I think the Amnesty Bill was intended to apply only to those susceptible to scips."

"That sounds interesting."

"Amnesty was just an afterthought. The focus of the bill was to equitably dispose of hundreds of millions of previous crimes discovered by the ACIP and to prevent violent crimes in the future by increasing the penalties. It wasn't written to catch more criminals, since it was already impossible for lawbreakers *not* to be caught."

"Okay. I'm with you so far."

"They added a grandfather provision, including amnesty, to reduce the stigma associated with pre–Truth Machine crimes, since most pre-ACIP criminals were no longer considered dangerous."

"I think I'm starting to see your point. Keep going." David too now appears totally alert.

"The grandfather provision allowed that crimes committed before January 1st would be punished less severely if the perpetrator confessed by the end of 2031. Again, the word 'confess' is misleading. The drafters of the bill must have assumed that everyone who'd committed crimes would automatically be caught next time they were scipped and would thereby be *forced* to confess. Overlooked was the possibility that somebody might not be vulnerable to scipping. Therefore, we can argue that the deadline shouldn't apply to Pete."

" 'Light dawns on Marblehead,' " jokes David. "I get it now. Were there any violent criminals eligible who *didn't* confess and receive amnesty?"

"None who were mentally competent. Eventually everybody has to apply for a job or public assistance or a license of some sort. Nobody could leave the country without passing through customs. By 2031, there was no way to avoid getting caught. As best I can tell, Pete was the only murderer who survived the year without confessing."

David is jubilant. He kisses her forehead and embraces her. "You're a genius."

Diana smiles. "I have my moments, don't I?"

David contacts two of the former Senate aides who helped draft the bill. Both agree to sign affidavits supporting Diana's theory.

In spite of their lack of sleep, the Wests decide to stay up all night. They intend to file the appeal document the next morning.

WORLD TRIBUNAL—August 3, 2050—Thomas L. Mosely

Most businesses, especially those requiring physical presence of workers, are closed today. The others will doubtless accomplish very little; few of us are capable of performing any real work until the appeal verdict has been rendered. The appeal arrived at the World Tribunal on July 23 and was challenged by Carlton Shaw four days later. Today's decision will be discussed in every historical text covering this century.

The entire world will watch in real-time as Pete Armstrong learns his fate.

The World Tribunal, currently based in Cairo, Egypt, consists of 11 justices, six women and five men. Every active judge in the world participated in their selection and all 11 were carefully chosen for wisdom and steady temperament. The Chief Justice this year is Molly Skylar,[27] the former President of Holland. The Tribunal decides an average of 16 cases per day, usually from written documents, only rarely allowing testimony via holographic transmission. They never invite any defendant or attorney to appear in person.

The Tribunal is in many ways the most powerful of all government bodies. It is the final arbiter of the most momentous controversies, many with abstract, highly intricate ramifications. Therefore nothing it does can be secret. Every deliberation is open to public inspection. David West himself saw to that. "The key to sustained democracy—and to justice itself—is freedom of information," he argued nearly 15 years ago. "Our highest court must never keep secrets from those of us who are subject to its decisions."

Yesterday the Tribunal released results of a probability analysis by their state-of-the-art artificial intelligence machines. Five of the most interesting conclusions are paraphrased here for any readers who are statistics aficionados. Keep in mind that these assertions are speculative. But I hope they're correct, considering how much it cost to build those machines.

Results of World Tribunal Probability Analysis, released on August 2, 2050

1) Without the ACIP in use, the chances that civilization as we know it would not have survived until now are 1 in 10.4675. That means there is about a 9.6-percent chance that Armstrong's Truth Machine has

---

[27] For the sake of international uniformity, the spelling of her last name was legally changed from Schuyler to the phonetic spelling, "Skylar," during her second presidential term.

already saved the human race from total or near-total annihilation.

2) Without the Truth Machine, installation of a World Government would have been statistically impossible without overwhelming military force. Even with force, the chances for its long-term success would have been only 1.4 percent.

3) There is an insignificant chance—less than 1 in 10 million—that any other living person on earth, excluding Armstrong, has been able to circumvent the ACIP. The world may assume the ACIP is still 100-percent effective.

4) The probability of a random individual (excluding Armstrong) being able to circumvent a Truth Machine during this century is less than 1 in 17 trillion. The odds that even one individual throughout the entire world, other than Armstrong, could achieve that ability within the next 100 years is only 1 in 92.

5) Should the Truth Machine or World Government now fail, apocalyptic war would become virtually inevitable. In fact without them there is only a 34.12-percent likelihood (barely one chance in three) that humankind will survive beyond the 21st century.

David West is troubled by the announcement. The statistics, although supportive of the ACIP and of Pete Armstrong's contribution to humankind, also suggest that the integrity of the Truth Machine must be the foremost goal of the Tribunal's decision.

The Tribunal has asked Pete to submit to questioning. Six technicians, two of them human, assemble a Kodak Holographic Module in his home and also install a CyCare Truth Machine. Maya, David, and Diana will watch from another room while Pete testifies. No one is permitted to advise or communicate with him during his testimony. While the world watches him through a one-way current of digital bits, Pete himself will be deprived of all outside data.

He enters the chamber, its seamless ebony walls surrounding him. Upon being seated and sworn in, he begins to rock. Now that he has a chance to survive on his own terms, he appears more nervous than when he seemed to have no hope.

The 10 Associate Justices on the Tribunal dictate continuous notes into their digital network. These notes, which will be analyzed in detail by the press over the coming days and weeks and years, are synthesized into questions by an IBM System 778 logic processor. Chief Justice Skylar reads the questions as they appear on her screen. She is the only member who maintains direct contact with Pete. But her words are formed through a team effort of the Tribunal, almost as though Pete were being interviewed by a single person with 11 brains.

"Mr. Armstrong, why did you appeal Judge Lezar's verdict?"

Pete answers slowly and deliberately, reciting a memorized response to an anticipated question. "F-For over eight years I've d-devoted all my working hours to the creation of a series of computer models. I hope these m-models will allow scientists to conduct aging research more efficiently than presently possible. I need at least five more months, maybe longer, to complete the models. My work requires total recall, an ability I currently have. The treatment prescribed by Judge Lezar's verdict would compromise that ability. It would be impossible for me to f-finish the project after receiving treatment for IDD."

"Would you have killed Charles Scoggins had you not been able to circumvent the ACIP?"

Pete continues rocking. "N-No. I'm p-positive I would not have c-committed *any* of my crimes if I had known I'd be caught right away."

The Truth Machine light remains green.

"Mr. Armstrong, can you assure us you will never,

under any circumstances, try to circumvent the Truth Machine again?"

For the past several weeks, Pete has considered how he would answer this inevitable question.

"I d-d-don't *think* I ever w-would. I have no intentions to do so t-today, but how can anyone give such open-ended assurances in a world that's always changing?"

Now Pete rocks more intensely, no doubt worried that his answer has sealed his fate.

Skylar's questioning continues. "Have you begun performing any of the calculations necessary to circumvent other Truth Machines?"

"N-Not when I'm awake, but I do them automatically in my s-sleep."

"How does that work?"

"Ever since I was about s-seven years old, I've developed algorithms and written s-software code in my sleep. I go to b-bed with a problem to solve, and by the time I awaken each morning, I usually have a solution in mind."

Skylar pauses while the rest of the Tribunal ponders the situation. Finally another question appears on her screen. She asks, "Can you teach yourself to think and dream about something else?"

"I d-doubt it. I've rarely dreamt about anything other than software for over 50 years. For example, Justice S-Skylar, could *you* ever force yourself to stop thinking about l-law or government? The Truth Machine's been a major part of my life; I can't help thinking about it."

I cannot communicate with him inside the KHM and I doubt that I'll speak with him before my self-imposed deadline of 10:00 a.m. tomorrow; therefore I can only wonder what's going through his mind right now. Perhaps he's recalling his recurrent dreams of flying from childhood before his brother's murder.

"We all understand we cannot police people's thoughts, only their actions and intentions," Skylar allows, a rare ad lib. The Chief Justice knows that billions are watching, so she is clarifying the Tribunal's basic legal precepts for the audience.

Once again, she reads from her screen. "How long do you think it will take you to develop the ability to circumvent the Truth Machine?"

"No less than two years, and that assumes all other Truth Machines function in the same manner as the ACIP. Otherwise I'm not sure I could ever do it."

"That confirms our own analysis. Thank you, Mr. Armstrong."

The Justices enter their opinions and reasoning into the digital network. Maya, David, and Diana linger in the purgatory of their doubt; for them the seconds seem to progress with all the blinding speed of a tree growing, or as Pete might say, a winded snail. After an agonizing 6 minutes and 11 seconds, Skylar prepares to announce their decision.

"Mr. Armstrong, we Justices of the World Tribunal unanimously agree that we cannot risk the possibility you might someday override other Truth Machines. The stakes are too high to allow an indispensable component of our society, indeed of our ability to survive as a species, to be jeopardized."

In tears, Maya stares at David and Diana, looking to them to repudiate her own prediction of doom. Their dejected expressions betray only blighted hopes.

Pete's face remains frozen, constant.

"Mr. Armstrong, you've certainly been thinking about this: Is there any 100-percent certain way we haven't thought of to prevent you from learning how to override other Truth Machines?"

"Nothing I've b-been able to c-c-come up with."

Skylar continues, "Do you have any questions, or is there any statement you wish to make before I pronounce sentence?"

"N-No, Justice Skylar."

"We will now sentence you in conformance with guidelines in effect during the year 2031."

Maya, David, and Diana can barely believe their ears. *Guidelines in effect during the year 2031!*

Of course. What other decision could the Tribunal possibly make? They can't take the life of a man whose invention might have saved the human race; neither can they abide an ability to render useless his great gift to humankind. History would never forgive either transgression.

Pete appears stoic, his expression still barely changed. Perhaps it hasn't yet sunk in that he is not going to die, or maybe he knew all along that this final outcome was inevitable. Or is he already mourning his impending loss of memory that in some ways may be tantamount to losing his very soul?

Skylar continues. "We cannot hold your actions to a standard that was created as a result of the ACIP, since you were not subject to its scrutiny at the time. You have already made monetary reparations to Renaissance Corporation's shareholders, the only proven victims of those crimes. Therefore, under the terms of the Amnesty Bill, there will be no further punishment for the offenses of fraud, perjury, and obstruction of justice.

"For the murder of Charles Scoggins, we request that you submit to IDD treatment within one year of today. Our analysis suggests this treatment will be both salutary and beneficial, generally speaking, and will remove any future danger you might pose to society. If you fail to so submit yourself, you will face incarceration until we find another way to guarantee that the Truth Machine remains foolproof, or until you are willing to receive the treatment. In the meantime you may continue your work for as long as you wish—even if you decide a year from now to go to prison rather than accept treatment. Mr. Armstrong, we thank you for your many contributions to humanity and wish you the very best of luck."

Pete's expression remains inscrutable. He simply answers. "Thank you. You've been more than f-fair."

THE DILEMMA—June 15, 2051—Thomas L. Mosely

I imagine writing software is like any other form of writing; you can keep editing forever and it still won't be perfect. Take it from me, I know about the obsessions of writers. Perfectionism usually arises from a quest for something other than perfection.

Pete's computer models were published 31 days ago. I've discussed them with several researchers on aging, all of whom believe the models are astoundingly useful. But Pete insists he has more work to do. Furthermore, his nervous tics, which had subsided for a while, now seem to be getting worse. I'm no psychiatrist, but I suspect Pete is reluctant to give up his perfect memory.

I call him. He returns my call about an hour later and grants me a short interview.

I ask in my usual less-than-tactful way, "You and I both know the models are plenty good enough. What's *really* going on?"

He hesitates before answering. "Maya, David, and Diana tell me I should just submit myself and get it over with. Tilly called it a no-brainer, which she later admitted was a terrible choice of words." He laughs good-naturedly.

"My friends are right though. I'll have to get the treatment eventually. First of all, I think I do have IDD. Probably had it all my life. They say the treatment'll help me become a happier person—more relaxed mentally— you know, more balanced. That doesn't seem too bad. Secondly, the latest estimate from the Department of Medicine is that it'll be at least 10 years before they can come up with a formula to allow me to keep my mnemonic skills intact and still guarantee I could never override other Truth Machines. I could always go to prison instead, but I couldn't spend 10 weeks away from

Maya and my little boys, much less 10 years. No sense going at all if I don't have to."

"So you'll submit to treatment before the deadline?"

"I th-think so."

"Are you having trouble accepting that you won't be able to work at the same level?"

"Maybe. In a way, I think it's selfish of me to accept the treatment because of that. I've always believed I had a responsibility to help the world solve its problems. Maya refers to it as my 'God complex,' which I hate to repeat because it sounds so egotistical. She might be right, though. All my life I've thought, 'I have to do this work for humanity's sake. Can't let the world down.' But what's a 'God complex' really, other than an oversized ego? My ego is what got me into trouble in the first place. And I guess that's even harder for me to abandon than my memory."

"There must be positive things about the treatment. Most IDD sufferers take it voluntarily."

"I can see both sides. But f-frankly I'm scared for more personal reasons."

"Tell me what you mean."

Pete ponders for a moment. "Are you aware that in most wild animal parks, they neuter all tigers by altering their hormones?"

"No, I didn't know that."

"They do it to make them more serene. It allows them to live together more harmoniously. It's actually a healthful process that measurably improves and lengthens the tigers' lives. But when they do it, they also r-remove part of whatever it is that makes them tigers." (Pete *loves* animal metaphors.)

"Tom," he continues, "I've had total recall almost my entire life. It's part of who I am. I can remember every word of every conversation I've ever had with Maya, every sound and gesture my little boys have ever made, everything I've ever experienced since before my third birthday. Of course I could record whatever occurs in the future and play back what I want to remember, but much of the past will be gone f-forever. If I can no longer evoke those memories, what is it that makes me the same person?"

I don't have an answer for that one; it's too complicated for my pedestrian mind. But it seems to me that a perfect memory might be a curse as well as a blessing. Don't get me wrong—if someone offered me that talent, I wouldn't turn it down. But I imagine Pete has memories he'd just as soon forget. I'm sure we all do.

THE TREATMENT—July 20, 2051—Thomas L. Mosley

In a way, our judiciary is like a team of forest rangers using break-fires to fight fires. Combating injustice efficiently requires a certain resignation to it. Today's sentencing process barely considers the motivations or character of the perpetrator; hardly in keeping with the 20th-century Christian notion of equity under which my generation was raised. But with nothing less than the continuation of our species at stake, we are forced to stick with what works.

Pete Armstrong's good deeds will not go unpunished.

He awoke this morning, arguably the most intelligent person on the planet. Tonight when he goes to sleep, there will be hundreds of millions of individuals on earth smarter than he is. His formidable mind will have been irreversibly reduced by the very society he may have saved. This outcome seems a tragic betrayal. Yet it is also as happy an ending to this saga as anyone could have realistically expected. When you think about the nature of civilization before the ACIP, it might be a miracle that any of us are still here at all.

We humans tend to forget that civilization is a system of tradeoffs. The perfect world is an unattainable goal. Seldom can members of society gain benefit without exacting a cost, either from themselves or someone else. The human race has opted for survival over privacy, prosperity over individual rights. We have learned that these goals cannot be nurtured simultaneously.

Likewise, Pete made a difficult choice 27 years ago. Humanity reaped a great dividend from that choice, but Pete must now face the consequences alone.

The room looks like any other hospital ward: brightly lit, perfectly clean and sterile, pliant white ceramic floors, walls, and ceiling. All cabinets and desks have been melded into the walls for now, but a blue-uniformed technician presses a few buttons on the control panel by the door and the nanomachines get to work. A chair emerges from the floor.

The technician asks, "Mr. Armstrong, have you eaten solid food in the last three hours?"

"No."

"Please have a seat."

Pete sits in the chair, which adapts to his body perfectly. The ceramic materials comprising it invisibly reconfigure themselves, shackling his arms and legs. The set-up is now remarkably similar in appearance, I muse, to the execution chambers used during the early part of the millennium— after Swift and Sure, but long before the ACIP. Maybe the treatment is symbolic of an execution; when he leaves this room, a part of him will be dead.

"This'll be very quick," the technician assures him, "and painless."

Pete is calm enough to remain perfectly still.

Still, he must wonder, *Will I emerge intact from the treatment? Or will the person who rises from the chair no longer be me?* The quality that gives each of us our uniqueness is incomprehensible. Many religions still contend that each person has an eternal soul. But most scientists will tell you there is no such thing and there is now proof that all conscious thought is simply a form of electrical energy directed into highly complex patterns by the brain. When the brain dies, the electrical energy ceases and there is nothing more. If the scientists are right, Pete will indeed become a different person; the treatment will alter those patterns.

Then again, perhaps we all become different people over time anyway. Sometimes, when I look at my journals from college or other writings I composed many years ago, I think that the person who wrote those things could not possibly have been me. And yet it was, wasn't it?

Even in the Truth Machine era, some truths are unknowable.

The technician warns Pete, "Now the medicine is injecting. Please try to sit still. If you move, it may have a stronger effect than we want."

The potion goes into his jugular vein through the neck. It's painless. In fact, Pete would not be aware of it, except that the technician tells him exactly what's happening at each step.

"It'll take about 90 seconds for the medication to reach your brain. You'll notice very little change, even though the effect'll be almost instantaneous."

Pete waits for the treatment to take hold. Less than two minutes later he is unshackled, but his body does not begin to rock; he's absolutely motionless. This change takes me by surprise as I'm sure it does many of my fellow reporters. None of us ever expected to see Pete Armstrong sit completely still.

The technician warns him, "Don't get up too quickly, Mr. Armstrong. Most people experience some lightheadedness. Occasionally they faint."

Finally Pete stands and appears to be smiling. "I don't even feel dizzy."

Later, at the press conference, I ask him if he feels any different.

"Not really, Tom. Maybe a little calmer. My mind seems less cluttered, I suppose. But I'm definitely still Pete Armstrong, for better or for worse."

But I have never seen him look this, well, normal. He seems so relaxed, not at all fidgety. I wonder if he really *is* the same Pete Armstrong, and if he isn't, how would he know? I'm not even sure I understand exactly what I mean by that.

SIX MONTHS LATER—January 20, 2052—
Thomas L. Mosely

A few weeks ago I persuaded Pete to grant me real-time access to his digital archives for one day. With today's optic and audile technology, real-time means I get to see and hear exactly what he sees and hears, at the same time he does, with no editing. Pete treasures his privacy these days and such access is rarely granted. I guess he felt *The Truth Machine* might have helped him get amnesty, so he feels beholden.

We agreed I'd get the access today, exactly six months after he received treatment.

Maya and Pete have a solid marriage, but IDD treatment was not an easy adjustment, particularly for Maya. She had been so relieved her husband's life was spared that she never considered what its effects might be on her. Today Pete is more relaxed, his mind focused on his family rather than on saving the world. This attitude may be a side effect of the treatment, or perhaps he simply recognizes his new limitations.

He is, of course, no longer possessed of the same over-powering intellect, which Maya misses. By most objective measures, Pete is now less intelligent than his wife.

There were times when Maya questioned whether Pete was still the same man she had married. Who wouldn't wonder? In pre-ACIP days, such feelings in marriages would often fester until the relationship was no longer salvageable. Fortunately the Truth Machine forced them to confront the issue, uncomfortable as it was, head-on.

Pete had insecurities about his diminished mental

powers and was surprised at how easily he adapted to being "normal."

"Look, Maya," he'd said, "I'm still the same person I always was; just not as smart as I used to be. But in a way, I *like* it. I never knew I could be this happy." He'd grinned wryly. "There's a lot to be said for the quiet life."

Then they had both laughed as Michael's ear-splitting demand for attention rang through the house. Maya had risen, but Pete caught her hand and looked into her eyes. "I have *time* now—and I still love you and the boys more than anything in the world."

We humans do adapt to reality extremely well, once we recognize it. That may be the Truth Machine's greatest value of all: clarifying reality. Maya and Pete attended several weeks of professional counseling that, since money was no object, was supervised by a human therapist. They both believe the sessions were beneficial.

Pete later told me, "I came to realize that without the ACIP, my relationship with Maya might never have worked in the first place. We both would've fallen into patterns of deceit, as in all my pre-ACIP relationships. After the treatment the Truth Machine put us through a difficult time, but may also have saved our marriage."

Maya agreed. "The Truth Machine forces people to confront their feelings candidly. The treatment changed Pete and left him with less of the intelligence that had initially attracted me. At first I felt cheated. But soon I realized he was also less intimidating, more patient, and more sensitive. He'd lost some of his brilliance, but gained a certain tenderness. The new Pete was neither better nor worse, just different. I fell in love with him all over again."

Now they're contemplating having another child.

Maya continues to work at ATI, she and Pete sharing the position of CEO. Under World Law, the stock remains in his name until he decides to transfer it. New products aren't being developed as rapidly as they once were, but ATI still owns most of the best software franchises. The licensing fees are a money machine. ATI continues to be the most profitable company in the world, although its stock price has declined over the past several years.

Pete still donates to charities, particularly intelligence and aging research and health education programs. Recently however, he's begun to place most of his income into trusts for his sons; the bulk of his fortune will go to Leonard, Michael, and to other Armstrongs yet unborn.

A few weeks ago Pete explained his reasoning to me. "I'd always planned to give the money away myself. But after the treatment I decided that when our children reach adulthood, the trusts should fall under their control. It won't be long before they're more intelligent and I hope much wiser than I am. I'll let them figure out the best way to distribute the money, or even if we should donate it at all."

It's Saturday morning, about 9:30. Pete kisses his wife goodbye. Maya plans to work until 3:00 p.m., while Pete babysits their sons.

"What do you guys feel like doing today?"

Before Leonard can say anything, Michael shouts, "Disney Texas!"

Leonard grimaces. He would obviously rather read a book or go swimming. They've already been to the Galveston theme park a dozen times in the last six months. But he goes along with it.

"Okay with me."

Leonard is now four years old and Michael is two and a half. The boys adore their dad and vice versa. But small boys can be a handful and little Michael is the epitome of impishness. As you'd expect, they're both bright for their age. Michael is astonishingly quick and astute, although he doesn't have his brother's awareness of the effect he has on others. Or maybe he just doesn't care.

Leonard is a quiet child. When he does talk, he speaks like an adult, with clear pronunciation and excellent grammar. I'm told he reads constantly and is very sensitive, as his father was at that age. He also inherited his father's photographic memory, although that's not such a rare characteristic in small children. In fact only a small percentage of child prodigies ever realize the promised potential of their early years.

Pete dresses Michael, which is always a chore. Michael makes a game of it, taking his clothes off almost as quickly as Pete puts them on him. Pete laughs cheerfully, but Leonard, obviously less patient, decides to start a computer game. It's just a ploy, but a cunningly clever one.

Michael, thinking Leonard actually intends to play on the computer, commandeers it for himself and begins playing "Escape from the Zoo." The holographic animals appear in the center of the room. The zookeepers must employ a completely different tactic to capture each one and get it back into its cage before the next animal escapes. One false move and the zookeepers are overwhelmed, ending the game.

Michael is a pro at Zoo. It's amazing to see how he runs through each segment of the game without missing a stroke. I'm told he never loses, which would be unusual even for an adult. With Michael thus distracted, Pete finally begins to dress him for their excursion.

With nothing to do but wait, Leonard calls for Marvin, their cat. Marvin runs into the room and jumps into Leonard's lap. Leonard begins to pet the purring animal.

"Want me to tickle your belly, Marv? How's that?"

Michael sneers at the cat and goes back to the game. Pete continues trying to dress Michael while he plays.

Pete knows I'm watching; he laughs. "Tom, this is pretty much what my life's like now."

It's obvious he's loving every minute of it.

If Galveston were closer, they would use their gyrocopter, which is subsonic. Instead, the 300-mile subway trip takes 11 minutes, which is still enough time to test Michael's patience. The two-year-old demands relentless attention and Pete spends the entire ride reading Darryl the

Dinosaur stories to him. They have one of the new portable holographic screens and Michael's eyes are glued to the images. I can't tell whether he can actually read the words yet, or if he just remembers everything. Every so often Pete changes or omits a word just to tease him.

"Darryl wants to know why Carly eats eggs and lizards while Billy the Triceratops only likes leaves."

Michael is not fooled. He always corrects his father, pretending to be upset at his mistakes, which is also part of the game.

He giggles. "Daddy! Billy's a *brontosaurus*. Pay attention, Sluggo!"

Pete pretends he's insulted and Michael laughs. Throughout the entire trip, Leonard hardly ever takes his eyes off Michael. Obviously he finds his little brother fascinating. So do I.

When they arrive, Michael wants to go straight to "The Alamo." It's his favorite ride. It's Leonard's favorite, too, but even if it weren't, there's little doubt who would have gotten his way.

The walk takes four minutes, during which almost everyone they pass seems to recognize Pete. He's popular these days, especially in Texas. Most people just nod or wave, but a few greet him with, "I'm glad you got amnesty," or "I thought you deserved a medal, not IDD treatment," or something similar. Nobody says anything negative.

Pete always thanks them and occasionally adds something like, "I appreciate your saying that." He seems pleased when people talk to him. He even gives his thumbprint to a teenage boy, although he usually doesn't do autographs when he's with his kids.

When they arrive at the Alamo, there's no waiting. There never is anymore, even at peak times, since they added C30 logarithms to the people-mover software. They go right in and watch a seven-minute VR disc, which both boys know by heart. They recite all the words along with the announcer and act out the movements with Travis and Crockett and all the other heroes in the center of the room, now loading the cannons. A lot of children are doing the same thing, which used to be quite a problem until the Disney organization began installing soundproof microwave barriers around each cart.

Then their cart takes them inside to the main event. Pete finds the lighting a bit dark and they're too close to the action for his taste. He instructs his wristband to calculate the optimal setting for his digital contact lenses so he can see the show perfectly. I'm grateful for the adjustment too, since I see whatever he sees.

"Now that I'm over 60," he says, "I should probably think about getting automatic lenses."

He should indeed, but not because of his age. Neither of us yet realizes adjusting the lenses would actually be counterproductive. He spends 14 of the next 15 minutes watching Leonard and Michael rather than the show. He doesn't want to miss a single laugh or expression of wonder on their faces.

They have time for 15 more rides over the next four hours. The day goes by quickly and soon it's time to return to Dallas. Pete wants to be there when Maya gets home at three o'clock.

Apparently Michael has only two speeds: full and stop. He falls fast asleep in his father's arms as they walk back to the subway.

"What is it about the Alamo that you guys like so much?" Pete asks his four-year-old son. It's their first opportunity for a real conversation, since Michael, were he still awake, would never tolerate being anything other than the center of attention.

"Michael just likes the characters and the fighting and all the noise. But I like the story."

"What *about* the story, Len?"

"Those men were willing to die for a cause. They wanted to help their families and neighbors become free.

They wanted it so much. And they all died, but they still won. It's a *great* story, Dad."

Considering his age, I find Leonard's insight remarkable, but Pete must be used to it.

He simply answers, "It sure is."

That night, while Pete reads his sons their bedtime stories, he tries to think back to his own childhood. Did the legend of the Alamo affect him the way it now touches his older boy? He's sure he learned the story when he was young. Yet as hard as he tries, he can't recall exactly how he felt about it. He wishes he could. It's the first time today that he misses having his old memory.

(I know this because he tells me a few minutes later. I'll also speak to Pete, Maya, and Leonard again the next morning before I submit my final version.)

Michael is asleep and Pete has finished reading a bedtime story to Leonard. He doesn't want to leave him just yet. "How about one more story?"

"No thanks, Dad. I want to go to sleep now—and dream."

"What do you dream about, Len?"

"I always dream I can fly. It's really fun to dream about flying."

"I know it is. I remember."

Leonard looks surprised. "You used to dream about flying?"

"I sure did. A long time ago. When I was about your age."

Leonard stares at his father's face for a moment, then just smiles and says, "Good night, Dad. I love you."

"I love you, too, son."

These days, Pete still dreams about software, but now when he awakens he can no longer reconstruct the code. He remembers how he used to dream about flying and wonders if he'll someday dream such dreams again. He imagines his son's pleasure in the dream is much akin to his own delight 57 years ago, when an entire life of limitless promise lay ahead, spread out before him like a breathtaking, panoramic horizon at the onset of a long journey. A tear rolls down his cheek as he watches his son's eyes close. Leonard begins to rock gently from side to side, and within seconds, he's asleep.

Finally in his own bed, perfectly still, comfortably nestled next to the woman he loves, the woman he knows he will always love, Pete tries to recall the world he inhabited when he was his son's age. He remembers enough to discern a place where you never knew who were your friends and enemies; a realm of changing allegiances rendered even more treacherous by the fact that nearly everyone told you the truth almost all the time. But not always.

In this world you never knew which of your comrades, in professedly kindred formation beside you, secretly plotted your deathly descent.

As he drifts to sleep, Pete Armstrong harbors no bitterness against the world he tried to save, a world he perhaps did save, a world that still saw fit to remove a part of him. He feels lucky to have survived such a world at all. He cannot imagine how his life could have turned out any better.

Across the hall, Leonard Gale Armstrong sleeps, a pure slumber of innocent childhood, once again dreaming he can fly. And in Leonard's dream world, his powers are such that when he flies, anyone else he invites along is able to fly as well, so long as he wishes it so. The others gratefully join him as they soar over their gleaming Dallas neighborhood, waving and greeting the amazed onlookers below.

IS THERE A TRUTH MACHINE
IN YOUR FUTURE?

Nobody is likely to agree with every political idea, much less every "prediction" explored in this novel. Nor do I endorse them all myself. But my hope is that the story provokes thought. We cannot prepare for the future without contemplation, and like it or not, the future *is* coming.

The Truth Machine was my first work of fiction, written in 1995 as an amateur's pastime. It was self published in June 1996, and in July was discovered by the editors of Ballantine/Del Rey. I'm both gratified and amazed by the public's reaction to it.

I have considered myself a futurist since my early teens. I think most of us are. We wonder what tomorrow's innovations will be. Will they improve our lives, or hasten our end?

If we are to survive a world of nanotechnology, back-pack nuclear weapons, and designer viruses, I suspect that the human race might really need a truth machine. So long as the device remains foolproof (admittedly, a big "if"), it may well offer the best hope of preventing our self-destruction. Others might reasonably contend that if misused, the truth machine itself would become our enemy. But then what does that say about the value of truth versus deceit?

Either way, a truth machine, although scientifically possible, might take a long time to arrive. Politics and economics will likely influence the timetable of its development even more than will technological progress.

Business managers could decide the demand doesn't justify the research expense required to develop a truth machine. Politicians and others might feel threatened by it, although with everyone in the same boat, most pre-truth machine transgressions would have to be ignored. Some may disagree with the premise that a truth machine will create benefits outweighing its drawbacks. We will even hear the argument that it is our God-given right to lie. Either side of the debate would be easy to advocate.

Those who fear for their privacy, however, should bear in mind that privacy must dissipate regardless. Cameras, recorders, data storage, and communications devices of all description are becoming exponentially smaller, cheaper, and therefore omnipresent—with or without a truth machine.

If you believe, as I do, that having more people thinking about these issues helps, do talk about it. Give this book to friends. Or if you really liked the novel, send it to your senator or congressperson. (Mail me a copy of your cover letter c/o Ballantine and I'll send you a personal thank-you note.) Whenever you're in a bookstore or library, please ask the staff to check it out. Since there are thousands of other novels vying for attention, booksellers and librarians tend to be the most efficient advocates for books they like. And based on publisher surveys, I'm pleased to report that booksellers usually love *The Truth Machine* once they're persuaded to read it.

You can also post your opinions on numerous Internet chat and newsgroups, including the Truth Machine Forum at: www.truthmachine.com

I'm grateful to anyone who completes all or part of the Reader Survey that follows. No need to sign it unless you wish. I read them all, and answer some. If the Reader Survey is missing from this book, please write to: The Truth Machine, c/o Ballantine Books, 201 E. 50th Street, New York 10022.

—J. L. H., March 1997

AGE EQUIVALENCY TABLE (Ages are rounded to the nearest whole year and reflect appearance, vitality, general health, and remaining life expectancy.)

YEAR:	1990	2000	2010	2020	2030	2040	2050
	20	20	20	21	21	21	22
	25	25	25	26	26	27	28
	30	31	32	33	34	35	36
	35	36	38	39	40	42	43
	40	41	43	44	46	48	50
	45	47	49	51	54	56	58
	50	52	55	57	60	62	65
	55	57	61	64	67	70	73
	60	63	67	70	74	77	80
	65	68	74	78	82	85	88
	70	73	79	84	88	92	95
	75	78	84	88	92	96	100
	80	84	90	94	98	103	107

AVERAGE ADULT HEIGHT

	1990	2000	2010	2020	2030	2040	2050
Male	5'9"	5'10"	5'11"	5'11"	6'	6'1"	6'2"
Female	5'4"	5'5"	5'6"	5'8"	5'9"	5'10"	5'11"

(Heights listed are for 35-year-old Americans and are rounded to the nearest inch.)

DOLLAR CONVERSION TABLE

Each year's figure reflects $1,000 in present (2050) value after accounting for inflation.

1990	1995	2000	2005	2010	2015	2020
$12	$14	$24	$46	$79	$115	$206

2025	2030	2035	2040	2045	2050
$386	$482	$558	$689	$821	$1,000

(All statistics have been calculated as of January 1; monetary amounts are rounded to the nearest even dollar.)

Travis Hall's "Blackstone Address," June 5, 1998

Sir William Blackstone, the great English jurist who compiled the Treatise of British Common Law upon which the Constitution and Bill of Rights of the United States were based, once wrote: "It is better that 10 guilty persons escape than one innocent suffer." What did Blackstone mean when he penned those words? How do you suppose he would have accounted for those innocent people certain to suffer at the hands of the 10 freed guilty persons? Have we been taking Blackstone's words too literally?

Today we are at war. It is not a war waged against another country and fought on foreign shores. This armed conflict, far more dangerous than Vietnam was for my generation, is one we confront upon our own soil. Again, we are our own worst enemy.

In Vietnam our government had two sensible alternatives, neither of which were adopted. We could have admitted a limited defeat and withdrawn, while attempting to leave our South Vietnamese allies the means to defend themselves and negotiate reasonable terms of surrender. Or we could have set clear objectives, accurately determined what it would take to accomplish them, and committed all resources necessary to succeed. Instead, our leaders ventured an ill-fated compromise. They endeavored to win without properly judging or allocating the resources needed to win. Almost 60,000 of my fellow soldiers were needlessly killed and much of a generation was lost.

Are we making the same mistake now?

In our war against crime, I believe that once again we have two sensible choices, both better than the one we have chosen so far. As in Vietnam, it is the compromise between the two from which we languish. Drug cases overwhelm our police and our judiciary, making this war against violent crime impossible to win. Criminals congest our courts and well over a million Americans clog our prisons. Some can be rehabilitated but others will never be saved.

Our resources are finite and our will is in question. But there are two ways to rescue this generation. The first is to admit a limited defeat and thereby minimize our losses. We can legalize drugs, tax them heavily, and use the money for rehabilitation and education, both of which are far more cost-effective than deterrence. Then we can focus our efforts on fighting the remaining violent crime, a problem that will have been sharply diminished by the legalization and availability of drugs.

The second way is simply to stop tolerating violent crime. That would involve a top-to-bottom overhaul of our criminal justice system. It would mean going through a total cost-benefit analysis strictly from the point of view of the victims and potential victims of each type of crime. We would be forced to select the most efficient methods of removing criminals from our midst through rehabilitation, incarceration, or execution. It would mean farming out much of the prison system to private industry. And most likely it would mean putting many more violent criminals to death than we do today, without nearly as many expensive appeals or technical defenses. It might mean executing insane or retarded murderers simply because society cannot afford to keep them alive. It will result, on occasion, in the suffering of those innocents accused. But there would be far less suffering of the innocent under such a system than there is now.

Ladies and gentlemen, please keep one thing in mind as you journey into the realm of law. Everything we want from our government and our legal system has a cost. If we are really committed to saving this nation we must be prepared to pay the price. Due process, as we know it today, may be a luxury we can no longer afford.

Audrey Whitcomb Presidential Debate Summation, October 23, 2004

My fellow taxpayers. Violent crime is the scourge of our nation. But this scourge can be confronted in an enlightened, humanitarian way consistent with our national character. Please let us never forget who we are. We are the United States of America, the most powerful, the fairest, the most generous nation on earth.

Our crime problem stems from decades of neglect and misjudgment by politicians and bureaucrats, both Republican and Democrat. There is no easy solution, no overnight fix. We can overcome it only through careful attention and good sense. Our progress against poverty will soon start to diminish the crime rates—of that I assure you.

America's future looks bright indeed. Just look at what we've accomplished over the past three Democratic presidential terms:

We've seen our national debt fall by 12 percent in inflation-adjusted dollars.

Unemployment has been reduced from eight percent in 1992 to less than six percent today.

Fewer than 10 percent of our citizens live below the poverty level.

Homelessness, a plague of the 20th century, will be a memory within five years.[28]

We've prohibited health insurance companies from rejecting applicants because of pre-existing conditions. Now all American citizens can obtain private insurance regardless of their health, and as promised, administrative costs and premiums have actually fallen.

---

[28] This optimistic prediction was based on preliminary results of H.R. 1717, the Homelessness Act, an ambitious program that among other things offered subsidized housing, subsidized drug, alcohol, and mental illness treatment and job training, and guaranteed jobs to homeless persons or those in danger of becoming homeless. It would actually take 12 years before the homelessness problem was effectively eliminated.

We've created more opportunities for young people, a sure way to reduce crime. Through the National Service Act, all teenage high school graduates who wish to go to college can pay for it with government service, or contract to pay a percentage of their future earnings. This privately administered program benefits both the economy and the students. It was introduced by a Democratic president, and to almost everyone's surprise, has already booked a profit based on free market prices now bid for those future earnings contracts.

Here in America we have the best medical care, the best schools, the highest standard of living, the highest life expectancy. More than ever, we are the envy of the world.

Yes, we have crime, and it's terrifying. But imagine what our crime problem would be with the same degree of poverty and economic despair we had years ago, at the end of the last Republican administration.

If you elect me, we'll bring the same laser focus we applied to simplifying our crippling tax code to bear upon the problem of violent crime in America. But a Whitcomb administration won't use violence as a means to end violence. The death penalty is no deterrent; it is retribution that only legitimizes violence. Swift and Sure requires executing up to 40 persons in the United States every single day. That's over 14,000 human beings each year, most of whom could be rehabilitated to become useful members of society—and many of whom will be *innocent* of the crimes of which they're convicted.

Even if we surrender and accept such injustice as a necessary evil—as a price we're willing to pay to make our streets safer—still, Swift and Sure won't work. Ultimately it will only make things worse.

In the past, Republican politicians assured us that their "Three Strikes and You're Out" legislation would reduce crime. But Three Strikes worsened our crime problem. Can you really believe Swift and Sure will turn out any differently? We must never forget; easy solutions to complex problems create unintended consequences.

We all want a safer America. But don't we also want to uphold the American tradition of opportunity, compassion, and fairness? It's not too late. We can still have both.

Travis Hall Presidential Debate Summation, October 23, 2004

My friends, I wish I had Secretary Whitcomb's patience. I admire her accomplishments. In a different time she could have been a superb president. But not today.

Today we need less patience and more resolve. I'd like to tell you one reason why I'm so impatient. Many of you know of my close friend Solomon Kurtz. I first met Sol at a town meeting 11 years ago in Hamden, Connecticut. He asked me some tough questions at that meeting; afterward I invited him to my hotel to continue our discussion and we became friends.

Sol's politics were as liberal as they come, but that didn't matter; anyone on my staff will tell you how much I admired him. He was a true humanitarian. He never made any real money for himself—in fact he barely got by, but always tried to help others. He selflessly raised money for three worthy charities and volunteered for them, usually 60 or 70 hours a week.

Two years ago, my dear friend was murdered, shot through the heart by a man trying to rob him. Sol wasn't carrying any cash that night and it made the mugger angry. Solomon Kurtz wasn't murdered over money—he was murdered out of spite.

The murderer, who had a long record of violent crime, was apprehended and convicted. The defense attorney for this cowardly criminal never denied his client had killed my friend. But he asked the court to consider his client's alcoholic father and alleged abuse as a child. Solomon's own childhood held similar nightmares, but Sol lived his life according to a higher standard. A good man was murdered and finally his killer was imprisoned for life.

But think about this: the projected cost of keeping a 26-year-old man in a maximum security prison for the rest of his life is over two million dollars. That's *your* money. Couldn't it be better spent improving the lives of those more deserving?

I've said I admire my opponent but I do disagree with her. She believes criminals who rob and rape and murder are entitled to the same rights and protection as law-abiding citizens. This view seems to suggest *your* life is no more valuable than the life of a criminal. Criminals may be victims too, but I've seen many victims respond to tragic circumstances without violence.

Secretary Whitcomb says the death penalty is not a deterrent—and she's absolutely right! As a former Connecticut Attorney General, I admit the slow and unsure death penalty process of the past several decades has proven no deterrent at all. It's barbaric torture to those waiting on death row and the legal cost of their appeals is absurd. It's a travesty. Those funds should be available for education and enforcement, not legal expenses and imprisonment.

Those contemplating violent crime must know they'll be caught and that their lives will never be the same. A person found guilty of any violent crime should get no more than one chance at rehabilitation. Swift and Sure still gives the criminal more consideration than those criminals give their victims. I believe the commission of a second violent crime requires execution, swiftly and surely. One fair trial and one quick appeal. No excuses. No delays.

Even experts commissioned by the Democrats concede that homicides and violent crimes will be cut in half if Swift and Sure is enacted. Those same experts project

14,000 executions per year. If they're right, and I hope they're not, it still seems a fair price to save almost 100,000 innocent lives.

Unlike our current death penalty, Swift and Sure efficiently promotes safety through deterrence. It will reallocate money now wasted on incarceration and legal wrangling and use it for rehabilitation and enforcement. Swift and Sure seeks neither revenge nor retribution, but does offer our best hope for victory in the war against violent crime.

The most compelling argument the Democratic party's experts have offered is that about five percent of those executed won't really be guilty of the crimes they're convicted of. They may be right, but I have enough experience as a prosecutor to assure you the great majority of those so-called innocents are guilty of some other violent crime. Even so, for every one of those we wrongly execute, we'll save the lives of at least 140 potential victims and the safety of thousands more. No system is perfect, but Swift and Sure will deliver far better justice than we have now.

Do I care about violent criminals as human beings? Anyone who knows me knows I do. Most have suffered tragic lives. My heart aches over such wasted potential and I know our society is partially to blame. But most of us are productive, law abiding, responsible citizens. If *you* are, your government should care about your safety more than it cares about those who, for whatever reason, choose to break the law and trample on your right to a life free of their violence. If you elect us, we'll put your rights ahead of the rights of criminals.

Description of LottoPick, discussed in Chapter 18, dated November 8, 2008.

At the time, 46 out of the 51 states[29] operated lotteries. Each two-dollar ticket holder chose a group of numbers, for example: six different numbers from 1 to 50.

(Note: In this example, each ticket's odds were 6/50 x 5/49 x 4/48 x 3/47 x 2/46 x 1/45, or approximately 1 in 15.89 million —22g CP)

Then at a weekly drawing, six numbers out of the 50 would be selected at random, and tickets with all six would split a multimillion dollar prize. Every ticket had an equal chance of winning a share of the main prize. But not all tickets had the same chance to win the *entire* jackpot, a subtle but important difference.

LottoPick was an interactive system that chose a series of numbers for the lottery ticket buyer, instantly eliminating that series from the field of available future picks. It also analyzed patterns of commonly selected numbers and excluded them from its repertoire. LottoPick thereby assured lottery ticket buyers that, in the improbable event their ticket won, they'd be less likely to have to split the prize.

(Note: To illustrate the value of LottoPick, on November 8, 2008, a typical $2 Texas lottery ticket had a theoretical value of $1.04, a ticket with completely random numbers was worth $1.41, and a LottoPick ticket rated to win $1.89 on average. These calculations assume a 12-percent discount rate on the winner's share of a $28.8 million prize paid in 20 annual installments.— 22g CP)

The 7-Eleven convenience store chain had test-marketed LottoPick in Texas. It was a major success. The LottoPick concept was difficult to grasp, but once ticket buyers "got it," they became repeat customers. With only

---

[29] LottoPick was announced three years after the admission of Puerto Rico, but East New York and West New York still comprised a single state.

a $2 million advertising budget, 7-Eleven's market share of all lottery ticket sales statewide climbed from 19 percent to 27 percent in the first 60 days, thanks to the appeal of LottoPick. Educated customers realized that with LottoPick, their expected dollar winnings were at least 30 percent higher than with the totally random numbers supplied by the state's machines (and nearly twice as high as when selecting their kids' birthdays or some other group of non-random "lucky" numbers). Also, as LottoPick's market share increased, the viability of any competing systems disappeared. After all, unless the program eliminated a lot of duplicated numbers, what good was it? LottoPick became another ATI "software monopoly."

ATI had put up the entire $2 million advertising budget and paid for the ticketing machines. They received only 20 percent of 7-Eleven's profit from lottery ticket sales, and the stores benefited from increased traffic.

ATI and 7-Eleven soon rolled out the program into each of the 46 states offering lotteries.

It seemed like a high-potential, risk-free deal for 7-Eleven. In fact, their top executives thought the contract had been too tough on ATI. But they quickly discovered that Scoggins and Thacker had negotiated with exceptional shrewdness. 7-Eleven's exclusive in each state would last only two years (or less if 7-Eleven declined to do a national roll-out), after which ATI could raise its price at will and market the product to other chains. Then LottoPick would become a cash cow for ATI, conservatively projected to earn $1 billion annually.

Description of TrueDose, as mentioned in Chapter 19, dated August 15, 2009

Before the early 21st century, drug companies manufactured and distributed most of the medicines they developed. In 2005, the Wal-Mart organization convinced several major drug companies to license their products for a royalty, roughly the wholesale price of the drug minus manufacturing and distribution costs.

The arrangement was revenue-neutral to the drug companies. But the advantages to Wal-Mart were enormous. The giant retailer saved money through efficient manufacturing and distribution, enabling it to offer prescription drugs at lower prices. Wal-Mart's increased market share also created windfall profits on generic drugs it manufactured. But far more significantly, they could now custom mix for each consumer. For example, instead of having to remember to take three different pills twice a day, each Wal-Mart customer received all medications in one daily time-release pill or monthly arm-patch.

Pharmacies soon followed Wal-Mart's lead or were driven out of business. By 2010, no drug company still manufactured products for the United States market. Instead, they sold their manufacturing facilities to the pharmacy chains and collected royalties on their patents.

TrueDose was designed so pharmacies could interface with HealthFile, ensuring that patients would never receive drugs to which they were allergic or that mixed badly with other drugs prescribed to them.

It was a great product, but it flopped. The problem was that any software company could design a similar program and any pharmacy could interface with HealthFile just by asking customers for their ID numbers. ATI had no previous link to the pharmacies and therefore no competitive advantage. TrueDose never captured more than 20 percent of the market, even with free trial periods and aggressive cost cutting.

Legal Alternatives for Cryonic Suspendees, see Chapter 23, June 15, 2015

To avoid depositing funds with the government, you could assign money to relatives or friends, who'd pay taxes on such gifts and who might not be around when you were ultimately revived. Or you could deposit the money in a government-insured bank account, but all interest earned would be assessed at up to a 40-percent maximum tax rate. You could also lend money interest-free to a tax-exempt charity, but if the loan was ever repaid, it would retain a fraction of its original purchasing power. Or, perhaps the best alternative, if you had art, antiques, jewelry, rare stamps or coins, or other valuables, you could lend them to a non-profit museum to be returned if and when you were revived.

Text of Rev. Dr. Asia Jonas's January 20, 2037 sermon, noted in Chapter 39

There is an old joke about three statisticians who go hunting for deer with bows and arrows. They spot an old buck. The first one shoots. His arrow misses by two yards to the left. The second statistician's arrow misses by two yards to the right. The third statistician excitedly shouts, "We got him!"

To grasp the nature of the world, you'd have to put yourself in God's place, which is of course impossible. But in light of all the suffering that has occurred and continues to occur, I have always assumed God cannot control every individual event. For a long time now, I have considered that maybe God is a statistician.

When I was a young girl, America was a land of both optimism and fear. We all anticipated longer, healthier, and more prosperous lives than our parents enjoyed. But this was during the cold war and every child also knew about the bomb. With dread, I envisioned World War

Three, wondering whether human madness or miscalculation might end all life on earth.

As I grew into young adulthood, I watched the AIDS epidemic take many friends and acquaintances, their lives untimely robbed of such promise. I watched the news in horror as wars, and the famines and epidemics brought on by them, claimed millions of innocent human lives in Ethiopia, Somalia, Rwanda, Bosnia, Serbia, Holland, Iraq, Ghana, Ivory Coast, Columbia, Spain, and many other nations. How I mourned for those fellow human beings with families and work and goals I knew were just as important to them as mine were to me.

Around the turn of the millennium, I feared for my own life during America's war against crime. And I watched reports of religious cults and political terrorists murdering hundreds, even thousands of innocent people at once, in nearly every country including the United States.

Yet throughout those years, the statisticians assured us that things were improving. People all around the globe were living longer every year—on average. Technology improved our lives and prosperity every year—on average. The world was becoming less politically repressed every year— on average. All true—but it would hardly seem that way to anyone who happened to be dying of AIDS or who lived in Baghdad during that terrible October barely 30 years ago.

Today the nature of humankind is different. We can *tell* that things have improved, even without statisticians proving it to us. A machine and a united world have appeared almost simultaneously and these two miracles have finally lifted us above the rest of the animal kingdom. We have been compelled—literally forced, as though at gunpoint—to think in terms of community. For the first time in history, every human being is held accountable for his or her intentions.

We are subject to the forces of nature and we still die from accidents, natural disasters, disease, and old age.

We often disagree. But we no longer start wars or thoughtlessly infect others with our diseases.

Still, many of us, those of my generation especially, mourn a loss of privacy and self-determination. We can no longer keep secrets or have them kept from us, even things we do not wish to disclose or know. Our families and friends and perfect strangers know almost as much about us as we know ourselves. And we have discovered too much of the darker side of human nature, our emotions, thoughts, and motivations—our natural tendency toward hypocrisy and greed, jealousy and spite. In a way, we've had truth shoved down our throats, and not all of us like it.

But if I put myself in God's place for a moment, I like the idea a lot. Statistically speaking, being forced to confront the truth about ourselves has improved our lives in countless measurable ways. It's not comfortable to deal with the truth, but for all it's given us in return, discomfort has been a small price to pay.

ACKNOWLEDGMENTS

While writing the outline for this novel, I polled many of my smartest friends, relatives, and colleagues for their visions of the future, asking questions like: What year do you think they'll invent an AIDS vaccine? When will cryogenic freezing become legal? When will they introduce commercial supersonic airline flights across the United States? When will we colonize the moon? I sent these same people (and others) copies of the manuscript in various stages. Q. David Bowers and Jason Carter were particularly helpful, each contributing hundreds of editorial suggestions. I also received great feedback, editing, and/or research assistance from the following "Friends of *The Truth Machine*:" Ellie Baker, Tom Becker, Jean-Louis Brindamour, Ph.D., Marc Emory, Sam Foose, Sondra Horton Fraleigh, Jonathan Fritz, Ronald Guth, David Hall, Rev. Dr. Laurel Hallman, Hugh Hixon, Bill Holter, Steve Ivy, Davar Khossravi, Ph.D., David Munro Jackson, Penn Jillette, Steve Mayer, David McLane, Cherri Mclamed, Ruth Minshull, Dr. Edgar Phillips, Dr. and Mrs. Dan and Patty Pickard, Greg Rohan, Mr. and Dr. Hugh and Sima Sconyers, Gayle Scroggs, Ph.D., Lynde Selden III, Michael Sherman, Dr. Robert Sternberg, Carlton Stowers, Andrew Tobias, Scott Travess, Gary B. Walls, Ph.D., Douglas Winter, and James R. Zimmerman, MD.

This being my first attempt at fiction, I was fortunate to happen upon Jennifer Miller, a talented and successful screenwriter from Seattle. To prevent me from becoming discouraged, she coached me by telephone and insisted I fax her my pages every morning; she corrected them (always with restraint and tact), occasionally rewriting entire passages. Without her, I doubt I would have finished *The Truth Machine*.

I also received writing and editing help from Donnell Brown, Joyce Engelson, Jerry Gross, Richard Marek, Tom Stephenson, and James O. Wade. Unlike Jennifer, these people did not refuse payment for their work. They were worth the money though, and I would recommend any of them.

I am forever grateful to the following friends and experts, who either suggested ideas for the story, read the manuscript and made suggestions and corrections, or both: Don Bagert, Stephen Bridge, Richard Brodie, Thomas Donaldson, William Dye, Marc Emory, Robert Ettinger, Abigail Halperin, Edward Halperin, Gayle Ziaks-Halperin, Marjorie Halperin, Penn Jillette, Steve Mayer, Ralph Merkle, Jennifer Miller, Max More, Mike Perry, Will Rossman, Roderick A. Carter-Russell, Brian Shock, Jeffrey Soreff, Andrew Tobias, Paul Wakfer, Brian Wowk, and especially Edward C. Root.

I would also like to acknowledge the following professionals associated with the publishing industry who have been instrumental in developing my skills and furthering my newfound career: Ellen Archer, Shannon Atlas, Joyce Engelson, Jean Fenton, Joel Gotler, Ellen Key Harris, Teri Henry, Timothy Kochuba, Kuo-yu Liang, Richard Marek, Gilbert Perlman, Shelly Shapiro, Heather Smith, Pamela Dean Strickler, and Scott Travers.

My parents, Ed and Audrey Halperin, and sisters, Dr. Abigail Halperin-Swenson, Marjorie Halperin-Rosenfield, and Sharon Halperin-Peureux, patiently read several drafts of *The Truth Machine*, and made gratefully accepted corrections and suggestions. My beautiful wife, Gayle Ziaks, a professional dancer and choreographer, provided similar help as well as a sounding board for my ideas. She overlooked the unpleasant side effects of the creative process and, along with the rest of my family, provided constant encouragement. Which any writer will tell you is more important than food, shelter, or air.

THE TRUTH MACHINE—READER SURVEY

Just seal and mail by affixing the proper postage. For more information, visit our World Wide Web page at http://www.random-house. com/delrey/

Do____ Do not____ add me to the DRINK mailing list.

Name _____

Address _____

City _____ State _____ Zip _____

Phone number _____ Fax _____

E-mail Address _____

Please rate the following aspects of the story on a scale of 1-10 (1 is terrible, 10 is perfect).

Plot___ Character development ___ Believability___
Philosophy___ Excitement ___ Scientific credibility___ Philosophical stimulation___ Educational___ Forecasts___ Computer narrator___ Conflict___ Introduction___ Drama___ Social Importance___ Ending___

I liked *The Truth Machine* because_____
_____
_____

I disliked *The Truth Machine* because _____
_____
_____

As a consumer, I would be interested in the following products based on *The Truth Machine* (rate on a scale of 1-10, 10 being the most appealing).

Feature film___ Television series___ Comic book series ___
On-line forum___ Board game___ Television movie___ Radio show___ Video game___ Other_____

I first learned about *The Truth Machine* from(fill in specifics if you remember, otherwise, just check):

Newspaper _____Magazine ad _____

Newspaper review _____Magazine review _____

Word of mouth _____Bookstore _____

Internet _____Radio_____Television_____

Other _____

Age _____Gender _____Occupation_____

You have_____do not have_____my permission to reprint my comments in promotion for *The Truth Machine*.

Signature _____Date _____

What would it mean to be human if you could
live forever?

THE FIRST IMMORTAL.

by James L. Halperin

This multigenerational saga follows the fortunes
of the Smith family from the Depression through
the rest of the twentieth century and on into a
future filled with technological marvels. Led by
Dr. Ben Smith, who becomes one of the first
humans to have his body frozen in the hopes of
later revival, the Smith family becomes pivotal in
the development of cryogenics technology,
cloning, and nanotechnology—the sciences that
will one day be humanity's fountain of youth. But
even as they marvel at the miracles of future science, Ben and his family come to realize that the
deepest ethical and emotional dilemmas of
humankind—and of their own entangled lives—
remain unsolved.

Published by Del Rey Books.
Available in your local bookstore.

Join us online to find out even more about

THE FIRST IMMORTAL
by James L. Halperin

Visit us at

www.randomhouse.com/features/firstimmortal/

**to talk with the author, cast your vote in a
cryonics opinion poll, get future news updates,
and much more!**

✎ FREE DRINKS ✎

Take the Del Rey® survey and get a free newsletter! Answer the questions below and we will send you complimentary copies of the DRINK (Del Rey® Ink) newsletter free for one year. Here's where you will find out all about upcoming books, read articles by top authors, artists, and editors, and get the inside scoop on your favorite books.

Age _____ Sex ❑ M ❑ F

Highest education level: ❑ high school ❑ college ❑ graduate degree

Annual income: ❑ $0-30,000 ❑ $30,001-60,000 ❑ over $60,000

Number of books you read per month: ❑ 0-2 ❑ 3-5 ❑ 6 or more

Preference: ❑ fantasy ❑ science fiction ❑ horror ❑ other fiction ❑ nonfiction

I buy books in hardcover: ❑ frequently ❑ sometimes ❑ rarely

I buy books at: ❑ superstores ❑ mall bookstores ❑ independent bookstores
❑ mail order

I read books by new authors: ❑ frequently ❑ sometimes ❑ rarely

I read comic books: ❑ frequently ❑ sometimes ❑ rarely

I watch the Sci-Fi cable TV channel: ❑ frequently ❑ sometimes ❑ rarely

I am interested in collector editions (signed by the author or illustrated):
❑ yes ❑ no ❑ maybe

I read Star Wars novels: ❑ frequently ❑ sometimes ❑ rarely

I read Star Trek novels: ❑ frequently ❑ sometimes ❑ rarely

I read the following newspapers and magazines:

❑ Analog	❑ Locus	❑ Popular Science
❑ Asimov	❑ Wired	❑ USA Today
❑ SF Universe	❑ Realms of Fantasy	❑ The New York Times

Check the box if you do not want your name and address shared with qualified vendors ❑

Name _____
Address _____
City/State/Zip _____
E-mail _____

halperin

PLEASE SEND TO: DEL REY®/The DRINK
201 EAST 50TH STREET, NEW YORK, NY 10022
OR FAX TO THE ATTENTION OF DEL REY PUBLICITY: 212/572-2676

DEL REY® ONLINE!

The Del Rey Internet Newsletter...

A monthly electronic publication e-mailed to subscribers and posted on the rec.arts.sf.written Usenet newsgroup and on our Del Rey Books Web site (www.randomhouse.com/delrey/). It features hype-free descriptions of books that are new in the stores, a list of our upcoming books, special promotional programs and offers, announcements and news, a signing/reading/convention-attendance calendar for Del Rey authors and editors, "In Depth" essays in which professionals in the field (authors, artists, cover designers, salespeople, etc.) talk about their jobs in science fiction, a question-and-answer section, and more!

Subscribe to the DRIN: send a message reading "subscribe" in the subject or body to drin-dist@cruises.randomhouse.com

The Del Rey Books Web Site!

We make a lot of information available on our Web site at
www.randomhouse.com/delrey/

- all back issues and the current issue of the Del Rey Internet Newsletter
- sample chapters of almost every new book
- detailed interactive features of some of our books
- special features on various authors and SF/F worlds
- ordering information (and online ordering)
- reader reviews of upcoming books
- news and announcements
- our Works in Progress report, detailing the doings of our most popular authors
- bargain offers in our Del Rey Online Store
- manuscript transmission requirements
- and more!

If You're Not on the Web...

You can subscribe to the DRIN via e-mail (send a message reading "subscribe" in the subject or body to drin-dist@cruises.randomhouse.com), read it on the rec.arts.sf.written Usenet newsgroup the first few days of every month, or visit our gopher site (gopher.panix.com) for back issues of the DRIN and about a hundred sample chapters. We also have editors and other representatives who participate in America Online and CompuServe SF/F forums and rec.arts.sf.written, making contact and sharing information with SF/F readers.

Questions? E-mail us...

at delrey@randomhouse.com (though it sometimes takes us a little while to answer).